HOPELESS KINGDOM

About the Author

Kgshak Akec is an avid storyteller. Born in Sudan, Kgshak spent her early years living in Giza, Egypt, before migrating with her mother, father and her eight siblings to Australia in 2003. She now calls Geelong home. As a first-generation Australian, Kgshak's work seeks to explore the inner workings of what it is to be Black and African in modern Australia, to capture the truth, the pain, and the magic.

Kgshak is also a passionate member of the theatre and performing arts community, but the art of the written word remains to be her first and true love.

HOPELESS KINGDOM

KGSHAK AKEC

First published in 2022 and Reprinted 2023 by
UWA Publishing
Crawley, Western Australia 6009
www.uwap.uwa.edu.au

UWAP is an imprint of UWA Publishing
a division of The University of Western Australia

ISBN: 978-1-76080-215-8

A catalogue record for this book is available from the National Library of Australia

Cover design by Mika Tabata
Typeset in 12 point Dante by Lasertype
Printed by McPherson's Printing Group

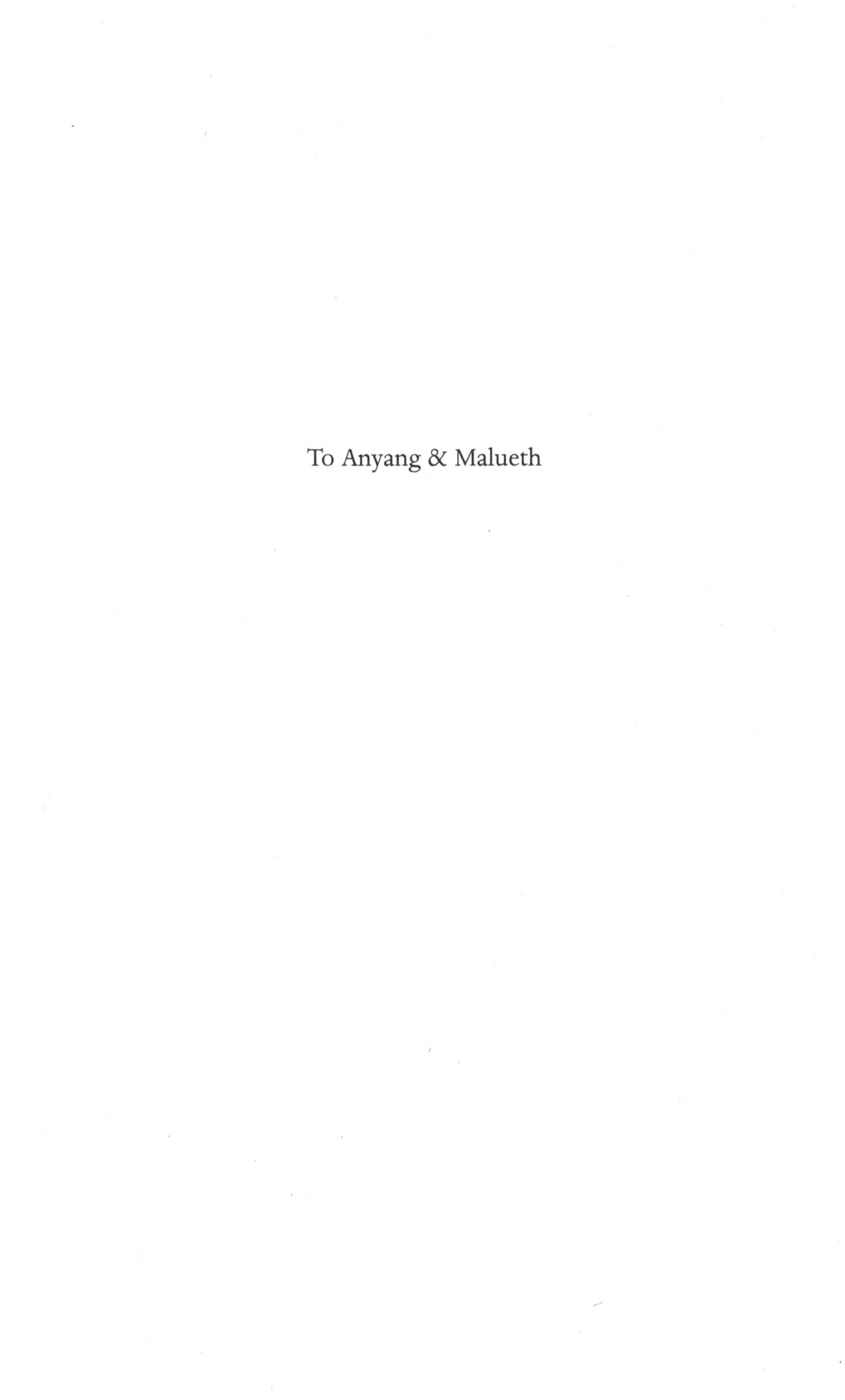

To Anyang & Malueth

Chapter 1

Cairo

Akita

'Go on then, you stupid girl,' he seethes, 'do it!'

I want to.

Very badly.

I want to punch Samra's brother in his ugly fat face more than I've ever wanted to do anything in my short little life. I want to strike him with all my strength, maim him with all my might. If I could just do that, I'm sure it'll be worth his retaliation; the punching, the kicking and the hair-pulling I'll suffer by his hands.

I've seen how he fights, filthy like the muck between his yellow teeth.

The only thing that stops me is the trouble I'll land myself in because of it, because of him.

Besides, he is a boy – two, maybe even three years older than me. He barely stands taller than I do, though he is much, much wider. Samra's brother's one leg is bigger than the two of mine combined, his punch will stain my skin longer than my scratches will mark his, and he smiles at me tantalisingly because he knows it.

I hate this school and everyone in it.

I hate the greyish-beige no-colour-having buildings surrounding this dirt courtyard, caging us all in. I hate the students who pick fights for no reason and the teachers who do nothing about it.

Samra's brother has been looking for a reason to hurt me more than his words do ever since I started here, and I, accidentally, fell into his trap this morning.

Samra is his younger sister, and she is the nastiest girl I have ever met. Samra, like her brother, has made it her life's mission to make mine a misery. I don't often react – Mama says it isn't worth it. She says that people like Samra and her brother only ever try to get the worst out of people like us.

Today is the first day I let Mama down.

Samra pulled on my hair as I entered the classroom this morning, for no reason except that she wanted to. It was the first time she'd lain a hand on me. My confusion quickly turned to rage, I pushed her hands away and told her what I really thought. That with a chin so long and eyes so beady, the least she could do is be nice so that people weren't to think she was a gremlin.

Those unkind words spewed out of my mouth like lava and enveloped her.

It was very strange. I've never seen myself become so angry.

I'd be ashamed too if I didn't think Samra deserved it.

Almost every day it's a new taunt from her – of the blackness of my skin, or the coils of my hair, wrapped and twisted into intricate braids that her eyes never seem to make sense of. While the heads of all the other girls in this school are covered with fine, royal blue scarves bordering their sand-coloured faces, my dark, braided hair falls loosely down my back. Thick, black strands like the branches of an obscure tree silhouetted against the blue of dusk, or the blue of my school jumper.

To my absolute horror, Samra cried and told our teacher, Miss Hanna, and anybody else who would listen. Naturally, by now, lunchtime, everybody in the whole school knows, including Samra's older and chunkier brother.

He stands a few feet before me in the gravel courtyard. When I look around, I see some of the girls in my class sitting by the steps of the classroom, a few boys in the years above absentmindedly kick a ball between themselves nearby, everyone else is scattered amongst the courtyard, pretending not to look even though every eye is turned this way.

Sweat gathers on the peach fuzz above his lip, his clenched fists shaking slightly, itching to act out the harm he means me.

'What's wrong, little monkey? Scared?' Samra's brother hisses, talking half a step towards me. 'Look at her face! She's so scared!' he laughs, his mouth spraying spit. A crowd of baby blue shirts and royal blue scarves begins to gather around us, most of them laugh with him. I look to them: at their nauseating joy in my forthcoming crucifixion, their delight in my misfortune.

He's going to hit me, I'm sure of it. I'll join his long list of victims.

I'm curious to find in all that is unfolding that I am not scared, even though it resembles most nightmares I've had. No chords of my fear have been struck. My hands don't shake and my knees keep me upright and steady. I breathe into it, welcoming this unexpected revelation with open arms as I stand before Samra's brother, still and complacent to whatever is going to happen.

He walks about, holding the attention of our peers. He is making a show of this, trying to agitate the lioness in the colosseum, even though it's he who should be tamed and bathed by the looks of it.

I watch as he walks from side to side along the gravel, his heavy footsteps kicking up clouds of dirt. Once more in my mind, I replay the series of events that led to this very moment, trying to connect the dots and grasp the ridiculousness of my reality. My decision of instinct, of reason, is the stone I threw into the water; only, I expected ripples, not this hurricane.

All for what? The entertainment and revere of a couple of our fellow students who have varying degrees of hatred towards me?

When Mama and Baba talk about power, they use simple words to try to make me understand. Power is the delicate and invisible energy I hold in the palm of my hands, feel it buzz from my fingertips. Everybody has it, some more than others. *It is power to act, just as it is to stay still.* That's what Mama always says. Neither is inherently good nor bad, that part is up to me.

But I'm seeing that it's one thing to understand an abstract concept and another thing completely to be in the eye of it. I hope I'm doing a good thing, and I hope they forgive me if I'm not.

'Hey monkey,' he chants malevolently. 'Didn't they teach you how to speak in the wild?'

The boys surrounding me guffaw loudly; some of the girls do the same, giggling unapologetically. Samra stands directly behind her brother, squinting eyes and a menacing grin on her pudgy face, sure to catch all the action. There isn't a teacher in sight, which is typical. When something like this happens, when I'm in dire need of one of them, they are never here.

A wicked smile tugs at the corner of Samra's brother's mouth. He watches me carefully with his beady eyes, eager to get a reaction. He wants me to cry and run away or scream and attack. I see the hunger in his eyes, looking at me the same way I'd imagine he'd look at a sandcastle before destroying it or a balloon before popping it.

As much of a soft-brained imbecile Samra's brother is, he knows one thing; he cannot throw the first punch.

'Say something, midnight!' he squeals, the agitation building in his small, round body.

I stare at him blankly. There isn't a word in this language I know that could properly describe the evil Samra and her brother are. I would say it's in their blood, but the truth is, cruelty runs deep within all those around me, not just the boy in front of me. The difference is that he and his sister are the only ones who openly act on it. Maybe that is what's in their blood.

'I said,' he repeats, bending over, picking up a small rock and hurling it at me. 'Speak!'

I instinctively shield my face from the incoming rock, leaving it to collide onto my wrist bone with a dull crack. A sharp pain shoots up my arm and around my back, and I recoil as the onlookers erupt in laughter and cheers. When I uncover my face and bring down my arms, some of the boys shout, egging Samra's brother on to do it again with a bigger rock and to throw it much, much harder.

I stand with my wrist in my hand. Frozen.

The clever thing would be to run. To cry and run, even if he runs after me, throwing rocks from behind.

But it seems I've forgotten how to do that. I've forgotten how to do anything.

Fear creeps its way in from my throbbing wrist, spreading all over before I catch my next breath.

I've lived nearly six years of this life, and I am about to die at the hands of the person I hate most in the saddest place I know.

I take a full-bodied breath, my feet standing before an invisible line. Should I surrender? Accept defeat and the bashing that comes with it? Or should I fight back?

Before I know it, I'm bending down and picking up the largest rock I see. I hold it in my hand for a moment, squeezing today's heat into my palm, staring as my fingers wrap around the jagged edges. The growing audience reacts loudly; some of the girls exclaim, others gasp in disbelief. Most of the boys cheer, knowing this means they'll witness something that more resembles a fight.

I look up at Samra's brother's face. He beams and narrows his eyes in focus. He sinks his feet into the gravel and bends his knees.

I'm giving him exactly what he wants.

I look at the rock in my hand for a while.

It is power to act, just as it is to stay still.

Everyone around me screams so loudly I can barely hear my thoughts.

I stare and stare.

Really hard.

Then something shifts.

The noise around me dulls down and distorts, until it is blanketed in soft silence. I feel as though I'm underwater, in the brief moments before resurfacing. My heart pounds in my ears. I feel it throbbing in my wrist, feel it beating within the rock in my grasp, as if it's my own I hold in my hand. Somewhere in the distance somebody calls my name.

I sigh deeply.

I can't do it.

I can't hit him, not even with this rock.

As much as he deserves it, I don't really want to hurt him.

I look to my hand, unfurl my grasp and let it slip between my fingers. As it falls to the ground, I start coming back to myself, feeling like I might faint under the heat of the sun.

When I look up, I see Samra's brother, charging at me with a force that makes my knees shake.

This is it. This is how I die.

Samra's brother's large frame is going to crush my body in a matter of seconds. The assemblage cheer belligerently. The sun feels hot on my skin, burning holes in my bones. A voice calls my name again, only it doesn't seem so distant anymore; actually, it's rather close, and it sounds like San–

I feel it before I see it. The weight of it tears through the empty space.

I turn and catch a glimpse of a small brick flying past my shoulder, feeling the wind it creates against my skin. I watch as it hits Samra's brother's face with a toe-curling smack.

He drops to the ground with a heavy thud, summoning clouds of grey ghosts from the dirt.

I stare at his unmoving body as the dust settles, in complete horror.

I try to form thoughts that make sense of what I've just seen. The courtyard falls silent and unnervingly still. For a moment it feels as if we're in another world, a world of grey dirt, grey skies, grey, visible air. I stand above his body as the sinking feeling deepens.

I've killed him.

I've somehow summoned a brick with my thoughts and killed him.

I'm going to be locked away forever.

I didn't mean it. I thought I wanted him dead moments ago, but I was wrong.

Then I hear a voice calling my name, a voice I instantly recognise. When my mind finally connects the dots, I breathe a bated breath, turning, searching for the thrower of the brick.

My eyes find Santo, the only other sunflower among this sea of roses.

Skin dark as night, my big brother, with another brick clenched in his fist.

'Stay away from my sister, Antony,' he sighs, walking past me and crouching down.

Santo leans closely to Antony, who I still think might be dead.

'You dirty, little pig,' he whispers, his voice dripping with venom.

'Are you alright, Akita?'

'I … uh, I don't think he can hear you, Sunny,' I say, anxiously gripping and twisting the hem of my dress.

'He's not dead, Kita,' Santo laughs, his teeth gleaming, 'but the rest of you will be if you don't piss off!' he shouts, and they disperse.

When my eyes meet Samra's, she shrinks back, looks to her shoes, and joins a group of girls making a hasty escape.

Where relief once was, weariness now takes place. I'm relieved that I'm not dead, and that Santo is here with me, but my stomach twists in knots every time I look down at Antony.

We're in trouble – my god, *huge* trouble, expulsion level trouble. Mama and Baba are going to disown us.

Then, as if summoned by the sin of the only two black children in the school conversing, we hear the distinctive sound of the vice principal's heeled shoes crunching on the gravel towards us. It's only a few precise steps until Madame Atef is towering over Santo and me with a look of disgust etched onto her leathery face. In this school full of awfully mean teachers, Madame Atef is the meanest of all. The scariest, too, mostly because I never see her coming.

'Animals!' she speaks, looking down at us from her large nose, her every word like a dagger. 'All you're good for is causing trouble.'

My body goes rigid at the sight of the terrifying woman. She eyes Samra's brother, who apparently is not dead, with little emotion. She turns to Santo and grabs him by the ear, then she yanks me forcefully by the collar. Santo snickers as we're dragged along, amused by Madame Atef's enmity, but stops when he sees my legs fail to keep up with her long strides. I stumble and fall on my belly, Santo reaches a hand to help me up, his ear still between Madame Atef's bony fingers, but she pulls him away without missing a step. She clings onto the collar of my dress chokingly and drags me along the gravel courtyard at a pace that makes it impossible for me to rise to my feet or catch my breath.

I whimper as my knees scrape along the hot, jagged earth. Tiny rocks scratch bits of skin off my knees, bruise my ribs and shins.

Santo kicks the vice principal, but she does not stop until we reach the bottom steps that lead into the sandstone building where her office resides. She dusts herself off and straightens her blazer. I feel her cast a long, foul look at Santo and me before walking up the few steps and disappearing into the building.

I push my palms, red and raw, against the hot asphalt as Santo puts his arms under mine and helps me up. He dusts himself off as I examine my injuries. Blood seeps through the new holes on the front of my dress where my knees were, running down my legs, staining my favourite pair of frilly white socks. I bleed from my left elbow, and, curiously, down my shoulder too.

'It's not yours,' Santo says, pointing to the bloodstain on my shoulder, reading my mind. 'It's mine,' he sniffs.

I look at him and see blood dripping from his nose the same way rain drips through the holes in the living room ceiling.

I take a deep breath, then let out a giggle, picking the last of the tiny rocks out of my palms, blowing cool air on them.

'Shut up,' Santo says, closing his eyes and shaking his head, turning away to conceal the smile that spreads across his face. 'Don't say it, Akita.' He grins, averting my eyes, blood staining his large white teeth.

'I knew it!' I cheer victoriously.

'No, you didn't,' Santo argues, wiping his nose with his pale-blue school shirt. 'I haven't had one in weeks!'

'Yeah, Sunny, I did know,' I retort proudly. 'I had a dream about it.'

'You had a dream that I got a nosebleed?'

'Yuh-huh. So, I was right.'

'Okay, Kita, okay.'

'I knew your nose was going to bleed today,' I say, laughing a little less.

Taresai

I'd be lying if I said I was surprised to receive a call from the state school with an urgent request to pick up my eldest son and daughter. It was 12.53pm on a Monday after all.

It's not yet been a week since the birth of my fourth child, but alas, I've been told there was some sort of incident.

From my experience, the word: 'incident' is code for 'we've had enough of dealing with your spawn for today, kindly, take them away.'

The phone call I'd predicted, and the request I had intuited as well. Atef's tone and disposition, however, had caught me off guard. She sounded placid on the phone, instead of her innate scornful manner and her proclivity to forget that I am not one of her students.

Atef becomes easily and unnaturally livid over little things Santo does, like calling a teacher by their first name, class disruptions, "bullying" other kids that start on him first.

Something else that struck me in that 40-second phone conversation was that Atef had said 'your children.' Plural.

I expect trouble from Santo every other day of the week at that wretched school, but Akita? Not my girl, not the child who is often presumed mute. She wouldn't swat at a mosquito, let alone a brat, even if they deserved it.

It pains me to think what lows that school has fallen to for my Akita to have landed in the vice principal's office.

I let these thoughts bubble as I sit in a sterile hospital room at the end of the children's ward, staring at my newborn as she spends her first week of life asleep in a rectangular glass womb. Her chest rises and falls, willing her every limb by the power of it, her cloth diaper too big for her small frame, her beanie too small for her head of hair. Every day I'm seeing it takes her a little less effort to breathe, the same could be said for me.

Ashanti arrived seven weeks before we expected her, unprepared for the world and far too fragile for it. I want nothing more than to bring her home, to have her sleep next to me, in my protection.

I want to touch her, to hold her, to let her know that her mother is in her grace.

The nights away are the hardest. Falling asleep is like falling into an abyss with nothing to break my fall. I spend most of my days here when the kids are at school and their father is at work, and on the rare occasions when I'm not needed at home.

I stand and press my hands against the glass, saying my goodbye to Ashanti for the day.

Her eyes flicker beneath her tender skin and her mouth opens slightly.

I lift a silent prayer for strength: for Ashanti, and for me too.

I step out into the cobblestoned street; the heat of the day instantly sticking to my skin. A soft breeze blows in the smell of Giza, of the sandalwood perfumes and ground spices.

I loosely wrap an orange scarf over my hair and around my shoulders. The heat of Cairo is akin to that of my home, but while Cairo's sun beats down on those below, Juba's sun glows with a warm intensity, heating you up from the inside out.

I wave down a taxi driver when I make it to the other side of the busy street, a familiar feeling of emptiness hallowing in the pit of my stomach.

My pregnancy was joyous, but when time came and Ashanti was out into this world, I become the bearer of towering grief, the withholder of all earthly pain.

It comes in waves, and when it peaks it's debilitating. It takes hold of everything inside me, rendering it impossible to feel any other emotion, trapped in its stillness.

My first were twins. A boy and a girl. I carried them to full term, lost them both overnight. Causes unknown, though I could make a few intuited guesses. That was in Sudan, where life and death walked hand in hand.

They were four days old.

I fell pregnant a year later, I lost her too before the third trimester.

At twenty-five I began feeling like I was cursed, like my body couldn't carry the children I'd dreamt of having, back when having children of my own was my only dream.

I prayed night after night, talked to the stars and cried to the moon.

I would feel a weight on my lap, warmth in my hands, and kicks in my belly; but the only children I had back then existed on a different plane.

I became pregnant again and I treaded with caution and apprehension every step of the way. That was until the thirty-ninth week when the pain in my womb shot to my every limb and wrapped itself around me, becoming so unbearable I was sure it would split me in half.

Santo was born a month after I turned twenty-six.

Then we welcomed Akita when Santo was two, then Amara when Akita was three. All three births were difficult in their own way. I was in labour for thirty-eight hours with Santo, Akita was born at home (the nearest hospital was three days away) and Amara developed severe eczema in the days following her birth.

Despite this, despite it all, every time my child was placed on my chest – heart beating, lungs breathing, their body shaking from the might of their cries – I've been content, heart full.

Something is different this time, something inside me. Unrelenting sorrow bleeds into my every thought, every memory, every emotion. I can't speak of this to anyone. I can't say the words out loud, not even to Santino. Sharing my pain won't alleviate it, it'll only grow his. Though I can't be certain he doesn't see it behind my eyes.

I have much to be grateful for, I remind myself. I have three healthy children and one that is in good care. Ashanti is getting stronger each day.

It is a tribulation, and though it is great, it's one that'll pass, an affliction that she will overcome; even if it's the first thing life has given her, a struggle before my embrace.

I am alright. I must be. I have four children.

I take a deep breath and stare out the window as the high-rise buildings disappear behind me and the school's gates come into view. The high metal spears stick out from the earth intrusively, resembling anything but a place of learning.

It will pass. If not today, perhaps the day after.

All of it.

Akita

Madame Atef stands over us in her plain office, informing Santo and me of the phone call she's made to our mother, sparing no detail in describing how disappointed Mama is in us.

She gives us strict instructions to go to our classrooms and retrieve our belongings, pinching my arms throughout for not looking at her when she speaks.

It's disrespectful, she says, and I know this, but the sight of the woman truly terrifies me. Madame Atef is disturbing to look at. If I stare at her too long, her face will be what my nightmares are made of for the coming weeks. It's the way her skin sits like old leather, so close to the bones beneath it, how her eyes float in the sunken pool of their socket.

Skeletal, from her rigid stance to the way she makes my blood turn to ice.

Madame Atef is the only teacher in this school who doesn't wear a scarf. Her jet-black hair is smoothed into a slick low bun, not a stray curl in sight. She looks as if she was made, not born. All razor-sharp edges, no softness, not even in the fabric of her suit.

She tells us to get out of her sight, that our mother is on her way to talk about the consequences of our actions, our punishment and then to take us home to enforce them. I turn away from her and walk hastily out of her office, crossing the courtyard in a panic.

I've never been in this much trouble before.

My teacher, Miss Hanna, doesn't really like me yet. I've only been attending this school for a few weeks. She helps everybody but me and disciplines only me – and for stupid things too. Stupid things that other kids do, like colouring outside of the lines in art, or when I take a little bit longer to figure out what comes after the number 43 even though half the class can't even count to 30. But not even she has ever spoken to me like Madame Atef just did. I thought I'd like Miss Hanna after seeing how nice she was to the other kids; she's also a lot younger and rounder than Madame Atef. But after having her as my teacher, I've made up my mind. She is not a kind person. Whenever Samra picks on me, she doesn't interfere as I know an adult should. I had dreams of what it would be like when I started school, but there hasn't been a day that's been close to what I imagined.

I knock three times on the grey door of the classroom and wait outside until I hear Miss Hanna's voice calling me in. I open the door and shuffle in, the room falling silent as I enter. I feel every eye staring at me; at my torn dress, my bleeding knees, my blood-stained socks, with my hands clasped and my head to the floor. I walk to my desk at the back of the classroom and I empty the little content of my tub into my bag, feeling silly under the scrutiny of their gaze and the silence of their tongues. Miss Hanna tells the class to go back to their tasks and work quietly, then I hear her heavy footsteps approach. She stands over me as I clear my desk, placing one of today's artworks – the paint still wet – into my bag.

'Has someone come to collect you?' Miss Hanna asks.

I nod and avert her eyes.

As I pick up the last of my belongings, she places a single, meaty finger on a portrait I drew this morning. I slowly follow her finger up to her arm with my eyes, then to her shoulder, until I'm looking up at Miss Hanna's round face. She stares at me blankly, then speaks.

'Your drawing, Akita, it isn't very good,' she says simply. 'It's unrealistic. The shoulders are too round.' She traces the portrait with her fingers, smudging all the colours together. 'And the nose is far too big.'

I look down at the portrait, all smudged and murky.

'It's you, Miss Hanna,' I shrug. 'I was only drawing what I saw.'

Taresai

The rigid woman sits before me in her pristine office. Madame Dina Atef. The beige walls are empty, save for a single, framed certificate, most likely her degree. Her shelves are neatly patterned with books, perfectly aligned in height order. Her files are colour coordinated, her mahogany desk polished, her grey suit tailored, her dark hair slicked. With her edges so sharp, Atef looks like she's an object of this unadorned office, not its occupant.

I've landed in this room many times in the two years Santo has attended this school, though I can't see myself ever feeling comfortable in its familiarity.

'Mrs Deng,' she exhales.

'Please, call me Taresai.'

Madame Atef exhales sharper, louder. 'Taresai, much to our disappointment, the staff and students of this proud school cannot endure Santo's antics any longer. We understand that he is a troubled child, but his actions today were inexcusable, even for him.'

Her tone is forbidding but there is a satisfaction on Atef's face, as though it gives her great pleasure to speak these words to me.

'I simply cannot accept this sort of behaviour.'

The way she speaks of my son makes me want to do bad things to her with my bare hands, but I know it isn't how this school works, how this country works.

She does this, plays this game, and the only way I can have even the smallest of victories is if I play along, because the education of my son and daughter comes before my pride, before this woman's disillusionment and her inflated sense of self.

'Remind me again, Madame, what exactly happened?' I say, a fake tone of worry in my voice.

'Santo is a negative influence on Akita. He is teaching her his ways. Just today, the two of them beat up poor Antony Diab.'

She's denser than a donkey if she expects me to believe any of this. She takes me for an absolute fool. Atef's face moves in a way that tries to convey emotion – sorrow would be my guess – but she's just a fraction out of practice.

'I'm afraid I draw the line at hitting another child, Mrs Deng – with bricks and stones, I should mention.'

Santo hitting a kid with a brick. That I can believe, but never how it was unprovoked. In these instances, I'm always struck by her failure to mention all the other times my son has been hit by another child and her galore of excuses then.

'Madame Atef, with all due respect, Santo is an eight-year-old boy and Akita is a few weeks shy of turning six. They're *children*. Surely, you don't think they'd be capable of beating a kid simply for the like of it. I just–'

'Mrs Deng–'

'Taresai. Madame, can you see no other reason?'

Because heaven forbid my children try to defend themselves.

Madame Atef exhales heavily. 'I've been in this line of work for longer than you've been alive, as hard as that might be to believe.'

As hard as believing the sky is blue.

'But, one thing I know is,' she continues, 'never underestimate what a disturbed child is capable of. I mean, all the bad people of today were once bad children, were they not? Bad children who were never taught right from wrong.'

'I trust that you don't mean *my* children are disturbed?'

'No,' her face unmoving. 'Your son is. With Akita, there is a real possibility for change. We can mould her to be an outstanding student. For Santo, however, the boat has sailed on that young man.'

I feel my grip tightening around my self-restraint.

Santo is a *boy*. A boy.

I gaze at Atef, at her black eyes, and I'm amazed to see that she believes every word she speaks.

She belongs to that dangerous breed of man who make up their own reality and believe it with such conviction, so remarkably blind to the truth even when it's right before their eyes. What makes them dangerous, is their efforts to make you believe it too.

Atef must mistake my silence for shame or guilt, because she starts speaking in soft words. 'Oh, you mustn't blame yourself,

Taresai,' she says. 'Circumstances considered, you're doing extraordinarily.'

She tries to soften her brow, but it only makes her look angrier, deepening the lines around her lips and the hollows of her cheeks. 'For someone who has no previous education, Taresai, my dear, who cannot read or write, yet you're in Giza and your children are in school. For you to be where you are is truly significant.'

The venom of her words, synthetic and vile, poisons the air. I feel the walls closing in.

This is the part where Atef expects me to grovel. To smile, accept the punishment she suggests for my children, and express my thanks for her time and charity of letting them attend this school. Instead, I stare at her with ruthless eyes, burning holes on the face that looks like the remains of the dead.

There is an evil I see lurking behind her dark eyes, enough to drain my soul and freeze over the torridness of this room.

She is beyond words, beyond hope.

I walk out of Atef's office and down the corridor to where my children wait. Santo lies belly-down on the seat of a rickety wooden chair, his arms and legs dangling precariously. Akita sits on the neighbouring chair, too roomy for her little frame, in a uniform too big for her tiny body, with her large school bag spilling over her small lap. My daughter meets my gaze and I see a swelling of relief in her large brown eyes. This alone is enough to break my heart, but it shatters when I see the bloodstains on her socks. I follow them up to her blood-stained school dress. What once was freshly washed and ironed is now ripped at the hem and torn in the knees, which both seem to be bleeding.

Akita nervously fiddles with the zip of her school bag as Santo grins with his large teeth in my direction, his nose bloodied and swollen. I felt a pulling this morning, from my intuition, to keep the kids home from school. I only ignored it because I thought it was for this reason, another nosebleed on this scorching day.

I bend down, tear a length of fabric from the bottom of my orange scarf and wrap my daughter's knobbly, scraped, and bleeding knees.

'Miss Deng? … Miss Deng?'

It's a few long seconds before I notice the school receptionist is speaking to me.

'Hmm?'

'Before you go, would you mind signing Santo and Akita out? Just on the register here.'

She's young, mid-twenties maybe. Dark hair underneath her brown scarf, red lipstick and a strong jawline. I stand and Akita tightly grips my hand.

'It's just for our records,' she continues. 'Their attendance.'

'No, thank you,' I smile, 'my children will never see this place again.'

* * *

Santino was good friends with the principal, Abdi Samir. It was how we got our children into the school. When Abdi fell ill a few months ago, Madame Atef took over, running the place as some sort of dictator. My children were at the bottom of the hierarchy, so naturally she had to make their schooling life more difficult than this country already does.

We are the onyx among the topaz, two colours of the same thing.

Hours and millions of thoughts later, I still stand by my decision to pull Santo and Akita out of that poor excuse for a school, though I'll admit that pulling Amara out of kindergarten may have been inordinate on my part. I figure if I am going to hasten the demise of our future in this hopeless city, I may as well push past the point of return, begin burning our bridges. Even if it is impulsively executed and without prior discussions with their father. With all our options exhausted, all we can do is wait until we find somewhere else to live, be it the next town over or halfway across the world. I'm hoping for the latter, although it's been months since our last correspondence with immigration. We're asylum seekers in this country, refugees; no respectable job or amount of silk scarves will make us as these Masarians are.

I could become their teacher. There's no telling if it would be good or bad, but I must admit that thought alone makes my stomach drop. I didn't birth my children into a life where their only options are to be educated and oppressed or uneducated and shielded from oppression until Santino and I are gone. All I want is for them to be free, for us to be free.

But until that day comes, Santo, Akita, and Amara will call me their teacher as well as their mother, I suppose.

I'm already the finest rum-maker in all of Cairo and I braid the hair of most the Sudanese women in the province, so how hard can teaching be?

* * *

Akita sits in the warm bathtub as I clean today's stains off her skin.

She says nothing, her attention instead on the bubbles sitting atop. She opens and closes her hands underwater and giggles softly when some of the bubbles pop or float away.

My daughter hasn't strung together a single sentence since we stepped out of that school. She uttered her baby sister's name, whom she's yet to meet, in the taxi, and when I shook my head in response, she retired from speaking for the rest of the night. When I asked her what happened to her knees, Santo answered that it was 'Angry Atef' who'd been the cause. Akita had three spoonfuls of her dinner before giving the rest to Santo, and when I announced it was bath time, she didn't mind going last, second to Santo, and third to Amara.

It hurts to imagine the thoughts that consume her mind after the horrors of today, and I feel a lifetime short of knowing how to soothe them.

'Akita, darling?' I say gently over the quiet sound of bath-water sloshing. She looks up at me, the thinnest layer of water sticking to her face, making her bronze skin look chromatic under the dim bathroom light. 'Do you want to talk about what happened today?'

She blinks slowly, her dark eyelashes fluttering, and she shakes her head. Her face is calm and unreadable, but there is much to be understood beyond her eyes.

'Are ... Are you sad?' I ask, feeling rather silly for being at a loss for words.

She shakes her head again.

'How are you feeling then, Kita?'

Her brown eyes move around the room as she considers this question. Akita simply shrugs and looks at her palms, observing their distortion underwater. I stare at her for a long while, thinking of the right words to say to get her to open. Is it normal for an almost-six-year-old to be this closed off from her own mother? Or is it a symptom of neglect?

'Okay ...' I whisper. 'Okay.'

I shift my stool so that I sit behind Akita, focusing instead my energy on washing her hair and bonding with her through the unspoken language of love.

'Akita ... you are beautiful. You are so full of light and you're ... so, so loved.' I feel her tense up by my words, but then she relaxes under my touch.

'Do you know why Samra's brother wanted to fight you today?'

'Because they don't like me,' Akita says quietly.

'Do you know why?'

Akita doesn't say anything, she just sits in the water with her head down, her shoulders rising and falling as she breathes.

'In this life, Akita, there will be people like Madame Atef, like Miss Hanna, like Samra and like Antony. People who look, speak and sound different to you, and they're going to treat you differently because of it. But I want you to know that there isn't a thing in this world that you can't do. You have powers, you understand? Know who you are in that heart of yours and you will always be okay. Okay?'

I let out a sharp exhale, breathing out air I didn't know I'd withheld. With each second that passes without a response, without some sort of reaction, my heart shatters for the umpteenth time today.

Then she quietly sniffs. 'Mm-hmm. Okay, Mama.'

I wrap her hair into a single cornrow and move to face her, staring at her bulbous eyes.

'Okay?'

'Uh-huh.'

'Is there anything else you want to say?' I asked, cupping her face in my palms. 'Anything else you want to talk about? Anything you want me to know?'

'No …' she shakes her head.

'Are you feeling better?'

'Mm-hmm …'

'Okay … good,' I breathe.

'It's just …'

'Yes?'

'I'm still a little …'

'A little what, Kita?'

'I'm a little … *annoyed,*' she says irritably, and I'm taken aback by the suddenness of it. 'I'm annoyed that my brand-new flower socks got messed up, and now, now they won't be nice like they were before.'

* * *

I put Amara to sleep and allow Santo and Akita to stay up and wait for their father to come home. Travelling straight to the hospital from work to be with Ashanti for a few hours has become part of his daily routine.

Santino works in administration at the mayor's office. It's a soulless job, mainly paperwork for people who believe we're second-class citizens but cower behind their denial of it. It puts food on the table and clothes on our children's backs, so all my complaints are made in private. Santino made some connections with immigration several months ago, to see what it would take for our little family to move to a place that offers more than this.

Sure, we have a place to sleep and food in our children's bellies, but I would give anything for them to have everything. A life without this one's limitations.

It's onerous to feel the touch of freedom when we're 14 storeys above the ground in a two-bedroom apartment with four young children.

Immigration sent countless forms for Santino to fill in, asking all sorts of questions: from the age of our youngest, to the medical history of our eldest, whether we're considering having more children, which Santino and I haven't even thought of or discussed yet. We never do really; pregnancy just sort of happens.

Now, a few weeks on, with multiple forms signed and lodged, it seems that our early dreams of freedom could well be a possibility. There hasn't been any word from immigration yet, but I know our days are numbered in this hopeless city.

Santino arrives home a little after nine. He holds Santo and Akita in a gentle embrace, kisses me on the cheek, then excuses himself to the bathroom. I reheat his supper and set a place for him on the dining table.

I sit down across from him while Santo and Akita watch cartoon reruns in the other room. I tell him everything, from the stiffness of Atef's shoulders to the blood on our children's uniforms. He smiles sadly, beams warmly. I take in the tiredness of his eyes, the new creases forming around his smile. It's a precious thing to grow old with one's love, but Santino is too young to look this old. It's too soon for grey hairs.

'You did the right thing Taresai, pulling them out of that school,' he says. 'I only wish we'd done it sooner. I just thought, well, I hoped that Abdi would've been back by now, and that Atef's reign was short-lived.'

'No. It's Atef's school now.'

'I'm sorry they had such a tough day. I'm sorry you had a tough day.' He runs his fingers over his moustache, flattening the black bristles.

'All our days together have been tough, Santino. Every single one. But … we make it through.' My voice grows distant, weak, speaking the words more to myself than to him. 'We always do.'

Santino closes his eyes, nodding as if surrendering to sleep.

'Are they okay?' he finally asks, opening his eyes and taking another spoonful of rice and lentils.

I think on this question for a moment.

'The worst of it is over. Santo will be okay, though we won't know for a few days. Akita might still be in a bit of shock, but … never again if I can help it.'

'Hmmm.'

'How was Ashanti? I didn't see her much today.'

'She's well.' A smile emerges from the corners of his tired face. 'She's getting stronger.' Santino pauses and studies my expression. 'Any day now, Taresai, I'm sure of it. In no time, she'll be sleeping in our room and Amara will have to move in with her brother and sister.'

I laugh, wiping away the tears welling in my eyes.

'May heavens help us with that. Amara will force herself between us before she moves on to a bed of her own.'

We laugh together, just for a moment. When silence falls, Santino puts his palms over my hands. 'Have some time to yourself, Taresai. I'll take them two out to see the stars,' he says, nodding to Santo and Akita, who lie with their bellies on the rug, eyes on the tv screen.

'Okay,' I breathe, slowly packing his dishes into the sink. My body finally gives itself permission to feel the full weight of exhaustion, so much so that I don't hear Santino call my name.

'Taresai,' he says my name again, but this time in a way that pulls my eyes to meet his, and I already know what is about to be expressed was forgotten news.

When I turn to him, Santino suddenly doesn't seem so tired, saying the words and filling it with worn tones of excitement. 'I've received some news from immigration.'

When I don't say anything, he continues. I find I'm too bewildered to speak. Today's the first day in four months that I haven't asked.

'They say we're eligible for permanent visas in three countries,' he says, his eyes begin to cast a gleam, one that I haven't seen for a while.

My heart halts then beats wildly like a drum.

'Bristol in England, Toronto in Canada …' he scratches the back of his head and squints his eyes, 'and Sydney in Australia.'

Akita

Baba comes home later from work these days.

Most of the time, Santo, Amara and I are asleep when he arrives, so, when Mama let Santo and me stay up I knew it was going to be a good night. It's nearly eleven o'clock when Baba finishes his supper. He tells me that it's the last hour of the day, which means that it'll be tomorrow when the clock strikes twelve. I find that hard to believe, because the sun doesn't rise at twelve o'clock, so how can the next day begin?

When Baba tells Santo and me that we're going out to look at the stars, I nearly jump out of my skin from excitement. We used to look at the stars from the balcony of our living room, on the very top floor of this very tall building every night, sunsets too. Everything changed when Santo watched a man jump from the roof of the building across from ours. It must've happened more than that one time, because ever since Mama and Baba forbade us from going out into the balcony. They think we don't know why, but we do.

Mama and Baba are also much more tired now than they used to be, since the baby came. She's a girl, her name is Ashanti, and even though I've never met her, I already know she's the cutest baby on this planet. She's going to come home when she's old enough, which is soon I hope, and I can finally be her big sister too.

Amara, my other younger sister, is two. I think she's still a baby. She's also pretty cute, she just makes it difficult to be nice to her. Amara's really loud, and she throws tantrums all the time and takes my things. I know with Ashanti it's going to be different.

I grab my favourite velvet cushion and I follow Baba into the balcony with Santo at my heels. The cold night air washes over us like a tidal wave, blowing off the sticky heat of the day's sun. It's a quiet night; the clamour of the street is muffled and distant from this high up. I lie on the farthest side out of the balcony, against the wooden railings. Santo lies closest to the living room door and Baba sandwiches in between us, his elbows out for us to rest our heads on like pillows. I look up and breathe out a hot breath into the starlit air.

There they are. The top of our planet that looks like the bottom of a wishing well.

There are so many of them. Tiny sparkling specks scattered across the endless sky, too similar to the coins Mama has in her purse. Baba once told me that those stars are actually rather big, bigger than me; they only look so small, smaller than my smallest freckle, because they're so far away.

'I hear you were a little fighter today, Akita,' Baba says to me. 'Are those your battle wounds?' he asks, nudging towards my knees, which are still wrapped in white bandages that almost glow in the dark. I nod and smile at the sky.

'I was too, Baba. I saved Akita from this ugly, pig-bodied boy called Antony.'

Baba chuckles. 'Of course, Santo, you always are. You're a good boy for standing up for your sister like that.'

Baba and Santo continue talking, but their voices fade out and the starry night sky fades in. It's so still, but the stars move in their own way without travelling anywhere. I can never quite understand it. I won't be upset if I never do.

I wonder what it's like to be up there, wrapped up in its stillness, to see this world and its movements, its colours, from so far away. I wonder if the stars can see me staring back at them, even though I am much smaller than they are.

Or can they only see me when I'm not looking? When the sun's out and I can't see them?

I begin to drift, float upwards towards the stars.

I bask in their twinkling stillness, their reverberant silence. I reach for their light until I'm touching it, the line between a dream and awake completely blurred.

Chapter 2

Cairo

Akita

The second week of Mama as our teacher and the living room as our classroom is coming to an end. It's Friday, and our lunch break is on the horizon.

Mama is a great teacher, better than Miss Hanna anyway, who's the only other teacher I've ever had. In this lesson, we're learning numeracy. It started off well, but Santo's attention is beginning to dwindle like it always does at this time of day. He's doing his work in comical bubble writing, drawing his answers on the lined pages like the graffiti we see on the street. I don't know why he does it when pencilling normally takes less effort, but Santo is Santo.

I'm using small wooden beads for numeracy because I don't yet know how to write or read, though numbers are much easier than letters. I don't miss school at all, not the gravel courtyard, not the sand-coloured buildings, not the nasty teachers, and certainly not the mean kids that go there. My regret is only small; in Miss Hanna's class, we'd just begun learning how to write our names.

I was so close.

'Santo, focus,' Mama says, returning to her seat after checking on Amara – she too is very hyperactive during this hour of the day. 'Only ten more minutes then we'll have a lunch break.'

Santo mutters and groans under his breath about it being some sort of violation to starve one's children. Mama ignores Santo's inflated remarks, so I try to as well.

I'm counting my second set of 15 beads when we hear the sound of Amara's cot creaking from Mama and Baba's bedroom, followed by her agitated cries.

Mum sighs defeatedly, 'class dismissed.'

Santo and I are sent to our bedroom until lunch is ready – which will probably be after she gives Amara a bath. Amara soiled herself for the second time this week; it seems being potty-trained isn't on her list of priorities.

Our room is nothing special: two small metal beds and a window. I have yellow sheets with pink hearts all over and Santo has blue sheets with clouds on them, though he says they're 'smoke puffs', not clouds. It's not a very good place to be bored, especially with Santo. Environments like this – bare and boring, are conducive to his creation of new games to play – which are only fun for him because he always wins and makes the rules up as he goes. And those rules only ever apply to me.

All our toys are kept in the living room where Mama and Baba can keep eyes on Santo and make sure he doesn't do anything stupid with them. Santo lies on his bed and blows a long raspberry. I sit on my bed, legs crossed, watching him, my stomach rumbling.

'This blows monkey turds,' he complains, and I nod in agreement.

He sits up and parts the mesh curtains all the way. I watch attentively as Santo opens the latch of the window with ease, as if he's done it countless times before when nobody's looking. The window swings open and the heat from the street immediately rushes in with a breeze.

'Santo, don't. You know we're not allowed to,' I say nervously.

Mama and Baba have said that under no circumstances should we ever open any window in this apartment. We live very high up, on the very top floor, and our bedroom window is large enough for Santo or me to easily fall out of.

'Oh, calm down, Kita, I'm just looking at the view.'

'You can look at the view with the window closed. That's why they make it see-through.'

'Yeah, but you can't smell and hear through a window, can you?' he asks, resting his palms on the windowsill. 'Come have a look for yourself.'

I slowly walk over to Santo's bed and sit beside him.

'See? It looks so different from way up here. Those people look like fat ants.'

It's true, everything big seems so small from this high. I look down at the laneways and alleys of our little village, lined with shops and stalls and fat ants moving to and fro. When I look up to my left, I see the large window of Mama and Baba's room, perfectly aligned and wide open. Their neat bedroom looks odd from here, familiar but out of place.

I gaze out to the horizon and into the desert, where the pyramids tower in the sand over our city like castles in the sky. I've had guesses at what they might be. Three triangular shaped rocks? I can see them most of the time, always somewhere in the distance, too far to detail, but always close enough to see. I wonder how they came to be. Are they fallen stars? Were they dropped from the sky? Were they built by giants who left them here as a gift?

'Hey, wanna play a game?' Santo asks, grinning with his entire face, his eyes shrinking and the dimples on his cheek deepening. I'm yet to adjust to his newly grown big-boy teeth.

'Hmm?'

'A game, wanna play?'

I get a sinking feeling in the pit of my stomach, the same feeling I get when I'm in trouble. The two of us sitting here, staring out the open window, so high from the ground, has inspired Santo to think up some sort of game. The way he smiles at me prickles my skin. 'Look, all we have to do is jump from this window into Mama and Baba's room through their window.'

My heart jumps out of my chest.

'Santo, no,' I plead, wanting to cry, not wanting to cry, trying not to cry.

'It's not even that far. I've seen you jump further and higher with your skipping rope, come on! Don't be a wuss.'

Truth is, it really isn't that far: it's two, maybe three small steps away. It'd be easier to land than to fall, I think, but still, one wrong move, one misstep …

Santo waits for me to say something. When I don't, he continues.

'I've done it before, I'll even go first if you like.'

'What happens if you fall?'

'I won't. I saw it in that film where the man flew through the window to catch the bad guy.'

'He had superpowers, Santo.'

'No, he didn't, he's no different from me, Akita, just watch.'

Only, the man in the film *is* very different from Santo; he probably practiced for a long time to jump like that and not die. But this is something Santo does: he tries to copy things he sees on tv, done by people he wishes he could be.

'You'll be okay? You won't fall? You won't die?' I question, shrinking into myself.

'I cross my heart.'

'What happens if *I* fall?'

Santo pauses when he rises to his feet and thinks on this for a moment.

'Well … don't.'

My body goes rigid when Santo steps onto the window ledge. I instinctively try to stop him, but I'm frozen and the words won't come out.

He stands up confidently and smiles down at me with his large teeth.

I feel like I'm going to be sick.

My heart begins to thunder loudly in my chest, Santo bends his knees and grips the ledge with his bare feet steadily.

Nausea churns in my belly and I feel like I'm made of jelly and stone at the same time.

One moment Santo stands, the next, he's flying through the air and everything goes in slow motion.

I can't bring myself to watch; I'm really going to be sick.

When I whip my head around, I catch the tail end of Santo, a flash of a black boy in an orange shirt and blue shorts flying through Mama and Baba's window, and landing on their carpet with a thud. I wait a few moments, then let out a stale breath when I hear him laughing from the next room. He rises to his feet and sticks his head out the window at me.

'See?' he beams. 'Easy! I didn't even jump that far. Now, you go.'

I rise to my feet and stand on the window ledge. I don't look down, or out, I just look at Santo's face grinning from inside Mama and Baba's room, making way for my landing. I hang on to the edges of the window as the gentle wind brushes my cotton skirt along my legs. I stand on my tippy toes and leap from this window to the next.

I crash land into my parent's bedroom, feeling the wounds on my knees from last fortnight reopen and a new gash on my elbow screaming for attention.

'That was the coolest thing I've ever seen!' Santo exclaims as he helps me to my feet. I feel blood seep out of the new wound and out of the old ones in burns and stings.

I assess the damages to my body, nothing too major: though I'm sure the new tear on my skirt will upset Mama.

'I can't believe you actually did it.' Santo beams.

Nor can I.

But we're in big trouble, I can feel it already.

There isn't a chance that Mama didn't hear all that, but even if she didn't, our neighbours downstairs most definitely did.

'Wanna go again?' Santo grins.

'Not even if I was on fire.'

'Hmm. Suit yourself.'

Santo climbs onto the window ledge, and I keep an eye on Mama and Baba's bedroom door, expecting Mama to fly in any second and give me the beating of my life. But she doesn't.

I jump when I hear a loud crash coming from where Santo was, and run to the window in a panic. At first, I can hardly believe my eyes, then I almost faint when I see a massive, Santo-sized smash in our bedroom window, which I could've sworn was open. The wind must've blown it shut.

'Santo?' I croak.

'Akita,' I hear him pant through the windows. 'Go get Mama. I hurt myself real bad.'

I run out of her bedroom and down the hall in search of her. I slow down my steps when I realise how quiet the house is. It's as if nobody's home and my footsteps are too loud; like someone is going to pop out of the walls and shush me. I tiptoe around the corner until I hear Mama's voice. She sounds angry, vexed, but not at us.

She's talking to someone. A man. I poke my head out from the hall, peering through the kitchen by the front door. 'I'm warning you,' Mama says to a man I don't recognise, her voice dripping with fury I've never seen. 'Leave!' she hisses.

Mama holds the broomstick threateningly towards the man who walks and bounces towards her like the floor is uneven, keeping him from entering the apartment. His clothes hang loosely off his frame. He tries to say my mother's name, but he slurs his words. I've seen some people act this way before. He's had too many drinks of the 'happy' juice Mama makes for grown-ups. Santo says it's like apple juice, but for adults, only it smells bad, and I can imagine it tastes worse, and this man doesn't seem so happy. He seems frighteningly miserable.

'Taresai, please,' he says, his tongue flopping out of his mouth. 'One more caseful and you – and you won't ever see me again.' He takes a step too close to my mother.

Fear freezes my every limb for the second time today. I try to think of ways to rescue her, but I'm too scared of what the man might do. I stay hidden, silent, my heart pounding so loudly I fear I might be seen.

'Get the hell out of my house, Seb!' Mama whispers, with such a ferocity it makes my stomach drop. She shoves him out the front door and slams it shut in his face. A moment passes and we hear him tumble down a few steps of the endless flights of concrete stairs, both knowing it's a long way down before he reaches the bottom. Mama leans the broom against the front door and sighs heavily. She scans the area and stops when she sees me.

'Akita! … what are you doing? Are you alright?' she asks, straightening her skirt. 'I'll have lunch ready in a minute.'

I don't say anything, I don't even move. Mama walks over to me and kneels down; her eyes widening when she sees my knees.

'What's wrong? What's happened?'

'It's Santo, Mama. He's hurt.'

Chapter 3

Cairo

Taresai

Manuela and I sit in the waiting room of the maternity ward. She, flicking through a magazine as I fiddle with the stray fabric of my chiffon scarf. We received a call yesterday afternoon from Helena – the senior paediatric nurse who's been caring mostly for Ashanti. She asked that we come to the hospital to discuss our daughter's progress.

I stare at the clock. The appointment was set for noon, sharp.

It's fifteen minutes to two.

Giza public hospital isn't tremendous at service as much as it is with care, but still, I've never been made wait to see Ashanti.

Every other day I'd simply sign in and the receptionist would let me through. But today, Layla at the front desk asked us to take a seat and said that Helena would be with us shortly. That was nearly two hours ago, before Layla clocked off and another young woman clocked in.

She hasn't said a word to us or so much as looked in our direction, instead greeted the other thirteen visitors in the waiting room who have come and gone and waited no longer than three minutes or so.

I rise to my feet when I feel the pulse of my anxiety quicken.

I stand by the window and watch the cars on the street below. It's rather quiet for a Thursday.

Santino's at the office, he couldn't get permission to take today off. Late notice.

When I asked Manuela to come with me, she dropped everything at once and had her cousin Ali drive us here.

Santo, Akita, and Amara are being watched by my mother, who I hope isn't being given too much grief. Although Santo is not nearly as mobile now with his stitched and bandaged arm.

I'm quite foggy on the details of what exactly took place, still. Santo keeps changing his story and Akita won't speak a word of it.

I start pacing the length of the waiting room.

I simply can't think about that right now.

'Taresai, will you stop that?' Says Manuela, eyeing her magazine. 'You're making me uneasy.'

I stop in my tracks. 'Making *you* uneasy?'

'Yes, my friend, I'm trying to finish this crossword,' she says lightly. She looks up at me and tries to conceal a smirk.

'You'll have to actually start it first,' I chuckle. The chances of Manuela doing a crossword are about the same as lightning striking twice. She, like myself, cannot read.

'I have,' she says, trying to keep herself from giggling. 'In here,' she points a finger to her temple.

I stare at Manuela seriously until a laugh escapes her and I follow suit. Our moment of relief is only broken when the young woman at the reception clears her throat loudly in disapproval.

Manuela looks in her direction and procures a fake laugh, exaggerated in volume and length, sounding more like a hyena than a woman.

I giggle quietly and take my place next to my friend.

She unravels her purple scarf from underneath her arm and tosses it over my shoulder, pulling me into her embrace. Manuela kisses my cheek repeatedly until I'm smiling again.

This is the way we've been since we were girls in our little village in Juba. Manuela is the youngest to three older brothers, all of whom are still in Sudan. We found pieces in each other that just fit. She was adored and protected by her mother, her father and all her brothers and she, at twelve, knew that Taresai, at fourteen, hadn't felt that in her short life.

She had no interest in schooling like her brothers, so she spent most of her time with me.

We were joint at the hip and people in the village would joke that we were twins in every sense except physical.

Manuela, short and plump with honey brown skin next to me, tall and slender, as dark as the night sky.

'This is ridiculous we've been waiting for nearly two hours,' I say, suddenly exhausted.

'Patience Taresai,' she says soothingly, and I shoot her a look.

'I'm sorry. But it's going to be alright, it's probably good news even.'

'How could you know that?'

'I don't, but is it so bad to allow yourself to think so?'

'Maybe. But why must it take so long? I mean, why set an appointment time at all?!'

I must've said that too loudly because the receptionist finally voices her disfavour of us.

'Excuse me miss, is there a problem?' She questions loudly and before either of us answer, cuts in.

'I suggest the two of you keep it down.'

'I beg your pardon?!' Says Manuela, turning with her whole body to face the receptionist.

She's square in the face and wears magenta lipstick that clashes terribly with her hospital issued cobalt headscarf.

'This is a maternity ward, miss,' retorts the receptionist.

She can't be older than twenty-five.

'Do I look like a 'miss' to you?' Questions Manuela.

'Do I need to call security?'

'Say another word in that tone and you just might have to.'

'Manuela,' I put my hand on hers to settle her down and give her a look of warning.

'It's not worth it, Mani.' I whisper.

The receptionist picks up the phone angrily and begins punching in digits, but before she finishes, the large blue double doors open, and Helena emerges.

'Taresai' she smiles, tucking a golden-brown lock behind her ear and I've never been happier to see her.

'I'm so sorry to keep you waiting' she says, ushering Manuela and I through the maternity ward and into her office.

'We delivered triplets to new parents last night that were expecting twins!' She laughs, taking her seat behind her desk.

'But enough about that, how are you? Can I get you some water?'

'No thank you, Helena,' I smile. 'You called about Ashanti?'

'Yes!' she says, tucking another stray curl behind her ear and fetching a file from her draw.

My heart starts feeling heavy and beating loudly.

'The paediatric team have agreed that Ashanti is fit and healthy to be discharged into your care, Taresai, as soon as tomorrow.'

Then everything stops. My heart, my breath, time.

'Ashanti has been off the machines for over ten days now and she is self-regulating all on her own. Congratulations.'

Helena smiles with every inch of her face which wobbles through my welling eyes.

'Mashallah,' Manuela breaths, and I sense that she's about to cry too.

* * *

Ashanti arrives home on the same day we decide to move to Australia. After correspondence with immigration, we were told that a house would be ready for us in a place called Sydney by the start of next month and that settled it.

We were humbled to have been given more than one place of refuge and planting our roots. But I had to be honest with just myself in my feeling that Australia was the only place I could see us, and I felt that in my every limb. I never voiced this, so that's all they ever were, feelings and thoughts that I kept to myself. But now they're coming to fruition.

They say when it rains, it pours, and so when it shines, it blinds. I can't trace the last time I've felt this way, this joy that is so dizzying, I don't know which way is up.

If it's a word, it is hope and it glows within me like a soft light.

Though it's warm, I approach it with apprehension, because it's a feeling I've learned only to deny. It always hurt more to have it extinguished than to not have it at all.

There are things we must think about now, movements that must be made and things put in place. Do all we can to prepare for our new life before we pack our things and move to the other side of the world.

It all frightens me, but not enough to stop me from moving towards it.

Akita

Today is the day.

Mama and Baba are finally bringing home our baby sister; today I finally meet her. Up until this point, Ashanti has felt like a figment of my imagination, a mythical character in one of Mama's stories that she tells us before we fall asleep. But here she is, cradled in Mama's arms, the cutest and littlest person I've ever seen.

She's small but chubby in pink ruffles and white bows. Baba says she looks like me, but it's hard to tell. Ashanti's skin is very pink, like a brown-ish pink, and all the features of her face look almost swollen. Her hair is as dark as mine but there is a softness to it that mine's grown out of. I sit next to Mama in my baby-blue dress and my new frilly socks, breathing in the scent of my newborn sister.

I only wish there weren't so many people around. My grandmother and my aunts are here, Aunty Anette and Aunty Asélle – Mama's sisters. Mama's best friend Aunty Manuela is here too, and they all get to hold and kiss Ashanti before I do. They decided to throw Ashanti a homecoming party, which is stupid because Ashanti is a baby and doesn't even know what a party is. She only knows how to breathe, sleep and poop. My cousins are here too, but that doesn't matter so much because my favourite person, my Uncle Messai, isn't.

Uncle Messai is to Mama what Santo is to me. Her big brother. He'd always throw me to the ceiling when saying hello, and he'd leave little chocolate sweets in my palms when he'd say goodbye. Some time ago, he said goodbye and I never saw him again. Mama says he moved away, somewhere very, very far from here, to be with his family.

We're all gathered in the living room with tea, biscuits, cake, and a fruit platter on the table in the centre of it all. All eyes take in the newest and cutest family member, passing her around like she's some newfound treasure. The kids are supposed to be playing in the other room, but my girl cousins – there are five of them – are all here, while my boy cousins are in the other room, with no interest whatsoever in a newborn baby.

'Psst! Kita!' Santo whispers behind my ear. 'Ditch the oldies and come play with us.'

'They're not all old, Santo. Aunty's daughters are here too.'

'Yeah, but they're *girls*. Come on, please?'

'I'm waiting for my turn to hold Ashanti.'

'Akita, you have the rest of your life to hold that baby. Besides, everyone's going to go home soon, and Ashanti isn't going anywhere, so you can hold her then.'

He has a point.

'Okay,' I say, sliding down from the couch as conversations between Mama and her sisters continue without disruption.

I follow Santo into our bedroom that Baba's set up with toys. Amara plays with our cousins Joseph and Bilal, who I think are the same age as her.

Anei, Aunty Manuela's son, emerges from behind the door and tries to scare me. I don't like him very much; he isn't even my cousin. Aunty Manuela is Mama's best friend since childhood, so I have to call her Aunty even though we're not related.

Anei is a rotten kid, and he's more annoying than Santo. He once stuck a penny between the small gap in my two front teeth, which Baba had to slide out. Anei always has something to say about the things I can't change, like the one freckle I have above my lip and the largeness of my forehead.

He thinks I care – I don't. They're the things about me that make sense. When I look at my reflection, I know that my gap and my freckle and my hair are the parts of me that come from my Mama, and I never have to search to find her in me, so he can shove it.

I look at Santo, trying to communicate to him without words my disapproval of Anei being with us.

'You look like a little lamb in that dress, Akita,' Anei smiles.

He thinks he's so funny. There are so many things I can say about his appearance, like how his eyelashes curl so far back they look like caterpillars perched on his eyelids, or how his pink gums are funny looking, or how the redness of his brown skin makes him look like he's blushing like the white people on tv. Or how the clothes his mother dressed him in make him look like an old man.

I don't say a word. I don't so much as look at him.

'Knock it off, Anei, only I can make fun of Akita,' says Santo.

'Alright, whatever. So, what's the plan, San?' he says, hands in his pockets.

'I think we should ditch this baby tea party and go down to the night market.'

I didn't know exactly what Santo was going to say, but I knew it was going to be a bad idea. Santo beams and crosses his bandaged arm from last week's accident, over his good arm, exceedingly proud of his plan.

'Santo, no,' I whisper, tugging on his good arm.

'Oh, don't be such a baby, Akita. It'll be fun,' says Anei, who's only one year older than Santo.

'But it's after sunset, Santo, and it's Friday. You know Mama and Baba never let us go when it's dark out.'

'It won't be dark, that's what streetlights are for.' Santo smiles.

'What could go wrong?' Anei chimes in.

So much could go wrong. Too much. I'm still trying to recover from what happened last week. I don't know how Santo seems so fine with his sliced-up hand in bandages serving as a reminder.

'Come on, Akita,' Santo sings. 'I'll buy you something nice?'

* * *

We sneak out through the front door without anybody noticing. My heart thumps wildly in my chest as I follow Santo down the concrete steps, with Anei annoyingly close behind. When we step out onto the street, we're instantly allured by the sound of music and cheap firecrackers, the smell of honey on warm bread and the bright lights of the market, all just one block away. Friday nights are when our little village in this run-down part of Giza comes to life. I usually watch it all from my bedroom window, seeing all the lights and the people dressed in colourful fabrics dance through the streets, all the way down here while I'm way up there. We walk into the markets, through the winding laneways lined with stalls that tower over us like wooden castles in a wooden kingdom.

Lights hang from every corner against the dark night, glowing so brightly I can barely see the stars. People dance in the streets to the sounds of bells, flutes, drums and many singing voices. There are stalls for everything imaginable: fruit, sweets, even candied fruit. We walk by a sugar cane stall, a stall that sells dresses, jewellery stalls, but only one makes me stop in my tracks.

There's a rickety wooden stall tucked away in a corner, where a dozen china dolls drape. I walk over to it, peering up at the dolls that hang from above like angels. I have plenty at home, but none quite like these: dolls with pale, breakable skin and moving eyes. I stand on my tippy toes, reaching up to the closest one.

I trace my fingers along her blanched cheek, cold to the touch. She has eyes like the sea and hair the colour of sunshine. I glare at her and retract my touch, scared for a moment because I feel her staring into me as if she were alive.

'Looks creepy,' says Santo, before pacing over to a stall nearby selling miniature sports cars.

'Hello there, young miss,' the stall-owner emerges from a corner. 'For a moment I thought one of my dolls had come to life and was trying to wander away.'

I smile and look at my shiny black shoes and my stark white frilly socks.

'That's a very pretty blue dress. Are you with your parents?' The old man smiles, his skin the colour of honey, his eyes with a grey film over them. When he opens his mouth I see he is missing a few teeth, but his smile is one of the friendliest I've ever seen. I shake my head.

'Are you lost?'

I shake my head again and point to Santo, who is transfixed by a duo-chrome sports car with silver wheels the size of his palm. Anei stands nearby, asking a Masarian kid where he got the powdered halawa he's eating.

'Ah.' The stall-owner beams and stares into space wistfully. He takes a bow from the doll's hair, a blue bow, almost the exact blue as my dress.

'Well, I hope you three have a wonderful night,' he says, clipping the bow to a braid on the side of my head.

I grin at him, baring all my teeth, even the wobbly ones, in thanks.

We move through the village that is lit from within, stopping at nearly every stall before we find the stall with all the cakes, puddings and pastries. Anei buys a large vanilla and chocolate swirl cake and divides it into three. With our bellies full, we march through, dancing towards the sounds of the music, painting the night with our vibrant colours.

In the distance we notice people gathering around a single belly dancer and we follow, slipping between their tall figures and arriving at the front. At first, I'm struck by the dancer's beauty as she moves her body like a rattlesnake. I'm struck once again when I catch a closer glimpse of her face, she looks like a character from my dreams – beautiful, with long dark hair that falls to her bum, a dozen gold bangles that line each wrist and a ring on her belly button. She wears a high-cut red top ornamented with golden embellishments, and a matching red skirt that drapes over her feet, the golden hem cascading along the sandstone cobbled pavement. Her lips are red, her skin is brown and the dark eyeliner she wears around her green eyes makes her look otherworldly, as if she has magical powers, like she will turn into a lion when the clock strikes twelve.

Countless more people surround her as she dances and twirls, twisting her body to the rhythm of the music. She is pure magic, hypnotising the masses with her powers. I could watch her forever.

She unravels an emerald scarf wrapped around her hips and tosses it into the air. It dances in the lights for a moment, moving through space and time ever so delicately, then she catches it on the beat of the drum. She twirls and twirls and then her eyes lock with mine.

She can't be looking at me, and yet, our eyes are fixed on each other.

I'm stunned when I see her moving towards me. She dangles the scarf before my eyes, and without a second thought I grab onto it. She pulls me into the circle, into *her* circle.

All eyes fall on me.

I freeze.

What now?

When I look around for the answers, I realise that Santo and Anei are nowhere to be seen.

My heart feels like it's going to come out of my mouth.

The music continues, it's rhythmic pattern unbroken by my intrusion – the drums, the tangerines, the bells. I feel it reverberating around me, beating in my chest, buzzing beneath my skin.

The belly dancer looks at me and smiles. She has so many teeth. She moves her body ever so slowly and I imitate her movements. The crowd starts clapping and cheering and whistling. I dance with the gorgeous woman who looks like she could be a queen under the warm lights.

She puts her hands under my arms, picks me up and spins me in the sky. The world twists and spirals and I squeal with delight. Then she sets me on her hips with ease as she moves her body, and I move with her. The people gathered around throw money and flower petals at us. With my legs wrapped around her hips, I feel her every movement bounce from her body into my bones.

I stumble when she sets me back down on the ground, momentarily unused to the sensation of the earth beneath my feet. She picks up a note and places it in my hand. She smiles at me, a smile so beautiful I want to stare at it forever. I can see why all these men are going crazy for her. Then she spins and twirls away, the sequins at the hem of her skirt dazzling like the sun in the middle of the night.

I step back into the crowd in disbelief and in absolute awe of such a woman. I hardly notice how late it is, or that I'm all alone. I go to follow the belly dancer when Santo emerges from the crowd and grabs my wrist.

'Run, Akita!' he pants. 'Run!'

I run as fast as my little legs can carry me before thoughts come to my mind. Anei runs the fastest with Santo leading closely behind, slowing down only for me to catch up. We zig-zag through the stalls, drawing more attention than we should.

'This way!' Anei shouts. 'It's a shortcut.'

We turn a corner and walk into a dim and narrow alleyway. We catch our breaths while hiding in the dark from whomever they – Santo and Anei – were being chased by.

'Santo, what did you do?' I pant, unsure if it's the running or my galloping beats of panic that's responsible for my shortness of breath.

'Nothing,' he breathes. 'I just took this from old man Omar,' Santo holds up a large bottle of mango juice in his injured hand.

'Why?'

'Because I was thirsty, Akita,' he says to me, very slowly like I'm stupid.

'But why didn't you pay? Mama gave you pocket money yesterday.'

'Yes, but I left it in the pocket of my home jeans, not these fancy ones she made me wear today.'

When we capture enough air in our lungs, we walk silently back to our complex. Anei is the first to speak when we're making our way up the stairs, and for once, I'm relieved by it. Anei's words distract me from the bloodstains on the concrete steps, blood of the man Mama called Seb.

'I know you're moving away,' Anei says, his voice echoing through the staircase.

'What are you talking about?' Santo enquires, short of breath as we reach our tenth flight of steps.

'Mama told me,' Anei responds, in that annoying know-it-all tone his voice has. 'She said your Ma told her that you guys are moving away. Not to another house or another neighbourhood. You're getting on a plane and flying to another country. A place called Australia. It's in Europe. Full of white people.'

I wish Anei would shut up. He's always been a fibber. But something feels different. Usually, he only plays tricks on me. Why would he also be tricking Santo?

We sneak into the house and nobody notices that we've been gone, not a single head turns our way. Everybody is how they were: too loud and invasive of Ashanti's personal space.

* * *

That night, after my bath, after I hold Ashanti in my arms for all of 20 seconds and kiss her 21 times, I lay in bed, thinking about the things that Anei said tonight in the stairwell.

'Hey, Sunny? Are you awake?'

'Hmm …' he groans.

'Do you think what Anei said is true? Do you really think we're moving away from here?'

'I don't know … Do you want it to be true?' he muffles sleepily through his blanket pulled right up to his nose.

'Yeah. I think so. I don't know.'

'Then yes. I think it's true.'

I lay my head on the pillow and stare upwards into the blackness of the room.

'Do you think we're going to like it there? … Sunny? … Santo?'

Santo snores in response, fast asleep.

We might really be moving away, somewhere far away. A new school, new friends. We're going to live in a new place. We'll have a new house, one that's probably close to the ground.

Chapter 4

Cairo

Taresai

It seems the news of our upcoming departure has travelled far and wide during this past week. When Santino and I attempted to break the news to the kids at breakfast, a few days after Ashanti settled in, Santo, with a mouth full of cornflakes, had cut us off, saying 'we know,' before Santino even completed his sentence.

I told the kids that this move is going to be the biggest one of their lives – heavens, our lives too. Australia is an entirely different country – and continent, so I've learned. We're not getting into a car for a few minutes or jumping on a train for a couple of hours. This'll be a two-plane ride, three-day journey. The first time on an aircraft for all of us.

We're going to live in a country where everyone looks different from us. Our lives as we know them will become inconceivably unfamiliar. Australia will be our new home.

Santino reassured the kids that though it's going to be quite an adjustment, so long as we have each other we will be alright.

* * *

The first few nights of sleeping next to my newborn are blessed.

To be with her washes over any reminder that I was ever without.

Ashanti is unlike any other child I've had. All she does is sleep. She only ever cries when she needs to be changed, when she's hungry and in the ten seconds when she goes from the bathtub to the towel.

She very much resembles her father, with her large brown eyes, head of black curls, and her chubby cheeks, but her nose, her small button nose, is all mine.

Santo was a screamer, he kept us up all hours of the day and night. Akita had separation anxiety from her father and me – which she only outgrew when Amara was born.

Amara is all the above. Still very high in her needs, both physical and emotional. In truth, and as predicted, I feel her need for attention has heightened now that she has what her mind could only comprehend as competition.

All my children lie in their beds, fast asleep. Santino has retired for the night after spending hours filling in more immigration forms.

It's a little past midnight, the only time I can brew my rum in the safety of solitude.

I lift the lid to the large pot tucked away in the corner of the kitchen counter and the delicately bitter smell of fermented medjool dates fills the space around me.

As I pour the cloudy liquid through a strainer, separating the medjool dates from their essence, I think about my eldest two.

I wonder what their new lives mean for them, what lies ahead. Santo seemed explicitly nonchalant about the news; you would've thought we'd just told him about the weather forecast for the day. His reaction doesn't concern me, but it doesn't relieve me either. He expected this news to come, he's been expecting it since we moved to Cairo from Sudan three years ago. But my firstborn conceives delayed reactions to things. He acts in the moment and his emotions catch up with him later, like the aftershock of an earthquake. It always leaves me wondering if there's more to come. Akita didn't say much, though I saw the slight smile that tugged at the corner of her lips when her father finally confirmed her suspicions. I think she's happy. I can only hope she is. Amara is too young to understand what's happening. She and Ashanti are on the same boat of oblivion sailing the sea of bliss.

As for myself? I'm as much thrilled as I am terrified. Terrified of the unknown and of all the things I *do* know. Australia is so different from any place I've ever been, but it's where we will raise our children and spend the rest of our lives, planting our severed roots into that foreign soil.

I set the pot on the stovetop and stir the dark-brown liquid that glimmers ominously under the yellow kitchen light. As I inhale the sweetened scent drifting upwards, I feel the familiar warmth it brings to my face.

This has been my way of survival for the past three years. Santino's cheques from work covers the bills, the food on the table, clothes on our back, while the cash from this illegally run business of mine pays for all of the things in between. With our life savings put together, we have enough to survive in Australia for at least two months, and that's not counting all the extra money I've pocketed recently as news travelled about this gig coming to an end. Business is humming and people are buying my rum in bulk. I've even had a few generous offers for the recipe, but there's been none I haven't respectfully declined.

I want to keep this one thing for myself, I want it to disappear from Cairo when I do. Everything else we've earned and built in this city will belong to someone else before our feet have left the ground. But not this.

I started brewing the first week we arrived here. From then on, all the characters of Cairo became acquainted with my rum, if not with me. Word travelled far and wide in the first few months and landed on one of Egypt's most revered musicians, Amr Sayyad. He too joined the list of loyal customers, though the only exception is we've never met.

I've heard the man sing, but never speak my name, and he has only tasted the rum, never shaken the hands that make it.

Every second Sunday of the month, Amr Sayyad's driver, a well-mannered gentleman named Sammy, arrives at my doorstep at exactly 2.15 pm to pick up a month's supply of rum, and leaving a generous tip that is often twice the cost.

Profit from Sayyad's money alone helped us pay for all the 'embellishments,' Santino calls them, when we first settled into this very apartment.

Sayyad is a mere stranger, and yet he's been a key element of our survival in this city.

I've always thought, as embellishing as they can be, it's not all they ever are, because what good is keeping the lights on without a comfortable place in the house to sit or sleep?

I let my mind wander for a moment, to a place I've been too scared to tread, watching the pot as it boils, turning from cloudy to clear.

In Sudan, I survived by running. From bullets and people who meant me harm.

In Egypt, I survive by making.

How will I survive in Australia?

When the rum cools, I fill up six bottles and set them aside on the countertop, ready for Sammy to pick up tomorrow afternoon.

Chapter 5

Cairo

Taresai

My mother, my two sisters, Anette and Asélle, and their children have come over for supper. Evenings like these, though they are intimate, are few and far between, and require a lot of energy. Too often I find that I must focus a little more, think much sharper, look deeper; because the truth always lies in the unsaid.

I adore my sisters and I'd do almost anything for them. I also don't blame them for being the way they are; our formidable upbringing is the root of it. Still, there are times I resent them for not abandoning their archaic ways of thinking and doing. These gatherings are almost unbearable without our older brother Messai. Almost.

He moved to Sweden with his wife Leena and their three children two years ago. It broke all our hearts to see them go, but it's an unspoken law between those who are in struggle, that one with a ticket to higher ground, take it before the waters rise.

It brings me great solace knowing he is leading a life someplace better, but Messai's absence leaves the scales unbalanced.

My sisters Anette and Asélle are twins, born a year and a half after me. Anette has four children. Her eldest two are also twins, nine-year-old Evelyn and Emmanuel, followed by seven-year-old Atem and four-year-old Joseph. I've never met the father of my niece and nephews. Anette ran off with him – the faceless man – when she was seventeen. She disappeared for sixteen years, and only reunited with us two years ago.

We don't speak of it, we never mention him, even if his ghost hangs over us, even if the truth is written in the air with invisible ink. He took all her money and left in the night, without a word to her or his children.

We aren't to truly know if she ever saw the signs or what conclusions she's drawn to gain an ounce of closure.

Her children are so very polite, so obedient, so neat, and unnaturally clean for ... well, children. In the short time that I've come to know them, I've never seen a hair out of place, they've never stepped a toe out of line. All their personalities merge into one.

My semi-mute Akita has more personality in her one finger than all those kids have combined, which is an awful thing to say, I know. I just wish that Anette was raising those poor children instead of training them. But Anette is a single mother with very young children. Who am I to judge her parenting? Besides, I can only imagine the thoughts she has about my offspring.

In Anette's eyes Santo is an absolute menace, a bad influence on her sons, which is why she rarely lets them play together. She thinks I don't notice, but heavens, is she wildly mistaken.

Akita is too rough around the edges for a little girl; she can never keep her dresses clean or her hair neat, running around and playing with the boys.

'Akita is so lucky to have younger sisters now.' Anette said to me the night of Ashanti's homecoming, which translates to: 'There's hope now for poor Akita. She's been running wild and untamed as the boys do.'

My relationship with Anette is unequivocally the most fragile, the most strained, the one that requires the most reading into. Sixteen years' worth of unspoken words between us remain unsaid, and every other word we speak to each other is a deeper stab into the wounds of our damaged relationship.

It doesn't help that we were both raised by two very different sides of our mother. She, the favoured child, was allowed to finish her schooling, went all the way to college. I, the firstborn daughter, was pulled out of school to be a second mother to my siblings. To cook, to clean, to feed, to bathe, to change, to raise.

I was eight.

Then, when our mother got sick the following year, she sought treatment at the nearest hospital, which was in the next province.

She stayed there for two years, and I stayed home, holding down the fort. I was ten by the time she came back. I didn't ask to go back to school, because I already knew that hell would freeze over before I sat in a classroom again.

So, we sit across from each other on the dining table, Ashanti in my arms, Anette's purse in hers, smiling and speaking meaningless words to one another, too afraid to unravel the mess we pretend does not exist. Anette, dark in skin, slim in the face, is a spitting image of our mother. With her black hair braided close to the scalp, she sits with a straight spine, though her shoulders cave in slightly. Her faded blue scarf sitting tightly on her head.

Every time I look at her, I fear that once we open those floodgates, the flooding won't stop.

Asélle sits beside me, her hair straightened, her lips red and her complexion a synthetic light-brown, erasing the resemblance she once bore to her twin sister.

Asélle and her husband, Ibrahim, also have twins. Their marriage caused a stir in our mother, primarily because it was

Asélle's first act of defiance. Ibrahim is Moroccan and therefore unworthy of our mother's approval like anybody else who isn't Sudanese. Their eldest two are nine-year-old's, Heema and Halima, then eight-year-old Samira, five-year-old Ines, and their only son, four-year-old Bilal.

Asélle's daughters are very sweet; their only habits of concern is that they think they're above everyone because they're a few shades lighter than their cousins. I don't fault them for this, it's this country that rots their brains into believing that garbage. I also fault Asélle, partially because she is their mother, but mainly because I know she believes it too, though the words will never be said.

I'm yet to know if she truly believes that her skin becoming five shades lighter since marrying Ibrahim and having his children has gone unnoticed. With her pale brown fingers and dark knuckles, Asélle strokes my daughter's face and gushes over Ashanti's beauty, pretending it has nothing to do with her lighter skin compared to my other children.

Despite her flaws, Asélle and I have always been close, from childhood to motherhood. She unabashedly adores my children and I adore hers, but I don't want them too close to mine. I don't want Akita thinking her cousins are better than her simply because their faces change colour when they blush.

I've always felt that I can be honest with Asélle, but never open, not since her marriage. I can't be when I never truly know what lurks behind those eyes.

Lastly, there's my mother. The well-respected Adele Deng.

The woman who birthed a village and created a kingdom.

A warrior of a woman, a monster of a mother. A titan and a tyrant, to me at least.

There are horrors I've witnessed at the hands of my mother, moments I still have nightmares about, memories that freeze my every limb. In her older age she's become gentler, has grown in patience, and I have been secretly searching through the depths of my heart to find forgiveness, but it's something that won't show itself easily.

She loves my children so very much. What love she kept from me she pours into them, and they, without hesitation, love her.

Though the void my mother's neglect created inside of me is still gaping, I allow her into my life, not for her sake, nor for mine, but for my children.

My mother sits across from Asélle, next to Anette, glaring at her eldest daughter who most resembles her first love. As she looks at me, I see her eyes glistening with feelings of grief, and thoughts of saying goodbye to my children, her grandchildren.

'Much congratulations on the approval, Taresai,' Anette says with a smile. 'It's a relief to know they're not particular about who they let in.'

The resentment in her tone cuts through the air. Anette is hopeless at hiding how she truly feels. Her words, or lack thereof, always give her away, washing up her truth to the surface. It's clear enough for me to see, though I pretend to be fooled by the disguise she casts. She's wondering in her little mind why we received the golden ticket before her, seeing as how her children are obviously better candidates.

'I assure you, Anette, it was very difficult,' I smile simply, breastfeeding Ashanti, 'the amount of paperwork that goes into these things is unheard of.'

Anette eyes me with false curiosity.

'Besides,' I say, injecting lightness in my tone, 'I imagine Santino being an English-speaker has something to do with the fact.'

'Has he secured a job over there?' My mother asks.

'Yes. He'll be working in a government office as an interpreter,' I say out loud for the first time, trying to imagine what that might be like. Santino working for Australians and migrants alike.

'Aren't you worried though, Tsai?' Asélle asks. 'Being unable to speak the language?'

'Well, I'll learn, won't I? And so will the children.'

It's a ridiculous question, I already speak five different languages in three different dialects, so what's another?

'Australia,' mother says quietly, almost to herself. 'So far away. I won't see the children grow up.'

Huh. She never ceases to surprise me.

Where was such regard when she forced me to grow up? Where was she?

'I'll send pictures,' I say bitterly.

A silence falls between the four of us, sitting heavier by the millisecond. There's not a person in the world that can push my buttons like my mother. The difficulty is that I know she doesn't mean to. I know she doesn't deserve my acrimony.

'Do you need any help packing?' Asélle asks sweetly, instantly dissolving the tension.

'Yes, that's a good point, what exactly are you packing?' Mother asks.

'Just the minimal necessities. Clothes, books, photos.'

'Oh. That's all?' asks Anette, seemingly more interested in her cup of tea than this conversation.

'Yes. I figure anything else we need, can be purchased there, couldn't it?'

'Heavens, this is really happening, ey?' whispers Asélle, 'It's strange how it goes. We become whole again, then Messai leaves, and now you.'

She smiles, but her eyes water. As the eldest daughter of Adele, I cannot relate to the feelings Asélle expresses, and as Adele's youngest daughter, she will never understand the emotions I'm grappling with in these moments and all the other moments before it.

She was sheltered and I was overexposed.

We have never been whole. There was always someone missing, someone absent in every stage of our lives. First, it was our father – before Anette and Asélle took their first breath, then our mother, then Anette, then Messai, and now me. And I have no ill feeling or remorse about it.

'Chey!' I laugh. 'We're still a family, are we not? We're not moving to the moon, Asélle. We'll see each other again, I'm certain of it.'

Profoundly certain because for once I'm not the one getting left behind.

'Well, my sister,' she beams, wiping her eyes, 'leave me in charge of your farewell celebration!' Asélle puts an arm over my shoulder, and I see Anette roll her eyes from the corner of mine.

Akita

Mama says today I'm not allowed to only play with Santo because my cousins are here. She says it's one of the last times that we'll see them for a while, so it's best to spend it together before we go in a fortnight's time.

I think it's a silly thing to ask because we've lived close to our cousins for more than a year, yet I only see their faces every once in a while. I also don't like them very much.

Moving to Australia won't change any of those things – in fact, being far away from them feels more natural than forced company. They're nice enough – nothing like the gremlins at the school, but still. I prefer playing with Santo – even though he is annoying and grotesque sometimes, I understand him. Santo is clear, straight. But my cousins are twisty and confusing. They say things they don't mean, and do things they *do* mean, but sometimes in secret, and they become really annoyed with me when I get their names mixed up.

The six of us girls sit in the living room while our mothers and grandmother are having supper on the four-seat dining table. Santo is in our bedroom with the boys, playing with our toys, while I slump in one of the plastic chairs Baba's put around the coffee table for us.

Everyone else sits up straight, pretending, mimicking our mothers in the room next door.

'You must be so excited to have a new baby sister,' says one of the older twins, could be Heema or Halima. It really doesn't help that they're dressed in the same pink skirts and white long-sleeve shirts with pink hearts on them. I nod.

'She's a very cute baby,' says another cousin, not one of the twins but their younger sister.

'Oh yeah, the cutest out of all of you,' says the other twin, looking away with a satisfied smile. The twins and their younger sister – whose name is either Ines or Samira – scoff and giggle.

'Obviously,' I say slowly. 'She's a baby. Babies are usually cuter than their older siblings.'

My cousin – who I know isn't their sister – sitting closest to me, laughs. She's been quiet the entire time, watching us. I know she's my Aunty Anette's daughter because her skin is as dark as mine, not orangey like the other four.

Her name I know. Evelyn.

'So, you're going to live in a house? Like a proper house?' asks Samira / Ines.

I don't know why she asks the question like that. As if this house isn't a proper house, a proper home, as if they too don't live in a skyscraper. A skyscraper is still a skyscraper no matter how close you are to the ground when you live in it. I shrug my shoulders and nod, trying to beam signals telepathically to Santo in the other room to come and rescue me.

'Where are you moving to again?' asks a twin, as if she doesn't already know the answer. They just want to laugh at my attempt to say the word.

'Austral-Australia,' I say, trying to sound confident.

'Oh! Only there? That's so funny!' says the one called Samira or Ines. I can already tell this is going to end badly.

'The president of Australia actually asked us to move to his country months ago, but Mama wants us to stay here, isn't that, right?' she turns to her twin sisters.

I'm not surprised that the president asked them months ago, but I'm surprised at Aunty's Asélle's silliness for saying no.

'Samira, stop telling lies,' Evelyn says simply. 'It's impolite.'

In this singular moment I learn a lot about the people around me. Samira is the name of the girl who looks a bit older than me, and Ines must be the one born after me, the one who hasn't spoken.

Heema and Halima are like two versions of the same person. I think they share a brain. And Evelyn, though she's the same age as the twins and a lot smaller, there's only one of her, and in this moment she's bigger than the two of them combined.

Our uncomfortable silence is disrupted by a loud bang, quickly followed by Santo's cheering, coming from our bedroom. Everybody jumps.

I watch Mama get up from her seat, muttering things about Santo being the death of her. As Mama disappears down the hall, I catch Aunty Anette speaking into my grandmother's ear, saying she's pleased her sons won't be around Santo for much longer.

Taresai

I dry the last of the plates and put them away, exhausted from the day, though my legs feels as if they could carry me as far as the night.

Santo had convinced Anette's eight-year-old boy, Atem, to place a plastic bowling pin on his head as he hurled objects at him, from chess pieces to small fruit, Akita's teddies and the miniature toy cars he collects.

Mother, my sisters and their children departed soon after I'd confronted Santo and comforted Atem who took a large Lego block to the temple.

On any other occasion, I would be disappointed in Santo for exhibiting such behaviour, but I was relieved to see them go, so tonight I'm grateful for my son's rejection of most things good.

With all the kids asleep and Santino in the shower, I tread shallowly in the deep pools of my thoughts. If I don't look too much into it, I can trick myself into believing that my sisters are genuinely happy for me – for us, that we've finally found our way out, that freedom is within arm's reach. But Asélle's small question sits heavily on my mind. How will I live in a place whose language I do not speak or understand? I don't worry for the kids; they'll pick it up within a year. And Santino has the gift of speaking, reading, and writing English.

As for me?

My mother tongue, Dinka, was the first language I ever spoke, then I learned Nuer when I was Akita's age and we moved to the south, then Shilluk a year after. Then I learned to speak Nuba, and Arabic when we moved back to the north. Five languages I could speak before I was ten. I couldn't write in any of them, but I used my tongue as a tool, and at times, as a weapon like most women in the world do when fallen into situations unprotected by our skin. In this country, we are outsiders, but we survived because we speak their tongue.

In Australia, how am I going to survive if I can't communicate?

I jump when the house phone rings, irritated by the echoing sound at this late hour.

I walk across the cold tiles of the kitchen floor.

'Hello?'

There's a short silence before a man, whose voice I've heard a million times, speaks.

'Why am I the last person in Cairo to hear that our finest rum-maker is moving across the world?' Amr Sayyad speaks out of the phone.

I catch a breath, and my composure before it falls.

'This life of rum-making was never meant to last forever,' I say into the phone.

'Congratulations, Taresai.'

It feels strange to talk to the man who I've only heard on the radio and seen on tv. Our only interactions have been through another person, yet it feels like we're long-lost friends. And now we're saying goodbye in the same breath we say hello.

'Listen, I won't keep you long. I know it's late and you have young ones and a newborn. I want your recipe, Taresai. For the rum.'

My stomach twinges. It's a moment before words roll off my tongue.

'I really appreciate your call Mr Sayyad, and the offer, but–'

'Name your price.'

I think about this for a moment.

'Ten thousand.'

I'm surprised by my words. My initial thought was to decline, but it seems my mind was not yet made.

Sayyad is quiet on the other end of the line for a couple seconds that seem to stretch on forever. Have I set too high a price?

'For your recipe, Taresai?' he says. 'I'll pay triple that.'

'I'm pleased to make the deal, Mr Sayyad,' I say, in utter bewilderment.

That's more than I make in a year.

'I offer you and your family my blessings. Australia will be fortunate to home you.'

Chapter 6

Cairo

Taresai

This time next week, we will have spent an entire day underneath the Australian sun and a full night sleeping beneath the Australian sky, in our Australian home, next door to our Australian neighbours.

But for now, it's time to celebrate our last Friday in this village of Giza, in the city of Cairo.

Nadene, the old woman who lives on the rooftop of our apartment building, has invited us over for a farewell supper.

When I first met Nadene I thought she was a nasty old witch.

There are still times when I feel that way, but when I gave myself permission to get to know her, look deeper into her layers, I realised that she was quite exceptional.

I met Nadene at the market on the streets below a week after giving birth to Amara. It was on the tenth anniversary of her daughter's death. She was dressed in all black with a matching scarf that covered her hair. Nadene bought a bottle of my rum at the start of the evening and returned for another as my last customer for the night. We talked as women do and she mentioned that she owned a complex nearby. I didn't know at the time that it was the very building we'd been living in for the past month.

Up until that point, the landlord had been a mystery. All our dealings to secure the place were done through estate agents. We never once heard from, or spoke to the landlord, just knew that her name was Nadene, and she owned the building.

No one else in the complex seemed to know her either, only whispers about her living on the rooftop.

When the pool of my customers began to expand, I started brewing from home.

One night, when the sky was clear and the breeze that came in through the windows was cool, I brewed my rum with Santino at the dining table reading over some papers. The children were peacefully asleep on their beds. I remember it was the first time I felt like we had a chance in this country.

Then there was a knock on the door.

I was reluctant to answer at first as it was well after midnight.

When I did finally open the door I found Nadene standing there and I instantly recognised her from the street. She asked to come in, and I gently refused. She stood at the threshold, her face stony and cold. With her brown skin that folded over her greying eyes and her chin up high, she opened her mouth to speak.

She told me to take better care of my children. That they have kept her awake all hours of the night, kicking and screaming.

It was only then that I realised it was her. That woman from the street was the landlord living on the rooftop. I was taken aback by her words; they were so far from the truth. Santo was my only handful back then, and he slept like a boulder. I apologised and promised it wouldn't happen again; in my mind, I deemed her as a senile old lady for being so wildly mistaken, for hearing things that weren't happening.

The very next evening, Amara's eczema had flared up worse than I've ever seen it, Santo had a fever of 41 degrees and Akita had refused her meals all day. I was certain it was a curse, certain that Nadene was a witch. Amara was screaming all night, bleeding very badly from the rash spreading all over her skin, Santo sobbed and whined in Santino's arms and Akita had fallen asleep on the tiles of the kitchen floor.

There was so much chaos that I hardly noticed Nadene had slipped in. She held Santo on her lap while Santino put Akita to bed. She stayed up all night with me as I rocked Amara to sleep.

For the next few nights as things settled down, Nadene left linen cloths at the door for Amara to sleep in, ones we couldn't afford at the time, and 'something small' she'd get me from the market. Be it nail polish or the raw nuts she knew I liked. I refused to accept these things at first and I was upset with Santino for not understanding why. I feared that Nadene was providing these things for me, for my children, because she assumed I couldn't provide them myself.

As weeks turned into a month and Nadene's visits and drop off's became less frequent, I began unravelling my thoughts that had been so tightly wound up. I was troubled upon my understanding of how things could turn so quickly, how people could change so quickly. How the things we spend lifetimes constructing can crumble in an instant.

Then I realised – I was wrong. I was wrong for assuming that we were out of harm's reach because we finally had a stable roof over our heads. It turned out that I was wrong about Nadene too. She didn't make the greatest of impressions, but I realised that even if she did, I still wouldn't have let her come in that night, let alone offer me any help when she simply owed me none.

I wouldn't call her a friend, and she's not quite family but in the almost three years I've known her, she's become someone dear to me.

I still struggle with Nadene from time to time as the currents of her bestowing waters interfere with my denying waves.

I don't yet know what she sees in me, it doesn't bother me if I never will. But it seems that in all this time, I haven't quite figured out how to deal with an older woman who makes no apologies for speaking how she feels and shows care for me in the way she does.

Santino follows me up the stairs to Nadene's rooftop. Amara's hand in his, while Akita and Santo trail closely behind. I hold Ashanti, who is wrapped up in a cotton blanket in my arms, fast asleep.

A grand sandalwood fire burns in a pit on one side of the rooftop, and a large metal pole sticks up from the ground on the other. Mixed fabrics hang from the pole and extend to the railings on the edges like a tent, a castle of fabrics. Yellow chiffon, crimson velvet, orange silk and brown linen dancing to the shape of the wind.

Inside the tent there's a bed made of large pillows and sheets. Beside it lay six large suede cushions circling a small round table decorated with food. Nadene, the eye in the sky, dressed in black, sits in the inner-most cushion, grinning as she welcomes us out to her home.

I settle into my cushion and place Ashanti into Nadene's reaching arms.

She taps on Ashanti's nose gently to wake her.

'It may be the last time I'll see these eyes,' says Nadene, sensing my discontent without batting an eye in my direction.

I place a bowl of rice, chickpea, egg, and diced tomato in front of Santo and one in front of Akita with a portion half the size of her brother's.

Amara sits on her father's lap with a fistful of purple grapes that she feeds into her mouth between spoons of brown lentils.

'What do you think of my home, Santo?' she asks as Ashanti reaches for her hooked nose.

'I like it,' decides Santo, peering outside the hung fabrics, 'you can see everything.'

'Correct,' she smiles, 'and nobody can see me.'

I know it brings Nadene great peace to live somewhere so open, yet out of sight, but it makes me weepy. I can't fathom the loneliness that might plaque her.

'What about you Akita?'

Akita looks to Nadene then looks to the food she's barely touched.

'Do you like it up here?'

She smiles awkwardly and nods.

'She's scared,' says Santo, not to be cruel, I sense, but to be helpful.

Akita looks to her father then to me.

'You've got no walls,' she shrugs and Nadene cackles so loudly that Ashanti starts to cry.

When their bellies become full, Santino leads the older three through the fabric castle to watch as noon turns to dusk.

It's a warm evening, but the breeze that comes in from the east is cool.

'Giza will miss you,' says Nadene, rocking Ashanti back to sleep.

'Don't be silly Nadene. We won't be missed.'

'I'm not talking about them,' she says simply, eyeing Santino and the children. The fading light settles in the gold of her eyes.

'Santino is a fine gentleman, but unremarkable.'

I go to speak my disapproval of her sentiments, but she swiftly continues, unscathed by my diffused reaction.

'And the children you made together are beautiful. But there's no telling who they are yet.'

I shake my head and turn my gaze away from her, though her words draw me back.

'You, Taresai, have left a mark, even if the streets are too stubborn to admit it.'

'I suppose I have in a small way.'

'Oh please, spare me your modesty. There's nothing more I distain. How far has modesty gotten any woman in this world of men?' She flashes a grin, and I can't help but titter.

Nadene leans in but doesn't lower her tone.

'You made this life here, Taresai. You.'

'*We* did Nadene. Santino and me. All we have gained, and lost and built, we have done together.'

'But it is ingrained in women like you. Just as it is ingrained in Santino to fly close to the sun.'

I let Nadene's words flow past me, my chest feeling warm and heavy, not by their meaning, but because this will be the very last time I'll hear them.

The Egyptian sun paints the sky in an explosion of oranges and pinks as it dips behind the great pyramids, drenching the city in gold, making everything look like it's draped in the finest layer of silk.

Nadene places Ashanti in my arms, fast asleep and somewhere in a world of her own making.

'From disparity you built a home for yourself and your children here in Giza and in Australia, from hope you will build nothing short of a kingdom.'

I watch as my three children dance with their father in deep marigold sunlight to the music coming from the street.

A smile tugs at the corners of my mouth and I feel a sting in my eyes as they begin to water. Every inch of my body feels light.

For the first time, I have enough air in my lungs to see this side of the world in all its glory, to breathe it in and slowly breathe it out.

Chapter 7

Cairo

Akita

It's our last night in Egypt, and despite mine and Santo's protestations we are going to the farewell celebration that Aunty Asélle organised.

Tomorrow morning, we'll be on a plane flying to a place with a name I cannot yet properly pronounce. My imaginings of this magical Australia feel as real as my memories of yesterday.

We've spent our last days here packing, cleaning, and erasing our existence from this place. All our things are packed in suitcases and trunks neatly stacked by our front door. The house feels empty, even though the furniture it came with remains. We've plucked all the bits that made this house ours. All our toys, our photos, our clothes. The smell of Mama's cooking, the smell of her brewing, all of Baba's papers and notebooks filled with his squiggly writing, all the dents Santo put on the walls, plastered over. All of Amara's chewed-up pacifiers, all of Ashanti's little socks, all my teddy bears, pastel-coloured dresses and the flowers I'd picked and left to die underneath my bed.

We walk down the stairs and through the streets in the night. Santo and I trail behind Mama and Baba as they hold Amara and Ashanti in their arms.

My legs are tired, and my eyes are heavy by the time we arrive at the front door of our cousins' apartment building on the nicer side of Giza. We walk into the bright lights, balloons, and long tables full of food and coloured fizzy drinks. People I hardly recognise welcome us in, hugging Mama and Baba, and, regrettably, kissing us. I can't remember how many occasions I've been to Aunty Asélle's house, but I know that it looks different every time I'm here. There's always a new couch or a larger tv or both.

Anei makes his way through the crowd, his face covered in powdered sugar.

'You're finally here, Santo!' he says. 'Nice to see you too, Akita.'

I don't think I have the energy for Anei's shenanigans tonight, even if this is the last time I'm seeing him.

I walk right past Anei to find a couch to sleep on. I slither through a cluster of people, then, somebody grabs my wrist. It's one of the twins, Heema or Halima. She drags me into a room where all the other girls are before I can stop her.

'Hi,' I say blankly as a dozen pairs of eyes glare at me. I recognise my five cousins, Heema, Halima and their sisters Samira and Ines, and my other cousin Evelyn. But the other seven girls I have never seen in my life.

'This is our cousin,' says one of the twins.

'She's the one who's moving to Australia,' the other twin continues, showing me off like a newborn baby.

'Why are you wearing pants?' asks Samira, her face scrunched up in disgust. 'Your mother usually puts you in nice dresses.'

'I'm tired,' I say, 'I didn't want to wear a dress.'

I turn around to leave the room when one of the twins says, 'We're moving to Australia as well! Mama has already put us in English classes!'

She says some other stuff too, but I don't hear the rest of it as I walk out of the room and close the door behind me.

Santo and Anei find me before I find an empty couch or bed without a child or an infant already sleeping on it.

'Here,' Santo says, handing me a sugarcane stick. 'Enjoy it while you can. Anei just told me they don't have these in Australia.'

'It's true,' Anei smiles.

I take the stick from Santo and smile a thanks to him.

'Me and Anei are going to drink some of the grown-up people's juice. Wanna come?'

'No, Sunny. I just want to sleep.'

'Suit yourself, Kita.' Santo disappears into the figures of big people who walk around us like we're not here. Anei hangs back.

'I'll miss that gap-tooth of yours, Akita,' he says before following after Santo.

I'm walking around in circles tiredly, pushing through flocks of people as they sing and dance and cry, finding my way about the confusing layout of this house, when two strong, but soft arms lift me from the ground.

It's my grandmother, my Haboba.

'Where are you off to, little one?' She smiles, the skin around her eyes crinkling as she plants several kisses on my face, her lips soft and pillowy on my skin.

She wraps me up in her sweet scent of cinnamon and soap. I lay on her lap and instantly begin to drift, gazing upward at her misty grey eyes.

'You've got a long journey ahead of you, my sweet girl. Haboba will miss you,' she says, her voice as gentle as a whisper, as soothing as a lullaby.

'I'll miss you too, Haboba,' I say tiredly, suddenly overcome with overwhelming sadness. I love my grandmother, probably as much as I love Uncle Messai, and it's only clear to me now that she's someone I'm not ready to say goodbye to.

My heavy eyes take in the sight of her face, every inch of it, so I remember it in my mind when I start to miss her. Her wide nose and lips, her silvery small eyes the one freckle above her eyebrow that I reach up and touch with the tip of my finger. Haboba traces her thumb along my face until she's touching my freckle too.

'That was a gift,' she smiles kissing my freckle, 'I passed it down to your mother and it landed on her cheek, then she gave it to you, and it landed above your lip.'

'A little star on my face,' I mumble, and Haboba repeats my words.

The world goes quiet, and the back of my throat starts to burn.

'Don't cry, Akita,' Haboba says. 'I'll always be right there with you.'

'How?' I ask, my eyes closed and my body limp.

'I'm a part of you, my girl, the same way the sun and the moon and all the stars are part of the sky. And you are part of me.'

Haboba's voice is the only thing I hear, like it's just her and me in this world, floating down a starry river.

'There will be days when the stars hide behind the clouds, when the sun will set behind the rain. But they will always be there, following you around wherever you go. Watching over you, even if you can't see them.'

I feel her soft fingers wipe away my tears.

'So, when you miss me, Akita, all you have to do is look at the stars and I'll look right back at you. And when I miss you, all I am to do is look to the sky, see your face in the clouds that pass and feel your warmth from the sun.'

Chapter 8

Cairo

Akita

I'm out of bed before the sun is up.

My teeth chatter in the cold, my eyes itch with tiredness and I can't stop yawning.

Today is the day.

Baba quickly bathes Santo and me and dresses us in neat and comfortable clothing. When everybody is ready we wait by the door for the taxi-man downstairs. When he arrives, he and Baba make trips up and down the stairs, loading our suitcases into the van while Mama waits upstairs in the house with us, Ashanti asleep in her arms and Amara sitting on her lap, sucking her thumb.

When Baba comes back up to collect the last of our things, Mama calls for us: it's time to go.

'Can me and Akita have one last look around before we go? Please, Mama?' Santo's wearing the red beanie that Mama makes him wear when it's cold outside. He hates it because it makes him look funny, with his big ears and small pea head.

'Okay,' Mama smiles gently. 'Don't be too long.'

Santo walks slowly around the house and I follow him from the living room to the dining room, then to the bedrooms, travelling up and down the hallway, the spine of the house, each tile a vertebra.

I remember jumping from one tile to the next with Santo on the long days of summer when we'd get bored from staring at the tv screen. We'd pretend the floor was made of lava or boobytrapped with poisonous snakes.

We wander out of Mama and Baba's bedroom into the kitchen, then to our bedroom, the laundry, and finally the bathroom.

The bathroom is probably my favourite place in this house. It's the only room with colour on the walls and wobbly shaped tiles.

Santo walks up to the mirror and waits for me to stand beside him. We stare at our reflections. Santo isn't much taller than I am even though he's two whole years older. He says I'm tall for a six-year-old when really, he's pretty short for an eight-year-old. I watch as Santo's eyes fall to the sink. He inhales deeply and slowly opens his mouth. Santo, with great thought and intention, spits down the drain of the sink.

'Ew.' I recoil. 'Why'd you do that for?'

Santo wipes his mouth with the sleeve of his jumper. 'Just leaving a little part of me in this place,' he says with a grin. 'Now you go.'

I stand on my tippy-toes and I try to spit, but it comes out as a pathetic dribble. I haven't had as much practice as Santo. We don't have time to dwell on it, though. Baba is calling our names, hurrying us along so we won't be late.

Taresai

The cold of the night still lingers in the dawn. The sun is yet to rise and warm the whole city. We usher into the van and drive through Cairo for the last time.

Akita

Everything takes so long. We wait in lines that go on forever, moving from place to place within this massive building called an 'airport.'

I fall asleep in Mama's arms and wake up in Baba's. Santo thinks of new ways to annoy me to rid himself of his boredom, and I grow more agitated by the minute. Agitated by all the people around me, by Amara's crying, by Ashanti's reeking diaper, by Santo poking his grotty fingers into my ear.

At last, we board the plane, just as I'm about to cry tears of frustration. I hardly believe it as I'm walking down the aisle, following Mama with Santo at my heels. I've never been on a plane, I've only ever seen what they look like in films, so I wait for this moment to feel real.

Mama, Baba, Amara and Ashanti sit on the row in front of us. I sit directly behind Baba, right by a window, and Santo sits next to me, finally settling down from his morning of hyperactivity.

When I look out the window and see the men on the ground dressed in bright orange vests, moving about and waving sticks, it all suddenly clicks, and I feel excitement course through every inch of my body.

I can't believe I'm actually sitting on a plane.

I'm going to fly in the sky.

A few moments pass and I feel everything start to rumble. The plane begins moving slowly down the runway and I struggle to settle the grin plastered on my aching cheeks, then the plane jolts with a speed that makes my heart thump wildly in my ears. The engines roar louder than anything I've ever heard. Before I know it we're up in the air and suddenly, panic-stricken, I want to get off.

Baba hears my whimpering and tries to calm me from his seat, reminding me how to breathe and trying to convince me that it's all going to be alright. The cereal that Mama made me eat this morning churns uncomfortably in my stomach. How do people do this?

We've not been in the sky for more than five minutes when all I've eaten today comes back up. I bend forward and vomit all over my violet corduroy pants.

The relief I feel is immediate, but I'm suddenly overcome with a shake, the kind I get when I'm about to cry.

Baba takes my hand and walks me to the small airplane restroom. He cleans me up, wiping my pants and my shirt, and washing my hands and around my mouth with warm water. Then Baba holds my crying face in his hands and assures me that the worst is over and I've been brave so far. He walks me back to my seat with a handful of lemon drops and a bottle of water. I shuffle back, my eyes on my shoes, sitting down without a word. I turn and stare out the window to distract myself from everything that just happened.

My eyes fall on the pyramids, they look so small from up here; they don't even look like the triangles I've known them to be. They slowly float further away.

'Hey,' Santo says tapping me on the shoulder. 'Are you feeling better?'

I nod, avoiding his gaze, waiting for him to make fun of me: to call me a cry-baby, or tell me not to vomit on him. But he doesn't.

'Are you scared, Kita?'

I nod again, searching his face for a clue as to where he might be going with his questioning.

'Don't be,' he smiles knowingly. 'How many times have you been scared?' he asks, leaning in.

More times than I could count. I get scared at least a dozen times a day.

'A lot,' I say.

'But you've always been alright, yes?' Santo asks and I nod.

'Remember that time when we went to the market after school and we got chased by that man with only three fingers because I gave him one-pound for a five-pound drink?'

I nod again, smiling at the memory that was terrifying at the time.

'And what did he say again? That he was going to find us and chop all our fingers off?'

I laugh, nodding enthusiastically.

Santo holds up his ten fingers in front of him and then points to mine when I do the same. 'Well, he didn't, did he?'

'Nope!' I giggle.

'We're going to be alright, Akita,' Santo says to me in the voice that he uses when he's stating the obvious. Only this time, it doesn't annoy me.

I close my eyes and let Santo's words melt into my thoughts until I believe them.

Taresai

This is the highest I've ever been off the ground. I hold my baby close to my chest and rest my head on Santino's shoulder, who is fast asleep with Amara resting on his lap. I listen closely as Santo uses his words to comfort his younger sister.

Chapter 9

Sydney

Taresai

I sit quietly in the sunroom folding the girls' clothes, still warm from the sun.

Most of Akita's jumpers are worn and faded but possess that beautiful sense of familiarity that old and loved things do. I separate a pale blue jumper that was once indigo in colour, decorated with pink butterflies down the sides, holding the shape of my daughter that it knows so well. I trace my fingers along the inside, wondering how many breaths Akita has taken in this.

Ashanti and Amara's shirts and sweaters beam with freshness and possibility and a fate of being outgrown in mere months.

Cairo seems worlds away, but it's only been four days.

We arrived at our new home on a quiet street in a suburb called Silverwater, in New South Wales. 23 Edgar Street, a three-bedroom Victorian cottage, like the kind I'd see in those old American movies, surrounded by the most greenery I've seen with my own adult eyes.

The house has a front yard with a garden full of flowers, weathered stone fountains and a gravel driveway that leads into the backyard where Santino can teach the kids to ride bikes. We arrived in the early afternoon, our brains obtuse from jetlag, and our bodies confused by the strange phenomenon of being plucked from one side of the planet and thrown into another. Santino and the kids rushed inside and collapsed onto their beds the first chance they got.

I stood at the threshold of the door for a long while.

Suddenly, the reality of it all, washed over me and I was overcome by it. Our own home and everything we've ever needed is firmly in our grasp, and I'm standing close enough to reach for more.

I turned and walked out into the garden, took off my sandals, and sunk my feet into a damp patch of grass, planting my roots, savouring each second that passed of being this close to the earth. My heart wept tears of joy. The peace that I've spent all my life searching for, the peace my ancestors could only dream of and only feel in death, I have finally found.

⋆⋆⋆

When we landed at Sydney international airport, we were welcomed to the country by a young, blue-eyed man named Nathan and a young woman called Kathleen, who I was surprised to learn was Filipina.

Nathan and Kathleen had been in correspondence with Santino; they're workers for an organisation who help newcomers adjust to their new lives in this country.

They gifted us with a week's supply of food and necessities, a drive to our new home – fully furnished – and donated items: clothes, books, VHS tapes, toys, and appliances.

The first couple of days, Nathan and Kathleen drove us around the neighbourhood, showed us where the local food markets were, enrolled Santo and Akita at the local primary school and Amara at day-care and registered Ashanti at the children's hospital nearby.

One afternoon, Nathan and Kathleen suggested that I attend the local English classes held for new arrivals. Though my first instinct was to politely decline, out of fear more than anything else, that night they left me with pamphlets for those programs, written in words I could not read.

* * *

I watch Akita squeal when a ladybug lands on her finger.

She's playing in the garden with her feet bare, braided hair, in her yellow dress, which already seems to have grass stains at the hem.

Santo searches the bush for lizards and crocodiles. Santino is inside with Amara, who's probably playing with her new toys, and Ashanti, who is fast asleep. It's a little after supper and the afternoon sun has started to dip. We had chicken, bean stew and rice, made from my very Australian pantry.

'Santo, Akita, five more minutes!'

'Ten!' Santo demands.

'No, the mosquitoes are going to bite your little legs off. Five minutes. Are you listening, Akita?'

'Yes, Mama,' she giggles, twirling in the last of the afternoon's sunlight, dancing with the flowers and flying insects.

My little black girl, dressed in yellow, swimming in an ocean of colours.

That night, after all the kids are bathed and tucked in bed, I hear Akita call for me from her bedroom.

'Mama?' she beckons softly over Amara's gentle snores.

'Yes, honey? Can't sleep?'

She hesitates under her blankets, pulled right under her chin. She stares up at me, wordlessly pleading for something she can't voice. I just have to kneel in the space between hers and Amara's bed, stare back at her patiently and wait for her words to come out.

'What is it?' I nudge.

She opens and closes her mouth, her little teeth gleaming in the dark.

'Can you, can you please … read this story for me?' she asks, pulling out a book from under the blanket. On the cover is a fish with rainbow-foiled scales that shift colour in the dim light of the room.

'Please?' she whispers, staring up at me with her bulbous eyes.

'Akita, honey, you know I can't read,' I say, my heart breaking a little. 'Do you want me to get your father?'

'No, Mama,' she shakes her head, 'you don't have to read the words.'

Akita opens the book enthusiastically and points to the rainbow fish on the page.

'Just look at the pictures on every page and make up the story as you go.'

She holds the book up to me with her tiny hands, her small, tender fingers.

Akita looks at me with the whole world in her eyes.

Her face explodes with light when I take the book from her hands. I open it to the first page and begin telling a story in a way that it was not written.

Chapter 10

Sydney

Akita

Today I learned to spell and write my full name in English.

Akita Amal Santino Adolé.

I've learned so many other things too in the time we've lived in number 23 Edgar Street, Silverwater. I've learned that there are twenty-six letters in the English alphabet, though counting to one hundred came to me a lot easier.

Spelling and writing in English is difficult, much more than speaking, which I, Akita – seven years old – am most certain in my fluency.

Though, I suppose, I cannot be absolute until I'm speaking a sentence and I realise I don't know the next couple of words that come after. But that hasn't happened in a while.

I am now in Grade Two at St John's Primary School, which is in the next suburb over.

On our first day, Santo and I walked through the gates without a single English word familiar to our tongues other than 'hello,' 'goodbye' and that one swear word that Santo taught me. I couldn't understand what anybody was saying for the first couple of hours, floating from place to place until I was led and introduced to everyone in my class.

That's where I made my first friend. Her name is Awien. Her skin is as dark as mine, and her hair is braided too. For me, the sun shone wherever Awien stood because she speaks both languages. She spoke Arabic to me and translated my words into English for my classmates and teachers. It was Awien who told our teachers that my name is pronounced 'Ah-kee-da' not 'Aki-ta' and Santo is 'Sun-toe,' not 'San-no.'

Everybody in first grade wanted to be my friend. They didn't care that I looked nothing like them, spoke nothing like them, and didn't eat the same food they did.

Now, after a year of being at this school, my closest friends are Awien, a girl named Ashra, which means the number ten in Arabic, and Eliza. Ashra's family is from a country called Nepal, a place with high mountains and snow.

Eliza has hair the colour of fire and hazel green eyes that change in the sunlight.

My teacher's name is Miss Hart – as in the thing that beats in your chest. Even though it isn't spelt the same way, nor does it mean the same thing, I can't help but see that when I look at her.

Miss Hart is wonderful. She wears great big glasses that make her eyes look hilariously large, and her blonde hair falls down to her waist; some parts of it curl, other parts don't. She sings to us on most days, and she's always kind to me, even when I don't know the answer to things.

There are many things I love about Miss Hart, but what I adore most is that she never treats me better or worse than the other kids.

I really like St John's Primary, even though I didn't expect to. In the weeks leading up to our first day, I'd stay up all night, butterflies in my stomach, hoping that St John's wasn't as rough as our last school in Giza. Hoping that I'd survive.

Since that first day I've found in every week all the ways that it's the opposite.

I like going to school, learning about the world, and how to do things. A few times a year, we go on excursions outside the school. This term we've been to the aquarium, and the museum in the city, where we looked at artifacts from the olden days.

The weather in Australia is very odd.

There's summer, which is their normal season. It's warm, as the world should be with a giant flaming ball of fire above us. Then there's autumn, when all the leaves die, followed by winter, which is the wildest thing I have ever experienced. The sun disappears for weeks at a time, it rains all hours of the day, and the air just about turns to ice. Last winter, our first winter, we all got sick. Santo was afraid his ears would fall off – though he'd never admit it. There were times I caught him going to bed with Ashanti's socks covering them.

There are a lot of white people here, with their cool-coloured eyes and hair in a rainbow of light and dark hues. But some of the people I see on the street, most of the kids that go to this school, they're from all parts of the world. In my class alone, there's a girl from India called Melinsa, a lot of kids from Lebanon and a place called Vietnam, and a boy who looks like me, but different. His name is Michael and he's from Nigeria.

I was entranced and befuddled with fascination upon my discovery of all the other colours of this land, all the cultures. It gave me a feeling I couldn't place, but it felt like home.

I see Mama in the way Melinsa's mother carries her young daughter, the swing of her hips when she walks, and the way she smells like perfumes and mixed spices.

I see Baba in the way Ali's mother scolds her son, and I see Santo in the way Michael tries to beat me in everything, from sports to spelling. I see myself in Eliza, my red-haired, green-eyed friend, in the hopes, the dreams, and the wishes we share.

* * *

'Come on, Akita, please?' Eliza pleads, sitting cross-legged on the asphalt. It's the second half of lunchtime, and Awien, Eliza, Ashra and I are playing hopscotch by the pond.

'Eliza, why don't you tell Nena to bug off yourself?' says Ashra.

'Because she only listens when Akita tells her to!' Eliza says, her face going red.

'No, she doesn't,' Awien butts in, throwing a stone on the farthest square. 'She just picks on you when no one else is around.'

Ashra laughs. 'Why do you care what Nena says anyway? She's mean and stupid.'

Eliza folds her arms over her chest and looks away. Her cheeks redden and her eyes swell, and I already know she's about to cry.

'Okay, okay,' I say, picking up a stone and throwing it onto the seventh square, 'I'll tell her off.' I hop to the seventh square, bending my knee to pick up the stone with one leg in the air.

'Hey,' Awien says, looking past my shoulder as I hop towards her. 'Aren't those your parents?' I turn to where Awien is looking: to the old red brick building where the library and the principal's office reside. I squint and stare.

'Yep,' I breathe, gazing at the two familiar figures walking up the steps and disappearing behind the large wooden doors.

Santo must be in trouble again.

Taresai

Santino and I have been called into Principal McDonald's office for the third time in six weeks.

I like the principal; she has my respect.

She is very fond of Akita: she told us the very first day we met her that our little girl has 'exceedingly high potential.' I never asked how she came to think that, but she's the principal. She probably says that about most kids. She greeted Santo with the same kindness, but offered no words about his disposition or his qualities.

We sit in her office, opposite a large window that oversees the playground. The room is decorated with framed certificates and photos of her with students, some of which look decades old.

Her shelves are lined with leatherbound books and countless awards made of glass and synthetic gold. She wears tortoiseshell reading glasses that make her blue eyes appear comically large. Soft lines appear around the features of her thin face – lines of age, of smiling too hard, speaking too much. Her hands are wrinkled but smooth, as though the only struggle they know is writing with a stiff pen.

I listen to her speak to us, but I only understand every couple of words. Though it's only Santino who responds to her concerns, the principal includes me in these discussions, which is much more than I can say for anybody else: doctors, shop assistants, bank tellers. I may not fluently understand the language of this country, but I can always grasp the essence of things. I read the deep lines between Principal McDonald's eyes, which grow deeper when she says certain words, in it, I see her sorrow and confliction. In the tightness of her lips, I read her frustration, and in her eyes, I see her trained discipline and honed decisiveness.

That's how it's been for the past fifteen months. I must read people, instead of listening or speaking to them.

Santo's done something. It's not as bad as the first time we were in this office, but not as benign as the last. Principal McDonald has decided the consequences of Santo's actions, but she is opening it up to us for suggestions as to how Santo's future at this school and the future of his education, can be bettered by us.

Santino turns to me when Principal McDonald finishes speaking.

'Santo was being disruptive in class. He coloured the entire whiteboard in black permanent marker during recess and pressured a boy into gluing his hand to the desk.'

Oh my.

I tell myself not to be surprised with what Santo is capable of, but every time he reaches new levels of anarchy.

'The principal is suspending him for the rest of the week, but she wants us to alter the way we parent Santo at home so that behaviour like this doesn't happen in the future. If Santo doesn't change his ways then she'll have no other option than to expel him.'

I look to Santino, then to Principal McDonald, and nod solemnly.

'I'm sorry,' she says, her hands clasped on her polished walnut desk, uttering the first words I understand.

We walk out of the office and into the hallway, where Santo sits on a chair, his blue school shirt covered in black and blue marker, navy-blue school shorts stained with remnants of dried glue.

'Hi, Mama. Hi, Baba, what are *you* doing here?' he smiles nonchalantly.

'Not another word, Santo,' I say through clenched teeth. 'Up. Now. We're taking you home.'

Santino catches the next train into the city back to work, and I walk Santo back home. It's a Wednesday, the only day of the week Ashanti is in day care; if I'm grateful for anything today, it's that. We walk silently through the streets of Auburn, my sandals shuffling on the pavement. Santo asks if we can dine in at one of the cafes we pass. I tell him there's food at home.

I soak Santo's uniform in the laundry sink while he cleans himself up in the bathroom. No tv and no riding his bike until the end of the week. He is to sit in his room and think about what he has done.

Santo is not a bad kid, I know he isn't. But I don't understand why he's losing more control of his impulses as the years go by. He defies all, even the voices in his head that tell him right from wrong. He'll be ten in five months. I expected him to have grown out of this unpredictable phase by now. This environment has been more nurturing to him than the rough streets of Giza. My only thought is that he's having trouble adjusting and this is his only way of expressing it. Or I might just be a mother in denial of some deeper issue.

But for the most part, the children have adapted with grace and ease into their new life. Santo has his bike and his confidence carrying him through the days, and Akita has made so many new friends at school. Seeing this new world and feeling a part of it has aided her in coming out of her cocoon, bursting with so much personality. She doesn't often speak, but when she does the words pour out of her, and it's hard to get her to stop.

Everyone in the house who can speak is fluent in English. Except me.

Santo and Akita speak English to each other and to their father, Amara, and Ashanti. They only speak Arabic with me.

It worries me sometimes that as they grow they'll forget their other language, and that the bridge of communication between us will collapse into itself.

What of Ashanti? She speaks more English words than she does Arabic. Will she have to speak to me through her father? Will all my children have to speak to me through their father? I shiver at the thought and push it to the back of my mind. I make a silent promise to myself to take up those English classes as soon as Ashanti is in day-care for at least three days a week. We've been in Australia for a full year and three months. My children have turned another year older, celebrated Christmas for the first time since leaving Sudan, Easter last April, and a blessed year of milestones.

When the sun is out, and kids are at school and Santino is at work, I spend some of my time wandering through the neighbourhood. I know the area of Silverwater and the surrounding suburbs like the palms of my hands. I know where all the shops are, I know which buses to take to get to the city, to the hospital, the dentist. I know how to get to the train station, the library, the park. So, when the kids or Santino say they want to go somewhere, I know where they're going to be and how they're going to get home.

I've met three Sudanese families in the area, and I've become great friends with all of them, but mostly with a woman called Achol, whose daughter Awien is in the same class as my Akita. Achol is a good woman. She reminds me of home, of Sudan. On days I feel the ache of unfamiliarity and foreignness, when the weight of loneliness becomes too heavy to bear, I connect with Achol. She reminds me of all I've lost, all I've sacrificed.

My mother, my brother Messai, my sisters Asélle and Anette, my best friend, Manuela, and all my friends in Cairo, seem worlds away, drifting further apart as the days pass. Our attempts to make contact with them have been persistent and plenty. Santino began writing letters seven months ago and sent it to Asélle's address, to my mother's and then to Anette's. Entailing our travels and our settling, assuring that we were in good health and asking after theirs.

When we received no word back, we tried again and again, letters to all three addresses and one to our old apartment in Giza for good measure.

I grasped onto every bit of my withering hope for a few weeks, spent the nights praying that we had not been lost to each other. I checked the letterbox daily, and still, nothing.

After several months I stopped checking, I couldn't defy the crushing weight of my deep aguish and disappointment every time we'd sort through the letters and find no words from them.

My grief lies dormant, my sorrow stays silent, instead burning holes in my chest until I'm empty.

Akita

I walk home accompanied by the spring sun and my own thoughts. Without Santo over my shoulder, I look forward to times like these, at the end of the school day when I can skip home in the warm sunlight and take in my quiet neighbourhood.

The magpies call in their fluty song from the treetops, and I hear the bees buzzing busily when I pass Mr and Mrs Oliver's white rose garden. I feel the gumnuts stuck in the grooves of my shoes rattling as I try to skip from one square of the pavement to the next, basking in the symphony of my neighbourhood.

I stop and stare up at a tree that stands at the end of my street. I reach up high and brush the red bristles with my fingertips, the low hanging leaves licking my forehead. I've gotten taller over the winter. I lost most of my baby teeth, too. Where two small teeth at the front of my gums, slightly gapped, used to be, two large teeth have taken their place. I'm still getting used to my new front teeth, which never seem to stop growing, although I'd rather have big teeth than no teeth at all.

Santo calls me Bugs Bunny and it annoys me to no end.

Amara turned four last month. She's okay sometimes, but mostly it seems like she exists to annoy me. She can speak now, so naturally, she never shuts up. She wants whatever I have and takes up all the space in our room. There are times, though, in the silent nights when I just watch Amara sleep peacefully, so, so quietly. That's when I feel I'm able to love her loudly.

I skip down the street until I reach the gates of number 23 Edgar Street, the white house nestled behind all the trees on the end of the street, my castle in this magical kingdom. I walk through our front garden, between the cracked stone fountains, and climb the wooden steps up the verandah.

I smell Mama's cooking before I even open the front door. I dump my shoes and school bag at the entrance and race to the living room, my socks slipping on the tiles. Santo's lying on the couch with his head to the carpet and feet in the air, grinning when he sees me enter.

'Hi Akita, honey,' Mama says, popping her head out from the kitchen.

'Hi Mama,' I say.

'Food will be ready soon.'

'Mm-hmm.'

'If you're hungry, there's zabadi in the fridge.'

'I'm okay.'

Mama nods, dries her hands on her apron and disappears back into the kitchen.

'You got in trouble today, didn't you?' I ask, sitting legs crossed on the carpet next to Santo.

'Yep.'

'What did you do?'

'I glued Elias's hand to the desk.'

'Why'd you do that for?'

'It doesn't matter. Mrs Declan is foul for getting me in trouble. She's so sensitive. I wasn't even that bad today, she's just weak.'

I don't agree with anything Santo's saying. From all my encounters with Mrs Declan, I've gathered that she's a very lovely lady. She's small and round and laughs at a lot of things. Maybe she is sensitive, but that's not a bad thing, I only pity her for it – it makes dealing with Santo that much harder.

I just wish Santo would be good at school. I really like it there and I don't want him to spoil the teacher's impressions of me because he's my older brother.

'Hey,' Santo says suddenly, 'can you do me a favour?'

'It depends on what it is.'

'Can you get the tv remote from Ma?'

I look at Santo, his arms dangling, his feet floating, then I look toward the kitchen.

'Only if you stop practising those wrestling moves on me,' I say.

'Deal.'

I get up and walk into the kitchen again.

'Mama, can I please get the tv remote?' I ask in the sweetest voice I can. She finishes chopping an onion, washes her hands, dries them on her apron, reaches above the fridge and hands me the remote.

'Make sure you're out of your school uniform before you sit back down.'

I hand Santo the remote and go change. I come back to the living room, with Santo on the carpet flicking through the channels, his face drooping with boredom. He blows a raspberry.

'Nothing's on.'

A silence falls between us, filled only with the buzzing of our minds as we try to think of something to do before supper. Then my mind hatches an idea that zaps through me like lightning.

'Wanna sneak into Ms Nora's backyard?' I grin.

Ms Nora is the lovely old lady next door who's always giving Mama lemons and pears and peaches from her trees. She has a large backyard with a seesaw, a swing set and a trampoline. She lets us jump over the fence and play in her backyard all the time, but her pink-faced, pudgy grandkids, a boy, and a girl, who often visit, always kick us out in a not-so-polite way – by throwing lemons at us.

I only jump into Ms Nora's backyard when her grandkids aren't there, but that seems to be the only time Santo wants to go.

He beams at me with mischievous delight. 'You're on, Bugs Bunny.'

Chapter 11

Sydney

Taresai

Every so often, we have a family outing. Last month we went to Taronga Zoo, which was Santo's pick. Today we're at the Japanese Gardens – Akita's pick. It's only a taxi ride away from Edgar Street. She invited her friends from school, all three of them. Awien, Eliza and Ashra. I watch as they play by the lilyponds. Akita kneels on the grass, trying to catch an orange butterfly. Santo stands on the opposite side of the pond with Awien's older brother, Deng, a sweet boy. He seems to have reached the age where most things have clicked; the world in his mind makes sense, or maybe his composure is because he's far from it. Either way, he's older than Santo, which means any influence he'll have on my son will only be good.

After all, I've never met a 'Deng' I didn't like. Amara and Ashanti play on the crochet blanket laid on the grass by my feet, feasting on egg sandwiches, jam biscuits and juice boxes. I like Eliza's parents, Bob and Shirley. They sit on a picnic table closest to our daughters. Eliza's mother adores Akita. She says her daughter didn't have many friends before my daughter, and she's glad that Eliza finally has a friend to play with.

Shirley didn't tell me this directly, of course – Santino translated, but my memories are of those words coming directly from her mouth.

Ashra's father hardly looks in my direction, deep in conversation with Santino, who sits beside me on the picnic table. Achol – Awien and Deng's mother, sits across from me, staring fondly at my two youngest.

'Ahh. I miss when they're that age,' she says, smiling with her whole body.

Amara has just turned four and Ashanti will be two in a few months. I suppose they are at a beautiful age, but they're both very high in their needs of me in different ways, so I never really get the chance to be still and enjoy it.

Achol has been in Australia for seven years. She speaks English very well. There's an accent that sticks to her voice in a way that makes her every word sound like it's hers and hers alone. It's the same with Santino and Ashra's father.

Achol reminds me of my old friend Manuela, reminds me of all the good things about her, the way she speaks with unambiguous emotion and unfiltered expression. Her gentle heart, unbridled humour, roaring laughter, but what made Manuela my greatest friend was her bad traits too. Not a day goes by where I don't miss her. We've never been this far apart, and with every tomorrow it's the longest we have gone without seeing each other. Time only seems to be making it harder to forget her.

A small part of me does wonder if it's because we grew distant before distance became.

It was inventible with all that was taking shape in our last months in Cairo, myself with four children under ten, and she, a single mother with her Anei.

Besides, it is innate to become so comfortable with the constant presence of someone at every turn of our lives. I've known her since I was fourteen and she were twelve.

So much so that the severing of those ties caused by this great move didn't even cross my mind.

It becomes imprudent to deny my growing feelings of guilt that expand as the picture becomes clearer. I hadn't noticed the distance between Manuela and myself at all then, though it might've been all she was feeling.

'Does it get easier?' I sigh softly.

'What? When they get older?' Achol asks, brows furrowed.

'No, not motherhood,' I chuckle, immediately feeling the need to weep. 'I mean … culturally. The … foreignness of it all. I feel like no matter how hard I try, how much I learn, adapt …'

I feel like it won't ever be enough. I'm still just a guest in this country, so far removed, no matter how many bus timetables I memorise or what colour notes are what dollar value. But how do I say this out loud?

'I feel like I'm falling behind. It doesn't yet feel natural … I guess I'm just wondering when it will.'

I close my eyes and clear my throat, realising I'd been staring out into nothingness for too long.

'Well,' begins Achol, breathing an empathic breath, 'you never stop standing out, if that's what you're asking. You never really blend in, you just … somehow became a part of this culture, as an extension of it, by holding on to your own.'

I look out at my daughter instead of the empty space that keeps drawing my gaze, watching as Akita digs her knees into the grass, sniffs the daisies, then scrunches her noise confusedly. Her lavender dress is painted in muddy grass stains when she stands; I can see it from here, though she seems to be none the wiser.

'But yes, it does get easier, Taresai. In time, things become … ordinary. You adjust.'

But do you ever stop missing home? I want to ask, but I'm afraid I already know the answer.

'I've well-adjusted to doing things, knowing where things are and understanding the natural rhythm of life around these parts. I just can't speak.' A laugh escapes me.

'Taresai, that's the hardest part,' Achol admits. 'Even so, there's no magic to making a place feel like your own, you just have to wait and let time do that for you.'

I let her words marinate into my thoughts.

Achol watches Amara and Ashanti for a while, and I feel her aura shift. When she looks at me there's a solemness in her eyes that envelops me into her same energy.

When she finally speaks, her voice is quiet, but her words are loud. 'Don't forget, Taresai, there's a stillness that only women like you and I know and have,' she says, an intensity in her eyes that pulls on parts of me that I keep hidden. 'A stillness that's been beaten into us, one that will soon force you to learn. To perfectly adapt. To speak. Out of survival, if desire is too feeble an incentive to suffice. Sooner or later.'

I'm taken aback by Achol's words.

In Egypt, I never had the luxury of worrying about such things. I never dwelled on wanting to belong. Those thoughts weren't worthy of occupying my mind, when at the start of every week I'd have to make enough money to last us to the end. Be that as it was, having less to worry about here and now doesn't mean I have no worries at all, it only means there's room for smaller ones to rise to the surface.

Akita

I watch intently as the ladybug crawls from my fingertip to my palm, its little feet tickling me as it marches the terrain of my hand. It moves like a little red planet against the galaxy of my obsidian skin.

Eliza is telling us the story of how Angela, her former best friend, made everyone in the school hate her.

'She spread around a rumour that I had nits and that I gave them to her when she slept over.'

'Did you give her nits?' Ashra asks, staring at the koi fish in the pond.

'No,' Eliza says, her face scrunched up in disgust. 'Well ... I don't know. Maybe.'

'Then it's not a rumour,' says Awien, eyes closed, lying on the grass with her face to the sun. 'But it's not fair. Why didn't anybody pick on her the way they picked on me? She had nits too, for god's sake.'

'People are stupid, Eliza, don't worry about them,' Ashra says reassuringly.

'Besides, you have us now,' says Awien, her eyes still closed, 'and me and Akita can't catch nits even if you have them.'

'That's not true,' laughs Ashra.

'Yes, it is. Isn't that right, Akita? Black people can't get nits. It's science.'

'Yep,' I say, the ladybug now circling my forearm.

'That's cool,' says Ashra, her attention back to the fish.

'Is it because it's in plaits?' asks Eliza, her eyes glistening curiously.

I shrug. 'I don't know. Probably.'

Sometimes it feels like Eliza is the baby of the group, even though they're all eight and I'm still seven. I always feel like I need to look after her, protect her in the same way that I'd protect Amara and Ashanti.

Taresai

All the parents are now gathered on the one picnic table, Bob and Shirley, Nav, Achol, Santino and myself. I hold Amara on my lap as Achol cradles Ashanti. They're all exchanging stories of travel, of how different things are in different parts of the world. Achol and Santino take turns translating to me what has been said in English if they aren't the ones speaking.

Bob and Shirley travelled the world before they had Eliza and her two older brothers. Ashra's father, Nav, talks about his young years in Nepal, and Santino tells them about his time growing up in Sudan and travelling through the villages to get to school.

Then the conversation takes a turn that I cannot follow, not even if I spent all my time reading every single person's moving face. Achol talks to Nav intently, who then pans a question over to Santino, who exchanges a few long-sounding words with Bob as Shirley and Achol exchange a glance, and then I'm lost. The discussion chugs along without any of them realising that I've fallen off the train. A few minutes pass, then Santino says something that makes everyone fall silent then erupt into raucous laughter, scaring the nearing birds away.

* * *

That night, I do a lap around the house. I close Santo's bedroom window as he sleeps on his bed, open-mouthed, snoring away. I swap Akita and Amara's ceiling light for their night light. I walk into our bedroom and pull Ashanti's blanket under one arm and over the other. Santino sits up in bed, reading Santo's school report. We haven't spoken much since returning from the gardens. He sensed too much in the air between us to know something isn't right.

He puts away Santo's report when I sit on my side of the bed and turns to me.

'That was nice today, wasn't it?' he smiles, taking off his glasses and setting them on the bedside table.

'Yes. Beautiful.'

He picks up his glasses again and fumbles with them. I can feel his mind in contemplation, deciding what he might say next.

'I'm sorry, Taresai,' he exhales finally.

'For what?' I ask quietly, slightly taken aback back by his apology, which usually comes after an explanation from him or I.

'For today, I should've … involved you more, been more attentive.'

'It's fine. I figured if what was being said is really important, you would've remembered to share it with me.'

Santino is quiet, again, contemplating his next words.

'Taresai, maybe it's time that you … I think you start taking up those English classes. The kids are all growing up. Ashanti will be two soon, so you can increase the time she spends at day-care.'

'I've always had the intention of learning English, Santino. I don't like that I don't know how to speak it, it just hasn't been a priority.'

'Can it be?' he asks gently.

'You mean alongside keeping this household going without falling apart?' I shoot back, suppressed frustration flaring up inside me. I can't put a finger on why my words of choice must be so candid tonight.

'I know,' he breathes calmly. 'I'm not trying to shrink that, Tsai, that isn't at all my intention. This family has only survived this long from place to place because of you.'

I let his words cool me.

'I'm just saying, now could be a good time to start.' He looks around the room, his eyes rest on our maroon curtains. 'In case I'm not around,' Santino says in a voice so distant it takes me a moment to realise what has been said.

'What do you mean by that?' I ask softly, but he doesn't meet my gaze. 'Santino, talk to me.'

He rests his glasses on his bedside table and smiles softly at me, before turning off his bedside table lamp.

'It's alright. Goodnight, my love.'

He lies his head on the pillow, his face towards the curtains, and I'm left in the dark room, oceans away from anyone. The loneliness that's been gnawing at my insides finally grips me and swallows all my thoughts of bliss into its abyss.

Chapter 12

Sydney

Akita

Tonight, I have my very first sleepover.

This morning Mama helped me pack my school bag and placed my overnight things in my Bratz duffle bag. I felt the ground buzz beneath my feet as I walked to school, both bags over my shoulder like I'd seen so many girls in my grade do all year.

I walked into the classroom with my chin to the ceiling, welcoming all presumptions that *I* was going to a sleepover tonight. It's all Eliza and I talk about for the rest of the day.

We've been trying for the longest time to convince Mama to let me stay over at Eliza's house. Ever since she finally agreed last week, we've been talking and daydreaming about nothing else.

When the final school bell rings we jump out of our seats, gather our things, line up at the classroom door, and run to the school gates as soon as we're dismissed.

We skip down the steps and wait outside the green school gates for Eliza's mother to pick us up. The car journey to Eliza's house feels strange. Eliza and her mother do most of the talking, blabbing on and on about our plans for the afternoon and evening, what's for dinner, what film we're going to watch, what games we're going to play, and I can't bring myself to utter a single word. It's like I've forgotten how to speak. I'm still excited of course, just a little less.

We climb the steps into Eliza's house. Eliza's mother takes our bags from us and places them on a shelf in the living room. She asks me what I'd like for afternoon tea.

'Black tea?' I shrug.

I've never drank it before, only Mama and Baba drink tea in our house but obviously they do things differently here.

'No,' Eliza giggles heartily. 'She means what do you wanna eat before dinner?'

'Oh,' I say, smiling at the silliness of naming a meal after a steaming hot beverage.

When I look from one to the other and shrug my shoulders blankly, Eliza makes an eager request for fairy-bread, which I can only imagine to be a glitter sandwich with wings.

'Come!' She says excitedly, grabbing my wrist and leading me into her room.

Every inch of space in Eliza's bedroom is taken up by her existence. Teddy bears, barbie dolls, baby dolls, a giant pink toy car that looks like it's big enough for Eliza to drive. A triple-storey dollhouse and a desk with nail polish, glitter pens, strawberry-scented stickers and glitter makeup. Her walls are pink with white daisies, her curtains are a light purple and her bedsheets are yellow.

Eliza's got more things in her one bedroom than Amara and I have in our whole house. 'What do you want to play first?' She beams, twitching as if at any moment she will burst from excitement. I don't think it matters what I answer, as long as she and I can do it together.

Taresai

I've been attending English classes at the community centre every Tuesday and Thursday for three weeks now. There are a lot of women my age, some older. Most are from Arabic-speaking countries like Lebanon and Syria.

The first few lessons were overwhelming. The speaking I understand, moreso than the reading and writing, though English words still feel as though they don't belong on my tongue.

Still, the best way to learn is by doing. I've been picking up more English words and phrases as the days go by. My teacher, Anne, says that watching Australian television will help, so I've been doing just that.

There's one show in particular where most, if not all the characters are blue-eyed and tanned, living in a town by the beach, and another about neighbours that seemingly have no respect for keeping their noses out of each other's business. I can't imagine living in either world.

I sit at the dining table. The children are home from school, burning time before supper. I try to get a start on my homework.

I told Anne that speaking English is more important to me than reading it, at least for the time being, so she sent me home with some CDs. All I must do is listen to the phrases and repeat after them. This routine is becoming familiar to me, but something about tonight has me distracted. Ashanti and Amara are playing in the living room next door, Santo is riding his bike around the neighbourhood, Santino will be on his way back home by now and Akita is staying at her friend Eliza's house overnight.

I feel I may have made a mistake by allowing her to spend the night away from home with people I don't know so well. I've just been trusting that they're good people.

Sometimes I forget that she's so young, still only seven. She really wanted to go, she's begged for weeks, and I thought, what's the harm? She's been such a good kid – she's a star pupil at her school, and never makes a fuss at home even when it's justified. She's the one child I forget about from time to time because she requires such little effort. She senses it too. Akita knows she doesn't get as much attention as her two younger sisters and her older brother, but she doesn't seem to mind or take it to heart. It's like she understands that they need it more than she does. Akita is often the least of my worries, and maybe my guilt over that has manifested in a way that compelled me so.

Her absence is felt in the walls of the house, in the bones of my body. It's almost silent without her, the loud kind of quiet that can only be conjured when someone is missing; my Akita hardly makes a peep.

I stop the CD player and massage the bridge of my nose. My mind has decided to dwell on other matters tonight.

Akita

Eliza and I sit at the dinner table, still in our school uniforms, our faces covered in gloss and glitter makeup. I'm beside Eliza, across from her older brothers, Jace and Jordan, who share the same ginger hair, green eyes, and freckles, though Jace – the eldest, has far less.

'Here we go,' smiles Eliza's mother as she sets some food on the table before us.

'You know what this is, don't you darling?' she asks as she takes my plate and piles it with chicken nuggets and steamed vegetables.

'What? Chicken nuggets?' I ask, confused.

She grins and nods.

'Yes, I'll eat them,' I respond, feeling like I didn't properly understand the question she was asking. After we eat our nuggets, mashed potato, and steamed vegetables, we change into our pyjamas and flick through the cabinet in the living room staked with about three hundred DVD's. After little consideration, Eliza and I agree to watch The Incredibles. I've already seen the film about a dozen times with Santo and Amara, but for a reason I can't understand I'm very drawn to watching the superhero family tonight, especially the daughter who can vanish into thin air whenever she wants.

Eliza's father comes home from work when we're halfway through the film.

He eats his dinner on the couch with a glass bottle of what looks like apple juice but smells nothing like it when he pops the cap off.

Eliza falls asleep on the beanbag next to me before just before the villain is brought to justice, but I stay up and finish the rest of it anyway. Her father carries Eliza to her bedroom and I trail behind them. He tucks her into bed and makes room for me next to her.

'Jump on in,' he smiles.

I crawl next to Eliza, and he walks towards the door and turns off the light.

'Goodnight, you two.'

On Eliza's ceiling are about a dozen glow-in-the-dark stickers shaped like stars.

Sleep feels like a distant memory of a past life, a life I've left behind, something I don't do anymore.

I try to take deep breathes as a feeling of unease settles heavily on top of me. Then I suddenly get a rush of uncomfortable feelings that I have to quickly make sense of.

I feel lost, I think, and displaced, like I was plucked from my life and thrown into this one. I miss everything about home. I miss Mama, I miss Baba, I miss Ashanti, I even miss Santo and Amara. I miss the little things that bring me comfort and I don't think I've ever gone this long in my life without them. Without the things that make me, *me*.

A shiver slithers down my spine as Eliza quietly snores. I love my friend very much, but tonight I've realised how different our lives are. It disturbs me for a reason I can't articulate.

For a while I thought our differences were only skin deep.

It's taking everything in me to stop myself from crying for my mother and waking up this entire house.

Another string of thoughts emerges, making my body tremble. My life, as I know and love it, is ever so fragile – if one night away is all it takes for me to miss what is. And I can lose it all in the blink of an eye.

In a few weeks I'll move up to the third grade. Miss Hart won't be my teacher anymore.

I liked change in Egypt, all that time ago, because it was good change. I liked when the sun would set and the stars would come out, but as I lay here I can't think of anything worse than these ugly green glowing stars in the dark of Eliza's room.

It's then I realise the reason I don't want things to change is because I can't see how they will get better.

Taresai

I turn off all the lights in the house, kiss my children goodnight and rest my head on the pillow, trying to ignore the strange feeling inside me. Next to me is Santino, with Amara and Ashanti in the spaces between us. It took a while getting Amara to sleep without her big sister. I didn't expect her to yearn for Akita this much when all she does is annoy her.

The feeling doesn't go away, that a part of me is missing, and it's a while before my mind can surrender to sleep.

Chapter 13

Sydney

Akita

'Grade Three is easy, Akita. Piece of cake. I didn't have Miss Sandra, though. I had Mr Richards.'

I'm relieved when Santo tells me this because I know he gave his teacher a difficult time when he was in Grade Three. Miss Sandra is a new teacher, younger too, which is why we call her by her first name. My class is meeting her today at assembly.

Santo and I are on our way to school for the last day of the year, my last day of second grade, first day of summer.

As we walk along the pavement, I try to get the same number of steps in each square.

'You're going into Year Five,' I say, squinting up at Santo.

He's had a growth spurt and I haven't grown much recently, so the gap between us has become more apparent.

'And soon you'll be in high school with all the big kids.'

'What're you talking about, Bugs?'

'Stop calling me that, Santo.'

We turn a corner and approach our school gates. The early summer sun paints the old brick buildings on campus with fresh daylight.

'I am a big kid, though. Too big for this school, anyway,' he looks around contemplatively.

I go to walk away, having nothing else to say to Santo's nonsense.

'I'm not coming back here,' Santo says to nobody and everybody.

I turn to him, but he doesn't meet my gaze, his eyes instead on the large building in front of us. The building where the library is, where all the teachers' offices are, including the principal.

'What do you mean?' I ask.

'I'm going to do something.'

'To get expelled?'

Santo nods.

'Do what?' I press.

'I'm going to get Miss Declan back for what she did.'

'What did she do?' I ask, panic rising from my feet to my chest.

'She got me repeated, Akita,' he says, unnervingly calm. 'Wants me to come back next year and do Grade Four again.'

This is the first I'm hearing of this. I can't say I'm surprised; I haven't known any kid to have been repeated, but if it were to be anyone, Santo makes sense. Though I must admit, Santo being just one year above me would be strange.

'Sunny, don't do anything stupid. Please,' I say, hoping with all my heart that he doesn't ruin things for me here. As much as he hates it, St John's is still my school. I love it here, I have friends here, I learn things here.

'Santo, please.'

But Santo doesn't look at me, doesn't even hear my voice.

His eyes stay fixed on that building.

Taresai

I've just put Ashanti to sleep when I get a phone call from Principal McDonald.

Santo has slapped his teacher.

Akita

It's awful seeing a teacher cry. My insides turn when I see Miss Declan's face, red as a tomato, dripping with tears. The Grade Four classrooms are across from the Grade Two classrooms with a small courtyard between us; we can see through their windows from ours. So, when we heard a ruckus and a grown woman scream, we ran to our windows to see Miss Declan, a hand to her crumpled face, half-running towards the principal's office.

Santo has really done it this time.

He's expelled for sure, and he's going to get the whooping of his life tonight. The worst part about all this, about this nightmare that continues to unfold, isn't even the fact that now I'm sure to inherit all the hate from the teachers. It's that Santo doesn't even seem sorry or ashamed.

I watch him stand on the table, pounding on his chest like he's seen those American wrestlers do on tv.

He seems happy with himself, satisfied, as if a weight has been lifted from his shoulders, as if he has accomplished a life-long mission.

Chapter 14

Sydney

Taresai

The summer days are long and the nights are still.

I have the children to myself from the moment the sun rises to when it dips into the horizon in an orangey haze.

We have picnics in the park, take trips to the market and the town square, and walks to the local cafes – Akita reads out the menus to me and Santo places orders for the five of us.

He has settled nicely into his summertime routine of wearing t-shirts and canvas shoes instead of his old private school uniform and eating whenever he's hungry instead of 'when the bell tells him to.'

He's also taught Akita how to ride a bike. She'd fall, a lot at first. But within a week, she's riding up and down our gravel driveway, the scratches on her shins and knees indeed not in vain.

I open all the windows in the house to catch the warm afternoon light and sit out in the verandah as supper cooks on the stove on low heat. The crickets begin to chirp and Amara walks towards me, her short legs taking high strides off the grass. She sits beside me, grasps the hem of my skirt, and pulls herself up onto my lap.

'Everything okay?' I ask gently. She shakes her head and points to Akita.

'Akita won't put flowers on my head.'

'She can't, bubba, it's bad for your skin.'

Amara can't be in the grass for too long; her eczema is starting to flare up again. The doctors say it's because of the change in season, from winter to spring, spring to summer.

She suffers great pain, but in the moments she doesn't she knows no such thing. She laughs joyfully and plays fearlessly, incapable of falling victim to that which ails her.

But still, it troubles me greatly to cut all of her hair off each time it grows, to dress her in hypoallergenic cotton pants and long-sleeve shirts on days as hot as today. To strip that which makes her look and feel as her sisters do. Amara looks at me, lips pouted, tears welling in her eyes.

'How about you help me check on supper?' I say, standing and resting Amara on my hips. 'And tomorrow, we'll go to the market, and I'll buy you the prettiest hairband you want.'

We step into the kitchen and Amara sets two plates at the table before she grows bored and re-joins her sisters in the garden again.

I'm caught off guard by the humidity that clouds the air when I set the rest of the table and follow suit.

The sun of Australia rivals the one of back home with its nuance. Some days, the sun's glow lights me up from the inside, and on other days it makes my clothes stick to my skin.

This is what most afternoons look like, the girls play in the front garden and Santo bikes around the neighbourhood. After weeks of practice and with the help of Akita, Ashanti can now walk. I watch as her chubby, wobbly legs carry her across the yard in small steps. When she falls on her bum, Akita and Amara plant daisies in the thick coils of her dark hair.

Akita's been reading books with less pictures and more words, and picking out puzzles of a more complex variety. She speaks less now that school's over. At first, I thought it was because she misses her school friends, so I suggested a playdate. Akita shook her head and smiled, replying that she can see them back at school in a few of weeks. When she isn't playing with and looking after Ashanti (when my hands are full with Amara), Akita spends hours playing in the garden, her marvel still lingers from when the wildflowers graciously bloomed from every corner in spring.

Santo's been enrolled at the public school in the next suburb. Auburn Primary, a bike ride away. He got a tour of the campus and met his Grade Four teacher, Mr Andrews, and his guidance counsellor, Mr Peter who, to our pleasant surprise, is a Sudanese man.

There are more Sudanese kids at Auburn Primary than St John's. I hope that counts for something as far as Santo can see.

Santino has been working longer; his workload has increased inadvertently over the summer, so he leaves home earlier and comes home later. He works the same job in the local government office as an interpreter for new arrivals. I'm gathering that perhaps at this time of year there's an influx of migrants. Santino barely has time to spend with the kids.

I appreciate all he does to keep this family afloat, because unlike in Egypt and Sudan, there isn't anything I can do here except study my English with the hope of pulling equal weight sometime soon. This means that every day our children grow, I'm fortuitous in witnessing it all in detail, in such colour. Santino is deprived of these experiences. These moments that are slipping him by.

Then, as if summoned by my thoughts of him, I hear the tyres of Santino's new car crunch the gravel as he pulls into the driveway.

He emerges and I notice him leave his leather work satchel in the passenger seat of the gold Camry. Santino kneels his ironed slack pants on the grass and all three of his daughters race to his embrace at varying pace.

He plants a kiss on Akita's forehead, scoops up Ashanti from the grass and takes Amara's hand.

'Let's go inside before the mosquitoes come and get us.'

Akita and Amara usher inside giggling and Santino places Ashanti in my arms.

'It smells divine in there, darling.' He says, kissing my cheek.

'Beef and bean stew,' I beam up at him.

A smile spreads across Santino's face, revealing his perfectly aligned teeth, stained slightly from age and too many cups of tea.

'You're home early,' I say, bouncing Ashanti on my knee.

'Yes. Quiet afternoon, a few of our clients cancelled their appointments so Paul let everyone have an early start to their weekend.'

Paul is the manager who oversees Santino's department.

All of Santino's mentions of him have been pleasant although infrequent.

Paul sounds like a good man, and I can only imagine how much he might value Santino's work, but I can't see Santino inviting him over for supper anytime soon.

He's been trained to keep those two parts of his life separate, and it seems not even Australia can change that.

'Nathan and Kathleen are coming tomorrow. We're taking the kids to the beach.'

'Has that come around already?'

'Yes,' I chuckle, twirling the tufts of Ashanti's coils between my fingers. 'Can you spare some time to come along?'

Santino peers down at me, his smile turning sad. 'I don't think I can, Tsai. I'm sorry.'

I don't say anything, I don't speak my disappointment nor my irritation. I don't even bother asking why.

'You'll have Santo and Akita,' he reassures. 'And they put my interpretation skills to shame.'

Santino laughs and I soften my face meeting his gaze.

'It's not myself that I'm bellyaching for Santino, it's them,' I say, tilting my head towards the opening of the house.

Santino's smile grows sadder. He looks up to the faint passing clouds and exhales softly.

The setting sun paints the sky with colour to welcome in the night.

Neither of us say anything for a while, then the moment is broken when we hear Santo, his bike tyres racing along the gravel driveway.

'San-man,' says Santino, wrapping his arm around Santo's neck.

'Come on,' I say, standing and resting Ashanti on my hip. 'Supper is ready.'

* * *

I continued going to my English classes twice a week during the summer holidays. On those afternoons, I'd take Ashanti and Amara to day-care and leave Santo and Akita home alone. That routine was going fine until a few weeks ago when I fell ill.

I felt waves of energy and plateaus of lethargy. I didn't bother going to the doctor as it seemed like more trouble than it was worth. Instead, I would lie down whenever my head hurt so much it started spinning, I opened all the windows in the house when the air felt too heavy, and I drank ginger tea when my stomach churned with nausea.

I only realised that I'd fallen pregnant in the fourth week, when the symptoms did not stop.

* * *

I look around the table, at Santo's swollen cheeks stuffed with his supper, at Akita using her fingers to push her food onto her fork, then into her mouth. I see Amara, so content, sitting on her father's lap, eating from his plate, at Ashanti, biting down on the carrot with her two bottom teeth in her ferocious two-year-old's grip.

When I look back at Santino, I see the way his eyes shine when he looks at me, the way his soul glows when he is in the presence of our children.

I cast my love inward, to the life that is growing within me, a secret until the time's right.

When the children have been bathed and put to sleep, the dishes washed and put away, Santino lies in bed and I sit in front of the mirror table on the other side of the room.

He can fall asleep at the drop of a hat. Throughout our entire marriage I can't recount more than a few instances where I've fallen asleep first. Santino is always exhausted from work, and my mind is always wide awake at night, overthinking the day. It takes a lot of concentration, or lack thereof, to lure sleep.

Tonight, though, Santino is restless, quiet, and staring silently at the ceiling.

He gets like this when something deep, be it a suppressed thought, memory or emotion, has been looming and brewing; and I can already feel the crashing of those waves coming in to shore. I know him through the secret language of spouses that only two people can create, one where I understand what lies behind every stroke of the skin, beneath the feeling of every word, the texture of every thought.

To be a man is to protect your family, even from truths, in Santino's eyes.

In all my years of knowing him, he has never presented me with a problem that he hasn't already found at least three solutions or answers to.

At times I feel like I'm being kept in the dark, instead of being protected from it, and other times, times like this, when he speaks little of any issues at all and then unscrews the cap to a million; they're the times when I feel like I am darkness itself.

'Something on your mind?' I ask from the mirror table, twisting my hair into a braid. Santino sits up and looks at me from the bed, into my eyes in the mirror through his glasses. We haven't spoken properly since that night all those months ago, when he said to make learning English my priority in case he is not around.

I haven't asked again what he meant, instead I've been thinking about it almost every night for months on end, trying to make sense of words he may have forgotten ever voicing.

Recently we only speak about the kids, about Santo's new uniforms, about Akita's upcoming birthday, about Amara's eczema, about Ashanti's doctor's visits.

We haven't spoken about us, outside of what we feel like for supper, how work or my Englishes classes are going. Boring spousal small talk is a luxury of living in a place where you can worry about things like that instead of how to keep yourself and your family alive.

'No,' Santino smiles, as if caught off guard by the question. 'No,' he says again, this time to himself.

I observe him closely.

'The kids are getting big,' he says suddenly. 'Santo is nearly my height.'

'Yes,' I smile, turning to him, unsure where this is coming from. Santo's last growth spurt was about a month ago; he hasn't grown much since. He's tall for a ten-year-old, but he's barely past my shoulder, never mind 'nearly' Santino's height.

'Akita is such a big girl now. Reading chapter books? Brilliant.'

'Yes, she is,' I respond, an emptiness to my tone.

Santino looks down at his knees, deep in thought.

'How are your English classes going, Tsai?' he asks, shifting to the edge of the bed towards me. *They're going fine, just as they were yesterday when you asked*, I feel like saying.

'Great. I can understand it a lot better than I can speak it, but, with time ...'

Santino nods, looking away from me, his face etched with something I cannot yet read. I feel a pulling in my stomach, the underlying energies of this conversation poke through this innocent facade. I turn to face him.

'Santino?' I say, quietly. 'Are you happy?'

He doesn't look at me when he speaks.

'Happiness is … futile, Taresai. A hopeless … dream,' he chuckles dryly. 'Something I cannot afford.'

When I don't say anything, he sighs very deeply and continues. 'I'm happy that I have four healthy, beautiful children who have the opportunity to grow up and be all they can be. I'm happy that I have you, that we have this.'

I flatten the fibres of my nightdress, listening, waiting for the truth to reveal itself.

'I'm happy we have food, a place to rest my head. But happiness? … Tsai, we both know that trying to chase it will only break us like we have been broken before … and yet, to be without it …' Santino looks away, his face pained. 'It eats you up until there's nothing left.'

I turn away from Santino and look at my reflection in the mirror. I busy my hands, unravelling the braid I've tied my hair into, and I start twisting it again.

I've always thought it important to keep certain thoughts to oneself, even in a sacred union, a fifteen-year marriage, with four kids, soon to be five. I expected a lot of things to come out of his mouth tonight, but this, I truly find disturbing.

It seems that the stable world we have built for our children has fragile foundations.

Santino rotates the gold wedding band on his finger. I go to turn and face him, but I find that I'm unable to.

In this short conversation, this small exchange of words, the future of our family, our children, is on the brink of collapse.

When I feel the slightest ounce of courage, I turn and look at Santino, really look at him, for the first time in a while, as he willingly casts his veil away. I see him, beyond his dark eyes, neatly trimmed beard, hair so dark it catches the low light of the room.

'Tell me what's really on your mind,' I say, suddenly overcome with anger.

Santino takes off his glasses, massages the bridge of his nose, then puts them back on. He looks at me, his eyes apologetic, his mind made. Whatever he's about to say or suggest or ask, he's already spent nights thinking about.

'When we were in Sudan, when you'd just had Santo,' he begins, reminiscing about a time over a decade and three countries ago, 'I was an architect, just finished my master's degree.' He takes a slow breath.

'Then we were forced to move to Giza, on the next train before the ashes settled. We lost … everything, we had nothing, Tsai, but we kept moving forward. Always forward.'

I stare firmly at Santino's brown eyes, how they seem to quiver in the light.

'I got a job as a land surveyor; no architecture firm would hire me, but it didn't pay well, so I worked at the mayor's office.'

My mind swirls with countless thoughts. Why is he recounting all our hardships? Retelling me all these stories as if I wasn't an integral part of it?

I stand and close our bedroom door, even though I'm certain the children are well into their slumber. I take my place in front of the mirror table again, inching away when Santino leans closer.

'We come here, and what am I?' he asks me, his voice strained with turmoil. 'An interpreter, Taresai. A form-filler. All those years I spent studying, all those nights I went starving because I'd paid for my tuition and my books instead of food or shelter. All of that just to come here and be in the corporate trenches. What good is all that I have done, all that I have sacrificed, when it isn't recognised?'

My head spins and my heart feels as if it might burst from thumping so hard. I don't know if it's the baby, or if it's my body preparing itself for news I don't want to hear.

'Santino,' I say firmly, 'what are you saying?'

'Tsai, I am not happy. Happiness was Sudan. It was my position as the youngest architect on the team, the most revered young man in Khartoum. To chase happiness would be to travel to the past. I can't do that, so I'm considering the closest thing to it.'

I get up from my seat and turn to walk out of our bedroom, in complete and utter shock, disbelief, and absolute horror.

'Tsai, wait,' Santino says, grabbing me by the wrist. 'I'm sorry,' he says, his eyes swelling with tears. 'I must go back to Sudan. Only me.'

I shake his hand off my wrist and look down at him as he sits on our bed. I've never hated this man more in my life than I do at this very moment.

He would leave me? He would leave his children? He would choose to become absent in their lives in search of something that he thinks is a greater sacrifice?

My blood runs cold. No love in my heart could warm the words that come out of my mouth.

'I don't have to search for happiness anymore, Santino,' I say as I walk towards the door. 'I created it.'

Chapter 15

Sydney

Akita

Santo was right. Grade Three isn't so bad. It feels like quite a leap, though it's still only the first term of school.

We don't have nap times anymore, and Miss Sandra doesn't sing to us like Miss Hart did. We get homework – worksheets that we have to do at home and bring back by the end of the week. I don't think I mind it, though; it makes me feel older, more responsible, and there are advantages, I've learned, that come with such responsibility.

We have our own library cards, which means I can borrow up to five books from the school library, we can spend lunchtimes indoors in the classroom and we're allowed to play the top-shelf boardgames. In our art classes we've moved on from finger-painting; we're learning art techniques like shading, shadow and light and texture to make objects look real.

It was nice to go back to school and see all my friends. They all looked so different. Awien has grown an entire inch and she now wears her natural hair out, her afro's neatly brushed upward and pushed back with a headband. Ashra has grown too. We're no longer the same height, but her hair is still the same – jet-black, cut pencil-straight just above her shoulders. Eliza didn't grow much at all, which makes me feel a bit better, but her ginger hair is much longer, and she wears glittery gloss on her lips to school nearly every day.

I don't feel like I've changed much. I'm still 115 cm tall no matter how much milk I drink and how many stretches I do. My hair is in the same hairstyle it has been for as long as I can remember: six neat little cornrows falling to my back. Sometimes Mama braids eight if she has time.

It seems like over the summer all my changes were on the inside. I can read a lot faster, even the bigger words, and my handwriting is much neater than Santo's. But nobody can see those changes so it feels like I'm not growing at all.

On the bright side, it is my birthday next week.

I'm turning eight. Two lots of four.

I know, I just know, that the day I turn eight everything will change. Even if I don't get taller it won't matter because I'll be a whole year older. I'll be the same age as all my friends and everyone else in my year who hasn't already turned nine the year before.

Also, Mama's finally agreed to let me pick my own hairstyle. I've finally outgrown the cornrows.

When she asked me what hairstyle I wanted for my birthday, I told her I wanted box braids, and she agreed, although reluctant. I sit on a stool between her legs on this Friday night, an hour past my bedtime, as she finishes braiding my hair.

Taresai

The past couple of months have been fleeting.

It was disorientating to go from the ease and steadiness of the summer right into the madness of back to school with two primary schoolers, a pre-schooler and a toddler. Before I know it, the leaves are changing and the air gets crisper. It is the first of April, a week before Akita turns eight.

I haven't spoken to Santino properly since that night over two months ago. I haven't forgiven him, either.

He slept on the couch that night and I stayed wide awake in our bed.

I woke him just as the sun began to rise. We both agreed that we did not want the children to see. As he carried his blanket into our bedroom and closed the door behind him, I asked him when he is to leave.

He answered that he wasn't sure. He wasn't sure of anything just yet. Only that he's certain that he, alone, must go back.

To chase something that he has left behind, but I think no longer exists.

It took a few restless nights before my mind could come to terms with what Santino has decided. And that was it.

We've both made a silent vow to keep things civil in the face of our children, though I know they can sense the shift in energy.

I mustn't dwell on that which I can't change, especially something that might take some time to unfurl, so every day I try to put my mind to appropriate things.

My days are spent in class, my afternoons are spent with the children, and my evenings I spend with myself and the unborn child in my womb, watching Australian soap operas, only retreating to the bedroom when I know Santino has fallen asleep. The weekends are the hardest to avoid Santino; our conversations are mostly about the kids. We discuss whether Santo is settling in well at his new school, if he likes his new teachers, if the new ointment for Amara's skin pains her more than the last. Whenever our conversation drifts outside the bounds I've built over the weeks, I retreat, change the subject, leave the room, or tend to one of my children's endless needs.

I'm yet to tell him that I'm thirteen weeks' pregnant with his fifth child. I'm yet to tell anybody. Not Achol who insists on coming over every second day, not my mother, not my sisters, not Manuela, not even my brother. Not that I possibly could anyway.

Our connections remained severed and with every day, with each passing moment, I feel the pain of their absence deepen.

Messai was always one of the first people to know when I was with child. But now, nearly three years without hearing his voice, hearing my sister's voices, even my mother's, I feel unfathomable waves of loneliness wash over me, pulling me under.

I don't know how much longer I can keep this up, being disconnected from Santino. But I fear that if we come back together as equals, to try and meet in the middle, he'll say and do things that make me feel lonelier than I already do.

Akita shifts between my legs.

'Getting tired, bubba?' I chuckle softly. 'Your hair's nearly done.'

'No,' she says sleepily. 'I'm okay.'

Her soft voice brings me back to this moment, to this space in our living room, to the yellow ceiling light, squashy brown couch I sit on and the red Turkish rug Akita rests her bottom. I push my worries away. Moments like these are for me and my daughter, and what a huge moment this is.

I have, for the first time, allowed Akita to pick her own hairstyle in honour of her upcoming eighth birthday. Of course, she's picked the most grown-up one she could think of. Box braids. I can only oblige.

Akita's head jerks back suddenly in a fight of sleep.

'Almost done, honey,' I whisper.

'Mm-hm.'

'How's school going?' I ask, in an effort to keep her awake for this last little while.

'It's good. Miss Sandra is really nice. We're reading Roald Dahl.'

'That's great honey,' I say, having no idea what Roald Dahl is.

'Do you feel okay? Going to school without Santo?'

'Yeah,' she laughs. 'Sunny was naughty. It's nice to go to school and not worry about him.'

I'm surprised to hear this.

I'd never known Akita to feel this way because I never thought to ask the question. It hadn't occurred to me to consider how Santo's behaviour could've impacted Akita at school, and yet it makes perfect sense that she harbours these sentiments.

She was tethered to him out there as much as she is in here, and without him, of course, she feels a relief. I feel a twinge of shame for not having recognised this sooner.

It's only times like this that I can properly spend with Akita, with my full, almost undivided attention on her. I forget she feels things because it rarely seems like anything is troubling her, but maybe I'm just not looking deeply enough, asking her the right things, connecting with enough effort.

'I do miss walking with him to school. Now he rides his bike the opposite way.'

Something about the way she speaks of her big brother makes me smile.

'Santo will always be your big brother. You have each other forever,' I say, hoping that my words bring her comfort. She shows no sign that it does.

My Akita, harder to read than a book. I search my mind, trying to think of another thing to say, to make use of this rare moment that I get to bond with my eldest daughter.

Akita's head falls gently on my lap, defeated by sleep. I smile to myself and finish off the last couple of braids, twisting her hair into patterns, the strands falling down her back and around her face like small snakes dangling from a tree.

When Akita was a toddler and her hair fell over her eyes, I started braiding it into little cornrows. When she turned four

I started putting rainbow beads at the ends of her braids, then iridescent baubles when she turned five. I only stopped putting them in her hair when that school in Giza forbade her from wearing them.

Now, here she is, at the brink of becoming another year older, with a head full of box braids.

I wake her when her hair is done.

'Can I see?' I ask as she gets to her feet. She rubs her eye with her knuckle then gives me a toothy grin. I try not to gasp too loudly. I now understand why I'd said no to this hairstyle for so long.

She looks so grown up. My daughter, my Akita. Eight.

Chapter 16

Sydney

Akita

It's the afternoon of my eighth birthday.

We've finished decorating the house and setting up, so Mama sends me to my room to get dressed. On Monday Baba picked me up early from school and took me to the shopping centre in the city. I got to pick out a dress to wear today.

I stand in front of my bedroom mirror in my underwear, my frilly socks and my dress shoes. I pick up the dress from my bed, unzip it and step into it, pulling it up over my shoulders and sticking my arms through the short sleeves.

It's light-pink, made with layers of different fabric that change colour under the light. It's got puffy sleeves, a full skirt and white flowers around the waistband. It's the most beautiful thing I own.

Once it's on, I step back and get a good look at myself.

I look so different with my new hair, in my new dress. Grown up. I twirl and dance in my dress until Mama knocks on my bedroom door, announcing that my friends have arrived. I'm pretty sure this is the happiest day of my life. Our house is full of friends: mine from school, kids that belong to Mama's friends, some of Santo's friends from his new school, and kids around the neighbourhood. Mama even made me invite our neighbour Ms Nora's grandkids, Evan, and Annabelle.

We decorated the living and dining rooms with pink and white balloons and yellow streamers. Our supper table is full of sweets, chocolate, biscuits, cupcakes, coconut bread, the special rosewater donuts Mama makes and soft drinks every colour of the rainbow. Baba puts the presents I receive in my bedroom, all wrapped in colourful paper, their contents a secret only I can uncover in the comfort of my own solitude later tonight.

Gifts like I've seen so many other people receive.

My friends and I play outside in the garden wearing paper crowns. I wave my wand – a fallen twig from a nearby gumtree – and turn each of them into a magical creature of their choosing for five minutes. Eliza into a mermaid, Ashra into a unicorn, Awien into a fairy and myself into a fire-breathing dragon.

Mama calls us in just as the sun starts to set.

Everyone gathers around the table. Santo sits to my left, Amara to my right. Mama stands me up on a chair so everyone can see as Baba walks towards me with a white-frosted cake. It's the most beautiful thing I have ever seen, decorated with pink flowers and my name written in strawberry jelly, holding eight candles, golden flames flickering at their tips. I never want this day to end, and yet I can't wait for the next second to unfold.

Taresai

I watch Akita's face closely, all lit up. With her uneven smile, shiny new braids and the pink dress too big for her small frame. I don't think I've ever seen her this happy. It makes me want to weep.

Her face twists pleasantly when the whole room erupts, singing her a happy birthday in the first language she ever spoke. Akita's rabbit teeth protrude, and she places both hands on her cheeks. She locks eyes with me for a moment, then she continues scanning the choir.

She's got a smile that could stop time.

Amara stands on top of the chair on her big sister's side, her hand holding the skirt of Akita's dress in a chocolate-covered grip.

Santo stands on the other side of Akita, holding Ashanti on his hip, trying with all his might to sing the loudest.

I take in every detail of this moment because I know it's going to be one that I revisit countless times in my memories, because that will be all it is before the night comes.

* * *

Later that night, when the guests have all left, and I've wrapped and refrigerated all the food, when Santo has taken out all the trash, and Akita – the last one awake – has unwrapped all her presents and fallen asleep from blissful exhaustion, I walk into our bedroom. Santino is wide awake, reading a book at the head of the bed. He looks up at me standing in the doorway. When I don't move or utter a word, he closes his book and sets it down. He takes off his glasses before he speaks.

'Are the children asleep?' he asks.

I nod and look away.

'Are you going to come to bed? I haven't fallen asleep next to you in months–'

'I'm pregnant,' I say, the words sharply cutting through the air. 'Fourteen weeks.'

Chapter 17

Sydney

Taresai

The weight of bearing an infant is heavier with each day.

I'm kept awake at night, grasping our forthcoming reality, when I bring another child into this world.

I'm almost four months along, due in September.

I can easily conceal the bump, but the baby within me is taking up more space with each day. This child is a secret between Santino and I, who, to my surprise, welcomed the news with glee. Since our youth, Santino has always expressed his desire for a large family. He wanted a few more children after Ashanti, but I doubt he expected it to be so soon.

Santino hasn't mentioned moving away and leaving us since that first time, instead he's awake at night, thinking of baby names and who in his family our unborn child should be named after. I've been apprehensive, reluctant to fall into prenatal bliss with him. Maybe welcoming another child into the world will be enough to fill the gaping hole in his male ego, and I can only hope that time will help me see him in a different light.

I'm keeping my pregnancy from the kids, partly because I think it's too soon, but mostly because I don't know how they might react.

Santo has just settled into Grade Five in his new school, Akita has only just started blossoming, and Amara has barely gotten used to having a younger sibling, never mind two. Ashanti, however, has been a dream since the day she was born, but who knows, maybe a newborn baby brother or sister will be the thing that sets her down the path of terrible toddler.

It's been difficult to come to terms with how I feel.

I think I'm happy.

When I examine the surface, there is primal joy around my fifth child. But below that surface my worries dwell. Despite myself, and all these years in between, there is still a fear which lingers deep in my bones: the fear of losing the life in my womb.

A healthy son and three healthy daughters later and I'm still taken back to the unrelenting horrors of my firsts.

It looms over me on most days, so I try not to think too deeply about it, even though it's becoming harder to ignore. In truth, if I tell the children they're going to have a new sibling in the next coming months, it's going to be much realer than I'm ready for. It's all they'll talk about and the thought of that terrifies me.

Not now, not yet.

If I'm honest, I worry most about Santo. He's a better older brother than he is a school student, and he always looks after Akita and tries to protect his little sisters from the harshness of the world.

Recently, though, he's been harder to predict. Santo's been on his best behaviour at school, but it has come at the expense of the natural rhythm of things at home.

The day after Akita's birthday, he threw a pebble at the wheels of her new bike as she rode it down the driveway, 'just to see what would happen'.

Well, she fell and scraped her elbows and her knee. He wasn't apologetic and Akita didn't make a fuss, but part of me wished she would.

Santo's also been practising more of his wrestling moves on her, throwing her around like a ragdoll. He's started listening to music entrenched in cuss words.

I don't know why he's acting out suddenly. Can he sense that things beyond his grasp are shifting, or is he simply growing? Whatever it might be, the news of a new sibling will rock him, and only time will tell if it's for better or for worse.

Akita

I ride my brand-new bike to the library to meet up with Eliza, Awien and Ashra. I've been eight for a couple of weeks and I think it might be my new favourite number. There are so many things that I can do now that I couldn't at seven.

I can ride my bike around the neighbourhood, even to the library on my own – which isn't that far; it's closer than school, but still.

Mama gives me pocket money for doing chores, I bathe on my own, and I'm allowed to use the microwave in the kitchen – not yet allowed near the kettle or the stove – but I can wash my own dishes.

I watch my reflection as I ride past the shop windows through the markets. I'm eight, I'm a big girl and soon I'll be a double-digit age like Santo. Seven seems like ages ago.

I listen to the songs on my CD player, which is another gift I got for my birthday.

It takes me two and a half songs to get to the library and four songs by the time I find my friends on the third floor.

They're sitting around a table on blue seats that are shaped the human hands.

'What happened to your knee?' Eliza asks when I sit next to her.

'I fell off my bike,' I say.

'Oh,' says Awien. 'Don't you know how to ride a bike?'

'No, I do. I fell because Santo threw a rock at my wheel.'

'Oh, brothers are the worst,' Ashra chimes in, rolling her eyes. 'Was it because he was jealous?'

'No,' I say, laughing at the silliness of the question. 'He just wanted to see what would happen.'

Santo has absolutely no reason to be jealous of my new bike or any of my things. Mama and Baba buy him gifts like every day is his birthday. When he gets a good grade on an assessment, he gets a new game for his console, a new WWE figurine to add to his collection or a CD player like mine. Just last week he got a new skateboard.

I don't mind; I understand why, even though no one's ever explained it to me.

Santo is special. Being good isn't as easy for him as it is for other people. When Santo does behave, he has to try harder than I ever will. Which is also why it's so easy for me to forgive him. I know he's being the best brother that he can, and when he does stupid things that leave me hurt I know he doesn't mean them. But I am finding it a bit harder these days to be patient with him. It's the school holidays so he's even more annoying than usual. I can't help but get sick of him when he's acting like a child even though he's double digits.

We break up and pull books from the endless, very high shelves of Auburn Public Library. I pull several books from the science section. One in particular draws my eye. I sound out the word on the cover of the book. *Astronomy.*

I turn to my friends, but none of them know what the word means. Judging by the hardcover of the large book, it's the study of planets, maybe. I look through the pages, reading sentences while sounding out the big words, the meanings of which I do not understand.

I feel myself getting nervous, thinking that with my older age has come a forgetful mind. I think for a moment that all the English I've learned in the past two years is falling out my ears. But when Ashra and Awien shrug their shoulders with cluelessness too, we laugh and abandon the words to stare at the pictures, and my worries are squashed.

I flick through page after page of planets that look like marbles. One of them, called Saturn, has a giant ring around it. I find it really hard to imagine such a planet exists. How has Saturn's ring not fallen off? What's holding it up?

In the quiet, when it's only me that hasn't lost interest in the book, I feel the weight of melancholy in my belly and around my shoulders. It's a little while until I understand why. Staring at these pages of planets and stars reminds me of my Haboba. I haven't thought of her for a while, and now that I do, I want to cry. I miss her so much.

I close the book and push it to the end of the table. I begin flicking through my second book. It's an atlas, a book about *this* planet.

I flick past Australia, even though it's my home and my favourite place in the world, and I'm sure nothing can change that. Australia is the only country we're taught about in school.

Kangaroos, wallabies, koalas, Uluru, our natural fauna and flora, Ned Kelly.

I flick to the continent of Africa and trace my finger along the country shaped like a fat chilli pepper made of Lego. Sudan. Where I was born, where I'm from. I find the page with pictures of Sudan. Yellow sand, red dirt, green savannas, mud houses with straw roofs. People in vibrant tribal fabrics with markings on their foreheads and such deep, dark skin.

As I look at the pictures, at the faces of my people on the glossy pages, I get a feeling that I don't understand. As I look at them, into their eyes, I feel a pulling. I want to reach into the book and grab them, but I don't know if I want them to pull me in or if I want to pull them out.

We hear a crash upstairs that makes me jump. Several voices shout over each other. Boys, high schoolers, probably. Starting trouble in a library? Pathetic, if you ask me.

Eliza tugs on the sleeve of my jumper.

'Can we leave?' she asks.

'Don't be a baby, Liza,' says Ashra. 'It's probably nothing.'

But just before Ashra can finish her sentence, we see a boy roll down the stairs from the fourth floor. He's young, but way older than us; he looks like a teenager. He holds the top of his head and lets out a wail. Older people sitting on the desks beside us run to his aid. Not a second later, I see an older Sudanese man; he looks about Baba's age. He walks down the stairs gripping the collar of a younger Sudanese boy who shouts profanities at the other boy who'd fallen down the stairs, a boy with a broken CD player and a bleeding nose. I let out a gasp.

'Santo.'

Chapter 18

Sydney

Taresai

I meet Santino outside the children's hospital in the city.

I've left Amara and Ashanti at home with Achol, and hopefully by now Akita too. It's been an hour since we got the call from Santo's guidance counsellor, Mr Peter, telling us Santo was involved in an incident at the public library.

Santo isn't badly hurt, but Mr Peter has taken him to the hospital for good measure. Peter was short in telling us the details of the incident, probably to ease our nerves on our way in, and though I appreciate the intention, the gesture is irritating.

An 'incident' 'involving' Santo could mean anything.

Has he damaged private property? Has he beaten up a kid, or has he picked a fight with someone and got beaten for it?

Santino and I race up the stairs to the doctor's offices until we find Peter sitting in the waiting area of the third floor.

'Santino, Taresai.' He stands and greets us with a firm handshake each.

'Where is Santo?' I ask, failing to muster an ounce of composure.

'He's fine, they just took him in for a routine check-up. He's in there with one of the doctors now.'

I'm relieved to hear this, but I just want to see my son.

'They assumed I was Santo's father, so they gave me some forms to fill out,' says Peter, handing Santino a clipboard.

'Thank you, Peter,' Santino says, and smiles earnestly. 'Do you know what happened?' he asks, already pushing pen to paper.

'He got into an argument with a group of boys at the library. Santo mentioned that they were having some sort of rap battle. One of the kids said a particular word and Santo didn't like it. He started punching and kicking the boy, then moved to punch all four of them.'

I find it extremely difficult to picture Santo putting his hands on another child and causing them harm, and yet it takes me no effort to believe it.

'The other boys,' says Santino. 'Are they okay?'

'They're fine. They're students at the high school I teach in. Year eights. They're probably a bit shaken by it all, but Santo sustained the most injury.'

I feel a galloping pulse of panic that makes my knees weak.

I don't know if I want to yell and smack some sense into Santo, or if I want to squeeze him until all his troubles fade away.

I fear I may burst at any second if I'm made to wait any longer to hold Santo. If I had all the English words firmly in my mind, I'd walk through those doors and see my son.

Santino nods, his mind buzzing with solutions to this predicament. When he doesn't say anything, Peter speaks. 'Listen, Santino, Taresai. I've been working with children both here and back home, children from difficult backgrounds. Santo is a good kid, but there is something about his behaviour that troubles me.'

'What do you mean?' I ask.

'Pardon my boldness, but I'd like to suggest you take Santo to a child behavioural analyst,' Peter says, first in English, then in Arabic. 'Child psychologist,' he says, looking from me to Santino.

I feel Santino tense up beside me. I'm sure he appreciates Peter's suggestion, although a man making one about another man's son might be crossing a line in Santino's eyes. He doesn't say anything, only glares at Peter intensely and nods.

'We'll make an appointment,' he says firmly, looking at me then back at Peter.

I've got so many things to say, so many questions to ask, but I can't bring myself to speak, to move.

A heaviness sets between the three of us. Something in the air feels permanent, concretised, broken only by Santo as he exits the doctor's office, shirt bloodied, a wide grin on his face, lollipop in one hand and a wrist brace on the other.

* * *

The next four nights I barely get a wink of sleep.

My worries of Santo swirl in the deep pool of my mind. I've always known there was something special about my son, something wild and untamed since the day he was born.

He once cried for two days without end when he was three weeks old. Our neighbour had grown so agitated from his screaming that she decided to come over and try her hand at soothing him.

Of course, it didn't work. But I was young then, a first-time mother after years of trying and miscarrying. I thought it was normal. Santo's had behavioural issues for as long as he's been Santo, but I thought that was normal too; he's a boy, boys are generally more hyperactive and temperamental. We have no other son to compare him to, only his younger sister, Akita, who has been his polar opposite since the day she was born.

I things like that became harder to notice and even harder to keep track of as children grow. They leave behind one phase and move on to the next, and I've been hoping for the life of me that Santo's destructive dispositions are nothing but a very long phase that he'll one day grow out of on his path to a gentleman. But I'm afraid hope, in this instance, is a fog that stops me from seeing reality.

What once seemed like harmless passing clouds has become a raging storm without our notice, and the older Santo becomes the darker those clouds get.

He is such a sweet boy, capable of so much, but there is something that clouds his thoughts, blurs his being, and I'm selfish because there is a small part of me that doesn't want to know what that thing is.

* * *

The next week, while Akita is at school, and Amara and Ashanti are in day-care, we take Santo to the town centre where Dr. Albert Abbasi's office resides. Peter recommended him because he is the best we can afford, and much to my elation, Abbasi is the only Arabic-speaking child psychologist in this side of New South Wales.

I nearly wept tears of joy.

I'll be able to understand every word and make of it what it is, instead of guessing the closest thing to it.

As Santo's parents, Santino and I share the same solicitude that bleeds into the day, though I don't think it makes him as uneasy to keep the appointment a secret from our son.

As far as he knows, he's out helping the pair of us run some errands.

Santo asked no questions beyond ice-cream being had and new shoes to be bought and we could only oblige, but heaven knows how today will shape him.

Two new shoes, three potato cakes and an ice-cream cone later, we arrive at Abbasi's office which from the outside appears to have once been a house.

The receptionist signs us in and we take our seats in the waiting room. Santo barely makes it to his seat, detouring when he sees a giant fish tank against the wall. He presses his hands and face to the glass and swivels his head back and forth.

We're the only ones here and I'm yet to know if it's a good or bad thing, my nerves instead making me too aware of the sound of Santino's pen scribbling onto paper, the smell of the vanilla candle burning that makes me ill with nausea, and the wig that sits uncomfortably on my head.

The air suddenly feels too heavy in this small waiting room, my clothes suddenly feel too tight and stifling.

Santino places his hand over my knee to settles my nerves.

I take a deep breath in.

When I meet his eyes, he smiles slightly, and doesn't say a word. I exhale and look to Santo, a silhouette against the fluorescent fish tank.

Then we all hear the click of the doorknob turning and Dr Albert Abbasi emerges from behind the beige door with his name on it.

* * *

Santo has ADHD and DMDD.

A bunch of random letters that meant nothing to me except maybe the first half of the English alphabet are now disorders that my son suffers. Illnesses that I cannot see. These acronyms are the answers, the causes of his behaviour. Something he was born with and hardwired into the inner workings of his brain. He didn't catch it like you would catch a cold overnight.

We sat there, across from Abbasi, in his neat office with half a dozen plants, a large window that looks out into the garden and his oak desk with framed photos and a drinking bird that instantly drew Santo's attention.

Abbasi, a brown, plump, older man with greying hair only on the back if his head, made small talk which Santino mostly responded to as Santo sat between us.

Dr Abbasi gave Santo a Rubik's cube before swiftly directing his questions to him.

It didn't feel much like an interrogation, which I feared it would, but more like a conversation and Santo answered truthfully to Dr Abbasi's disarming manner, tone and questions alike.

He was then sent to the garden to play as we were given his diagnosis.

He will still live a happy and full life, Abbasi assured us, so long as he takes his medication and sees a regular counsellor, so his condition doesn't manifest into something worse.

His medications aren't a cure, but rather a leveller. It contains all his negative impulses and balances out his moods.

While I remain hopeful in the face of Santo and his father, I am absolutely shattered. I'm scared for my son. Terrified. I don't know if I want to protect him from the world, to shield him from the harshness of it, or if I want to shelter the world from him. What breaks me is that I can't do either.

Santo will become what and who he is exposed to, I know that now, and that fact alone makes me want to wrap my arms over him like a blanket and soften his raging fire for eternity.

I can't, though. I shouldn't.

I turn over on my pillow for the last time and rise out of bed. 3.26 am.

I pace the hallway and follow the sound of Santo's snores into his bedroom. He sleeps on his back with his legs sprawled out and his mouth wide open. Santo's tartan blanket covers only one of his legs hanging off the bed, but it rests mostly on the carpet.

I close his window and run my fingers through the coils of Santo's dark hair. He leans into my hands and twitches.

A chuckle escapes me, and I have to cover my mouth to stop.

I pull Santo's blanket to his chin and breathe a breath into the night.

There is a silver lining in this predicament that not even I can deny, and it gleams brightly.

How fortunate are we to live in a place like this, a country where they have medicines for illnesses and disorders that the eyes cannot see?

Chapter 19

Sydney

Akita

Things are strange. They seem to be moving at a slow pace but shifting quickly at the same time. Everyone at home is changing, going through the motions, and I seem to be the only one smooth-sailing through the days without any major tides crashing my way.

Ever since that day at the library over a month ago, something shifted, causing every other day after that to be different.

Baba has been working a lot. I barely see him. On weekends he sits for hours in his spot at the dining table with countless books piled up around him. Whenever I walk into the room he barely notices me, and when he does, he looks up from his books, confused, as if I were a figment of his imagination come to life.

Mama has become uncharacteristically soft and very emotional. She nearly cried yesterday when I sang Amara back to sleep after she had a bad dream. Mama never cries. Ever.

She wears wigs now, too. She owns three, but they all look the same, very short and unalive. Mama's hair is much longer, which is silly, because I thought that was the whole point of a wig. I've never known anyone to wear wigs back in Egypt. It seems to be something that African women particularly do here.

I'm not fond of it, especially on Mama. It sits on top of her head intrusively, hiding her cornrows beneath, making its presence overly known. It bothers me because it's what I look at when I see Mama, not so much her deep silky skin, not her small eyes and high cheekbones or her wide smile and gapped front teeth. Just the wig.

Santo is now at his third school, Lidcombe Primary. He got kicked out of Auburn Primary for doing something, but Mama and Baba won't tell me what.

He too is being weird. Mama and Baba took Santo to the doctors and got some medication to help him behave better, but all it's done is make him really quiet and sleepy.

The house is almost silent without his nonsense, too reserved, and I can't believe that I miss his loudmouth and all the extra noise he'd have around him.

Baba says he'll go back to normal soon, he just needs time to adjust.

Amara lost both her front teeth; she doesn't look as cute as she did before. She looks rather funny, but I can't laugh at her because the last time I did that she kicked me in the face. Seeing Amara lose her teeth makes me feel sad for Ashanti. This is as cute as she'll ever get. Soon, she too will lose her teeth and be all funny-looking like Amara. For now, at least, she remains the cutest baby there is. She likes to run, though not very fast because she's quite fat and her legs are like sausages.

Even the weather is peculiar.

It's an unusually warm morning in late May. Mama's walking me to school for the first time in ages. I told her that I would be fine walking to school on my own, just as I have all year, but today she insisted on joining me.

She acts strangely, stares at me oddly, so much so that I find myself averting her eyes from the discomfort.

I'm bewildered when she speaks to me in English for the first time ever and smiles at me expectantly, like I'm about to burst into colours at any moment.

'How are you this morning, my daughter?'

Taresai

I'm freaking her out. I can sense it already.

I try to defy my doubts, but it shouldn't be this hard to connect with my own eight-year-old daughter for goodness' sake. Yes, things have been changing substantially at home, and the time Akita takes up in my day has been shrinking, but I refuse to let her slip through the cracks. I'm going to make sure that she's okay, and if she isn't, I'll be the first to know and do something about it.

It's a warm autumn morning, one of the last warm days before the treacherous cold descends upon this country. We stroll. My attempts to make conversation are strong in thought but come out as feeble words. I ask Akita how she is, and she glares up at me, smiling as if she expects me to read her mind and find the answers behind her eyes.

She might be uncomfortable because of how unfamiliar my voice sounds in English perhaps, I was, but either way, at some point I am to start speaking it with the children, why not today? I'm gaining confidence in class, and my tutor Anne says my English is excellent for a non-native speaker.

But Akita looks at me like I've just yelled at her. I take a deep breath in and try again.

'Akita, my daughter,' I say in what sounds to me like perfect English.

'I know things have been changing at home,' I say, reverting back to Arabic, 'but I just want you to know that change is good.' I smile.

'I know, Mama,' she says quietly, pushing down her school hat on her head.

'Your Baba and I,' I begin, in less than perfect English, 'we will always love you.'

I must've said the wrong thing or said it in the wrong tone because Akita eyes me warily, searching my face, taking everything in. She looks down my shoulder and glares at my belly.

Her eyes then drop to my feet and follow the pavement we walk.

I'm not sure what she's looking for. I'm showing, but with all the layers I drape over my body it's impossible to see my four-and-a-half-month belly, even if you know it's there.

Akita starts walking faster and further away, as if she's literally trying to escape this conversation. I have absolutely no idea what I'm doing wrong. Am I trying too hard? Did I say something that scared her? Damn it, why is she running?

I search my brain for something to say to bring her back, something to slow down time so we have more of it together, but it's running out, St John's Primary is just around the corner.

'Akita, wait!' I call out, the words of my pregnancy on the tip of my tongue.

Then I walk under a low hanging tree branch that hooks onto my wig and lifts it off my head on this lovely autumn morning.

I feel a cool breeze on my scalp.

Akita turns to look at me, her eyes wide with horror. I try to reach up and retrieve my wig from the tree but it's too far up.

When I look back to Akita for help, I see her sprinting the rest of the way to school, her bag swinging wildly from her shoulders, ignoring my calls to her, utterly mortified.

Akita

Sometimes I thank goodness that I'm not white, because if I was my face and probably my whole body would be red with embarrassment until my next birthday.

I ran away as Mama called for me, ran straight to school, pretending I didn't hear her cries for my help to get her wig down from that tree.

I feel bad for running away, but I think I probably would've felt worse for staying. It's not like I could've helped anyway. It was way too high; I couldn't have reached it. I hope she got the wig down, but hopefully this means that she'll stop wearing them now and go back to having her normal hair again.

Everybody is being strange at home, but maybe Mama's been acting odd because of the baby growing in her belly.

Taresai

I retrieve my wig from the tree just as Akita rounds the corner. I watch her run straight through the school gates as passers-by politely avoid my eyes.

I walk home with my wig in my hands. I didn't think I was terrible at connecting with Akita, but that was before this rude awakening. Yes, the wig in the tree didn't help, but running away like that?

Was it my English? No, it can't be. I practised this conversation with Santino last night and in the mirror this morning.

I'm disturbed too, by the way she eyed me, eyed my belly, as if she's trying to put the pieces together. Is it possible she already knows?

No … no.

Of course she doesn't, she cannot read minds and see what lies ahead, what am I thinking?

She's not telepathic, she's eight years old for crying out loud.

Even so, I was surprised by my inclination to tell her. To tell her about the baby. At first, I thought I was going to blurt it out to Akita in a panic, my mind jumping to its last resort to get her to stay.

Akita, your father and I are expecting another baby. You're going to be a big sister to a baby brother or sister.

But the more I think about it, on this walk home, the more it starts to feel right.

Maybe it's time that I tell Akita, only Akita that we're expecting.

Santo is far too fragile at the moment; he and the two younger girls can wait.

Maybe if I tell Akita how and why our lives are going to change in a matter of months before these changes occur, maybe it'll make her feel at ease and supported and a part of it. I hope she recognises my efforts to connect with her, and I hope I can conceal how much it pains me when they fall short.

* * *

We eat supper accompanied by Santino's mountainous paperwork, which he's pushed to the side of the dining table, its presence much more pronounced than the man who sits among it, his eyes scanning a very thick book.

Amara asks him what book he's reading, expecting the answer to pertain to some sort of fairy tale. Instead, Santino replies, 'Just records, honey,' as if she, at four-years-old, is supposed to know what that means.

He looks at me when the room falls quiet.

'For work,' he adds, to make me feel better about it. What else would it be for?

I blame my impatience with the man on my pregnancy hormones. It always happens, every time, without a miss.

I focus my mind on other things to stop myself from picking up a nearby book and throwing it at Santino's face so hard it shatters his glasses.

I look at Santo, sitting next to Akita, unenthusiastically picking out the chicken from the rice and veggie stew and placing it in his mouth. He gets tired around this hour of the evening. His medications are yet to balance out his moods and energy levels.

Akita inconspicuously eyes Santo when he's not looking, trying to conceal her worry. I watch as she takes some chicken from her plate and places it onto her brother's.

It didn't take much to notice in the past weeks how their relationship has evolved, gone through the broken waves of Santo's emotions. Through it all their love for each other has remained in place. Santo just doesn't have the energy to show it, doesn't have the energy to bond with Akita.

After dinner, I ask Akita to take out her braids and tell Santo to help, while I bathe Amara with her prescription soaps and ointments and Ashanti with her Baby Johnson's.

Once I've put both the girls to bed, I walk into the living room and find Akita with half her braids undone – the coils of her hair twisting upwards – and the other half still in box braids. Santo's asleep on the carpet beside her.

I glance at Santino, still sitting on the dining table, his nose in a book. I call for him to carry Santo to bed and I call for Akita to sit on her stool between my legs. I undo the rest of her hair.

Neither of us talk for what feels like an eternity. My mind starts to ascend into a silent panic without a clue as to what to say.

Do I acknowledge what happened today? Do I scorn her for running? Do I pretend nothing happened? I'm worrying about what to say until I don't have to anymore because Akita starts speaking first.

'Sorry Mama ...' she says quietly, her head hanging low. 'About today.' She turns around and faces me.

'It's okay, darling,' I say, as she turns away.

'I'm still getting used to wearing wigs.' I make the joke to the back of her head, and for the love of all that is good, Akita laughs, she *actually* laughs at what I said.

A comfortable silence falls between us. Akita leans her head on my thigh, and I feel her body relax, heavy with sleep.

'Akita?'

'Yes, Mama?'

'I'm pregnant. We're going to have another baby.'

Akita is quiet. Silent. For a second, I wonder if she heard me.

'I know, Mama,' she says.

'You do?' I whisper.

'Yes,' she says, nodding her head, 'but you should tell Santo. He thinks the bump is because you're eating too much.'

Words leave my mind as emotions fill my heart. Joy, relief, and the smallest amount of remorse. I have many questions to ask, but something tells me I shouldn't ask them. Be it intuition, or fear, or simply just learning and letting go.

After a while of silence in the room and sheer chaos in my mind, Akita opens her mouth to speak again. 'I think it's a boy,' she says, playing with her toes. 'I feel like it's a boy.'

'How do you know, honey?' I ask, unplaiting the last of her braids.

She rises to her feet and looks me in the eyes with her gravity-defying hair curling upward, shining like a halo underneath the ceiling light, twisted into the patterns of the braids it no longer-holds.

Akita looks deep into my eyes and says simply, 'I had a dream about it, Mama.'

Chapter 20

Sydney

Taresai

The months have been steady and unchanging, save for the growing life in my womb. We've fallen into a routine that everyone in the house has landed in the rhythm of.

It's been a couple of days since we've last seen the sun. This winter isn't as cold as the last, nor as wet, but there is a persistent fog that mystifies the mornings and clouds the evenings. One that I've grown particularly fond of.

On the mornings when I wake the children up for school and part all the curtains in the house, out the windows, we can't see past our front garden. In those moments it feels as if we're the only people on the planet or living in one that is completely our own.

Santo's medication has balanced, meaning he's arrived back to his prevailing self, full of energy and mischief, without the violent and destructive tendencies.

The light in his eyes has returned, the fire in his belly reignited.

Akita has been maturing as of late; the coming of her unborn sibling has seemingly inspired her to soar. She does her chores without being told to, she's been more patient with her younger sisters, and she offers help in doing things around the house that my six-month-old belly won't allow.

Akita has also become more comfortable speaking with me, asking about my favourite type of flowers and garden insects when I do her hair.

I told Santo the news in the afternoon before supper, when he was hosing down the wheels of his bike after a ride around the neighbourhood. He's been hoping for a baby brother ever since. When I told Amara, just after bath time, she threw a temper tantrum, which, to be honest, I'd expected, though a deep worry soon followed and lingered for a couple of days.

After a few sleepless nights with my anxieties brewing, I soon concluded that there is much to worry about but Amara's outbursts shouldn't be one of them. At least not for the time being. I know it in my heart and spirit that Amara does not have the same illness Santo has – she just loves attention; and when it isn't 100 per cent directed at her, she explodes. Her traits are developed, not innate. Habitual, not irrevocable. It's our fault; Santino and I poured too much of our attention into Amara, even though her needs demanded it.

My Amara is a sook, not ill, she simply can't help herself, especially tonight as we gather around the living room, discussing the matter of the baby, two months before her fifth birthday.

'Okay,' I say, shushing Amara.

Santino sits by my side on the couch and the kids sit on the carpet looking up at us, Ashanti on Akita's lap.

'Your mother and I,' begins Santino, 'are having a boy.'

'Yes!' Santo punches the air, Amara scrunches her face unapprovingly, Ashanti chews on her fist and Akita smiles up at me.

'I knew it,' she whispers to Santo.

'Yeah, well, I knew it first, Kita.'

Akita doesn't argue.

'How'd you know, Santo?' I ask.

'Because,' he says, 'it makes sense. It's math. Patterns and stuff. It goes boy, girl, girl, *girl*. It has to be a boy next,' he waves his hand knowingly.

'We should name him after me!' he says suddenly, eyes wide, slapping his knees with excitement over his brilliant idea.

'Santo, honey,' I laugh, 'you're named after your father, so to name your little brother after you would be … well, silly.'

'We can call him Junior, Mama,' Santo argues, nose in the air.

'Mummy, can we stop?' Amara groans. 'I'm hungry.' Her bottom lip trembles and her eyebrows furrow.

'In a minute, honey,' I say, scooping her up, laying her across my lap.

'What about you, Akita?' Santino asks.

'Hmm?'

'How did you know he's a boy?'

'Oh,' she says, playing with Ashanti's hair. 'I had a dream about it.'

'What else was the dream about?' I ask curiously.

'I don't remember,' she says looking up at me and shrugging, 'I dream about lots of things.'

* * *

I'm woken in the night by my unborn child. We must be speaking of him too much.

With his restlessness disturbing my blissful slumber, I roll over on my side and shut my eyes, hoping for sleep to visit me again, but it sails away when I don't feel Santino lying beside me. I switch on the lamp and blink at the empty space where Santino should be. I wrap on my dressing gown and step out into the hallway. The winter nights are especially chilly, colder than the desert nights in Egypt. The windows are fogged and the grass outside freezes over with the thinnest layer of ice.

I find Santino sitting at the dining table in the dark kitchen, illuminated by a single desk lamp that shines over the piles of books and paperwork. Santino sits still, eyes down on a piece of paper. On it sit his scribbles in blue ink. I cannot read, not in any language, but I know the patterns and shapes of Santino's handwriting. The sharpness of it, the way it slants and dances, elegant chaos, transcribed.

He looks at the piece of paper in such a way, as if the words stare right back. Whatever is written on it must be of great importance.

'Hi,' I whisper, unsure of what to make of the scene.

Santino looks up at me and smiles sadly. 'I didn't see you there. Did I wake you?'

'No,' I say, glaring at the books, the papers, the forms.

He feels a million miles away from me, so distant that his being before my eyes feels like my imaginings, like a dream, like if I were to reach out and touch him he'd fade into a cloud of mist.

'Santino ... is – is everything all right?' I ask, suddenly overcome with angst.

'Yes,' he says, tonelessly, not looking up from his sheet of paper.

'What are you doing? Why are you up so late?' I ask, trying to gain control of my voice.

'I'm working,' he says softly, as if to himself.

'On what? What in particular? Is every single sheet of this tedious paper hill just for work?'

'Taresai,' he says quietly, 'sit.'

'No.'

Santino exhales deeply, removing his glasses and looking up at me. He looks so tired.

I thought he and I were going well, I thought things were good. I thought he was absent because he was working more hours to bring in more money for this baby I'm going to have in a matter of weeks. I thought all was resolved, that I could be at ease. I thought I could finally breathe.

'I'm planning,' Santino says.

'What are you planning?'

He is quiet for a very long time, long enough for the deep cold of the night to seep into my bloodstream.

'I'm leaving, Taresai.'

It takes all the strength in me not to throw the closest thing at my reach at his face.

'No, you're not!' I shout. 'How could you? How could you leave me with our four young– five young kids? Leave me to raise them on my own? Santino?'

I'm hysterical at this point, my body shaking with rage, hatred, primal fear.

'Taresai, please–'

'Santino, you can't.'

He looks at me, a look the shatters my heart into a million pieces. A look I cannot bear to see because I know I've already lost, I've been defeated, there's no changing his mind.

'You won't be alone, Taresai,' Santino says calmly, almost smiling.

I wipe a tear as it streams down my cheek, catching it before it falls.

'What do you mean?' I ask softly, a wave of exhaustion hitting me so hard I almost collapse.

'Taresai, I … I found your sister, Asélle. Your mother too. They're here in Australia, in Victoria, the next state south.'

The room spins, and I lose my balance.

In this moment, I'm unsure if I'm still standing or if I'm on the floor, already fallen.

When Santino continues speaking, I know my body has not physically moved.

'They've been here, in Australia, for nearly a year.'

Santino doesn't say anything else. He doesn't need to.

In this landscape between worlds, where it is no longer the late hour of the night nor the early hour of the morning, these could be Santino's final words to me. I could go a lifetime with no further explanation because I already know what he means. Fifteen years I've been married to this man, seventeen years I've spent knowing him, loving him.

I see his mind at work, clear as day, his unspoken words strung together as his plan crystallises in my mind before I properly get to unpack everything else. The foundation we worked so tirelessly to build for our children crumbling right before my very eyes.

Chapter 21

Sydney

Taresai

I give birth to a healthy baby boy in the early hours of September 15.

Zandé Atem Santino Adolé is the spitting image of his father, moreso than the rest of my children. Jet-black curls, wide lips, large brown eyes.

I send photos of baby Zandé to my sister Asélle and my mother, who are living in a region called Geelong, about an hour away from the well-known city of Melbourne.

It's where we'll be moving in nine months' time.

I haven't told the kids yet; I think it might be too soon. Things have only just started to fall into place with a new family member in the house. The girls have finally adjusted to Ashanti's move into their room. Santo, for the first time, is doing well at school; he's on his best behaviour and he does his homework. Akita was just voted sports captain for the term.

Three years and four months we've been in 23 Edgar Street. We've spent less time here than we did in Egypt, as peculiar as that fact feels. But that's just it, this the very first place my children have called home.

The rooms of this house hold the most precious memories in their walls, a timeline of this family's milestones; losing baby teeth, growing new ones, taking first steps, learning to read, to ride a bike, Zande's conception, his birth.

I can't bear the thought of ripping them away from everything they have.

I'll tell them soon, I must, just not now, heavens please, not now.

Santino has asked that, for the time being, we keep his departure from the children. They don't yet need to know that their father is going back to Sudan. He's unsure when he might leave after we settle in Victoria, at this stage it's between eighteen months and two years.

Delayed by the move and his infant son.

Part of me wants to defy him – how dare he expect me to be part of the heartbreak he is going to inflict on them. But, regrettably, the other part of me agrees to keep them none the wiser and in total bliss as I see this time ticking away.

Perhaps I'm too hyperaware of these very strange moments of my life that I'm living through, for I have been mourning the loss of these things that I have not yet lost and celebrating the new life I have birthed.

It wounds me deeply to keep all this from the children, a truth that will flip their worlds upside down in nine months' time and then once more when their father leaves, and there's not a thing in the world they could do about it.

It's almost cruel.

Every time I see a grin on Santo's face, when his cackling vibrates into every room in the house, when Akita and Amara giggle in the garden, every time Ashanti smiles at me, there is an equal pain that swells in my chest.

These moments are numbered and will soon be no more.

I can't stand talking to Santino about anything other than our children. His finding of my sister was timely, because if I didn't have Asélle to talk to then my lonely hours would be months long.

I've been talking on the phone to my sister and mother daily ever since our reconnection. Asélle and the kids are well, and she says Victoria is beautiful. I've come to discover a lot of things speaking to her. My long-lost friend, Manuela, and her son, Anei, are living in Shepparton, another town in Victoria a few hours away from Geelong. Asélle's promised to find her number and send it my way.

My brother Messai is happy and well in Sweden. His eldest daughter Jamila got married a few months ago.

Soon, we'll all be together again – me, my sister, our mother and all our children. It's the end of a lot of things, the end of this quiet life of ours, but there will be new beginnings too.

Our family will reunite, and I so badly want to feel good about it.

* * *

When Zandé is six months old, a week after Akita's ninth birthday, Santino and I gather the kids around the dining table. It's just after supper but the autumn sky is already beginning to darken. Storm clouds hang in the sky, pronouncing the warm glow of the ceiling lights. I tell them we're moving away from New South Wales. Amara cries.

'I was going to start primary school next year,' she sobs.

'You still will, darling,' I assure her. 'You'll just be at a different school.'

Amara's been looking forward to starting at St John's.

She'll be six this winter. We've kept her out of primary school for the year because of the eczema that still ails her skin. Last week I caught her trying on some of her big sister's old uniforms. She looked so small, yet so grown up with Akita's sun-faded blue school dress draping over her ankles.

'And you'll all be together,' Santino chimes in. 'The three of you, all at the same school. Amara you'll be in prep, Akita still in grade four, and Santo in grade five.'

Santo nods slowly. 'Are we gonna get a new house?'

'Yes, we'll be moving into a new home. It's double-storey,' Santino beams. This wins Santo's and Amara's approval.

Akita is unnervingly silent. Her eyes remain fixed on the woodgrain of the dining table. I feel helpless.

When Akita looks up at me, I can't bring myself to look her in the eyes. I can't stand the sight of the heart I've broken.

After this announcement, life becomes a waiting game. We're counting down the days until we move, then counting down the days until Santino leaves, and then we count each day after that until there are no more days left to count.

Akita

A few weeks have passed since we learned that we're moving to another state called Victoria, to a town with a horrendous name. I looked it up in my atlas. It's at the bottom of Australia, along the coast.

We'll be leaving the first place I've ever loved. The first place I've called home. I'm leaving behind my friends, my school, my house with the magic garden and stone fountains. We're leaving behind the flowers in the spring, the peaches in the summer, leaves of the autumn and the dewy spiderwebs in the winter. I've cried every night since Mama and Baba told us. Baba was smiling as if this is something to be happy about.

So what if our cousins live in that place with an ugly name? I didn't like them very much in Egypt, so why do we have to move our entire lives just to be with them? If we wanted to be with them so badly, then why did we move halfway across the world from them in the first place?

Every day has been painful. I go out to the garden, I ride my bike past the shops, to the library, I walk to school, and the city of Auburn, the suburb of Silverwater, shines with so much colour it makes my heart ache. So vibrantly it hurts, sharpening the pain of having to say goodbye.

The only thing I can do is dim it. Stay inside most days and to pay less attention to it. To dim the colours, paint over it in grey, so that my numbered days are bearable.

Taresai

I sit on the verandah, Zandé asleep and wrapped in a blanket on my lap. Santino does laps around the house with Santo as his helping hand, ensuring everything is as we left it. I mind Amara and Ashanti playing in the garden and our packed bags on the driveway, ready for our move. We've been blessed with early afternoon sunshine that has warmed this winter day. They're excited, Amara and Ashanti, while Santo only cares about getting the largest room in our new home.

Akita still, is devastated. She's barely uttered a word in the three months since telling her. Much to her strain, this move is happening halfway through the school year.

It seems like nothing can soften the blow of reality. Not even her reunion with her aunt, her grandmother and her cousins. She's been crying oceans and rivers for this place.

I comfort her in the times she lets me, when she doesn't turn her face away as I try to wipe her tears or leave the room when I try to offer her some soothing words, though it's not without difficulty. Mostly I just feel at a loss that I can't mend her broken heart.

It's painful, but I must remember that Akita is only nine years old, she's sad, naturally so. I have to let her be and hope that this will pass.

I hear the gravel crunching underneath the tyres as the taxi pulls into the driveway. I cradle Zandé and hold on to Ashanti's hands as Santino helps the driver load our suitcases into the van. I call for Santo, who appears from the side of the house, and takes Amara's hand.

'Where's your sister?' I ask. 'Where's Akita?'

Santo shrugs. I look towards the house; the front door is wide open. I call her name, and sigh softly when I don't get a response.

'Santo, will you please go get your sister?'

Akita

I pretend not to hear Mama calling my name as I walk through our empty house. All our furniture got packed and taken on a truck yesterday. We had to sleep on blow-up mattresses. I barely slept a wink next to Amara, with her snores, her kicking and scratching the backs of my legs with her toenails.

But that was nothing to my thoughts of goodbye that haunted me all night.

I'm exhausted, and I'm so, *so* sad. I've cried every day because of today. I've said all my goodbyes. Yesterday, to my best friend Eliza – we played in the park for the last time; to Ashra – we read books in the library; and Awien – she and her mother came over for supper. I've said goodbye to all my teachers at St John's, and my classmates. They gave me a giant farewell card and a block of chocolate. I cried all the way home from school, and I haven't even thought about unwrapping the chocolate yet.

My final goodbye is to this house, this very small, old, rickety, magical house: 23 Edgar Street, Silverwater. The first home I've ever known, with its giant windows, tiny hallway and the front garden that I'm sure I will dream about every day.

On the ground, not 14 stories above it like Giza.

I've said all my goodbyes, but I apparently have not cried all my tears. Hot tears sting my eyes, blurring my vision, making these empty spaces that were once so full look all wobbly. I cry as another suppressed thought forces its way into the centre of my mind. I will never see my greatest friends ever again.

I hear a car in the driveway, and someone enter through the front door.

'Kita? You in here?' Santo yells, swinging around the corner, finding me in the empty living room. He stares at me. I expect him to laugh, like he always does when I cry. But he doesn't. Instead, Santo reaches his hand out to me.

'Come,' he says.

I take Santo's hand and he leads me to the bathroom. We stand in front of the sink. Through my tears, I peer at our reflections. Santo doesn't look much taller than me as he once did. His face isn't as chubby, his dark hair is trimmed closer to his scalp.

But there is something young in his dark brown eyes. Santo lets go of my hand and I watch as he stares at himself in the mirror for a moment. I inch closer to the sink when he does, feeling a pull to follow his lead. Santo then looks down at the sink and spits in it.

* * *

Santo wakes me when we arrive at the airport. I fall almost straight back asleep on a lounge chair at our departure gate and wake up when it's time to board. I collapse into my seat without a care. I start to drift off, but then Santo pokes me on the shoulder, begging to swap seats because he wants to look out the window.

We switch and I fall into immediate sleep, only to be woken by the plane announcements when we're taking off, and once more shortly after when we hit some turbulence. I hardly know which way's up when I finally feel myself start to drift off once more into deep, unconquerable, promising, sleep. I feel light as a feather as all my worries float away. Then I hear the sound of the plane's turbines, and I begin to feel the stiffness of the seat I'm sprawled upon.

For a moment I think I'm waking up, only my eyes don't open.

'Finally,' says a voice, sounding like nobody in particular.

At first I think it's the pilot making an announcement. But the voice doesn't sound scrambly as if it's coming from a speaker. The voice is soft, quiet, but very clear, as if whoever speaks it is floating right by my ear.

'Finally, what?' I ask, but I don't hear my voice at all. It's strange. This doesn't feel like a dream. I feel like I'm awake with my eyes closed, but the feelings of being awake, the feeling of my shoes on my feet, the waistband of my pants, I feel those things only in transient waves.

This 'dream' is too vivid to be a dream, but too vague and abstract to be real life.

'Finally, what?' I ask again.

'You're finally coming home.'

Chapter 22

Geelong

Taresai

We land in Melbourne, drive to Geelong and arrive in our new house in the late afternoon. Number 8 Hugh Court in a suburb called Corio. It's a two-storey, five-bedroom house built with red bricks, sitting on the curve of a quiet cul-de-sac. There's a garage on the side and grass in both the front and back yard.

Much to my relief, Santino arranged for the furniture – which arrived yesterday morning, to be assembled by this morning. Most of it is new and afforded with all the hours he worked before our move. The gold Camry is also long sold, we won't know yet if it was worth it, though I can't pretend catching buses and trains and learning new routes again doesn't excite me in the slightest.

We file in and Santino shows the children to their bedrooms. Santo races around the house excitedly and claims one of the two bedrooms upstairs. Amara and Ashanti follow their father outside and pace the backyard with him. I go to our bedroom to put Zandé to sleep. When I pass Akita in the neighbouring bedroom, I see her lying face down on a single bed, her bum in the air, snoozing away.

I put Zandé in his crib and I go back to Akita. I take off her shoes and her denim jacket and I pull the blanket right under her chin.

* * *

Asélle embraces me, holding on long and hard, trembling as she cries her tears of joy. She welcomes us into her home. We gather in the large living room, bordered by four large brown leather coaches, and two matching armchairs, embellished with a round Turkish rug, a large flatscreen tv on one end, and a grand framed photo of their children on the other. Ibrahim and Santino shake hands heartily. When I see my mother she holds me close for a long while, then she hugs my children, two at a time kissing their cheeks until they become agitated.

For a while it's all-consuming, simply too much. Asélle's children, my nieces and nephew – have all grown into themselves and out of what I remembered them to be.

It's quite jarring when my mother is sitting in the same room, looking exactly as I remember her. Dear Asélle, whose skin has never been so colourless, still bears the same wide smile and high cheekbones on her slim, card-board coloured face. My heart shatters for her and for me too. I didn't realise the vision I had of her in my mind in all these years had been so far from what sits before my eyes. I know what ails her to be so, the thoughts that poison her mind and compels Asélle to do such a thing. To bleach and harm one's skin because it is far better than being dark. As dark as me, as our mother, as dark as her twin sister. I know this, most people from our community do from a simple glimpse of Asélle, but what do you tell a zebra who dreams of being a horse?

Nothing.

And so, we, as her mother, sisters, and brother, mourn those parts of Asélle in private.

I'm grateful though, grateful that nothing can discolour or erase her beaming smile and fiercely loving heart. And that thought alone, balms my fleeting feelings of remorse.

When the children have migrated to the other living room, Santino and I sit across from Asélle, her husband, Ibrahim, to her right, and my mother to her left. The men engross themselves in a conversation that interests no one else.

'The children, Taresai,' my mother smiles warmly, her eyes swimming with such jubilation I find it difficult to look. 'They've grown so much.'

'Little Santo isn't so little anymore,' laughs Asélle. 'He's taller than me! How old is he now? Nine? Ten?'

'Eleven,' I smile, sipping some fruit tea. 'He'll be twelve next February.'

'And little Akita, still the same. Still so quiet.'

I take a breath, waiting for this to feel normal.

If things could just slow, if we could just have an hour of silence while my spirit catches up with my body, that would be entirely splendid.

'Taresai, why do you cut dear Amara's hair so short?' my mother enquires, a familiar hardness in her tone, cutting through me the same way it always did.

I'm interested in the revelation that I can have these feelings of familiarity without traces of normalcy. My instinctual reactions are still there, but the Taresai of Giza is not.

'Because of her eczema, Ma. It's worsened since Giza, but we're managing it.'

'She's such a happy girl,' smiles Asélle, 'and you're the cutest little boy ever, aren't you?' She gushes over Zandé, who plays with her gold necklaces dangling over his face.

How I've missed her, my youngest sister, her fearlessness in feeling so loudly, showing it so boldly.

She has a good heart, Asélle, I've always thought, and it takes courage to wear such a heart upon her sleeve.

'Oh,' Asélle breathes, her eyes still wet with tears, 'you have no idea how much we've missed you. How much I've missed this!'

She strokes Zande's curls lovingly and plants several kisses on his cheek.

'It's only a matter of time until Anette comes over here with her babies and we'll be together again.'

I choke on my tea. 'Anette?' I cough. 'She's coming?'

I haven't spoken to or thought of Anette as much since leaving Egypt, of course without intending to. I suppose we naturally fell back into disconnect the moment it broke. I get an awful feeling in the pit of my stomach.

'Yes!' beams Asélle, too wrapped up in familial bliss to catch the displeasure in my tone. My mother, who can read anybody's spirit in the blink of an eye, looks at me, but I do not meet her gaze.

I clasp onto my cup firmly and try to swallow down the feelings that have caught me by surprise. I distract myself by shifting my attention to something else, projecting my soul out of this space between heaven and hell. I zone in on Santo's voice in the backyard among the other children, the smell of sandalwood on my mother's skin, the taste of sweet tea, hot on my tongue.

Outside I hear a car pulling into the driveway, then the engine cuts off a moments later. In this dream state I'm struck once more by how strange this all is, and how ridiculous it seems to pretend like it isn't. I feel like I've travelled to another time, to another dimension.

Just this morning we were in our home on Edgar Street, my little family of seven. Now I'm thousands of miles from that old life; I am part of something bigger than my children and their father.

In the seconds of forced silence my mind slows, and I'm once again thrown into this reality.

We hear someone walk up the steps and through the front door. I didn't think Asélle, or Ibrahim were expecting any other guests.

A tall man walks swiftly into the living room as if he's done it countless times before. A man with a smile so beautiful, a smile I never thought I would see again. My brother, my Messai.

Akita

I was woken up for this? Sure, it's nice to see my grandmother, who hasn't changed, not even a little bit, and my Aunty Asélle too. But then I was whisked away, without permission, by one of my cousins, a girl, the one that's a little bit older than I am.

I find it much easier to differentiate between all four of them now. Even the twins look different from each other. We all sit in a circle in the playroom. Amara excuses herself to go play with Santo and our cousin Bilal outside before anybody says anything important and any real conversation starts. He's the same age as Amara.

The twins, Heema and Halima, are now twelve years old. Heema has a long face like Aunty and Halima has a monobrow; her hair is darker and longer too. Samira is the girl who's a bit older than I am, even though she's a lot shorter. Plumper too.

Then there's Ines – she's eight, and she has really small teeth and a lot of hair. They stare at me like I'm some sort of alien or exotic animal.

I wonder if I look different from how they remember me.

All of my teeth have grown in and they don't feel so large nor gapped, my hair is in box braids and tied into pig-tails and I dressed myself in this plum sweater, denim jacket with matching pants.

I sit cross-legged on the carpet, on the outer most curve of this circle we formed, my back closest to the door. The room is lined with containers stacked on top of one another full of toys:

dolls, Legos, and cars from what I can see from here and two doll houses in the corner. One pink, one white.

Heema holds Ashanti on her lap the same way Mama does. Halima and Samira sit on either side of her playing with Ashanti like she's a doll. They seem so much older than I am even though the gap between us hasn't changed in all this time.

They talk to me and ask me questions, and I answer them simply, not as enthused by this day as they clearly are. I feel bad about it, but not enough to mask the despair I feel. I'm too caught up in it to take in the world around me and enjoy it, or at least try to.

I feel like I'm still recovering from being ripped out of my world and thrown into this one.

'So, what was Sydney like?' asks Ines, inching closer. She sits the closest to me with her legs crossed like mine.

'Huh?'

'Did you see the Opera House? Go to Bondi Beach?'

'Uh … Yeah, yes. Went twice on a school excursion and once with Mama and Baba.'

'And Bondi Beach?' Ines asks, looking at me wide-eyed.

'Yeah … But I didn't swim.'

'What?' says Samira, looking up from Ashanti. 'Who goes to the beach and doesn't swim?'

'The water was salty,' I say simply.

'Can't you swim?' asks Heema. She scrunches her face up like it's something I should be ashamed of.

How she gathered that I don't know, but she isn't wrong.

I look around the room before I answer. 'I … no, I'm not very good at it …'

The room falls into a pitiful silence. I want the ground to open, swallow me up and spit me out into Edgar Street. I would be back to my place of peace, doing things I truly enjoy, to be with people who actually like me.

As I plot my escape out of this torture room, we hear the door open and I feel someone with heavy footsteps enter behind me. For a moment I think it's Baba, finally here to call on us so we could go back to our house on Hugh Court. But then the man behind me puts his hands under my arms and picks me up, throwing me into the air as if I'm made of fluff. He catches me then sets me down gently.

I spin to see the face of my favourite uncle in the world. Uncle Messai.

I hug him tightly, burying my face into his torso, I hold him close, closer than I've ever held anybody. I wrap my arms around him as if he's going to disappear the moment I let go.

Chapter 23

Geelong

Akita

It's a cold wintery morning and I would give anything to be back in bed.

Instead we trail after Baba – Santo, Amara and I, walking through the empty campus of our new school. St Paul's Primary. Baba talks to the principal, Mr O'Malley, as he shows us around.

We start here next week, in the third week of term three. St Paul's Primary is small, a lot smaller than St John's. Each classroom is a separate block lining the courtyard like shoe boxes. There's an oval though, and a playground and sandpit – something I haven't seen since I was five. There's also a one-storey library with a few shelves of books and bright orange carpet that's all fuzzy.

We walk back into Mr O'Malley's office at the end of the tour, and he hands the three of us large cardboard boxes with our names on them. Baba tells us not to open it until we're home. It's a surprise, he says, but Santo tries to poke holes in his box before we've even left the office. When Santo and I surreptitiously peer through the discreet holes he's made on the side of his box as Baba and Mr O'Malley continue their conversation, we see folded fabrics. School uniforms.

Forest green and mustard yellow.

Mr O'Malley stands up from his seat and shakes Baba's hand passionately before proceeding to shake Santo's, then mine, then Amara's. He beams as he looks around the room, grinning widely as he stares at our faces.

Mr O'Malley takes a breath and says he's thrilled to have us attend this school; we're the first African students St Paul's Primary has ever had. He grins at us like it's supposed to make us cheerful, but all I want is to disappear into thin air.

Taresai

'He said that?' I ask, setting the last of the plates on the dining table.

Messai has joined us for our first meal together in our new home, in this new town.

We've been in Geelong for three nights, and in the busy-ness of settling in, breaking bread together was a difficult thing to make yet happen.

Messai has been here for a week; he arranged the trip as soon as he learned from our mother that we were to be here too.

The children are still in their rooms, trying on their new uniforms.

Messai sits across from Santino and me, handsome in his navy-blue dress shirt. He inherited his height from the father we've never known, though the sharp features of his dark face very much resemble our mother.

It's been nearly six years since he moved away, resettling with his wife and three children in Sweden. Before then, we all lived together in Giza, with our mother and all our children. When Messai moved overseas, he'd visit and stay in Giza for weeks at a time. These visits became infrequent as time passed and Leena needed him at home, but he only stopped completely when I moved away.

'Yes, Taresai, but we shouldn't be alarmed,' says Santino calmly. 'He seemed genuinely pleased to have us there. Honoured even.'

'The last thing they need is to be gawked at by hundreds of white kids. As if being new in town isn't hard enough,' I argue.

'They'll be fine, Taresai,' says Messai. 'You forget that Santo and Akita were once the tough kids of Giza.'

'What if I don't want that anymore? What if I don't want my children to have to toughen up their way through life?'

'I'm afraid that's out of our hands, Tsai,' Messai chuckles, lightness in his tone, heaviness in my spirit. 'Maybe in the next lifetime.'

I breathe an exasperated sigh.

'It isn't so bad,' says Messai soothingly, flashing his white teeth. 'Leena and I were just as worried when we first moved to Gothenburg. You'd think that Europe would be the last place an African man would want to settle his young family,' he says. 'I'm not going to lie and say we blended right in, not even today, after all this time.'

I look at Messai, my face knotted with irritation. None of what he is saying is making me feel better; it's rather doing the opposite.

'But,' Messai continues, 'as much as we stood out, no matter how much attention we attracted, it was nothing like Giza, Tsai. They welcomed our difference and I feel like that's what it's going to be like here.'

I let Messai's words hang in the air for a moment.

'Yeah,' I sigh. 'I suppose you're right.'

I hear the kids' footsteps as they strut into the kitchen, dressed in their coloured uniforms.

'Oh my!' I smile, 'look at that.'

Amara and Akita are dressed in plaid green dresses and woollen green jumpers, the school's crest stitched in yellow on the left breast. Santo wears the same jumper in grey shorts and a yellow shirt.

'I like it,' Santo decides over our compliments.

'Green is a lovely colour on you, Santo,' I say. 'So handsome.'

'Green like the hulk,' he corrects me.

'Who?'

'A big ugly green guy who destroys things,' Akita says unexpectedly. 'And he's not handsome.'

They change back into their regular clothes, and we eat supper. The table is loud with sounds of Messai's stories to the children of his time in Gothenburg, Santo and Amara arguing over who gets the last slice of basbousa, and Ashanti crying on her father's lap; it's way past her bedtime. In and amongst the chattering I hardly notice that Akita has slipped out, her half-eaten plate sits silently by the sink.

We send the rest of the children to sleep shortly after.

Did you get a chance to speak to Ma at all?' Messai asks.

Messai, Santino, and I are sitting around the table in the late hour of the night.

'Not about anything beyond our wellbeing, no,' I shrug.

'Ah,' Messai breathes, turning his glass of wine contemplatively.

Messai is the only other person, besides Santino, to come close to understanding my relationship with our mother. He bore witness to the beatings, often wedging his slender frame between the pair of us to stop the wrath of our mother, Adele. She'd never lay a hand on him and he knew it.

He understands my complex feelings of resentment and undying affinity to her. But there are times when I feel like he must be a son before he is a brother.

'Why do you ask?' I say, the suspicion creeping in my tone.

I fear I may have already said something to upset her in the short time we've been here.

Messai hesitates for a moment then he speaks. 'Anette is coming. She'll be here in two weeks.'

'That much I know,' I say, relieved yet burdened at once.

'Great. Well, she's put all of her life savings in bringing the family here.'

'... Okay,' I respond, waiting for the words he dares say to come out of his mouth.

'She needs a place to stay, Tsai. She needs you.' Messai says, looking at me the same way he always does when speaking of Anette. His face is stern, but his almond eyes plead for my understanding.

'Messai, when has Anette ever needed me in her life?' I say coldly, anger rising to my chest.

'Every single day, Tsai. You know she's just too stubborn to believe it,' says Messai, a gentleness in his voice that melts the bullets I shoot at him with my eyes.

'Why do you always do this?' I seethe finally. 'Why do you always take her side?'

'That's not what I'm doing, Taresai,' Messai says, exhaling calmly.

'Why must I always be the one to rise above? Why do we always have to make room for Anette when all she does is prove how much she doesn't need us?' I ask, taken aback by my own words. It's one thing to feel this way, but another thing completely, to voice it.

'Do it for the kids, Tsai,' Messai pleads.

He places his hands over mine.

'It's never been about taking sides. I just have more faith in you. I can always count on you to do the right thing.'

My eyes sting as a lifetime's worth of heartache rises to the surface. How can I explain to Messai the thoughts in my mind when he knows every bit of what lies in my heart? How am I to refuse truly if he is the one asking?

We've lived many lives together, and landed in this one not by coincidence, that's what our mother used to tell us. Messai was Adele's first born and only son, I came a year later. We grew up playing in red dirt and swimming in the River Nile. Ever morning when Messai would wake to go to school, my mother would wake me too. As I'd fetch water from the river or milk the cows of the village, I watched Messai disappear into the orange horizon of sunrise, embraced by the world. Messai would come home just as I finished helping our mother make supper. He'd lay out all he'd done for the day and share with me everything he'd learned. I couldn't wait until it was my turn.

When I turned eight, Messai and I walked to the only school in our village in the blistering heat, with my sandals worn and our uniform sun-faded and covered in red dust.

I loved every single day.

I loved going to a place so small to learn about this great big world.

But my joy was short-lived. My mother pulled me out of school the next semester, Adele said it was Anette's turn to learn since she had come of age – Asélle would wait until the next year as she was ten minutes younger.

I was shattered, but still, I picked up my pieces and I did everything around the house, became the perfect daughter, begged, cried and pleaded with my mother so I could go back, but she had already decided that school is not where I belonged.

I spent the rest of my young years watching my mother put Anette through primary and secondary school – Asélle got pulled out before high school.

When our mother got sick and moved away for two years, I assumed her role. As time went on I became less of a sister and more of a surrogate mother to my siblings, doing all the things a mother would do, filling the void that hallowed my siblings, neglecting my own. Messai, Anette and Asélle excluded me from things; I don't remember if it was unintentional, but I suppose it would've been difficult for them to include me when there was more that set us apart than that which brought us together.

I didn't experience the things they did, didn't share in the privileges they had. Being deprived of schooling set me miles behind and worlds apart from them.

Besides, I had Manuela back then to keep the fire in my belly alight. She wasn't in school and had no desires to be which was a current that caused me to drift further apart. That was the structure that took shape for the rest of our childhood.

Through time, they came around and the grandness of little Taresai in their little lives is what strengthen the bond I share with Messai and Asélle.

But Anette became estranged, she looked at me with blind eyes that saw me for what our mother tried to make me, instead of who I was. Who I am.

'I'll do it,' I say. 'Of course, I will.'

Messai grins, his eyes swelling with love. 'You need each other, Tsai, you and Anette can help each other, especially now that Santino has decided to run off on you and the kids,' he says suddenly, pointing to Santino with his nose.

I see Santino's grip tighten around his glass, but he doesn't say anything.

He can't, after all, it's he who decided that making his wife's brother and sisters aware of his departure was a prosperous idea.

'You've spent your whole life looking after everyone, Tsai. Let me, let us, look after you.'

Chapter 24

Geelong

Akita

Today's a special day, Mama says. Our cousins and Aunty Anette are arriving from Egypt to live with us. She gives me a peach-coloured cardigan with a matching skirt to wear and Santo has to put on his dress pants and a button-down.

Mama stayed up all night cooking and spent all morning cleaning. I had to help get the girls ready, they wear matching yellow dresses as if they're twins. Santo was so loud with his complaints when Baba combed his hair using the afro pick – the one with the metal teeth and the black fist on the handle – that it woke Zandé up, so Mama tended to him

I think I remember Aunty Anette. She never said much to me, but I remember her eyes that shot daggers whenever she looked at me.

I remember Evelyn too. She was the only cousin who actually looked like my cousin. I know that she's a few years older than I am and she has a twin who is a boy and two younger brothers.

I don't know how I feel about them coming to live with us. I don't think I feel anything about it.

I just miss the things that I had. Back in Silverwater I had the garden, I had school, I had friends, I had the books in the library, I had my bike. Even though I could probably find those things here, or make them, it just isn't the same.

This house doesn't even feel like home to me yet; I don't care how much bigger and newer and nicer it is, it just isn't 23 Edgar Street.

Living with my aunty and with Evelyn and her brothers is just another new change that I have to get used to which is hard because there is nothing here that even feels like mine.

* * *

When Aunty Anette and my cousins arrive I wait in my room. I only walk into the larger living room – this house has two, and join everybody when Mama calls my name for the third time. I don't mean to exclude myself, but all the noise and emotion exploding in the air is something that frightens me a little.

The curtains are drawn in our new living room, the afternoon light spills in pleasantly and bounces from every corner of the room.

Aunty Anette pulls me in for a tight hug. She smells like mothballs and exhaustion. When she lets go of me I step back, eyeing her warily. I think it might be the first time she's ever held me.

Aunty Anette says hello and asks me a bunch of questions that I don't comprehend, my attention instead on every eye in the room that's on me. I smile and nod.

'Santo, Akita,' Mama says. She's smiling but her eyes glint with something serious, not to be tested. 'Why don't you two show your cousins around the house?'

Evelyn and her three brothers follow Santo and me from the living room to the other living room upstairs.

'Kita,' Santo begins when we walk into the space, 'this is Evelyn and Emmanuel – they're twins,' he whispers.

Evelyn and Emmanuel look a little bit older than Santo.

'This is Atem,' Santo points to the triangular-faced boy who looks younger than him but older than me, 'and this is little Joseph,' says Santo, pointing to the little boy who hides behind his older sister Evelyn. The boys share the same neat haircuts, the same ironed denim pants and brown corduroy jackets.

'I'm Santo and this is Akita.'

The four of them stare at us blankly.

'Sunny, I don't think they know how to speak English,' I whisper.

'Then why are you whispering, Kita?'

I shrug and Santo sighs quietly.

'Okay, why don't I take the boys, show them where they'll be sleeping, and you take the girl?'

I show Evelyn to my room downstairs wordlessly. I point to the bed that Baba put in last week for her, identical to mine. I sit on my bed and she sits on hers across from me. Evelyn stares at me curiously and I stare back. It's the first chance that I'm getting a really good look at her.

She's wearing denim pants and a matching denim jacket over a red turtleneck. Her cornrows are neat, tied together at the nape of her neck. She sits up straight on the bed and smiles. She looks older than I remember. I don't know if she'd want to be friends with me. I don't know if I want to be friends with her. She doesn't seem as annoying as my other cousins, so that's something.

Evelyn opens her mouth up to speak. She says I've grown a lot since the last time she's seen me. I thank her and smile.

'You too,' I say after a while, my words filling the silence between us.

Evelyn stares at me, confused.

For a moment I forget she can't speak English.

In the second that it takes for that realisation to dawn on me, I feel a prickle of anger building in the pit of my stomach and rising to my chest. Great, just what I need, another adjustment I have to make to the way I live. I don't even speak Arabic to Mama anymore. She speaks Arabic to us, sometimes with a few English phrases, and Dinka when we're in trouble and she's yelling.

Mama and Baba speak all kinds of languages to each other, but for the most part we speak English at home now. I don't remember exactly when things shifted to the way they are, but it's been long enough for it to feel normal.

Anger bubbles underneath my skin as I sit on my cloned bed in the bedroom I now have to share with Evelyn, who only knows how to speak Arabic.

I close my eyes, stretching my Arabic-speaking brain muscles that I haven't used in a while so I can speak to my cousin.

Then I stop suddenly, irritated by the effort of it. In a brief flash of anger I decide not to bother.

I stare at Evelyn silently. She stares back, confused, trying to read what had happened in the seconds between my last words and now. She relaxes her shoulders and leans forward so that her eyes meet mine. She opens her mouth to speak.

'What's wrong, Akita?' she asks. 'Are you alright?'

I stare at her silently, and her face falls. There's a sad look in her eyes. 'After all this time,' she whispers, 'you still don't speak?'

Taresai

Messai's eldest daughter got married.

Jamila.

She married a man called John six months ago. The ceremony was beautiful. Messai was showing me pictures yesterday when he came over for supper. He's intending on staying for five short weeks. His wife Leena and their three children will join him in the last two.

My heart leapt and still does every time I'm reminded of this news.

Jamila, Ornella, Michael.

The last time they'd seen their Aunty Taresai, she was on the brink of a breakdown because of her infant's skin condition. Ashanti and Zandé were yet to exist.

They'll be here in a few weeks, the newlyweds, John and Jamila, Messai's wife Leena, and my nephew and niece Ornella and Michael, for a traditional wedding ceremony. That's all I've been thinking about – in hope to suppress everything else that Anette's arrival has triggered.

It worked all week. It worked last night as the children slept and I made seven dishes and baked two cakes and prepared a small batch of rum. It worked this morning when I scrubbed the house down and kept a watchful eye on Akita as she got herself and the rest of the girls dressed.

It even worked when Anette landed in the country and Messai and Santino went to the airport to pick her up.

But the moment I see Anette's face, standing at my door, the floodgates open.

It all comes back to me, rushing over me, and I sink under its weight. The heavy woes I've spent nearly all my life suppressing, Anette evokes with the look of an eye, the twitch of the lip.

I stand for a minute, smile, and welcome her into our home.

Time heals all wounds, but my wounds have yet to turn to scars; heavens, they still bleed.

Akita

Just before supper, Uncle Messai, my grandmother, Aunty Asélle and her children arrive. I hide in my bedroom again as I hear the stampede of people flood in through the front door. I stay within these four walls, waiting for Mama to call on me, only this time she doesn't.

I lie on my bed staring at the ceiling, at the strange-looking light shade on the ceiling light. It looks like a flower petal made of glass.

I look at Evelyn's white, metal bed by the window, so neat in floral sheets, like an artifact in a museum under the lace curtains.

I get up from my bed, take off my shoes, then I turn off the bedroom light and part the curtains. Outside the window a full moon shines brightly in the starless sky, its light is rivalled by the streetlamp that shines right outside our house.

There's nothing amazing outside my bedroom window, just the fence and the view of our neighbour's backyard.

Back in Edgar Street, the window of my and Amara's bedroom overlooked our front garden.

We were the first to see the sunrise and the last to know when the sun had set.

I sit on Evelyn's bed and stare into our dark bedroom, the light from the night spilling in through the lace curtains, making shapes dance along the floor.

I tiptoe back to my bed, and I lie in the shapes of the light and in the curves of the shadows, in my own little fortress of solitude as chaos ensues outside my door. I don't know how long I'm going to stay in here. Maybe until my cousins leave, maybe until forever.

It means I'll have to go to sleep without dinner, but that seems like a sacrifice I'm willing to make.

There's a knock on my door that makes me jump.

It quietly swings open as Evelyn's shadow pours in. She flicks on our bedroom light and closes the door behind her. Evelyn tells me that she's been looking everywhere for me. I go to tell her how silly it is that our bedroom is the last place she's decided to look, but before I can arrange the sentence in my mind she grabs hold of my wrist and leads me outside.

Evelyn pulls me to the bigger living room downstairs by the dining room where all the kids are except for Zandé, who snoozes peacefully in Baba's arms at the dining table with the adults. Evelyn drags me to a circle where all the girls sit, except for Amara, who's playing with Santo and our other boy cousins a few metres away. I've never felt more envy towards Amara.

Evelyn sits and pulls me down to sit next to her. She's very strong.

Ashanti spots me from across the circle. She crawls out of Samira's arms and walks towards me as fast as her three-year-old legs can carry her. She collapses on my lap, the weight of her nearly crushing my twiggy crossed legs.

She rests in my arms, soothing me in a way I haven't felt before. I don't even care that everyone else in the circle watches bitterly, probably wondering why the cutest girl in the world would like someone like me, her strange older sister who doesn't speak.

Taresai

I sit silently, taking in the scene at the dining table.

Santino sits beside me with our baby in his arms, speaking to Ibrahim about the oil and gold in the soils of Sudan. Anette and Asélle are engrossed in a light-hearted conversation (about knitting patterns probably). Messai and our mother sit at the end of the table speaking words of love to each other in the form of making sure each is going to the doctor, drinking enough water.

I'm surrounded by all my loved ones. We're finally here, in this place of freedom, peace.

So why do I feel so detached from it?

I look at my children and I see Santo's face, beaming as his youngest cousin Joseph tries to guess which pocket he's hidden something in, probably candy. Amara, with her missing front teeth, bites down on a soggy biscuit. Ashanti, sitting on her big sister's lap, too caught up in her own little world to take in her surroundings. My Akita sits silently and glares at her cousins as they speak to her. I breathe a sad breath. It's been three weeks since we moved from Edgar Street, but Akita still carries on like she's broken.

There hasn't been much that's excited her since seeing her grandmother and her Uncle Messai, especially when he appointed her the flower girl of Jamila's upcoming ceremony.

But once those things no longer serve as distractions from her sadness, she dives right back into it, headfirst.

I watch as Evelyn whispers something in her ear. My heart swells when a slight smile tugs at the corner of Akita's lip. One of Asélle's older twins then says something to Evelyn, who then scrunches her face up like she doesn't understand what's being said.

Asélle's other daughter, Samira, stands, walks over, and forces her way between Evelyn and Akita. I go to say something, to tell the girls off, then I catch Samira pinch Evelyn on the arm when she resists being shoved.

'Girls!' I say in an angry whisper, but nobody hears me.

Akita sets Ashanti away from the fight that ensues, stands and marches toward us. For a moment I think she's coming to me, running into my arms for comfort, but Akita walks right past me and marches straight to her Aunty Asélle.

She stares at Asélle until her aunt meets her gaze with a blank smile.

Akita, with a lethal look in her eyes, opens her mouth to speak and my stomach drops before she even says the words. 'Your daughters,' Akita says firmly, 'have no manners.'

The rooms fall silent. Even the children in the living room shift their attention this way.

Akita turns on her heels and walks the hallway leading to her room before I can send her there myself. Asélle smiles awkwardly and I'm completely lost for words.

'Well,' Messai breaks the silence, 'Akita has spoken.'

Santo is the first to cackle and then the room erupts into boisterous laughter.

Before I know it, the moment has passed and everyone in both rooms go back to what they were doing before.

Evelyn sits separate from Samira and has moved closer to Ines. Ashanti joins Santo and Amara, rising to her feet and trotting after them.

Messai pours himself another glass of wine, Asélle refills her plate with food, and I'm still stuck on the loop from minutes ago.

Chapter 25

Geelong

Akita

It's my fourth week at this school, and I still hate it.

On my first day into the lion's den, I got introduced to the class first thing, and by recess I wanted to go home because I got hit in the head with a basketball. A ginger-haired boy named Calum was the thrower of the ball – onto my fresh and tender set of braids that Mama did the night before.

I told her that I didn't care how she did my hair for the first day, so she braided it like she always has, since my eighth birthday.

Today, I'm in trouble because the same boy – Calum – purposely tripped me over during our morning PE session, and I, in a fit of rage, took off my shoe and beat him with it.

This school is a strange place.

The third and fourth graders are taught in the same classrooms with the same teacher. I'm in Three/Four Red and my teacher is a plump, blonde lady named Mrs Costa whose cheeks are always pink. She's nice enough, and she asks me a lot of questions about what goes on at home. I catch her staring at me from time to time. I don't mind it, though. I was a bit nervous coming to this school; I thought everyone would dislike us because we're a different colour, but it's almost the opposite.

Everybody loves Santo. He's charming, athletic and very funny – teachers love him too. They don't even get him in trouble when he deserves it, like when he bullies some of the weird kids nobody likes.

Amara is also very loved; how can she not be? She's so full of personality, she's the centre of attention always and the star of every show. You never know what she's going to say but you know it's absolutely going to be hilarious.

Then there's me. The odd sibling in between the two champions.

I don't have friends at this school, but I don't really care because it isn't for the colour of my skin.

Lunchtimes I spend in the library, even if the sun is out. In Sport I'm always one of the first kids picked to be on a team, and when I talk in class everyone listens to what I have to say.

At recess this morning I think I made a friend.

I sat near the sandcastles, and Danielle, a bug-eyed girl in my class who has a strange attachment to a stuffed bunny she takes everywhere, sat next to me and offered one of her Tim Tams. I declined, but I didn't tell her to go away like I did the first couple of times.

Danielle is in the grade below me, even though we're born in the same year. I'm in Grade Four and she's in Grade Three, so this friendship can only go so far.

I lay on the grass of the oval, eyes closed. It's 4.15pm.

All the other kids have been picked up. Me, Santo, and Amara are the only students left in the school. We're waiting for Baba, who's in the office with Principal O'Malley and Mrs Costa. They called him in to talk about what happened today in PE and the consequences I'm going to face moving forward.

Calum wasn't even badly hurt. I'm not sorry for what I did, either. He hit me once with a ball and tripped me the second time. Yes, I hit him with my shoe, repeatedly, but he walked away without a scratch. He didn't even cry, he just laughed and pushed me away, apologising to me only when Mrs Costa was within earshot.

He says both instances were accidents, but I'm the only one who believes they weren't. I don't know what Calum's problem is, but I see him do this to other kids as well, the loners, the quiet ones, the weirdos, the kids with no one on their side. He picks on them because he knows he can get away with it. Not with me though, never with me.

I feel Santo block the sun from my face with his shadow.

'Cut it out, Santo,' I whinge. He chuckles and sits beside me.

'So,' he begins, 'I heard you beat up the chubster.'

'Who, Calum? Nah … I didn't beat him up. I just hit him with my shoe a couple of times for tripping me this morning,' I say, eyeing the afternoon clouds rolling away towards the sun.

The heavily trodden grass feels nice on my back.

'Did he do that to you?' Santo asks, pointing to the beige-coloured band-aids on both my black knees.

'Yep,' I say.

'Do you want me to beat him up for you?' he asks simply, as if he's asking me what my favourite colour is.

'No,' I chuckle, 'don't worry about it.'

I see the way Calum looks at Santo, like he admires him, craves his approval, and he's probably using me to get Santo to be his friend. He thinks that he and Santo are alike, that Santo will accept that he's picking on his little sister because he thinks Santo picks on me too. What an idiot.

I'd love to see Santo beat some sense into Calum, to show everyone what a weakling he really is, but I know if Santo does that he'll go too far and get expelled.

I don't want that, not for him.

Santo loves it here. The teachers love him, everyone wants to be his friend, some of the girls in my grade even have little crushes on him – which makes me feel ill every time I think about it.

I don't want him to lose all of that just because of me.

Santo starts to laugh softly.

'What?' I ask, suddenly very exhausted, but very relieved that it's almost the end of this very hard day. The spring breeze feels cold against the unbandaged scratches on my elbows.

'It's just so funny how things have changed. I'm my teacher's favourite student and Baba got called into school today because of something *you* did. It's pure comedy.'

'Shut up, Santo,' I say, unable to stop the smile from spreading across my face.

Amara plays noiselessly in the sandpit nearby.

Santo is quiet for a moment, watching as a flock of birds fly across the blue sky.

I stare up at the powerlines where a group of magpies warble loudly. I eye them intensely, tempting them to come and swoop me.

'Why are you all different all of a sudden, Kita?' he asks curiously. 'You're more ... angry and stuff.'

'I hate it here, Sunny.'

'Yeah, everybody knows that. But you don't have to be such a baby about it.'

'Oh please, Santo, you're one to talk. You gave Mama and Baba a hard time for years. You still do, so don't tell me to be a saint.'

'Well, one of us has to be ... you know ... for balance,' he shrugs. 'I mean, look at Amara.'

We look over to Amara, who's filling her socks with fistfuls of sand.

I sigh, lacking the strength to tell Amara off for doing that today.

'Besides,' Santo says, 'I've got ADHD, I can't help the way I behave sometimes.'

'Oh, bullcrap, Sunny,' I cackle. 'Go suck a toe.'

He laughs and throws a stick at the sky, then he crosses his legs and plays with the grass. 'I like it here Akita,' he says softly, 'and I don't like many things. Just … just give it a chance.'

I'm quiet for a long time, my eyes to the sky.

Maybe Santo is right. If I give this place a chance, maybe I'll like it.

Yes, this school has ugly uniforms, and I don't like the way the classrooms are set up, and no, I don't like the ugly name of this town. But if I played outside more and rode my bike around the neighbourhood instead of just staying inside the house avoiding Evelyn, maybe I'll see that things aren't so bad. Or I can at least distract myself from it by creating something good.

'Are you going to miss Baba?' The words are out of my mouth before I even get a chance to think about what I'm asking.

Mama and Baba told us at the start of the week. They both looked really sad even though they were trying to hide it. Mama said it was best hearing it from them than anyone else.

Whatever that means.

Santo doesn't say anything. I think he didn't hear me, I think that I might've asked the question so quietly that the wind whisked the words away before they reached his ears. Or maybe I didn't speak it, maybe I thought it so loud I heard it.

'Hey,' Santo whispers after a while. 'Look.'

I sit up on the grass and look to where Santo is pointing. There are a dozen seagulls wandering along the oval a few metres away.

'There must be a beach nearby,' I say.

'Wanna chase them?' Santo asks, a glint of mischief in his cola-brown eyes.

In an instant I'm on my feet, racing towards the seagulls with Santo following closely behind. I hear him laugh hysterically as he trips and stumbles. A laugh escapes me, rattling my ribs and stealing my breath with its infection.

I stretch my legs, extending each step. I run faster than I've ever run, toward the flock of seagulls and they part and open their wings, flapping as they fly away. I spread my arms wide and my elbows sting, but I stretch them anyway. Santo and I sprint through the grass, laughing so hard I give myself a headache. In these moments I forget all my worries, all my troubles and I swear I could fly.

Taresai

My children's arrival from school has been delayed because Akita was involved in causing a 'disturbance.' The school didn't tell Santino what it was over the phone.

The Taresai of the past would've thought that some kid picked a fight with my daughter, but she took the fall, because even though she may have been smaller and younger, she is blacker, which apparently makes her the most threatening.

But the Taresai of today does not know what to make of it. I've been surprised by Akita's disposition ever since we got here. She's still a good kid with a great heart, she does all her chores, doesn't talk back, does her homework, helps her siblings when they need it. She's just quieter, quieter than I thought possible, with a deep anger brewing in that little body of hers, and it's not like I can tell her off for it.

I can't yell at her for not wanting to ride her bike or play outside, I can't scorn her for not caring what her hair looks like. So, I give her space and pray that her wounds heal themselves with the grace of time.

It's not easy to say goodbye to the first place you've ever called home, then to pack up and find another one – I more than anyone should understand that, but it seems that while everyone else has flourished because of it, Akita's spirit has been deflated.

I thought living with Anette's children would help, but Akita only talks to them when she needs to, otherwise she keeps to herself.

My other children seem to be getting along fine with their cousins. They attend Corio Primary, the local public school down the road, as St Paul's didn't have places available. Evelyn, Emmanuel and Atem always arrive from school earlier than my children. They're out of their uniforms before they greet their mother and immediately get a start on their homework or chores. A blind man can see that Anette and I have very different parenting styles; I just hope they don't clash.

In these few weeks living together I've been relieved as to not spend a heap of alone time with Anette, with her being driven here and there to set up things for herself and her children in this new country.

There is a conversation that has not yet happened, and because of that I'm glad, even though I know it awaits. We live under the same roof, but still I'm yet to see Anette behind the heavily guarded walls she puts up, greater than it was in Giza. I only see her in small glimpses when she speaks to her children and she thinks I'm not listening.

Living with her has left me feeling exposed. I remain as I am, unguarded in her face and in her absence. As I have my entire life. I laugh to myself as I put the last of the clean plates in the cupboard. After all this time, after all these years, there is no closure yet to be had? We live in the same house; we will be for a while. Should I find the strength to forgive my younger sister without an apology? Find closure without her guidance? Her permission?

My thoughts are disrupted when I feel two skinny arms wrap around my waist from behind. I spin and look down at Evelyn's smiling face. Her eyes are so warm, exuding much love.

Where did she get them?

'Aunty?' she says. 'When is Akita going to be home?'

Chapter 26

Geelong

Akita

The day my cousins arrived was the most excited I've ever been in forever. My cousin Jamila came with her mother, Aunty Leena, her new husband John, her younger sister Ornella, who's much, much older than any of my other cousins, and her brother Michael.

Michael is the youngest in their family, but the eldest boy in all of ours. He's seventeen. Uncle Messai's kids live in a country called Sweden where it snows all year round and the yellow-haired people speak two main languages, Swedish and English. Their English is very different from ours; they have a funny way of pronouncing words and putting sentences together.

Mama says I'm not supposed to have favourite cousins, it's rude, but Uncle Messai's kids are my favourite cousins. In the three times they've come over in the past week they've been so polite, charming and … foreign. They look like us, and yet they're so different, so extraordinarily unfamiliar. It's like they're from another planet, and I can't help myself from staring at them from time to time.

They're alluring in the way they act, even the way they dress.

Michael wore an oatmeal-coloured knitted vest without sleeves the first night I met him, even though it was freezing cold outside. Ornella wears her natural hair; she walks around with her afro out, curling around her face like a halo. Jamila is so tall, so beautiful and so polite. She looks the most like Uncle Messai, especially with her big, bright smile. She and Ornella aren't like my other girl cousins who ask me questions just to make fun of my answers. They ask me questions because they're interested in me.

I never have to worry about them not liking me.

I'm tied to them like I am to my other cousins, but when I think about my connection to Jamila, Ornella and Michael I get little butterflies. We all come from the same grandmother, the parts of Mama that make up me, Akita, are the same parts of their Baba that make them up.

One day I might be as beautiful as Jamila, as intelligent as Ornella and as charming as Michael.

* * *

I like being the flower girl.

I get to sit next to the bride and her bridesmaids; I get to look as beautiful as they are in my white dress with a pink waist ribbon. But I'm also allowed to be a kid. I'm allowed to eat as much cake as I want and dance the night away, while my beautiful cousin Jamila has to sit like a statue, smile and only speak when spoken to.

She can dance, but only with her husband, John, who is nice but isn't as beautiful as Jamila. I feel bad for thinking such things because John has been lovely since meeting him last week, but it's true.

They got married ages ago, at the start of the year. This is their second wedding ceremony because their first one was in Sweden and none of us went.

Most of the night has passed within this reception hall decorated with white floaty fabric and metallic gold florals. All my flower-girl duties are done, and now, with the cake cut and the drinks served, the music plays. The drums shake the ground as the beat bounces from wall to wall. Most people are on the dance floor, but I sit alone at a table I migrated to hours ago, the same table Santo was sitting on before he ditched me to go play with some boys.

Mama is a few tables away, sitting with my grandmother and all my aunts, Asélle, Anette, Leena, and a couple of other women I don't recognise.

I watch Amara and Ashanti suspiciously as they twirl stupidly on the dance floor. If I knew any better, I'd say they had some of that adult juice that makes people loopy. There are jugs filled with them on every table.

Aunty Asélle's daughters are sitting together on a round table on the other side of the dance floor. They haven't come near me all night and haven't spoken to me since that evening a couple weeks ago, when Samira pinched Evelyn.

I think they're still angry with me about what I said to their mother, that, and also the fact that only I was asked by Uncle Messai to be part of the bridal party.

I don't know where Evelyn is, though, which is strange because she's been following me around everywhere I go since I stood up for her. Mama says to give her a chance, that she wants to be my friend even though she's three whole years older than me, but I haven't yet thought to try.

I feel someone pull a chair near me. I must've summoned her with my thoughts. Evelyn sits beside me, smiling, a small plate of cake in her hands. She looks quite pretty tonight in her white dress with red cherries on them and a red cardigan. She offers me a fork.

'No, thank you,' I say, shaking my head.

I rub my belly; I've had enough wedding cake to last me at least a couple years.

She sets the cake down on the table behind us and we both watch Amara and Ashanti dance. We're quiet for a long time; this is now very typical. We share the same room, live in the same house and spend a lot of time together, exchanging few words, and most of mine to her she doesn't understand, and most of hers to me I don't respond.

Evelyn exhales softly. In the corner of my eye, I see her body deflate, her perfect posture slouches. 'Akita …' she says softly, 'why do you hate me?'

I see her face turn to me, but my eyes remain forward, feeling her gaze on the side of my face. I look down at my lap, my shame filling the air between us. I don't answer this time, not because I don't want to, but because I don't have an answer for her. I don't know how I feel about Evelyn, but I know that I don't hate her.

Evelyn sighs dolefully and looks away. 'I see the way you talk to Santo, to Amara, even to Ashanti. You've said more words to your toddler sister and your infant baby brother than you have to me.'

I feel like I'm going to cry. Tears well in my eyes and I blink them away.

I want to get off this seat and run into the horde of tall dancing people, away from this conversation, but I don't, I sit where I am because I know that there's no running from this.

'I don't hate you, Evelyn,' I say. My voice sounds foreign to my ears, speaking words in a language I haven't spoken in years.

Evelyn looks at me, trying to suppress the grin that fights its way onto her face.

'I'm just …' I start, trying hard to find the words, 'I'm just trying to get used to a lot of things.'

Evelyn smiles at me sadly. 'Me too.'

It all hits me at once with a force that nearly tips me over.

Evelyn has moved halfway across the world, she lives in a country brand new to her, and doesn't speak the language everyone else speaks.

I'm having a hard time here, but I've never even thought to think of all that Evelyn's been going through. If Geelong seems new and strange to me, I could only imagine what it's been like for Evelyn.

'I'm sorry, Evelyn,' I say. 'I haven't been very nice to you.'

'You have been nice ... well ... sometimes, but not talking to me is better than pinching me.' She smiles.

We laugh quietly. I feel rather silly for being so cold towards her for the past couple of months, pretending she doesn't exist and hoping she'd just disappear. She's my cousin, she'll be here for a long time, so I might as well give her a chance and enjoy her company.

'You know,' Evelyn says, cutting into the cake with her fork, 'you're about the only girl that could look like a princess with white-people-coloured band-aids on your knees.'

I laugh at the comment, but feel a little embarrassed as well.

'I didn't have time to colour them in,' I shrug, looking down at my knobbly knees decorated in beige strips.

Santo emerges from the dancefloor with an entourage of boys standing behind him.

'Sup Kita? Hey, Evelyn,' he says, his dress shirt untucked from his pants.

'Where have you been, Santo?' I ask, eyeing the group of adolescent boys behind him. One thing I can always count on, is Santo gaining a group of loyal followers wherever we go. At school, at the skatepark and now at Jamila's wedding.

'Around,' he smiles at me.

'Hey Evey, are you gonna eat the rest of that cake?'

Evelyn rolls her eyes and hands Santo the plate. He grins, bows his head in thanks, and walks away. The boys follow.

All but one.

A tall boy, about the same age as Santo, stays behind. He stares at me and smiles as if he expects me to say something.

I stare back at him blankly.

'Akita?' says the boy.

'... Yes?' I say, looking at Evelyn in confusion.

The boy's smile fades. He sighs softly.

'You don't remember me?' he says, tucking his hands in his pockets. I search his face for traces of familiarity. His chestnut skin, dark eyebrows, pink gums and eyelashes that curl far back.

'Anei?' I whisper, digging the memory of him up from the depths of my mind. I'd forgotten such a boy exists until now. I haven't thought of him in years.

'Yep, in living colour,' he beams.

I don't bother to enquire as to what that even means.

'When did your family get here?' I ask. With every second that passes his face feels more like a person and less like a memory.

'To the wedding?' he asks.

'To Australia.'

'Oh, a few years back. We left Egypt a year after your family did.' When he speaks I take in his whole face: it's a lot slimmer, his jawbone and cheekbones protrude more than they did when I saw him last, and his voice is a lot deeper too.

When he smiles I catch a glimpse of his pearly white teeth, and the smallest gap that you could ever see separates his two front teeth.

'Oh! I love this song, do you wanna dance?' he asks, his hands in his pockets, his nose in the air.

I look at Evelyn and she lets out a giggle.

'No thanks, gap-tooth.'

Taresai

At the start of the night our table was full.

Asélle was to my right and Santino was to my left. Anette sat directly across from me, with our mother on one side and Leena on the other. Santo and the girls sat on the next table over, and Akita was at the alter with the bridal party.

But now, as evening has turned to night and the air in this hall has loosened, people begin to scatter. Messai and Leena went to be with Jamila on the dance floor, Asélle, with Zandé in her arms, walks around the hall, table to table, talking to her many friends. I'd lost track of Santino hours ago. Manuela, my lifelong friend, and I finally reunited; we spoke for hours, laughed, and cried. She told me about Nadene, the old woman who lived on the rooftop of our building in Giza. She passed, less than a week after our departure. The news weighs on my heart more than I expect it to. I haven't thought of her in all these years, I hadn't even known she was sick, and yet, a selfish part of me weeps because she is no longer on this earth.

But even after these hours' long and lifetimes deep exchanges, Manuela too, got up and left. Slowly, each person drifted away from the table, until there were three.

Anette, my mother, and me.

The three of us engage in a shallow conversation; I go into autopilot to navigate my way through, my mind instead on other things, specifically how to keep myself together because this is the exact predicament I've been carefully avoiding since Anette got here, and retrospectively, all my life. I think of possible ways to escape.

Our mother looks out into the dance floor, chuckling when she sees Amara and Ashanti stomping their feet to the music. Then she looks over to us and points to Akita and Evelyn nearby, twirling with their hands joined, their skirts floating in movement with their bodies.

Akita. She did it.

I cast a glow of love and send it towards my daughter, relief swelling my heart.

'How sweet,' my mother laughs, 'they're all growing up so fast. Mashallah.'

'Hmm,' Anette says with a smile. 'They ought to slow down, or else one of them will be sick.'

'They're just dancing,' I say, 'there's not much harm in that.'

'Why weren't you girls ever like that?' mother asks, and I shoot her a look.

She's getting old.

She's forgotten the years of grief she's put me through, but I haven't.

'Because we had a different upbringing.' I laugh bitterly.

'We did,' Anette agrees calmly. 'It was a different time Mama, a long time ago.'

'How are the kids settling in?' Mother asks Anette. 'Are they enjoying school?'

'Yes. They're speaking more English with each day that comes. Evelyn and Emmanuel have been teaching me some of the things they learn.'

'Taresai,' Mother says, shifting her attention to me. My name sounds hardened when it comes from her mouth, like she's peeled all the soft edges away. 'I heard you couldn't get Anette's children enrolled at the good school Santo and Akita attend?'

'I had very little to do with enrolling my own children, let alone my niece and nephews.'

Anette clears her throat. I see her grip Mother's hand beneath the table.

'Of all the nicer places you could've enrolled them, why is it that they attend the public school down the street? How are they to learn proper English?'

I take a sharp breath, biting down hard on my tongue.

'Ma, that's something you should be discussing with Messai and Santino. They organised the children's place of learning,' I seethe, anger rising to my chest.

I shouldn't be surprised; I was a fool for expecting Anette to have grown out of her old ways. Of course she's gone behind my back once again to make complaints of me to our mother.

Using her 'favoured child' privileges and her plagued tongue to throw me under the bus.

I didn't even know Anette felt this way, how could I?

'As you know, Ma,' I say carefully, each word sharper than a knife, 'Anette can attest to this; my time and my efforts are purely spent in the kitchen.'

Tension buzzes in the air between us, palpable in the tinted lights of the hall.

I look into Anette's eyes, see her mind working to stop things from escalating, to diffuse the fire that has ignited.

I rise out from my seat and walk onto the dance floor, my eyes on my two youngest daughters.

I crouch down near Amara and Ashanti.

Ashanti squeals 'Mama!' when she sees me, and Amara grins.

'Are you girls okay?'

'Mm-hmm,' Amara nods.

'That's good, we're going to go home soon, okay?'

They moan and groan, and get back to dancing as soon as the next song comes on.

I walk back and sit at the childless kids' table nearby.

I feel Anette sit beside me.

'Taresai,' Anette says gently. She knows she's treading on thin ice. 'Mama means no harm, you know this.'

'Actually,' I scoff, 'I don't know anything.'

'She's just concerned, and angry, about my children and when she feels those things about one thing, she misdirects it towards another thing. *We* know this.'

When Anette speaks to me I don't ever feel like she sees me. Her words are empty, regurgitated, robotic, rehearsed. Instead of soothing me, they undo every bit of healing I've undergone, rewinding the clock and erasing all the time I've spent away from our childhood.

Just like that I'm back to being an eight-year-old, heartbroken because I'm the only child pulled out of school when the rest of my siblings were free to go, back to being the only child forced to mother my two younger sisters and older brother.

I'm back to being the only child who wasn't granted permission to be a child.

I know my mother, and I know Anette. I know that when Mother is angry about one thing she does indeed misdirect it at something else, but Anette fails to realise that 'something else' is always me.

I don't say anything, though.

I stay as quiet as I always have.

I stare ahead, stare beyond all the people on the dance floor, beyond the alter where Jamila and her husband sit, staring into nothingness and everythingness.

'Taresai …' says Anette, her voice distant. 'She knows … Mama knows about Santino, and she's concerned. We all are.'

'Is … is that supposed to make me feel better, because,' I laugh, 'you're doing a terrible job, Anette.'

'I'll stay,' Anette says firmly. 'I'll stay with you as long as you need me to when he leaves. I'll help around the house; I'll help you with your English–'

'Anette, just stop,' I whisper. 'Don't you understand? There will be no learning or studying English when he goes. I'll have no time for that. I'll have to get a job, heavens, maybe several.'

I take a deep breath and swallow the lump in my throat.

'I have to put food on the table, put the kids through school.'

Give them everything I never had.

* * *

That night I take a little extra time putting my children to sleep, kissing Santo as he snoozes, speaking words of love into Akita's ears as she dreams. Sitting between Amara and Ashanti's beds, singing to them in their slumber, holding Zandé in my arms, long after he's fallen asleep.

I walk around the quiet house, its emptiness in the dark a stark contrast to how it looks in the day with nine kids under the age of twelve.

It's three hours past midnight and everyone is asleep, but I'm wide awake, growing restless by the minute. The wedding celebration was beautiful. I wish my eyes could've seen more of my children celebrating and sharing their joy with their cousins and less of my mother's unneeded critique of the small things that are wrong in this big world of so many things that are right.

I slide open the back door and step out into the night, sitting on the steps of the verandah. I can count on one hand how many times I've been out to the backyard of this house. This is my first at night.

The air is cool, but soothing, washing over the bones in my body.

In the sky half a moon shines, casting a silvery light on the thin clouds that pass. Not many stars tonight.

Behind me I hear the door slide open then close again. Anette wraps a blanket over my shoulders and sits beside me. I'm so stunned by the notion that I barely move.

Anette looks up at the sky and kisses her teeth disapprovingly.

'The stars, you can barely see them.'

I'm too tired to respond, I'm too tired to pretend everything is okay, I'm too tired to rise above.

We sit in this silence for a while. Part of me wants Anette to leave me alone, to retreat inside and leave me to the night with my thoughts, but there is the smallest part of me that wants to lay everything out on the table, and overcome this lifelong burden. For my own sake and no one else's.

But this night could last forever, and there still wouldn't be enough time.

'Taresai ...' Anette whispers, and says nothing more until I meet her gaze. I can barely see her in the blackness of the night, only distinguishing the features that reach from her slim face and catch the moonlight in a way I don't see in the day.

'I'm sorry,' she breathes, her voice sounding frail, like speaking the very word itself has weakened her.

I chuckle softly. 'I think you're way past apologising for Mama, Anette.'

She stares at me with deep sorrow swimming all over the face I can barely see, her eyes glinting with so many words her mouth can't say.

'I was fed, out of all of us, Tsai, and you were starved. I know it. I always have.' She hesitates. 'I … I watched as Mama took things out on you, took things *from* you, and gave them to me. You did everything, you were everything, and I had no remorse.'

I bite on my bottom lip. Anette truly has a way with words. Nobody, *nobody* in this world can get underneath my skin as she does. Not even our mother.

'I was a kid, Tsai. Just a kid … But so were you, and for that, I am sorry.'

I turn to Anette slowly and speak my words carefully. 'After all these years, Anette, you're now having this epiphany?' I ask, the venomous bite of my words hangs in the air, devouring the softness of hers.

'No. No, I realised it a long time ago. You were given nothing, Taresai, and yet … Yet you defied us and made something of yourself.'

I look at Anette, really look at her. This facade, these walls she's put up in the face of everyone else, has crumbled and turned to ash. She is … envious of me?

'I'm sorry that I was just a bystander, Tsai, I'm sorry I never stood up for you, and I'm sorry I walked all over you to just get ahead. It's my karma that I've remained far behind you.'

I'm relieved that Anette has finally gained the strength to say all this to me, but I'm struck with the feeling that time has yet to grace her with the gift of wisdom.

'All I ever wanted was to go to school and learn,' I say. 'To read … to be able to write my name on a piece of paper.'

Resentment takes up a huge burden in my heart where my sister and my mother should be. Depriving one child of something, and giving the rest that opportunity so freely because of some arbitrary system that deems all but one worthy, is to me, unforgivable, and I must learn to live with that.

I look at Anette, and for the first time in a long time I see my little sister. I see that she needs me, I see just how much she needs my love, I see the faceless and silent pain she's endured in our years apart. Anette, with every fibre of her being, is yearning for my forgiveness, my words of comfort so that she may sleep peacefully for the rest of her days.

I offer her none.

I wrap the blanket tightly around my shoulders and I walk inside.

As I lay my head on the pillow, I realise how much lighter I feel. As if all I ever needed, in all these years, was for Anette to acknowledge the hardships our mother put me through and the hurtful hand she had to play in it.

Chapter 27

Geelong

Akita

Dad left two weeks after Zandé's third birthday, three weeks before Ashanti lost her first baby tooth, four weeks after Amara finally learned how to ride a bike, five weeks before Santo's major growth spurt.

It was six weeks before I graduated from primary school.

It's a day I don't like to remember, but every night since it replays in my mind until sleep finally takes me away and everything fades to black. I dreaded saying goodbye, hated it.

It was hard for me to distinguish it from death. I suppose, in a way, it was no different.

Not of a person, but the death of life as we knew it. The knock didn't come, but I'm certain the grief that we share is that only felt by the Grim Reaper's touch. Something very deep inside me feels like it has died. Like a light has been extinguished.

I knew for a long while that Dad's time with us was running out, I knew that we were only counting down until the day he went back to his home country to be the man that Australia couldn't let him be. I just wish that day never came.

For some time, it felt like it wasn't going to, nothing happened after Mum and Dad told us the news. Two years passed and he stayed.

It was only a few months prior, after we'd finished dinner and had a very ordinary day up until that point; that we were reminded.

My heart broke more the second time, I think.

Now, seven months later, the thought of holding him tighter for just a second longer keeps me up at night, and still I feel an eternity wouldn't be enough time to say goodbye.

The first night without him here was the hardest. I cried until the sun came up.

He calls every day, but it's not the same. It will never be the same.

* * *

It's a Thursday evening, Mum's at work, and Evelyn and I are babysitting Amara, Ashanti and Zandé. Me and Evelyn spend almost every day together, even though we haven't shared a bedroom in years. She and her family moved out several weeks after Jamila's wedding.

We both go to St Brigid's, a Catholic girls' school on the upper-middle-class side of town. She's in the ninth grade and I'm in the seventh.

'I don't care that you helped with the dishes yesterday, Amara,' I shout from Mum's room, 'the sooner you listen to Evelyn, the sooner we can all eat!'

I dry off Zandé, still dripping from his bath, and lay him on the towel as I fetch his bottle. This routine is usually easy, but he seems to be particularly restless tonight. Zandé kicks his legs in the air as I try to slip on his cotton onesie; he laughs hysterically, finding amusement in my fluster.

'Zandé, please, come on,' I groan.

Evelyn opens the door and stands on the threshold.

'Food's nearly ready,' she smiles, her beige sweater and blue jeans still clean. I don't know how she does that. Whenever it's my turn to get the food prepared, I'm always covered in it.

'Did Amara help?' I ask.

'Mm-hmm, she's setting the table.'

'And Ashanti?'

'Just got out of the bath, she's nearly dressed.'

Evelyn watches with sad eyes as I struggle with Zandé.

This time of the week is when I feel the most exhausted.

Mum works from Monday to Friday. In the mornings she works her job at the carpet factory, and during the night she cleans houses that are up for sale. The weekend is the only time I get a break from the kids, the only two days Mum's home and I don't have to deal with it all.

'Do you want me to try?' Evelyn suggests after a while.

'No, it's okay,' I lie. 'I think he's just had too much sugar or something. He'll be asleep in a minute.'

'Well, okay,' Evelyn says hesitantly. 'I'll set you a plate. Don't take too long.'

I shove Zandé's chubby legs into the onesie and zip it right up. With my hands under his arms, I pick him up and I stare at him with the meanest look my face can pull.

'I'm serious, Zan. *Go to sleep.*'

Zandé stares at me vacantly, shocked by the suddenness of my movements.

For a moment I think he's going to cry.

Then he reaches for my face and grabs my cheek with his chubby fingers, his nails pressing against my skin. When my face softens, he blinks as if he understands me, understands how exhausted I am. How hungry I am. How badly I want to put him to sleep so I can eat and then clean up and then put the girls to sleep so that I can be in bed before Mum comes home at ten.

Zandé blows a raspberry, spraying my face with his slimy saliva.

I throw him on my hip and walk to the dining room in an angry defeat. I eat my oven-ready pizza with Zandé on my lap. He drools and pokes his fingers in my food, soiling the onesie that I've just put him in.

Evelyn goes home before it gets too dark out. I leave Zandé with Amara and Ashanti in the living room as I stack the dishes in the sink, too tired to wash up.

I turn off all the lights in the house and make sure all the doors and windows are locked. When most the important things are done, I settle in the living room and place Zandé on my chest, his energy slowly fading. Amara and Ashanti lie with their bellies to the rug and their feet to the ceiling, eyes on the tv.

It's 8.07pm. I agreed to let them watch a movie in the hopes that they'll be asleep before the final credits. I don't pay much attention to the film, or the scrawny white wizard boy it's about. I feel the full weight of Zandé on my chest as his small body goes limp. I breathe a deep sigh of relief and run my fingers gently through his soft black curls.

He snores tenderly, gripping tightly onto the palm of my hand with all his fingers. I forget just how cute he is when he isn't being an absolute pain.

He looks like Ashanti did when she was a baby: lots of hair, soft as clouds, chubby cheeks and a button nose. He isn't as fat as she was, though.

Ashanti isn't much of a baby anymore. She's six and doesn't talk at all unless she needs to, especially since Dad left. I think she's confused as we all are, moreso probably. Ashanti would go to Dad for everything. I think she found comfort in just how much Dad spoke.

Even though she doesn't say much to me with words, Ashanti speaks to me with her eyes, with her hands, with her feet. The way she looks at me when I tuck her in, how her large brown eyes twinkle when I tell her stories of made-up kingdoms and little black girls with magic. The way she peers at me when her milk is too hot. The way she stands and hides behind me whenever we go visit our cousins, the way she holds my hand sometimes on our walk to the shops. Softly on a good day, tightly on a hard day.

Amara is still the same. Loud and annoying. She listens to me most of the time; she just has to, without fail, make a big fuss about it. To defy me for the sake of it.

Amara's popular at school. Her skin condition isn't as bad as it was when she was a baby, so Mum let her grow her hair out, and now it's nearly as long as mine.

Mum braids Amara and Ashanti's hair into ponytails, while I wear the same box braids I've had since I was eight.

I let Zandé sleep blissfully on my chest for a while, then I place my hand on his lower back and sit up. I rock him gently from side to side as I place him into his crib, tuck one arm under his blanket and one arm over, just like Mum taught me.

I walk back out into the living room and eye them both. Ashanti's seconds away from falling asleep; her head lolls from side to side and her eyes droop sluggishly.

'Alright, you two, bedtime.'

'What?' Amara whinges, 'it's not even nine o'clock yet!'

'Yes, it is,' I lie. 'Go to bed.'

'Please Kita, the movie's nearly finished, come on,' Amara protests.

I wish there was some way I could transmit my tiredness to Amara. That way she would be asleep in her bed, and I'd be wide awake.

'It's recorded, Amara, you can watch it tomorrow.'

'Fine,' she grumbles, rising to her feet. She helps me pick Ashanti up and walk her to their bedroom. I tuck them both in and bid them goodnight before I switch on their nightlight and flick off the ceiling light.

This is my favourite time of the night, when all the responsibilities of the day are done, and my only duty left is to sleep.

I go to walk to my bedroom when I hear a knock on the door. I know who it is before I even answer it. With a heaved sigh and a roll of my eyes, I open the door to Santo, a black hoodie over his red and white school uniform.

'Is … is Mum home yet?' he asks, his words slurry.

'Well,' I start, 'since her car isn't parked in the driveway, Santo, I'd say that, no, she isn't home yet.'

Santo laughs stupidly. 'Good.'

He's high again.

Santo does things to himself that stop him from thinking straight. He's been hanging out with those no-good friends of his from that no-good school he got himself thrown into after getting expelled from Delany College in Year 7.

Santo goes around huffing things that make his brain mushier than it already is.

He's an imbecile, an absolute fricken moron.

Santo is fourteen, two whole years older than I am, and yet I'm the one babysitting him. Puberty has turned him into a complete ogre. He's barely home, but when he is he either lazes around, eats all the food and makes a mess, or he comes home after spending the day with his friends in this state. I, for one, am so sick of it.

Mum doesn't see him when he's like this, and I'm not one to snitch, but tonight he's disturbed my peace, made things harder for me, disrupted my rhythm when I was so close to sleep, and I am too exhausted to let it slip.

Santo tries to walk into the house, but I don't step out of the way.

'What are you doing?' he asks, trying to deepen his voice.

'You're not coming in,' I say firmly. 'The kids are asleep, and … and you reek.'

He takes a step forward, towering over me.

'Move, Akita.'

'No.'

We stare at each other.

Santo isn't one to be tested, but tonight, nor am I.

Santo grabs me by my shirt and pulls me out of the way; I trip over him and fall on the stone steps of our front porch. I grab onto his ankle before I even grasp what I'm doing. Santo stumbles backward, his body falls down the steps, collapses on mine and all the wind is knocked out of my lungs. He sits on top of my belly and I kick at him furiously, pounding his backside with my knees and punching his chest with my fists.

Santo then rolls over me and pushes me away. He gets to his feet, walks a couple steps then he collapses face-down on the grass.

I watch him for a moment, his body a lump on the front lawn, black, in the darkness of the night.

I get up, walk back inside the house and lock the door.

Mum can deal with him tonight.

I check to make sure all the kids are asleep before taking a long shower. I examine the damage done to my clothes: my torn shirt and my scuffed track pants.

Santo always ruins my things, whether he intends to or not.

I lie in my bed. Wide awake. All the sleep has been beaten out of me. Santo and I fight even on good days, especially recently, and it almost always ends physically.

Truth is, I rarely ever win.

He hangs out with dimwits so often that he's turned into one. I don't know what's got into him. He's been off his medications for goodness knows how long.

Santo and I used to hang out all the time when we were younger. He'd share all his cool things with me, but now it's like he saves the best parts of himself for people who couldn't give a crap about him even if they tried.

Santo annoys me, and he makes it hard for me to want to be around him. I can't wait until he grows out of this phase, when he comes back to himself after realising the trouble his friends are. I hope it's soon because I really miss him.

I hear the engine of Mum's car pulling up the driveway, humming gently, like her personal fanfare. I pretend to be asleep when I hear her walk in, her footsteps echoing through the house, slow and considered.

Mum opens my bedroom door slowly, the light from the hallway spilling in.

When she speaks her voice is quiet but sharp, not to be tested. One wrong word in a wrong tone could land me in big trouble, I can feel it already.

'Akita,' she says, 'why is your brother sleeping on the lawn?'

I turn on my pillow to face her silhouette.

'Because I didn't let him in,' I say simply.

'Why not?'

'You should wake him. Ask him. See for yourself.'

Mum sighs and runs her fingers through her loose cornrows.

'Akita, you shouldn't have done that.'

'Mum, he wasn't in a good way.'

'All the more reason for you not to have done what you did,' she says in Arabic, anger brewing in her voice. She sighs again. 'Your brother is vulnerable right now, and more importantly, he's your *brother*, Akita. You know better than to treat family this way.'

'Why are you telling me this, and not Santo? He's the one that needs to hear it.'

'Akita ...' she says, a warning in her tone.

'No, it's not fair!' I say, my voice doing that thing it always does when I get upset. It goes all high and pitchy and I sound like I'm singing. 'Why am I the one that's always getting told off?' I say, swallowing hard, fighting back tears with all my might. 'Even when he's in the wrong?'

'Akita, that's enough!' she says in a loud whisper, her words cutting through the air, through me, like a knife.

'I'm tired,' she says quietly.

So am I, I want to scream. I'm so, *so* exhausted.

It's been hard to adjust to life being this way, but I'm doing my best and Santo isn't and it's just so unfair.

I say nothing more and lay back down.

Silent tears roll down the side of my face, puddling onto my pillow.

Mum grabs the door handle.

'I expected better from you, Akita,' she says before closing my bedroom door, leaving me in all-consuming darkness.

Taresai

Dragging Santo's large, limp body inside the house was like dragging a burlap sack full of bricks up a mountain.

I arrange the cushions and pull out several blankets, leaving him to sleep on the couch in the living room. I lay on my bed, showered and ready for sleep, exhausted from the day and drained from the night.

Usually I come home from work to a quiet house and leftover food in the oven for me. Usually, Santo and Akita save their fights for the weekend, but I suppose even the strongest of routines aren't immune to disturbance.

Things are difficult without Santino, several months on, which makes me laugh because it's not like he was particularly present when he was here. And yet, in his absence, this household has lost its order.

But when it's night and the kids have gone to sleep and the house falls silent, it all becomes too much. Loneliness sits on top of me, invading all my thoughts, until I feel so far away from my being.

If I were to scream, it feels as though no one would hear me.

When I fall into the deep abyss of loneliness, it tells me things, things like how our lives will never be the same, how I will never find peace again, not in this lifetime, not in the next.

These nights seem to last forever.

Until I hear Zandé's snores, or Amara's footsteps as she shuffles to the bathroom in the middle of the night. And every so often, I feel Ashanti crawl into my bed because she's had a bad dream. I feel the presence of my eldest daughter, asleep in her bed, and my eldest son, asleep on the couch.

Suddenly it isn't about me anymore. It's about them.

Suddenly the hallowing feelings of emptiness that have been awakened in the absence of Santino politely dismiss themselves, understanding that the kingdom of my soul is ruled only by my children.

My Ashanti is struggling the most with the adjustment. Santino calls twice a day, yet it seems like her separation anxiety from her father worsens with each day, each phone call.

Amara tries to be okay. For an eight-year-old she's extremely articulate when talking about how she's feeling, which makes managing her mood swings a lot easier.

Akita, though she speaks more than she used to when she was younger, can be quite a mystery to me, still. The words she speaks and the things she does are like pieces to a never-ending puzzle.

Time is not a luxury that I can afford to spend sitting down with her and talking until there's nothing left to talk about. She's helped in ways I couldn't have asked of her, with no complains or expressions of being burdened by the responsibilities I need her to take. Yet tonight was such a disappointing display. Leaving Santo out in the cold like that.

I can't blame Akita, of course. She's just a kid. She's twelve and a carer of her three younger siblings and an older brother who is absolutely no help. I can't even begin to imagine the kind of pressure she's already under.

Part of me is proud of her and another part of me breaks for her. I only wish it wasn't this way. This isn't the life I wanted for her. I wanted all my children to just be that, children, but fate had other plans.

Santo is going through his phases; this behaviour comes as no surprise to me. He has been refusing his medications and seeing his counsellor for almost a year. Santino and I fought it so hard that it began feeling like we were fighting Santo. Fighting his return to himself. He was thirteen and so, with trust, in him, in the universe and some higher power, we let him be.

There haven't been any major incidences or meltdowns that Santo has had, aside from his expulsion from Delany College.

He edited the pictures of his teacher's PowerPoint presentation during an entire school mass. The currents of his river have not changed, for better or for worse.

If Santo's father were still here it wouldn't change a thing; he'd still be behaving this way. It has afflicted him copiously to see Santino go, but in a way that I can't yet see, after all, how could a growing boy not be when abandoned by one's father?

I fear Santino's abandonment will show its face on Santo through time, and through time only.

The day his father left, Santo didn't even come out of his bedroom to say goodbye.

I get out of bed and into my slippers. It's a couple minutes to midnight. I walk to the chilly living room, throwing on an extra blanket over Santo and tucking it under his chin. I go down the hallway and stand outside the door of Akita's room.

I turn the doorknob slowly and step into the dark, cold space. Words can wait up to a lifetime in this household, but I just need to see her face, see her asleep so that I can too. It takes my eyes a moment to adjust to the darkness of her room. One second I'm looking at blackness, the next I'm glaring at Akita's empty bed and her wide-open window.

Akita

I breathe in the delicate cool of the night and try to breathe out my pyretic worries. It just gets too much; it's always too much, especially times like these.

Times when Mum takes Santo's side after all he does, just tips me over the edge. I find myself going for walks around the neighbourhood to calm myself, typically when the sun is out, but I guess there's a first time for everything.

I can't bear to think of how Mum would react if she knew I was wandering these streets at this late hour.

She worries about me, more than she used to when I was a kid. Mum worries about how some grown men look at me when I walk into a room, she worries about their hungry eyes and greedy hands. When I'm out on my own she cannot protect me from their gaze, and in the darkness of the night is where their foulness festers.

I know all this, and I should be scared, but tonight, freeing myself from the bondage of home is my highest concern. Tonight, Mum can worry all she wants; her peace of mind is not worth sacrificing my sanity over, especially since mine was sacrificed in Santo's favour.

I walk along the footpath dimly lit by the meagre streetlights of this rundown neighbourhood, casting dark shadows with its yellowy glow.

A full moon gleams bright, pressed into the autumn sky. The air is icy, and this hoodie is much too thin. I continue walking for a few blocks through the streets as my breaths come out in clouds.

We've lived in Corio for three years now. I was oblivious to its roughness until I started going to St Brigid's, four suburbs away, on the nice side of Geelong, where there's a beach, a pier, and the town centre. It seems that the further away the suburbs are from Corio the nicer they are. The further north or south, east, or even west you go, the more you'll likely find people living in stable homes. A mother and a father, two, maybe three kids if they're daring, a few cats here, an old dog there, and a bird if they're really bold, or they want to appear so. Those are places where everyday problems are: Sue from next door who keeps putting her bins out on our nature strip or the local grocery store discontinuing my favourite brand of bread. Normal people problems.

Despite it all, I like the rough edges of this neighbourhood, it took me a while to come to see it; but it's become a place whose chaos I am a part of. I like that this is where I come from.

The 3214.

I turn a corner and walk down a familiar avenue lined with leafless trees. I stop and stare at the moon, glowing in the sky like it owns it. Hanging over me, as if it's trying to whisper something in my ear.

I take a step forward until a low-hanging tree branch obstructs my view. I gaze at the moon through the branch. The longer I stare, the more it starts to look like a crack on the face of the moon, as if at any moment it will split in two and fall from the sky, exploding the night with iridescent white light.

I walk to the end of the avenue until I'm at the front door of my grandmother's house. I hesitate to knock. I have no idea what time it is, but I know it's late.

With a brief flash of courage, I knock, wait a few moments, and knock again. Then I hear shuffling footsteps, and see a light turn on from the window. Grandma opens the door and blinks at me, confused.

'Akita?' She asks, squinting.

'Hi, Haboba,' I smile, tears stinging my eyes.

She ushers me in and sits me down on one of her large, squashy armchairs that feels like one of her hugs, something I could sink into until I disappear.

She places a warm mug of black coffee in my hands and reignites the fire of her gas heater. She drapes a blanket over her knees and cups her own mug in her hands. I feel Haboba staring at me with her silvery eyes, and I find I can't bring myself to look up at her, so instead I stare into my reflection in the dark liquid.

Tonight's the first time I've shown up to her house at this late hour, unannounced. I wouldn't usually; my Haboba, gentle and loving as she is, above all, is a woman of order, and this surprise visit from her twelve-year-old granddaughter this late at night is anything but.

'I made it after supper,' she says, pointing to the mug in my hands. 'I roasted the coffee beans a little after six o'clock.'

'It smells good.' I inhale the steam rising from the mug, my body taking time to adjust to the warmth of her home.

Haboba eyes me, sitting so incredibly still.

When I feel a little braver, I study her face, study the soft lines etched on her mahogany brown skin, how her full lips naturally droop downwards in a stern frown, how the fluffy bits of her white hair look like cashmere. But I feel a reluctance to look into the pools of her eyes. Haboba's face, and every iota of her being, is sure, definite, absolute, and yet so impossibly hard to read. Whether disappointed or thrilled, her face is unchanged, never straying far beyond the image of her I have in my mind, from my earliest memories of her to these waking moments.

'So,' she says simply, 'are you going to tell me what's wrong, or are you going to sit there wordlessly?'

With her sharp tongue, words pelt out of her mouth like tiny asteroids, without the force of volume for a harder hit.

Whenever Haboba speaks, her every word presses itself firmly into my mind as if it belongs there. With such power it's easy for me to think of her as more a primordial phenomenon rather than a human being, someone who wasn't born but came into existence just as the stars do.

I shift uncomfortably in my seat, still unable to bring myself to speak.

'You know, Akita,' she says slowly, 'I can't actually read minds, despite what Santo may have told you.'

I smile, then I frown just as quickly.

'Santo doesn't tell me much these days,' I say, angrily wiping my runny nose. 'He behaves like a two-year-old. Even Zandé has more manners than him.'

Haboba sips her coffee without taking her eyes off me.

'He's no help at all, Haboba. It's just me and Mama – and she works most of the time, so it's mainly me. The three kids are hard enough, so I don't understand why Santo always makes things harder for me, and I don't get why everyone always takes his side! Why? Because his brain is half-cooked?'

I feel bad saying those things, and a little surprised that those words slipped out of my mouth. But I'm finding it hard to contain the anger rising in my chest. Recounting it and speaking about it in Arabic only fires me up even more.

'Why is it my problem, Haboba?' I continue, calmly this time. 'I'm happy to help around the house, because that's what big sisters do. But I refuse to look after a fourteen-year-old boy who knows right from wrong, who knows actions have consequences, yet he chooses not to obey.'

I take a deep breath, and Haboba watches me steadily, unaffected by the words I speak. 'Tonight, I got sick of it. I locked him out of the house. He fell asleep on the grass. I know it was wrong, but I'm not sorry. I don't regret it; I'd do it again if I had to. If Mama isn't going to discipline him then I will.'

I take a sip of my coffee and I set it on the table.

Haboba stares at me. We sit in silence, the intensity of my words hanging above us. It takes everything in me to hold her gaze, to refrain from running out of the front door and pretending I never came or said anything.

She drinks the last of her coffee and sets it down on the table. I don't know how long we sit in stillness for – a couple of seconds? Five minutes? Ten hours?

Haboba's face only moves when she blinks, her silvery eyes fixed on me, giving nothing away of the things they've seen.

She moves ever so slowly, wears her gold and patterned fabrics ever so proudly. Under the blanket and through the printed skirt draping over her knees I see the craters left on her skin from bullet wounds. Even though they're the same scars I've seen since I can remember, I catch myself staring and can't bring myself to look away. Those bullet wounds are secrets that whisper to me the pain my Haboba has endured, the fight she put up to survive, and serve as sobering reminders that one cannot live so long in a place so rough without having scars that kiss the skin.

I feel like surrendering to the armchair I sit on, letting it swallow me up into its folds. I grab my mug from the table, and then I grab Haboba's before I know what I'm doing. I walk them over to the kitchen sink and rinse them out with soap and warm water. I dry the mugs and set them on the dish rack. I look over to Haboba. Her eyes are still fixed on the dents my body made on the armchair, sunken with the weight of my ghost, as if I still sit there, as if I never got up and walked to the kitchen.

I dry my hands and walk back into the living room, the seat still warm when I sit back down.

'Did I ever tell you about your Haboba Akana? Your father's mother?' Haboba says finally.

'Yes,' I say, confused by the question in this context, but interested to see where it may go.

'You've told me lots of times. I'm sad I never got to meet her.'

'Sadly, she passed. Seven days before you were born.'

'Oh,' I say, 'I didn't know that.'

'Didn't know that she passed?'

'I didn't know she passed seven days before I was born.'

Haboba takes me in with her gaze and smiles wistfully, but I feel like she isn't looking at me, I feel like she's looking past me, beyond me, into a different time.

'I knew her since childhood. I didn't like her at first; I hated her, but we grew to be best friends. She had your father; I had your mother.'

I stare at Haboba's face in the softness of the warm firelight. As she speaks, I see her face in a way I haven't before. I see the striking resemblance she bears to my mother, or my mother, to her. I've always known that she's my mother's mother, but it's the first time I'm seeing her as such, and it's perplexing.

'Akana was a special soul,' Haboba continues. 'An otherworldly spirit. She would see things before they would happen, speak to people who weren't there.'

Haboba's gaze settles on me, and I watch us the dim colours of this dark room dance in her eyes.

'Akana had a loyal following of serpents at the foot of her dwelling. She would rub sesame seed oil on their heads, and they'd slither around her hut, warding off evil.'

I lean back on the squashy armchair with ease, from tiredness or enchantment, I yet don't know.

'Some people in the village including your father, thought her ill. But that wasn't it. Akana was a question to this world of answers were there were none for her. And that was how she liked it.'

I feel my eyes begin to droop from tiredness and my body itch with sleep as Haboba's deep and smooth voice cradles me in the memories she speaks.

'It was like she was placed in this world for a mission and taken out of it only because someplace else needed her more. Then, on the first day of the fourth month all those years ago, the serpents disappeared, and Akana was no longer in this world that she was not of.'

Haboba is quiet for a moment, in the silence, my tired mind wakes a little and tries to figure out why she might be telling me this. Then something changes in her eyes.

Haboba doesn't move, but in this very moment I know that she can see everything, all of me, from the tiny freckle above my lip to the last braid on the bottom of my head.

'When Akana parted with this world, there was a sadness we shared among the village, she wasn't loved by many, but she was respected by all, and the weight of her existence was something of a comfort to those who knew her.'

I feel a pull and I lean forward, my eyes on Haboba in this dark room, lit only by her and the flames of the gas heater.

'But along with that, there was a relief, a relief that lingered for years in her absence and nobody could put words to it. Not even I, nor your father, but it was palpable.'

She doesn't move, Haboba doesn't even blink.

'It's only a few years later that I reckoned with the truth that it was because Akana didn't belong here. Her soul travelled here for something, many things, and when she left, that was her homegoing.'

Her eyes flicker and land on me again, only this time, I'm not sure what she sees.

'She knew of you; Akana, knew before any of us did. She would speak to you, years before you were born. She knew of your arrival before your conception.'

I wait for Haboba to say more, to elaborate, to share with me some words of wisdom or guidance, anything. But she doesn't.

I feel the air around me shift as I come back to reality or ascend to another plane, or somewhere in between; suddenly filled with a need to go home.

Chapter 28

Geelong

Akita

My alarm wakes me with a start.

I groan into my pillow and blink myself awake. I sit up on my bed, staring at the carpet as last night's events come flooding back.

My stomach sinks into itself; unfortunately it wasn't all a bad dream. I pull the blanket over my head and wrap myself in it like a caterpillar in a cocoon, but without the promise of wings when I emerge.

I sink into my mattress and try to make myself as small as possible. I let a few moments pass, then I get up, walk into the bathroom and splash cold water on my face.

I go to Amara and Ashanti's room, flicking their light on and off until they wake up. I walk the length of their bedroom and part the curtains.

When the girls are dressed in the green and yellow of the St Paul's uniform, Amara in my hand-me-downs and Ashanti's in Amara's, I go to wake Zandé and get him ready for day-care.

I place the dishes from breakfast in the sink on top of last night's dishes, and I hurry them outside when I hear Mariam's car pull up the driveway.

Mariam is a friend of Mum's and a carer for the kids. She gets paid by the government to take them to school and pick them up.

It's 7.56 am by the time Mariam drives away with the kids in the backseat of her minivan. I have just over twenty minutes until my school bus arrives, the only bus that comes to this side of town to get to St Brigid's.

I walk back into the house and go to my bedroom. I place my textbooks along with my unfinished homework into my bag and go to pull my jumper over my school dress. The wool of my school jumper feels like sandpaper against the scratches on my arms, which hurt more today than they did yesterday. I make my way to the kitchen and put the lunchbox Mum packed for me this morning in my bag. I'm surprised to find food in there. After last night I'd expected Mum to leave it empty.

I pick an apple from the fruit bowl and bite into it. I've never been a breakfast-eater like the rest of my siblings. Food in the belly early in the morning coupled with a thirty-minute bus ride is a recipe for sickness. I do a lap around the house with my school bag on my back and the keys in my hands, making sure everything is locked.

As I walk to the front door, I pass the living room and only then realise that Santo is nowhere to be seen.

Taresai

Last night, sleep only came to me when I heard Akita's bedroom window slide open and close as she snuck back in. I didn't yell at her, didn't go to her room to talk to her, didn't even get up from my bed.

As relief eased my anxiety, it also gave permission for my worry to turn to fury. Akita knows far better than to wander through the streets at night, I don't care how upset she is.

She remains none the wiser to my knowledge of her sneaking out and I'm not yet sure what to do with that.

Shall I confront her and meet her with my scold or simply ask the question and see if she confesses?

She was gone for three quarters of an hour and though it was the first time I'd caught her in the act, a few weeks ago I noticed that her bedroom window is without a flyscreen.

I have so many questions for her, especially concerning tonight, but that must wait until I'm afforded time to ask.

So, this morning, I wake up at 5 am, I set out the girls' school uniforms, and packed their bags and their lunchboxes like I do every school morning.

And tonight, I'll come home and we'll have dinner. I'll take some time to talk to my daughter and afterwards, I'll ask her what she wants for her twelfth birthday which was almost three weeks ago and without a celebration.

Chapter 29

Geelong

Akita

I clip a gold pin into my straightened hair and smooth it down once more.

I'm seventeen today.

I take a step back and stare at myself in the mirror. My forehead looks massive. This brown lipstick feels like cement on my lips, the mascara heavy on my eyelashes, and my plucked eyebrows look unnaturally pristine. I adjust the neckline of my blouse, anxious not to show too much cleavage, and I tug at the hem of my skirt that floats above my knees.

Mum knocks on the bathroom door for the third time in ten minutes to let me know that my guests have arrived.

This is the first birthday that I've agreed to celebrate after the hot disaster that was my fourteenth birthday, when Santo drove Aunty Asélle's minivan through our front gate and broke his arm.

Lifetimes ago. It feels strange to be at the centre of attention again, to have everyone gathered here to celebrate my stepping into another year. I don't know what to do, how to be, how to act.

Outside the door I hear distinct sounds start to build on top of the music: chattering and laughing; some voices are familiar, others I can't single out. Damn, how long have I been in here? I love birthday parties and celebrations. I love blowing balloons and putting them around the house for Zandé's birthdays, I love hanging up pink streamers for Ashanti, I love wrapping Amara's presents. But I don't know how to be when everyone is celebrating mine.

I hear another knock on the door, too soft to be Mum's.

'Yeah?'

'Akita!' Zandé yells, mouth close to the door. 'Your white friends are here.'

I wash my hands and dry them, then I lather them up with Mum's floral-scented lotion. I step out of the bathroom and into the hallway. We moved into this new house three months ago yet its layout still confuses me. It's in Norlane, the next suburb from Corio, only ten minutes away from Hugh Court. To my right is the front living room, adjacent to the front door where my aunts, my mother and Haboba have congregated. To my left is the kitchen and back living room where I see five white faces among the sea of all my cousins. Four of those faces belong to my friends from school: Chloe, Emily, Isla and Jade.

I wave and smile apologetically at them, then Jacob meets my gaze.

I'm nervous enough as it is having my friends from school in my house for the very first time, in the company of my entire family, let alone my boyfriend, who, for tonight, has to pretend he's not.

I make my way to the living room to greet my grandmother and my aunts, to thank them for their coming.

* * *

Most of the night passes by and I catch myself having a good time for brief moments in between. I float from group to group, treading along the cusp, evenly spreading my attention to every single person who came here for me. Swimming far out, instead of diving deep.

There's not enough of me to indulge in a heated conversation with my school friends, to listen to Evelyn's quarter-life crisis, to dance until my limbs feel weak with Ines and my sisters, to be wrapped up in glee with Jacob.

Inviting him over is possibly the most daring thing I've ever done. Our entire one-and-a-half-year relationship has been in secrecy, and it's going to be kept that way. Throughout the night we find ourselves creeping along the baseline of safety, careful not to be alone together for more than a minute so long as to not raise suspicion. As far as anyone knows our friendship is purely platonic, and if anyone needs more convincing my backup plan is to say that Jacob is gay. It's foolproof, I hope, but I still sweat when I feel eyes on us standing less than a metre apart.

I spend most of the night sitting with Evelyn and Ines, avoiding my friends, all of whom have already turned eighteen and had expectations that there'd be alcohol.

Evelyn keeps me from hanging out with our other cousins, Heema, Halima and Samira, who she calls the wicked three. I don't mind keeping my distance from them, though Mum nags at me for having favourite cousins, especially when I show it.

Ines and I have grown close over the past couple of years. Once I learned to separate each of my cousins from the other, it became easier to decipher their differences, who is who, and what makes them who they are.

Ines is mild-mannered and subtle in everything she does, unlike her three older sisters. Samira, having no sense of identity, clings onto Heema and Halima like a third wheel, following their mean-spirited nature like one would a religion.

I often wonder how Ines lives with them, how she survives with her clean heart when she's so brutally outnumbered.

I'm filled with relief when Mum says it's time to cut the cake. They all sing 'Happy Birthday' as I stand awkwardly, smiling crookedly at everyone in the room, wishing for the everlasting song to come to an end.

Jacob is the first to leave. He doesn't have any cake.

I walk him out the front gate when his father arrives.

I'm not sure if it was the greatest idea to invite him, but he was eager to come, despite all the stupid rules I had to enforce.

'Goodnight, Akita,' he smiles softly, his eyes sad. 'Happiest of birthdays.'

Taresai

'Did you have a good time?' I ask.

'Yeah,' Akita smiles. 'And it seems like everyone else did too.'

It's 34 minutes past midnight and Akita and I clean up the remnants of what was apparently a good time.

'It was nice to finally meet all your friends,' I say, emptying the biscuits into a container.

'Yeah,' she says distantly, sweeping up the timber kitchen floor.

I worried about Akita being a loner for years. She would say she had friends at St Brigid's, but she'd never speak of them. She wouldn't invite them home the way Amara invites her friends, she wouldn't go to their houses like Ashanti goes to her friend's houses, she doesn't meet up at a park and throw footballs with her friends the way Zandé does with his.

It became hard for me to believe that they weren't made up, that she didn't do things with her friends because she had none. Tonight was a relief. Five friends came to her party.

'So,' I say, trying to sound casual, 'who was the boy?'

'Boy?'

'The skinny boy? Curly brown hair in the blue button-up?'

'Oh ... that's just Jacob.'

I have an inkling that Jacob isn't 'just Jacob'. You could feel it in the air between them.

Puppy love, and he stunk of it all night. I saw the way he looked at her, and the way she nervously averted his eyes. I don't know how I feel about it, but I suppose I'll act oblivious for as long as Akita wants me to.

'The one from Delany College?'

'Yep, that's the one.' She forces a very dry giggle.

'How did the two of you meet again?' I ask this because St Brigid's is an all-girls Catholic school and Delany's is an all-boys private school.

'Interschool athletics,' she says, smiling, not meeting my eyes.

'And the blonde girl?' I ask putting the leftover cake in the fridge.

'That's Chloe.' Akita breathes, relief in her shoulders.

'She's the one with a hippie mother, right?'

'She's not a hippie, Mum, she just has dreadlocks and doesn't eat meat.'

'Darling, every white woman with locs is a hippie.'

'She's probably my closest friend,' Akita says, holding the broomstick close to her chest. 'We've been pretty much inseparable since Year 7. Same goes for Emily.'

'Emily, she's the round one with the blue eyes.'

'Yes,' Akita says through gritted teeth. I should probably refrain from calling her friend round.

'And the short girl with the red hair?'

'That's Isla. Brainiac. We have this running joke that she's going to work for NASA or create her own version of it or something.' Akita laughs as she dumps the rubbish from the dustpan to the bin. 'And then there's Jade.'

'Ah,' I say, confidence in my tone. 'The Chinese one.'

'Vietnamese, Mum, *Vietnamese.*'

'Oh.'

'Yeah ... Jade's nice ...'

I wait for Akita to say more, but she doesn't. She yawns and absentmindedly smooths down her hair that was straightened at the start of the night. Now, as Akita's guard has fallen, her hair rises. She looks like a tired dandelion after sunset.

In the other room I hear my phone ringing. I go to answer it, leaving Akita in the kitchen. I instantly recognise the sixteen-digit international phone number stretched across the screen. I pick it up and respond with a 'Hello.' Then I wait three seconds until I hear Santino's voice on the other line.

I speak to him for less than a minute. Yes, I'm fine, the kids are doing great, nope, still no word from Santo, no. Zandé injured his wrist during basketball practice, not his ankle; yes, Akita had a good time today.

I walk back into the kitchen, phone in hand, Akita looks up from the sink when she sees me.

'It's your dad,' I say.

I can't be certain, but for a moment I think I see a flicker of light vanish from her eyes. Maybe it's because she's tired, but I wouldn't be angry at her if it isn't. This is the sixth birthday of Akita's that he's missed.

She takes the phone from my hand and begins speaking into it as if she hasn't done it almost a hundred times in the past six years.

I watch her as she paces back and forth, talking to her father the same way she'd talk to a distant relative. I notice how she tiptoes in circles, the way she pulls on her ear lobe when she's nervous.

Time has been kind to her, and unkind to me for moving so fast.

It seems like only yesterday she was eight, now here she is, a young lady before me, in her last year of high school, standing taller than I am, and all I did was blink.

Tonight was a celebration of thanks to her – for all the dishes washed, all the nappies changed, the meals cooked, the laundry folded. The hours of sleep she'd lost doing the things I couldn't do. I'm glad she agreed to celebrate this birthday, even though I know she did it more for me than for her own delight. She deserved it and so much more.

I can't say any of this to her. Not in any language. So, I smile at her and hope that she receives the beams of love and gratitude my heart is sending her.

I walk to my room to give Akita a private moment with her father.

Birthdays for me always have been when I feel the most sentiment, the heavy, bittersweet catharsis. I think on my sons and daughters. Watching them grow has been one of life's greatest gifts and privileges.

Even the ugly parts, even when things get so messy and obscure that it weakens me.

I pity Santino, I really do. Six years he's been in Sudan with nothing but phone calls to and the photos I send of our children. He's impeded to all of it, *willingly*. He's stuck in some sort of vortex with an image of who our children were, missing out on who they're becoming in each waking moment they breathe.

Akita

When Mum handed me the phone tonight, there was a small, irrational part of my mind that thought she was going to say it was Santo on the other side of that line.

It's stupid, I know, but in that short second, hope expanded in my heart like a bubble, glowing and growing in an instant, but that bubble burst just as quickly.

Now, as I lie in bed, this week, and seventeen years behind me, hurt takes shape in the place where hope once was.

I feel so exhausted. My body aches like I've been carrying the weight of the world for an entire season, tensed up with anxiety over a night that has finally passed. I feel a sense of relief when my body starts going limp, my mind swirling with thoughts before my arrival at sleep.

It was nice to talk to Dad, though; he calls every birthday. It's pretty much the only time of the year we speak. He stopped calling every day before a full year passed.

I haven't heard from Santo in ten months, it's my first birthday without him. The last time we saw him, it was a totally ordinary, un-special day. He came home as we were having dinner and he went straight to his room without saying anything to anyone. None of us batted an eye, that was normal by that point. He'd disappear for days at a time and stay at friends' houses that we knew nothing of.

I think by then too, Mum had already accepted that there was no pacifying Santo.

He landed himself in juvie, not long after that, for drug related charges. When Mum told us, she was neither sombre nor enraged, but there was the slightest note of relief in her tone.

Santo was then moved to a minimum-security prison just outside of Melbourne.

They must've released him because last I heard, Santo was couch surfing.

Mum said he can come home if he cleaned up his act. He must've decided against it, because his bedroom is now where Mum folds the laundry and keeps her treadmill.

We don't talk about him much in the house. We don't speak our pain; we don't share it. But he remains in my thoughts in private.

My god, how much I miss him. I miss how he was. There's no getting used to his absence.

I hug my blanket tightly around my shoulders.

A memory slithers its way through and sits in the centre of my mind. I think about the day Santo got expelled from St Paul's primary, all those years ago. He punched Calum in the nose, the boy who bullied me. St Paul's was the first school Santo liked, felt safe in. He had friends, he was popular and his teachers adored him. Yet he threw that all away for me.

Then I remember the time he shoved me into the pool and tried to 'fake' drown me, and the time he stole my thirteenth birthday money and I got smacked for it because he wouldn't admit he took it.

It was $345, Mum, Dad, Aunty Asélle pooled money together. Even Uncle Messai sent money from Sweden. I wanted to buy textbooks with it for the school year which Mum couldn't afford at the time.

I chuckle softly, semi-aware of the tears streaming, carving wet paths down the side of my face, dampening my pillow.

Santo, the biggest pain in my arse, but my greatest keeper. This is a quiet life without him, yet my life knows no peace. I wonder, as I sink deeper into sleep, where in the world Santo could be, wonder how many, if any, nights of sleep he has lost over me?

Chapter 30

Geelong

Akita

'Eighteen out of twenty,' Jacob smirks, setting the flashcards down on his desk. 'Not bad.'

'Damn it,' I whisper, sitting up on the rug.

I've got an economics exam tomorrow morning. Generally speaking, my marks for the year have been sitting steadily on the above average mark and though my grades in economics are promising, it's the subject I struggle with most since dropping maths at the end of Year 11.

'Read them to me again,' I say, lying back down on the rug, my eyes on the ceiling.

'Akita ...' I hear Jacob get up from his desk and shuffle toward me. He stands above my head, obstructing my view of his very fancy ceiling lamp and the ornate carvings around it.

'One last time,' I say with a smile. 'Please?'

Jacob softly exhales through his nostrils and lies down on the rug beside me, flattening his soft brown curls.

'Fine.'

I remember the first time I came to Jacob's house to study, back when he and I were just friends. I felt like I was committing a crime to be inside the bedroom of a boy I wasn't related to. That was when I was fifteen.

These days I'm here twice a week, and nearly every day when there's an exam on the horizon. That's pretty much all he and I do together. Study. We make a good team.

I did meet Jacob at interschool athletics – that part wasn't a lie. He was one of the only boys who was gracious in defeat. He wasn't bitter because he was beaten by me in the mixed-gender hundred metre sprint.

Jacob is exceedingly bright and extraordinarily athletic, but he's had no option to be anything else. Jacob's had tutors and personal trainers at his beck and call ever since he could talk. He was born with a silver spoon in his mouth, white skin to the bone and an XY chromosome. It isn't a bad thing, none of it is, though I am pretty much the opposite of what he is. He's had an upper hand in life, and I can't use my own to climb because I'm busy fighting off problems Jacob can't even imagine with his big brain and large blue eyes.

'Twenty out of twenty!' he chants.

'Yes!'

'Fifth time's a charm,' he grins, and I shoot him a look.

We lie on the rug, on the floor of his bedroom, staring wordlessly at the ceiling, letting moments of comfortable silence pass us by.

'Jacob?'

'Hmm?'

'Do you ever get scared … of like … the future?'

'What do you mean?' he asks softly. I see him turn to face me in the corner of my eye, but I only focus my gaze on the ceiling.

I'm unsure of what I'm asking or the feelings that provoked the question, so I stare upward in hopes of finding what I'm searching for.

'What do you mean?' he asks again.

'I don't know. Say I fail tomorrow's exam, say I fail all my exams for the year. Would it all have been for … nothing?' I clasp my hands, pressing my palms together to settle the anxiety that's trying to trickle its way out of me. 'Where would I go from there?' I look to Jacob. His face twitches slightly and he takes a prolonged blink.

'What?' I whisper when he doesn't say anything.

'No, nothing, it's just … I just thought you meant something else.'

'What did you think I meant?' I ask, sitting up on my elbows.

'I thought you were talking about us.' Jacob lets out a nervous chuckle.

'Why would I be worried about us? Wait, are you?!'

'No! no, no … not at all, Keeks. I'd say *excited* more than anything.'

'Excited? What for?' I ask, lying my head back down on the carpet.

'I want school to be over and done with so we could actually … you know … be boyfriend and girlfriend.'

'Jacob,' I scoff, 'what have we been for the past two years?'

'I know, and I guess what I'm trying to say is: I'm looking forward to having more time together when we graduate. We can actually hang out, do things together. This wouldn't be the only time I see you. Just you.'

I don't know what to say to that. It takes me so far away from my own worries because it seems like such a small thing to think about. A speck in the grand scheme of things.

Still, I didn't know Jacob felt this way, not because his feelings are deep-rooted and hard to find, but because I didn't think to look. We see each every week, at our schools' leadership assemblies or interschool recitals, and during afternoons like this to study. I only now see that it's not enough.

I don't know if I should apologise; it doesn't seem right saying those words, but to say nothing also feels wrong. There are parts of me that want to do romantic boyfriend/girlfriend things that people our age do, but the only way this works is if we're studying, if Jacob is somehow part of an element in my life that is integral, like my education. Otherwise, what's the point? I mean, what am I supposed to tell Mum?

Jacob knows I can't tell her that we're dating. 'It's not because you're white!' I'd say, it's simply because I don't think I'm allowed to have a boyfriend. Not in high school, anyway.

I don't know, it's all so complicated.

'You're going to do fine tomorrow, Akita,' Jacob assures after a while. 'Amazing even. Believe it or not, Year 12 isn't the be all and end all. Do the best you can, and you'll be fine.'

I will do the best I can, but that doesn't mean I'm going to be fine. I don't have the privilege for one to equal the other.

'Alright!' Jacob proclaims. 'That's enough studying for tonight.' He sits up and slaps me on the thigh. 'You hungry?'

We join Jacob's parents for dinner downstairs in their dining room, where a magnificent chandelier hangs from the high ceiling. Jacob is the only child to his blue-eyed, blonde-haired parents, Simone, and Chester Warren. Simone owns a chain of health food stores around the state, and Chester is an executive at a Melbourne print agency.

When I first met Jacob's parents I was petrified of speaking to them. I didn't even want to ask them questions about their lives in case they asked about mine.

And then what would I say? I'm the second of five children to a hardworking mother who I barely see and a runaway father who I talk to every birthday? Oh, and I have an estranged addict of a brother who I love dearly, despite his incapacity to love me?

I came to find that Simone and Chester are lovely. When time comes and they ask about my family, they don't pry, and more than anything they seem most interested in me, in Akita.

'Akita,' Chester announces when he sees me trailing after Jacob. 'I didn't know you were here.'

'Hi Mr Warren, Jacob and I were just studying upstairs.'

Chester is probably the same age as Dad, but there is something youthful in the way he looks. Healthy, but also the epitome of what a full life without worries looks like.

I sit next to Jacob, across from his father.

'Akita has an economics exam tomorrow,' Jacob says, placing a slice of vegan lasagne on my plate.

'Economics?' Chester looks up at me, his blue eyes set on the rim of his glasses.

'Yeah, I tried to be strategic with my subject selection this year.'

'Remind me again what your electives are, darling?' asks Simone, handing me the salad bowl. Simone, too, looks years younger than she is, but her youthfulness is also in her spirit.

'Economics, global politics, sociology, visual communication and English literature.'

'Have you had a think about what you want to study next year at university?' enquires Chester.

'That's assuming she wants to go, dear,' says Simone.

'Yeah, I have every intention of going to uni, and I've given a lot of thought as to what I want to study, but I'm still unsure.' I shove the lasagne in my mouth before it gets too cold.

'What about you, Jacob?' asks Chester.

'What about me, Dad?'

'After that gap year of yours, are you still keen on majoring in philosophy?' he says, in a way so patronising it makes my skin crawl. I have come to find very quickly that though Chester might look young in years, his thoughts of the world are merely those held by an old man.

'Yeah,' Jacob smiles cheerfully, without missing a beat. 'I feel like one can never know too much in this life. Not even you, Dad.'

In the pocket of my school dress I feel my phone buzz. I check the time on the ornate grandfather clock behind Simone. 6.37 pm. Mum's expecting me home before eight, so it won't be her calling.

I ignore my phone, assuming it's not urgent, then it buzzes again.

I dig it out, hoping I don't come across as rude, though at the same time I don't think the family I sit with are paying enough attention to notice.

A passive-aggressive discussion ensues between Jacob and his father as Simone tries to be the voice of reason. This is pretty much what it's been like in the Warren household for most the time I've been in their company.

I stare at my screen. Three missed calls from Evelyn. Followed by a text message with five short words, one simple instruction.

Meet me in the park.

I know Evelyn enough to understand that this is a distress signal, but beyond that I have no idea. It could mean anything.

For all I know she's run away from home for the third time this year, she's stranded, or maybe she needs someone to vent to about her mother, my Aunty Anette.

I excuse myself from the table and go upstairs into Jacob's room to grab my things.

'Everything alright?' Jacob asks, handing me my school jumper.

'I'm not sure, it's Evelyn,' I say slipping on my leather school shoes. 'I figured I'd call her back on the way to the bus stop.'

Jacob throws on a hoodie and slides on his runners. 'I'll walk you.'

We walk down the hills of Newtown in Geelong's west, through the neighbourhood's wealthiest residences, just as the sun disappears behind a mega-mansion in the distance.

'Did she pick up?' Jacob asks.

I shake my head. 'No answer.'

Jacob is the only person in my life who I confide in, second only to Chloe who I feel sometimes is too delicate for such things. He knows about Dad and the complex feelings I have about him, he knows about Santo, he knows about Mum and all my younger siblings, and how imperative it is that I keep him a secret.

He knows about Evelyn, how in the past couple of years she's shed the clean image of her strict upbringing and exploded into a 'problem child' in the words of Aunty Anette. I know that Evelyn is troubled, but I don't think she's a problem child. She's tired and nobody can fault her because who wouldn't be as the first and only daughter of the merciless Anette Deng?

We walk past St Brigid's, my school of six years. It looks eerie at night without the people and light of day. Large building blocks with high, panelled windows and expensive art sculptures tower over premium grass and high-grade asphalt behind tall, iron gates.

I remember my first day, stepping out from the bus and through these gates. I'd missed the orientation because Mum had to work. I had no idea where to go, but there Evelyn was, waiting for me in the courtyard. She showed me to the canteen, the toilets and all the important places on the junior side of the campus before we were called to homeroom.

'Are you gonna go see her?' Jacob asks as we walk around the corner and arrive at the bus stop, the same bus stop me, and Amara walk to every day after school.

'I don't think I have a choice.'

'You have the choice to go straight home?' He shrugs, and I shoot him a look.

'Look, I only say that because it's getting late, it'll be dark by the time you get home, and you've got your economics exam tomorrow morning.'

'Yeah, I know, Jacob. But she needs me, alright? She's family.'

In the distance we see the headlights of the number 10 bus arriving. Jacob squeezes me tight, and I promise to text him when I get home. I sit a few rows from the back of the bus, waving to Jacob as the engine coughs and the wheels roll.

The bus journey is slow. I stare out the window as the houses pass, trying not to breathe in the faint smell of urine and lemon air freshener. Bus number 10. Graffitied seats, sticky floor, scratched-up windows.

The buses that travel to my neighbourhood are always the most impaired; the newer ones are saved for the nicer areas with the scenic routes.

There's no one else on the bus, just me and the driver. Nobody from this side of town would want to go to Corio at this hour of the evening. I don't mind it, though. Bus number 10 is home to many unusual characters and altercations during the day anyway, ones I try to avoid.

It's the same one I catch since moving to Corio and then to our new house in Norlane.

There isn't much that separates the two suburbs, Corio and Norlane. You never want to be walking the streets alone at night. People still leave their unwanted furniture on the nature strip for others to have, and anything nice left in your front yard will be stolen by the morning. Poverty and camaraderie.

I step off the bus a couple of stops after my house and walk to the park where Evelyn and I have spent countless nights venting, underneath Corio's sky, about the ugliness of the universe.

I see her unmistakable figure sitting on a swing, rocking gently underneath the yellow streetlights.

I set my school bag down on the bark and sit on the swing beside her. Evelyn doesn't look at me, her gaze fixed on empty space. Her eyes are glassy, the tip of her nose shiny and wet. Cold wind blows, dragging dead leaves across the pavement, and dark clouds roll in the sky. The air reeks with the promise of thunder and rain.

'Beautiful night,' Evelyn says after a while, and I laugh because I think it's anything but.

'I love stormy weather,' I say, swinging slightly. 'When I'm in my room, at home and warm. I like my chaos outside.'

Evelyn looks at me and laughs. 'That's a cruel joke to make. I find my peace in chaos.'

'Okay, so talk to me, big girl, what's the matter?'

'Same shit, Akita.'

Evelyn wears a beanie and a crimson hoodie. She looks thin and cold and so small and frail, as if the wind could snap her in two.

'Your mum? Did you guys fight?'

'Yeah …' she says, her voice breaking. For a moment I think she's going to cry, then she takes a cigarette out of her pocket and lights it. Evelyn takes a long drag, the tip of the cigarette glowing in the dark like an orange beacon, a flare gun in the middle of the ocean.

'What?' she says, rolling her eyes.

'It's a filthy habit, Ev.'

'Oh please, Kita,' she laughs bitterly.

'What?'

'How's that boyfriend of yours? The white one? Told your parents yet?'

'You know I haven't, Evelyn.'

She looks at me like it's something I should be ashamed of, like having a boyfriend – a white one – is equally as shameful as a lung full of tar.

Evelyn's head drops. She looks at her lap, blowing smoke from her mouth.

'I'm sorry,' she whispers.

'It's okay,' I shrug.

We fall silent as the wind howls, leaves rustle and the swings creak.

'You know,' I begin, attempting to uplift her energy, 'I don't think Mum and Dad would care so much about *who* I'm with, it's more the fact that I have a boyfriend that would send them into cardiac arrest.'

'That's progressive!' Evelyn cackles. 'But why do you care what your dad thinks anyway?'

'Because he's my dad, Evelyn.'

'And, where is he?'

'He'll be back,' I say, feeling foolish for saying something so naïve.

'Right, and so will mine.'

I kiss my teeth.

'Ev, why did you drag me out here in the cold?'

'Man, what is it with African parents and boyfriends?!' Evelyn exclaims, ignoring me.

'I don't know,' I say. 'Fear of a daughter getting knocked up? Without a boyfriend, that fear is kinda … well, out of sight, out of mind?'

'So, they expect you to go your entire young adult life without one until they find one for you to marry. What? Is it only okay when it's on their terms?'

'It's all they know, Ev,' I say, already growing impatient. 'They were brought up in a different time, in a different place, in different ways.'

We both fall quiet. Sometimes I feel like talking to Evelyn is like talking to a brick wall. I often don't even know why she calls for me when she's having a crisis every other month. We always dance around what's truly bothering her; we talk about everything that's wrong with the world before she finally opens and tells me what's going on in hers. It takes a while before she lets down her guard and then it's like everything at once.

'Kita … do you ever feel like … you're not meant for this world? Like God – or whoever is in charge – made a mistake by putting you here?'

'Evelyn …' I say softly, my heart shattering, 'why would you say that?'

'Because it's true. For as long as I can remember, Akita, I've always felt it. I … I followed Mum's rules because I didn't think I had a choice. I wasn't defiant, I thought I'd burn in hell for all of eternity if I didn't obey her and I felt wicked for even thinking she was wrong.'

Evelyn puts the light out on her cigarette and places the butt in the pocket of her hoodie. 'Then I grew up, unlearned a lot of things, separated myself from her.'

Evelyn puts her hands in the pocket of her hoodie and hunches her shoulders to protect herself from the cold.

'I started asking questions, got beaten for them, started becoming my own person, got beaten for that, but I'm now at the point where I'd rather take a beating every hour of the day than be someone I'm not. Someone she's worked so hard for me to become.' She exhales sharply.

'But as much as she tries, I'll never stop being Evelyn, the med school dropout after a trimester of study, the one who refuses to marry all the rich suitors she can find, the one who would rather die than be a miserable housewife to a man I can't love.'

The wind blows the cold night air all around us, the clouds thunder in the sky, and yet, this moment feels so still.

'We fought again today. Me and Mum,' sighs Evelyn.

'I figured.'

'She slapped me and I slapped her right back.'

I gasp and she smiles.

'For shaving my head again, can you believe that?'

She chuckles softly. 'She still thinks she can tell me what to do with my body.'

'She'll lose her shit when she sees the tattoo on your thigh,' I say, and a smile creeps onto Evelyn's face.

I suddenly feel very tired.

'Come on, it's getting late, you can stay the night,' I say, putting my arm over Evelyn's shoulders.

Every time she runs away from home, I sneak her into my bedroom without Mum's knowing or permission.

The last time we got caught, Mum didn't speak to me for days and Evelyn still talks about the beating Aunty Anette gave her.

We walk in silence as the rain pitters around us. I don't know what tomorrow brings, but I know I'll sleep peacefully tonight, at ease with the decisions I've made tonight.

Chapter 31

Geelong

Akita

I shove my books into my locker and breathe out all the tension in my body. My shoulders ache, the same way they always do after an exam.

It's the third week of the third term and the intensity of Year 12 is kicking me. I feel like I'm in a constant state of burn out, but so does everyone else and at this point, I'd be worried if I wasn't. I've also been preparing for the stress of the final year since Year 9. Even so, I think it's a miracle that I'm keeping my head above the water.

I'm coming to terms with how quickly it's going by, the final year of my high school experience; whether I'm ready for it or not, the end is near. In a matter of weeks I'll take my VCE exams, then

I'll graduate, and then I'll no longer be a high school student, or a student at all.

Thirteen uniformed years gone, just like that. Six years of heavy textbooks, of red-penned borders and blue-penned notes, of math equations and cursive essays. Twelve years of waiting in line for canteen – tuckshop in Sydney – for the same snacks and hot lunch I always order. Which reminds me – I dig my hands into my pocket and pull out two five-dollar notes. One I forgot to give Amara this morning.

'How'd you go?' asks Chloe, leaning on the locker beside mine.

'Okay, I think. I answered all the questions, but I think I spent too much time on one worth only eight marks. What about you?' Chloe closes her eyes and shrugs nonchalantly.

She's naturally intelligent, not book smart, but very wise in the way she thinks and feels. Chloe does her best, not for the test marks (she has no plans to go to university or pursue tertiary education) but for her own sake, which I admire.

'I think I did alright, you never really know with English, and Mrs Ross is a really harsh marker.'

'I like that about her,' I confess.

We make our way to join the rest of our friends at our usual lunch spot.

I see Isla's hair in the distance, red as embers, incandescent in the sunshine against the grey of her woollen school jumper. Chloe and I walk and sit with Isla, Emily, and Jade underneath the giant pine tree, the tallest one in Geelong and probably just as old.

'What's wrong with her?' Chloe asks Isla, who's comforting Jade, in tears.

'It's Jonathan,' Isla whispers.

'He broke up with me!' Jade wails, burying her face into her knees.

'Again?' Chloe whispers, rubbing Jade's back. 'I thought it was because you failed your SAC or something.'

Jade sobs, and Emily looks at me as if to say that Jade did, in fact, fail her English SAC this morning because Jonathan broke up with her, either last night or this morning; details are still unclear.

'You don't need him, Jade,' assures Isla, half a liquorice in her mouth.

'Yeah, besides, it's too beautiful a day for you to be crying over some boy,' proclaims Chloe, and she's absolutely right. It's the middle of winter and the sun is shining, the air is cold, and the grass is dewy. We're sitting under our favourite tree we've sat under since the seventh grade, for the first time since the first term.

'He isn't just *some boy*, Chloe. You can be so insensitive sometimes!'

Chloe looks to me for help, but I shrug. Jade rises to her feet and storms off to the bathroom.

We glare at each other, thinking the same thing.

'I'm not going after her,' says Emily the second Jade stomps out of earshot.

'I went last time!' Isla whines. 'Chloe? Akita?'

'No way!' scoffs Chloe. 'She's been weird with me all week.'

'Akita?' Isla looks to me, her lips stained red from the liquorice.

'You know what?' I say, 'I just remembered, I was supposed to find Amara and give her lunch money.'

'I'll come with!' says Emily.

We walk to the junior section of the campus, letting Isla and Chloe rock-paper-scissors their way in and out of consoling Jade.

'What a train wreck,' I whisper to Emily. Her jaw drops, and she whacks me on the arm, deservingly so.

'Akita don't say that!' she whispers, suppressing a grin.

'Why? We're all thinking it. She can do so much better than that man. What's he doing dating a high-schooler anyway?'

'Akita, Jade's eighteen, Jonathan's twenty-two.'

I shoot Emily a look to convey my disapproval.

'He's certainly not someone to cry over, let alone fail an exam for. Her mother's gonna kill her.'

We don't find Amara around the Year 8 block, so we walk past the library and out onto the oval. Amara is as unpredictable as anything; she's like a nomad on our campus, she never stays too long in one place.

We walk out into the field; the wet grass covers our leather shoes with dew. Dozens of uniformed girls run back and forth, kicking footballs to each other, some catching them, others falling.

But I'm drawn to a group in the centre of the oval. I see arms swing and legs kick as two people grab on to each other in a fight; one of them is unmistakable. Amara. My shoes slip as I sprint on the grass, kicking up dew all over my kilt and stockings. Emily's footsteps follow closely behind.

I grab onto Amara and pull her off the blonde girl whose face is red with fury. Amara shouts profanities at her, hurling rapid-fire insults about her looks and the mediocrity of her parents. The other girl attempts to punch Amara but her fist dives into my lower-back ribs.

'That's enough!' I seethe, angry dripping out of me like lava.

Emily catches up to me and pulls the other girl away.

'Amara, what the hell?!'

'She started it, Akita!'

'Who hit who first?' I ask Amara, gripping her shoulders so she doesn't launch into another attack. Amara scrunches up her face and averts my gaze.

'That's so unfair,' she whines.

'So, it was you?'

'You didn't even hear the things she was saying to me, Akita, the word she called me!' Amara's voice breaks and tears bulge in her eyes. I don't have to ask to know what word she means.

I turn around and eye the girl, the thrower of a word so vicious in her mouth, so foul, a word that invokes hatred of hundreds of years. Her face is still pink, warped in a way that is so unpleasantly angry. The ugly of her insides manifested its way to the outer. I feel sick when her beady eyes look at me.

She sticks her tongue out and throws her middle finger up at Amara, who then pushes off my hands and slaps the daylight out of the blonde girl's face.

They both fall to the ground and Emily, and I are forced to break them apart again. I see Mrs Selwood, a strongly built woman in her fifties, running across the field.

'Girls!' she heaves. 'Demerits! Both of you!' She looks from Amara to the girl, her face twisted in shock.

Mrs Selwood grabs them by their wrists.

'Office! Now!' she seethes, storming away with the girls by her side, the blonde girl's hands crumpled into fists so tight that her knuckles are paperwhite. In the sun, I see a couple golden strands of hair in Amara's hands as they disappear into the distance.

* * *

I find myself unable to focus in fifth period. Global politics.

Emily and I followed Mrs Selwood to the main office, but by the time we got there Amara and the other girl were nowhere to be seen.

I stare out the window as if at any moment I'm going to see Amara emerge from the building that houses all the teachers' offices, including the principal's.

I have a sinking feeling in my stomach – I got it the second I saw Amara's hands on that girl.

I'm afraid I already know how this is going to play out.

The little white girl is going to be deemed as the victim, and little black Amara is going to be the provoker, the culprit, the shit-starter. It's going to be that way because that's the way it always is. Amara, to some degree, has been a good student. She has a mouth on her, but it usually gets her out of trouble instead of the opposite.

Mum has raised the best of us to always keep our hands to ourselves; Amara has never lain hands on anyone besides me every couple of times, and Ashanti that one time. But on a white kid? I just know that this is going to land her – land us, in more trouble than we know.

'Akita?' enquires Mr Hatcher, standing in front of the classroom, looking at me quizzically.

'Off with the fairies, are we?' he chuckles lightly. I like my global politics teacher; I like the subject and I like our current assessment topic. But I can't think of anything else but Amara.

'No, I just – sorry.'

'Just try to focus please, I know it's a Friday afternoon, but this is important. That goes for all of you.'

I don't believe my eyes when I see Amara walking in the distance. Her school bag is on her shoulders as Mrs Selwood closely follows her into the main building. I get up from my seat.

'Excuse me, Mr Hatcher,' I say walking toward the door. 'I've gotta go.'

I run down the steps and into the main building, my school kilt weighing me down around my ankles with every stride. I catch Mrs Selwood and Amara in the foyer.

'Um, excuse Mrs Selwood?' I announce myself from behind.

'Akita,' she looks at me accusingly, 'shouldn't you be in class?'

'… Yes … but I'd like to know what's going on with Amara?'

Mrs Selwood looks at me like she doesn't know who I'm talking about, like Amara isn't standing right beside her.

'My sister?' I say, eyeing Amara who looks at me desperately to save her from this house fire.

'Akita, can I ask that you go back to class? Amara will be spoken with accordingly.'

I like Mrs Selwood; she was my PE teacher in years 8 and 9. She's never given me a reason to hate her, even though most of the girls in the school do. But she, in this very moment, is trying my patience.

'How about the other girl?' I ask. 'Will she, too, be spoken with accordingly?'

Mrs Selwood looks at me for a long time with a glare that can cut me in half. It takes almost everything in me not to look away.

She scoffs and her eyebrows soften. 'Akita, let's not make this something it isn't.'

'I'm not trying to make something anything Mrs Selwood, but I saw what happened. I was there to break it up, and the other girl –'

'Tahlia,' Amara cuts in.

'Tahlia, is as much in the wrong, if not more, than Amara is, so by that logic she should face consequences for her actions too, no?'

'That's quite enough, Akita. I'm not going to argue with you. Amara is to stay in the principal's office after school until a parent or guardian is present to discuss how we move forward. The same goes for Tahlia. Understood?' I hold her stare then I nod.

'Now, go back to class.'

I turn to walk, the sinking feeling in my stomach deepens. There's not a chance the school has gotten a hold of Mum. She turns her phone off when she's at work.

* * *

'Hey, I got your text, everything alright?' asks Jacob, his school bag over his shoulder.

'No, Amara's in trouble. She got into a fight with a girl who called her the n-word.'

We're standing outside St Brigid's front gates as the general after-school chaos ensues. Kids running for their buses, walking to the fish and chip shops, or casually strolling home.

'Oh shit. Where is she?'

'Principal's office with the girl's parents. Mum's not gonna show so I have to go in there, whether I'm allowed to or not.'

'Well, I'm coming.'

'No, Jacob.' I laugh at the silliness of the suggestion. I simply sent him that text to let him know that I won't be walking home with him tonight, not because I need him to come with me. I'm not even sure if that's something I want, let alone expect.

'No, you're not.'

'Akita, yes, I am.' He grabs me by the wrist and walks me through the crowd of high schoolers dressed in different coloured uniforms from the other schools in the precinct. We walk through St Brigid's gates and into the main offices. Jacob leads me straight past the front desk and into Principal McCarthy's office. Without even knocking.

Mr McCarthy, a very large man both in height and width, sits on the polished timber desk, and Mrs Selwood stands beside him. Tahlia and her mother are on one side of the room, Amara sits on a chair on the other. Mrs Selwood glares at Jacob and I disapprovingly. For a while, nobody says anything, each waiting for the next person to speak.

'Should we be expecting Mr or Mrs Adolé anytime soon?' asks Mr McCarthy. His voice is deep, and even though he speaks carefully his words come out in bellows.

Mrs Selwood bends down to Mr McCarthy's ear and whispers something to him.

'Our mother can't make it,' I say, trying to sound as mature as I can.

'Akita,' Mrs Selwood begins patronisingly, looking down at Amara and me like she pities us, like we are so far below anyone she's ever seen. 'With all due admiration, you're a student. You're not Amara's parent or guardian, and since you're neither –'

'Yeah, but I am her big sister, Mrs Selwood. I'm the closest thing you're gonna get to either of those things, and I'm not leaving this office without Amara,' I say, walking forward, long strides, chin in the air, holding Mrs Selwood's heavy gaze.

'Neither am I,' says a voice behind me. It takes me a second to realise it came from Jacob. The room falls to an awkward silence. I know he meant well, and bless him for it, but I just wish that Jacob would've kept his mouth shut.

Mr McCarthy looks from me, to Jacob, to Amara, to Tahlia and her mother – who for a second, I forgot were in the room.

'Well, alright then,' Mr McCarthy decides, gesturing for me to take the empty seat beside Amara. Tahlia's mother is well put, in a coral-pink blouse, black leggings and a pair of thongs, her yellowy hair in a high updo. I thought she would've looked more like a bogan.

She stares ahead, eyes forward, at Mr McCarthy's face and no one else, fighting with herself to avert my eyes. I can't tell if she's embarrassed or afraid. Tahlia sits beside her, head down and lip quivering. Oh, for goodness' sake. I peel my eyes away and refrain from kissing my teeth. To nobody's surprise, Tahlia is not above crocodile tears.

'Amara,' Mr McCarthy speaks, his voice reverberating, dancing on my spine, threatening to make it snap. 'Why don't you recount to us the events which occurred this afternoon between Tahlia and yourself?'

* * *

We walk out of Mr McCarthy's office, shocked at the verdict. Tahlia's been suspended for two days, has one afterschool detention, and has to submit a written apology to Amara. My sister on the other hand, with the universe on her side, walked away with no further punishment other than apologising to Tahlia, which is mild even though Amara would disagree.

Tahlia's mother, Sharon, barely uttered a word. It was strange. She was neither dignified nor ashamed, but complacent. It confuses me, because often when I see ignorant kids they come from ignorant parents. I suppose Sharon likes to keep her prejudice hidden, and that disturbs me more than if she were to be open about it.

We walk down the hall and into the foyer, where we see Samira and Ines. It's rare that we cross paths on campus, which is laughably ironic considering not only are we related, but also the four of us are the only black kids in the entire school. Not to mention Samira and I are in the same grade.

We weren't placed in the same classes together after Year 10, so avoiding each other became easy.

'Hey?' I say, confused. 'Everything alright?'

'We should be asking you that,' says Ines.

'Huh?'

'We heard about Amara,' Samira says. She stares at Jacob suspiciously for a second too long, then back at me. 'How'd it go?'

Before I answer the question I feel footsteps behind me. I don't turn to see – instead, I look at Samira and the way she eyes them nastily. I know it ca be no one else but Tahlia and her mother. If looks could kill, Samira would be behind bars and the both of them would be six feet under.

'Good,' I breathe.

'Really?' Samira's hard face softens, and she uncrosses her arms.

'Yeah, I don't think any of us expected it.'

'When I heard Amara punched a kawaja, I thought expulsion for sure,' says Ines.

'We all did,' Samira says, and laughs.

We stand there for a second, the four of us with Jacob standing close behind me. In the silence we all feel how awkward this all is.

'We should probably be going home,' I say after a while. 'Wouldn't want to miss the bus.'

'Yeah, us too actually,' agrees Ines.

'Okay,' I whisper.

The five of us awkwardly shuffle out of the office. We part ways with Samira and Ines. When I can breathe clearly, I turn back to them as they walk the distance to the opposite side of the campus. A feeling swells in my chest; I can't put a finger on it, but I know I want to thank Samira and Ines for being there. I see they're too far to hear me.

We stand outside the gates of St Brigid's. The street is eerily quiet compared to how it was an hour ago, like a spell of silence has been cast.

I pull Jacob to the side and give Amara a look not to stand too close.

'Hey, is it okay if you don't walk me to the bus stop tonight? I wanna talk to Amara about what happened –'

'Of course, Akita,' he interjects softly, smiling like he understands, but I feel his regret.

'Thank you, Jacob for … for coming … and staying.'

Jacob smiles a smile that travels from his mouth to every corner of his face; he glows in a way that makes my heart feel like it's going to burst. He pulls me into his embrace, holding me tightly. We untangle ourselves from each other when we hear Amara making kissing noises. I wave Jacob goodbye and smack Amara on the back of her head.

'Hey-yuh!' she exclaims.

'That's for being an idiot today,' I say, draping my arm over her neck and pulling her into the side of me, 'and this is for standing up for yourself.'

'I got away with it too,' she says proudly, her nose in the air.

'Don't be stupid, Amara. You barely got away with it, we just got lucky.'

'I'd do it again, you know! I'd smack Tahlia in her ugly pig face over and over if she gives me a reason to.'

'No, the hell you won't.'

'Yes, the shit I will.'

'Amara …' I say stopping in my tracks. She turns to look at me, the smile on her face vanishing when she sees the weighty look of mine.

'Geez Akita, nobody died.'

The setting sun behind the dark clouds paints the sky in a cobalt blue, making everything look like it glows from within.

'Amara, don't you see?'

Amara looks at me, confused, trying to read my face.

'Do you think you would've gotten away with it today if Jacob wasn't there?' I say, my heart sinking when I say the words out loud.

'I ... I guess? I don't know.'

'How often do you get in trouble?'

'At least twice a week, but for tiny things that don't even matter, who cares?'

'And how often are you given a chance to explain yourself?'

Amara falls quiet as her mind wanders.

'Why was this time different? Think about it, Amara,'

'No, Akita, you're just talking crap. How do you know all this?'

'I just do.'

'But how?'

'Because I just do! I felt it. I saw it in his eyes, Amara. I saw the way Mr McCarthy's face changed when he saw him. I saw through it. All of it.'

'Well ... maybe you're wrong.'

'Did Mr McCarthy say anything to you before I got there?'

'No ... no he didn't.'

'Then why did he let you speak first?'

Taresai

I press the phone against my ear and wait three seconds for Santino's world to catch up to mine. I used to look forward to the days when I'd speak to him, but now, I dread our conversations. His voice is the only part of him I receive, and that stopped being enough a long time ago.

'It's fine here, how's the weather over there?' Santino asks, shouting into the phone as if I'm down the hall, not millions of miles away.

'This year's winter isn't as terrible as the last,' I speak into the phone. 'It's wetter, though not as cold.'

'Is that a good thing?' he asks after precisely three seconds of static silence.

'For a large part of the country it probably is.'

It's like the two of us are strangers. It's as if we haven't known each other since I was eighteen, as if we haven't been married for twenty-five years, as if we don't have five children together. It's strange how the space between us, how distance has made time slow, then come to a complete stop. Now, it feels like time is going backwards, like the father of my children is someone I must endure small talk with and prove my worth to.

'How are the kids?' he asks, the same question he has asked every week without fail for the past five and a half years.

'They're hardly kids anymore, Santino.'

Three seconds turns to six seconds, then to nine.

'They're good,' I say.

Three seconds, six seconds. Static. Silence.

'Are they keeping warm?'

'As warm as they can be.'

'Are any of them awake? What time is it there?'

'No … no, they're asleep. It's two in the morning. When are you planning on coming home?'

In the five years that Santino's been gone, this is only the second time I'm asking him this question.

'Two in the morning, eh? Can't sleep?'

'Santino, when are you coming home?'

Three seconds. Six seconds. Nine. Twelve.

'Akita graduates soon, Santino …'

Three. Six.

I feel like I'm talking to a ghost.

'Santo needs you. He never stopped needing you. Without you, he's … he's lost himself, Santino.'

Three. Six. Nine.

'Zandé barely remembers you, I … the kids need a father, they need their father.'

Three.

'Please Santino, come back. For them. Please.'

Three. Six. Nine. Twelve. Fifteen. Eighteen.

'Taresai … I will come back. I will.'

'When?!'

'Soon.'

My body goes limp in defeat, my heart flattened by a singular, four-letter word. The phone slips through my fingers and falls to the carpet by my feet. Santino's voice calls out to me from the floor.

Three. Six. Nine. Twelve.

He hangs up before fifteen.

Chapter 32

Geelong

Akita

I'm on a train home after spending the day at Melbourne University.

Despite persistent persuasion from my vis-com teacher, my Year 10 PE teacher and my Year 11 writing teacher, Mr Rian, I think I've finally decided what I want to study next year: Bachelor of Sociology and Social Sciences, with a minor in Politics. Much to their disappointment, which I am sorry for.

Being a star pupil comes at a cost, I've come to find. Each teacher tries to mould me into their protégé so that it's them I have to thank when I'm highly acclaimed or something. Be that as it may, there's no denying that I get my best grades in sociology. With the degree, I'm almost guaranteed a job, which means a career, which means security and not having to worry about the things I see Mum worrying about, the things that I worry about now.

MU is the third university I've been to this week; it's also the one I'm most drawn to. I can see myself there; I can get used to this: the train rides, the coursework, the campus, the people. All I have to do now is pass my upcoming exams, the first of which, English, is in less than two weeks. Then, when I get into Melbourne Uni, study for a few years and graduate; I'm almost certain it'll be smooth sailing from there. It's a foolproof plan to guaranteed success. A life of struggle comes to an end overnight, just like that.

I let my head fall back on the headrest and exhale the rest of my apprised thoughts. I need to start taking more day trips to Melbourne to get used to this, to become immune to the exhaustion. As the train sways from side to side, I look up from the pamphlets on my lap and out the window as we ride past the You Yangs, a small mountain range with three distinct peaks. The First People of this land, the Wadawurrung People, tell stories of the granite formation, calling it "the three sisters" that stand and protect the land, protect Geelong. Some people believe the hills are sacred. I know they are because they show me where home is.

* * *

I walk into my room to see Amara laying across my bed and Ashanti putting on lip gloss in front of my mirror.

'So, how was it?' Amara asks, sitting up on her elbows.

'Melbourne is huge! I walked for hours, and I still couldn't learn my way around.'

Before this fortnight, the only other times I'd been to Melbourne city was during Year 9 camp and on the annual school excursion to Melbourne Museum.

It's an enormous city both in size and in life. I've never had a good enough reason for Mum to take me when I was younger, and I never had a good enough excuse to go when I could.

I'm not even sure if Amara and Ashanti have ever been.

The closest to the city we've gone to together is Footscray, which is known for being a cultural melting pot. Every second Sunday of the month, when Zandé needs a haircut, when Mum needs African fabrics and we need things for our hair, we go to Footscray. We shop at the food markets for produce, herbs and spices we can't get from our local Coles or Woolies, and we eat at that one Ethiopian restaurant or the kebab joint with the baklava and semolina cake. We don't like Footscray as much as Mum does; Ashanti hates it in particular because of that one time she got lost in Footscray market, a three-storey fruit and veggie lot.

'Oh yeah?' asks Ashanti, jumping on the bed beside Amara. 'What was it like?'

'Cafés everywhere, trams on like every street, skyscrapers that look like they were built in the future, and cathedrals that look like they're older than the planet,' I say, throwing my bag on the floor and lying on the bed between them. 'It's like a movie.'

'Damn ...' Amara breathes, her eyes wide.

'When you say it like that, going to university doesn't sound so dorky.'

'The two aren't mutually exclusive, Amara.'

'Oh geez, Shanti, we've lost her, she's already starting to speak like one,' Amara laughs, and I throw a cushion at her.

'So, what are you gonna do? What are you gonna study?' asks Amara, her toes wriggling in the air.

'Sociology. The study of society and the people that make it. That's what it says on the pamphlet,' I answer, digging it out from my pocket.

Amara grimaces and scowls. 'Why?'

'What do you mean 'why?' I question, sitting up and looking at her.

'I thought you'd study something ... you know ... cool. Exciting.'

'It is exciting. And cool.'

'No, you should be doing something else, something that changes the world, not studying the changes *of* the world,' argues Amara.

'What do you suggest then, huh?'

'Didn't you used to paint?'

'And draw!' Ashanti adds.

'Yeah, when I was like fifteen, come on guys.'

'Why don't you do that? Study art?' Amara suggests, as if I, too, didn't have that thought when I was fourteen.

'And what? Struggle to sell my paintings for living? No thanks.'

'What about, um … a storyteller!' says Ashanti very proudly.

'Yes! Exactly! You used to make up stories all the time.'

'Yes when you guys were little and I'd struggle to put you to sleep, but I don't do that anymore, but even if I did, then what Amara? Become a black Brontë? Overnight?' Amara and Ashanti look at each other confused.

'A black Shakespeare? … No, look guys, with this degree I can get a high-paying job, look after you guys and Mum, maybe get involved in some kind of research initiative, and then in twenty years when I'm a professor at a university and I have my PhD, I'll write a book!' Amara and Ashanti look at each other, then they look at me like I'm trying to convince them that Santa Claus is real.

'What if –'

'Look, no, drop it, please,' I say, suddenly very fed up. 'Now … hurry up and get ready, Jacob's gonna be here soon.'

Taresai

I do the last of my rounds.

I like being a nurse. I feel like it's one of the things I was born to do, to care for those who cannot care for themselves. I just had to work harder for much, much longer to be where I am. I started studying English again two years after Santino left. I'd begin my shift at the carpet factory two hours earlier and drove to class the minute I clocked off. After that year I began studying community service and I took a few courses on nursing. Three years later, here I land, six days a week. My path was lined with strenuous difficulties, unfathomable odds which made a steady climb through the ranks almost impossible. Almost.

Some of the people I work with I adore, and the feelings are mutual, but others look at me with an envious eye. Those that pretend not to understand what I'm saying, even though my English remains unbroken and has been for quite some time. Those that loathe with everything in their being that I have earned a seat at this table, that I am at their level, and they are so far from being on mine.

I suppose I'm astonished, mostly by the fact that even in a hospital, a place this high up that works to bring order to the chaos, that exists to mend the ill and injured, a thing such as racism so prominently exists. It's like discrimination, prejudice, and every form of bias is primal, and envy is something interwoven in our DNA.

I used to endure abuse from all corners of Giza, from other makers of liquor and their families. They were all men, all lighter in skin than I am, some older than I was and more experienced in the craft. But all the privilege in the world didn't grant them what must be earned.

Not one could've survived a day as Taresai Deng, not one could brew liquor as such.

These days I speak more English than my native tongue. My spoken words are transfused only when I speak with my sisters and Messai, my mother and Santino. I reserve Dinka and Arabic for special occasions with my children, specifically when I'm yelling the life out of one of them for doing something idiotic. Zandé, bless his soul, who can only speak English, understood every word I spoke last week when he broke the washing line and I scorned him until he turned purple.

He'll be nine soon. My last-born. Growing up in such a hurry as if he has somewhere to be. Zandé has basketball tryouts today. I put in a notice a month in advance so I wouldn't miss it. Akita and the boy she won't admit is her boyfriend have taken the other two to watch.

'I'm going, Adeline,' I say to the elderly Irishwoman in my care.

She breathes shallowly and barely cognises my being near her.

There's more of her in the afterlife than there is here. Adeline, who has lived quite a life, now finds herself spending her ninth month in hospice.

I fluff her pillow and place my palm gently on her hands, wrinkled with age, calloused with years of revolting, fighting for liberties women like us weren't born with.

I feel her pulse weakening, feel the pull of her reigning and resilient spirit being needed elsewhere, in another universe, in another life.

Through the years I've worked more hours of the day than the opposite. I see tiny glimpses of my children during the big moments in their lives. Akita's award nights for her academia and athleticism, Amara's violin recitals, Ashanti's dance performances. My presence, my witnessing of those milestones is my blessing. My absence from moments where my children are purely existing, that is my sacrifice. I don't see the delight on their faces when eating their favourite meals, their joy when they're watching their favourite films, the light in their eyes when they're just being.

I must remind myself that those things – that all things – are possible precisely because I work so much, enough to afford stable foundations for the rest of their lives. It's also a blessing that my children never seem to need reminding.

I won't know if my youngest son has made it into the basketball team before the day is done, for my eldest is expecting a visit from me today.

* * *

I sit in the visitor's centre of Port Phillip Prison.

When Santo called this morning my earth shattered, for better and for worse. I heard my son's voice for the first time in too long, and in the same second I learned that he'd landed himself in hard prison. I was shaken, even though I've prayed in these years for anything other than death. I suppose in a way I was in denial; this is a path Santo has been travelling for a while. It is by no means a twist of fate that he is here, as harrowing as that might be to accept.

Landing in prison after years of juvenile detention is an effortless pipeline, moreso than coming home.

Santo has been here for two weeks, drugged up on prescribed medication to aid his instability and comedown from goodness knows what.

It's been two years since he was diagnosed. After a few manic episodes, Santo's worker, at the time, delivered the news that my son has schizophrenia. It only took a few manic episodes, though it's unknow whether it developed from the drug use or conceived from his pre-existing mental illness, or if it's woven in our bloodline. My guess is that it's an ugly mess of them all.

When I see my son I feel a pull of energy, a pulse in my womb. I'm utterly winded to no end by the manliness of my little boy.

He stands tall even as he hunches, shoulders broad, towering over everything in sight as he walks his heavy, shallow footsteps toward his birther.

Santo sits opposite me, his eyes unfocused, his stubbled cheeks hollowed.

'Hey, Ma,' he smiles. 'Long time no see.'

Words don't come to me easily; they hardly come at all.

'How are you? How's everyone?' he says, his jaw slightly locked.

'Good,' I force out. 'We're good, darling. How are you feeling?' I speak to a shadow of my son.

'I don't feel anything,' Santo says and laughs, his eyes closed.

I'm afraid I might weep, weep until the end of my days.

In my silence, Santo takes a while to heed my stern expression, to read my uneasy eyes.

'N-No, Mum, it's a good thing.'

'A good thing'? For the love of god, how is any of this is a 'good thing'?!

'Are they looking after you here?'

'Yeah. My social worker Daniel is pretty good.'

'Praise the heavens.'

'How are the girls? How's Akita?' Santo's tired eyes focus on mine and find a stillness that travels to the rest of his large, swaying body.

'Your sister's good. A little bit stressed with high school, but good.'

'Akita's always stressed,' snorts Santo. 'She's gotta learn to breathe.'

'Amara is well too. She's getting better at the violin. She's mostly good, but she gets into trouble from time to time.'

'A shit-starter?'

'Watch your tongue, Santo.'

'Sorry.'

'But yes, you're right, she is.' I exhale. 'And her eczema has cleared up. Ashanti and Zandé are pretty much the same. Just as you left them.'

'Huh …' I see Santo's mind work, bending to reach and unearth memories buried deep to the point of forgotten.

I stare deeply into his eyes, trying to understand my son, willing his spirit to come forward and speak to me, to see me, so that I may see him.

'It's nice to see your face, Mum,' Santo says after a while. 'You're getting a bit old.'

'Oh, am I?' I laugh, choking back tears.

'Yeah, but it's a good thing. Helps me see that some time has passed, you know?'

I don't know. I probably will never know or understand the world my son is living in.

'I wasn't sure you were gonna pick up the phone today when I called.' He rubs the back of his neck impulsively. My heart breaks.

'It's nice to see your face too, Santo.' I smile, fearing if I say anything else I might burst into tears, that I might show the pain Santo has caused in me.

We stare at each other and smile, taking each other in.

When the sun gleams through the window light bounces around the room, brightening the brown of Santo's large eyes, falling onto his dark coils, the same ones I'd pray over, catching the light as they did my prayers.

* * *

That night, when the kids are asleep, or at least pretending to be, I warm up the pasta bake Akita made for dinner. I lean on the benchtop as the microwave hums.

I cook most nights, Sudanese, sometimes Arab food. On the nights that I can't, Akita takes over, making dishes from recipes she finds online or things she's eaten at restaurants. Just last week she made two different types of quiches, a rather interesting dish made up of egg, spinach and bread.

Needless to say, it was quite delightful.

When the microwaves beeps I hear Akita's bedroom door open. She shuffles into the kitchen with a giant sweater and slippers on.

'Did I wake you?' I ask, adding an extra minute to the microwave.

'Nah,' she smiles tiredly, 'I'm still studying.'

'Oh … well, don't stay up too late. It's important to rest.'

'I'm making a cup of tea, do you want one?' she asks, shuffling past me and grabbing a large mug out of the cupboard.

'No thanks, darling, I'm about to sleep soon.'

'Okay.'

The tea kettle bubbles, and the microwave hums, and Akita and I stand across from each other.

'I went to Melbourne University today. I think that's where I want to go next year.'

'Of course!' I say, guilt spilling out of me. 'Today was open day, how was it?'

'Yeah, it was good. I think I know what I want to study.'

'And what's that?'

'Sociology. Social and political sciences.'

'Oh,' I say, trying to conceal the disconcertment in my tone. 'That's great, Akita.'

'Yeah. It's very promising, I'll easily be able to find a job once I graduate. A well-paying one.'

I don't know what to say to that – my heart breaks ever so slightly at the sentiment. After seeing Santo today, drugged up and in his prison blues, I want Akita to stay away from anything that remotely resembles that world. I want to protect her from it.

She's running into what I want her to run away from, even if it's only to study it for now and eventually become goodness knows what working for goodness knows who. But how can I tell her this without breaking her? How do I tell her about Santo?

'Well, I'm very proud of you, Akita,' I say, taking the pasta bake out of the microwave. 'I always will be.'

Akita smiles at me, though dimples form on her cheeks, and her eyes look so incredibly sad.

'Thanks, Mum,' she says, rotating the teaspoon between her fingers.

'Goodnight, darling,' I say, walking out of the kitchen and into the front living room.

I sit with the warm plate on my lap, realising only then that I've lost my desire to eat.

I set the plate on the coffee table, turn on the tv and try to indulge in some late-night television, switching between SBS, the ABC and Channel 10. The bright images on the screen can't drown my woes. I find that I'm too disturbed by that conversation in the kitchen, by seeing Santo, by missing Zandé's tryouts today.

What has happened to Akita? How haven't I noticed her evolution into being this way? She was talking about her future like she was reading an article from a newspaper. Is it my doing? Has seeing my struggle put out the fierce fire she once had in her soul?

I think back to when Akita was a child, how she used to talk about being this and being that, how her words would paint colours in the air, but now it's like they drain them.

Has growing up in uncertainty made her this way? Has ancestral trauma wrapped itself around her?

I'm disturbed because I feel Akita inching closer to resembling someone she is not. She is choosing a means of survival, not a way of life out of love and passion. I had no choice in that matter. My mother made me like that. And as much as I've sprouted, I'm still the seed Adele planted in infertile soil. I endured all my struggle with the intentions of setting my children free, setting Akita free. Free to make a life of her own creation, a kingdom of her own hope. I believed in all these years, being her mother meant so. But has what bound me all these years gripped her too?

Chapter 33

Geelong

Akita

It's been a year and five months since I last saw Santo, seventy-three weeks since I last heard his voice. It's strange – it feels like so much longer, seems like forever ago, but in the same mind it feels like no time has passed at all.

Life has gone on without Santo. Some days I don't think about him at all and other nights, nights like this, I sink deep into the hallow within me that took his place.

I wonder where he is, I wonder if his heart beats to the rhythm of mine. I hope, for the life of him, that he's locked up.

Prison is a horrible place to wish someone to be, but at least within its confines Santo will have a harder time doing in there what he does on the streets. I'd rather Santo be locked up for ten years than be free for ten days, because that's how long I expect him to survive with all the shit he shoots into veins, inhales into his lungs, snorts up his nose and grinds between his teeth.

As much as it would hurt, I would rather it.

This is the longest I've gone in my entire life without seeing him, and with each passing day that time grows by seconds, minutes and hours that we'll never get back.

I sit on a damp bench on the pier, shaking from the cold of the evening in my white silk dress. The celebration ceremony carries on in the double-storey hall that stands in the water, glowing like a lantern.

I graduated high school today.

St Brigid's have put on their annual graduation ball, which was fine to begin with. Mum, the girls and Zandé, dressed in their best attire, sat around the table with me, Evelyn, and Jacob. Everything was perfect, far beyond what I'd imagined. That was until Mum spoke, and I realised how very far from fine things are.

Mum decided she wasn't happy with me. She thinks I'm pretending to be content. She made it known to the whole table that studying the lives of people was a great way to waste mine.

Why today of all days? Why now?

Damn it, why open your mouth to begin with when all you've been doing these past few years is holding your tongue?

I thought she'd be proud of me. I thought she *was* proud of me.

I didn't say anything to that. I simply walked onto the dance floor with Jacob's hand in mine. I didn't care how much she doesn't approve of he and I, or how poorly it reflects on her that I'm seventeen, fatherless and have a boyfriend. I know she's afraid that it'll all come back to her, to her parenting alone, and if Dad were ever to come back then he too would point the finger at her for how tragic their kids have turned out.

I watched as she walked out of the hall with the kids. Amara and Ashanti waved sadly when they caught my eye. When I went back to the table, Evelyn was sitting alone, and six plates of uneaten desserts were spread evenly around the table. She was bent over, bawling her eyes out. Evelyn was upset about nothing in particular, everything in general. She's back at Aunty Anette's house. The champagne mixed with her fragility and intense emotions was a recipe for a meltdown. But I felt too broken myself to deal with her, too weak to be her pillar of strength, her rock, her shoulder to cry on tonight. So, I walked out, left Jacob to deal with her, and now I sit on this mouldy wooden bench, staring at the dark sea below stained with the lights from above that are dancing on the water to the shapes of the tender ripples.

I see Jacob's silhouette emerge from the hall, his head twisting from side to side in search of me. He strolls the length of the boardwalk and sits beside me wordlessly. We sit in silence for a while and it's nice listening to the gentle splashing of water over the harsh sounds of music from the hall in the distance. Jacob removes his suit jacket and lays it over my shoulders.

'You okay?' he asks softly. I scoff in response.

'Do you wanna go back inside?'

'Yeah, in a minute I just … I need some air.'

'Do you want me to stay?' The question breaks my heart, and I start to sob before I can stop myself. He holds me close and then lets me go.

'Can you please go in and check on Evelyn?' I ask, wiping my tears and smudging the makeup on my face. Jacob looks at me like I've slapped him.

'What?' I sob.

'Well, Akita, I'd rather be here with you.'

'Please?'

He stands reluctantly and walks into the hall with his hands in his pockets.

I should be the happiest girl in the world. I've graduated high school, performed well on all my exams. I even got an early offer from Melbourne Uni to study sociology next March. Security is finally promised for the rest of my life, firmly in my grip. And yet, in this moment, I want nothing more than to drown in my sorrows. So I do just that, drinking expensive French champagne by the bottle in my expensive white silk dress, sitting outside the most expensive venue in all of Geelong.

I drink until there's nothing left, until my stomach is full and my head is empty, until there is nothing but blackness. A single voice then speaks to me: it tells me I'm lost, that I live a dream and lie in a bed that is not mine.

Chapter 34

Geelong

Akita

I blow out nineteen candles.

Another year older.

I've invited a few friends for a small and intimate gathering at the back of an old Italian restaurant by the beach. Chloe and Emily from high school are here, albeit we're not as well connected anymore. I've got a couple friends from uni here with me too, though I went all last year not knowing their names. Dalia is my closest campus friend; she laughs at everything and never has much to complain about, other than her Sri Lankan parents. We find it easy to bond when most of our existential problems have similar roots. Christian is a blonde, French-speaking student from Vancouver, as pasty as they come. His mild obsession with extravagant food is what first drew him and I together. When I'd forgotten my notebook in the auditorium after a lecture in first year, Christian found me in the dining hall to return it. While doing so, he absolutely lost his mind when he noticed the lunch I packed – Mum's leftover coconut chicken curry. We shared my meal and almost every other meal after that.

Although, what I most admired about him in the at the start, is now something I find rather bothersome. Sometimes when we're roaming through the city I just want to eat a damn burger with a side of greasy fries. But no, over Christian's dead body. Instead, we dine in places that have main courses with names split into three words.

Maybe his antics annoy me because Christian is a man, or maybe all men are irritating to me as of this moment because I'm quite drunk.

Amara is here. 'I'm sixteen soon!' she pleaded until I finally caved in, inviting her and her best friend, Josephine (Amara's long-lost Liberian twin.)

Evelyn was here too, though she left a while ago, and so is my ex-boyfriend, Jacob. We broke up eight months ago. Our lives became incompatible, so it seems. Too different. He was taking trips around the world and I was studying in Melbourne and working at a shoe store. We spent less time together and more time apart, so much so that it was easier that way, natural.

I broke it off and we've managed to keep close. We hardly see each other, but when we d, it's like no time has passed, like we haven't evolved out of who we were and grown into who we are. It's like I haven't put my hair in braids again, like Jacob hasn't cut his brown hair shorter and grown stubble around his lips.

Our breakup wasn't tears and flying objects like I thought my first breakup would be. It was a series of honest conversations. I can't say that I wasn't hurt. I can't say I didn't hurt Jacob. Eight months on, he still can't look at me for too long and neither can I at him, and we can't talk about certain things because some wounds remain wide open.

Uni is great – I'm a month into second year and I'm beginning to let my guard down because I know what to expect.

Last year I was too hard on myself. I dedicated more time than what was necessary in all aspects, from assignments to doing extra readings that weren't on the syllabus every single week.

Though the expectations and the calibre of our assignments have significantly heightened from last year, I feel now that I'm better at adapting to it.

I smile around the table, cathartic from the wine. I remember when birthdays used to be special occasions. I would spend all year looking forward to it. It seems they don't come around like that anymore. That ship sailed before I was given the chance to say goodbye.

I'm overcome with a feeling of remorse that I can't quite put my finger on, a feeling I only experience on my recent birthdays. Right now I want to lie on the carpet of my bedroom, curl into a ball and sob until the sun rises, but I've got all these people here for me, celebrating with me, smiling at me, so I have to pretend to be happy, for them.

I give Amara and Josephine the rest of my birthday cake and go to ask the waiter for some more water for our table when I see someone approaching.

A man. A man I've only ever seen as a boy.

Anei.

For a moment I don't believe my eyes, thinking I've perhaps had one too many. To see he who only unearths every couple of years, washed ashore. The last time I saw Anei was at Santo's seventeenth birthday all those years ago the first birthday he had out of juvie. When Santo was locked up again a few weeks later, he was out of my life and so was Anei.

Until now apparently.

'Anei?'

'In the flesh,' he beams. He wears a maroon dress shirt over black jeans, almost the exact shade of deep red as my dress. I feel eyes glaring at us when we embrace.

'Um ... everyone, this is Anei ... a family friend.'

I take him in – the triangular shape his face now strongly holds, the eyelashes that curl so far back, his pink gums, and the smallest gap I ever see between his two front teeth.

'So, what brings you here?' I ask as he takes the seat opposite me, the seat that was Evelyn's. I can feel the heat of Jacob's glare from a few seats down burning a hole through Anei's temple.

'Well, it's your birthday, isn't it?' Anei smiles, pouring himself a glass of rosé.

'I mean ... yeah, but since when has that ever been a reason to see me?'

'Since always, Akita. Besides, you're mother told me you'd be here, and I was in the area.'

I glare at him suspiciously, put off by the sudden demonstration of audaciousness that seems to run in most men. We're friends on Facebook, he follows me on Instagram, he sees my posts and I see his, but we haven't spoken since we were children.

There's no substitute for that, which leaves me confused because he clearly thinks it is.

'Okay, enough with the flirting,' I say firmly, but with a smile, so it doesn't backfire, though my patience is wearing thin.

'How have you been?'

'I've been good, really good. I'm still at RMIT.'

'Oh yeah?' I say, unable to muster the enthusiasm that comes to me easily when sober.

'Yeah,' he retorts, without noticing, 'I took the last two years off to just chill and travel.'

'And how was that?'

'Amazing. But there's nothing like coming back home ... After a while the homesickness starts to feel good, it actually feels good to miss home, do you know what I mean?'

I do know what he means.

I miss the feeling of home so much, even though I have never left.

The only images I see of the world are through a screen, but how do I tell him that I've travelled to a place a million miles away from home without having left? How do I tell him that I'm still there?

'Anyway,' he says softly, suddenly self-conscious.

The room carries on, Dalia laughing very loudly as Christian, who is drunker than I am, does very bad impersonations.

Chloe and Emily are looking at someone on Chloe's phone, Amara and Josephine are savouring the last bites of the cake and Jacob is looking very sombre in the corner, staring into his cup as if it has all the secrets of the universe.

'Hey,' Anei says softly when he sees me staring at Jacob, 'do you remember when we were younger and our mothers always used to say that you and I would grow up to marry each other?'

'No!' I cackle, a little too wildly. 'Since when?!'

'Oh, come on, Akita! All the time! We were like little Romeo and Juliet.'

'Are we talking about the same childhood? Because I have absolutely no memory of such a thing.'

'Of course you do.'

'Nah, I remember you used to bully me.'

'That was how I expressed my like for you.'

'Please,' I snort. 'Stop. You were like a brother to Santo … and to me too … kinda.'

'Oh …' he says, his smile shrinking. 'Do you still feel that way?'

I take a slow sip of my drink, thinking of ways to answer the question, hilariously so because this wine only slows my thoughts, not time. I don't say anything for a long while. I stare down at the pale pink liquid in my glass.

'I'm sorry, by the way,' Anei breathes finally.

'No,' I sniff. 'Don't be.' I push the glass away when my eyes start to see things fade into another. 'It was a long time ago, Anei.'

'No,' Anei's smile fades to a stern frown. 'I mean, I'm sorry about Santo.'

'What's to be sorry about?' I say, looking about the table to distract myself from all that I sit on.

If only Anei knew the dangerous territory he treads. Please, for the love of all things good, don't say anything more about Santo.

I don't need this, not tonight.

'I am, Akita. Hearing that mustn't have been easy,' Anei says seriously.

What on this green earth is he talking about?

'Sorry? …' I squint at him cluelessly.

Anei's eyes widen, and his mouth falls open, a look of horror painting his face in red.

'Oh – I, you haven't – you haven't heard?' he chokes nervously, his body sinking into itself.

The last time I saw Santo was last December, four months ago.

He was in the city with a couple of dealers and users. I stupidly went up to him to greet him, having not seen my big brother for close to three years. It was a miracle I even recognised him. He looked so sickly and gaunt, like the only thing he was eating were those little white rocks. He didn't look like Santo at all. He told me to piss off, spewing words of anger, coming out like bile, all over me.

In the corner of my eye I saw one of his friendly associates take a knife out of his pocket and hang it by his side.

I went home and told Mum what I'd seen. She rang Santo, told him where we lived, urged him to come home. He promised he would, and he did, only to break in, smash all the windows and steal both our tvs among other valuable things.

I couldn't look at Mum for a week. I hadn't thought of him since.

'What about Santo?'

'Well – I … Akita … he's in the Roswell Centre.'

'The psych ward?'

'Yes.'

'Good.'

'Don't you want to know why?' Anei looks at me like he pities me, like his heart breaks for me, like I'm broken, and he wants to fix me. 'Akita … he, he overdosed.'

Akita

I swallow away the anxiety that flutters in the pit of my stomach and pull the roller doors of the shoe store down.

Nearly three years I've been working here, juggling my time between this and university.

I place the store key and my lanyard in my handbag and exhale hot air out of my mouth.

I get these feelings of angst most weeks, but today's spell has been dizzying. The worst part is it's for no reason I can detect.

Mum says it's because my intuition can sense ill fortune coming to fruition, but I just think it's the stress of my upcoming graduation.

Selling shoes is easy enough. All I'm expected to do is stand there, offer fashion advice when needed and process sales.

It's tedious and boring most of the time, but anything's better than being unemployed.

It's a shame the new manager is such a piece of work – Tyler, a flamboyant man who loves me one second and hates me the next.

I don't think he has the brain capacity to conjure up his own feelings about me, personally. So, he goes from liking me because it's a trend to like people of my complexion, to disliking me because I don't coerce every customer in spending an extra $25 on shoe care when they've spent double that for a pair of semi-decent shoes.

My conscience just won't let me do it.

Some of these people could be spending their paycheque on nice shoes for work, they don't need me to point an invisible gun at their pride.

I walk through the deserted shopping mall. It's the late summer afternoon, my favourite time of day: there's an ease in the air and still hours left of light. I step into my old but reliable car, a silver Ford. It's probably older than I am, and it looks like a sideways tear drop according to Zandé, but the elderly lady who sold it to me took good care of it.

It's as ugly as anything, but it's yet to fail me, it can't any more than public transport has over the years. I still catch the train to uni, but that'll come to an end when I graduate next month.

Now that I've got a car I've become the new taxi driver at home, taking Zandé to his basketball games, picking Ashanti up from her friend's parties, and shuttling Amara to wherever she kindly demands.

This is how life is now.

* * *

'Amara!' I shout from the kitchen for the third time in ten minutes.

'I'm studying!' Amara whines as she emerges from her bedroom, lying through her teeth.

'All I need you to do is peel the potatoes while I chop the onions.'

I don't believe Amara for a second. She fibs a lot; she has her entire life, but she's never gotten better at it. The problem is that she shoots for the moon instead of aiming over the fence. She gets decent grades, but she's never been much of a reader. Not even I was that pedantic with my Year 11 exams, so there's no way that her sudden attitude is sincere – it's all a feeble excuse to get out of things, and Mum seems to be the only one to fall for it.

Ashanti joins us in the kitchen.

'Oh hey, Akita, you're back. How was work?' she asks, her eyes glued to her phone screen.

'Slow Sunday, just the way I like it.'

'Have you heard anything from the places you've applied?' Ashanti asks.

There it is again. Anxiety, leaking into my bloodstream like poison, turning everything inside me into ice in a way so agonisingly slow.

'No ... no I haven't,' I swallow, trying to steady myself.

It seems like everyone on the brink of graduation has secured a job in their desired field. Though I've kept my grades high and consistent in these three years, volunteered for a few local non-profits and completed a two-week internship at the mayor's office, I'm yet to be one of them.

This uncertainty has been my biggest worry for the passing months. Sixteen years of schooling and nothing to show for it because no place wants to hire me. No matter how hard I try, it cruelly seems, I'm still going to be a failure.

'Put "Jane Smith" on the application forms, Akita,' smiles Amara. 'Then someone will probably hire you.'

I laugh at the sentiment to stop myself from crying.

I'll save these tears for my pillow tonight.

When we lived in Egypt I knew it wasn't home. I understood it as merely a pit-stop, a stepping stone to higher ground.

As young as I was, having little memory of what came before, and too wild an imagination to transparently visualise what was yet to come, my ideas of what 'was' were heightened. I knew, though the words were never said, never spoken into existence.

I saw it in the way Mum folded our clothes, how her hands, calloused with labour, would come alive when she'd cook for us. How her tired eyes looked at me while she dressed me for school.

I was six years old when I understood that we weren't like everyone else, even though we spoke their tongue, wore their fabrics, lived as they did. Six when I recognised that our skin was darker than everyone else's, much, much darker and no amount of layering would make us as they were.

I was six when I understood that was dangerous.

I was so young when I learned of our place in the world, and the thing is, I should be used to this by now, the rejection. But still, I hope for something that does not yet exist. I know that things are harder for people like me in this country; we battle invisible obstacles in the corporate world, we have to work harder to be seen, which is hilariously ironic because we stand out like sharks in a fishpond. I know all this, I've lived it, setting myself up to not get picked. And yet every wave of disappointment hits harder than the last.

I get Ashanti to prepare the salad and Zandé to set the table.

Mum works from the morning until the late afternoon; she's never home for evenings like these, she only catches the tail end of them.

I often wonder how she feels about everything. About herself. How she sleeps through the night knowing that she did it, conquered it all, how she wakes up each and every day with the weight of the world on her shoulders. I wonder how she keeps going.

A year after Dad left, when Mum's safety net had expanded beyond the baseline of our front door, she'd sit me down a couple of times a week and I'd read her our mail.

The electricity bill is due in a fortnight, there's a council election coming up, my Year 8 report is in, and I've failed Maths again.

One night Mum asked me to leave the opened letters out on the dining table. I didn't ask questions, I did as she wished. After a few weeks when the pile became too big, I took it upon myself to clear some space. As I filed the letters away I found on the back of almost every single page scribbles of the same two words in blue ink. It was Mum's handwriting, in English. She wrote her name, over and over and over again.

After that day I took notice of the little things. I watched as my mother started unravelling parts of herself that were once so tightly wound up. Her gaze was soft when I'd catch her staring out the kitchen window, she would sing to herself again as she folded our clothes, her steps were gentle, appeased when she walked about the house. There would be mornings when I'd sense her terror, but in the afternoons before dinner, when she'd cook a traditional Sudanese meal from her Australian pantry, terror's grip would loosen, the tides of her waters stilled.

My mother.

I stir the pot of tomato and potato stew, closing my eyes and inhaling its hearty aroma.

I do wonder, I wonder what she would say to me if I expressed to her my tired spirit, my anxious soul, my hopeless kingdom. I wonder what she would say to me, if anything at all.

My hill to her Everest.

I go to my room to call Evelyn. I haven't in a while, and I'm always met with a feeling of unease when I go too long without hearing her voice.

Evelyn isn't a great listener, so I never share with her my feelings of distress, but hearing her voice makes me feel human, like I am something to someone.

I give up after the third try, leaving her a short voicemail telling her to come over for dinner if she's around the area.

Evelyn moved out of Aunty Anette's house when her mother disowned her. Anybody could've predicted it, though from time to time I do wonder what the nail in the coffin was.

I haven't seen much of her since, she moved to Melbourne in the same week. Mum forbade me from seeing her so soon and watched me like a hawk. Soon enough, Evelyn too became someone I rarely see.

Mum and the rest of the family still speak to Aunty Anette, and they've been trying for years now to intervene and mend her relationship with her only daughter.

I remember when Uncle Messai came down about a year ago to try and build a bridge between them, but it was no use. There was no changing Aunty Anette's mind, and there was no manipulating Evelyn. She's her own being, and not even her own mother can take that away from her. All bridges have been burned, all love has been lost.

Mum, Aunty Asélle and Uncle Messai were very much on Evelyn's side throughout the entire ordeal. Haboba was complacent.

In spite of this, in spite of it all, Mum still doesn't want me hanging out with Evelyn too much. She won't ever say why, but I have a feeling the reason is something completely ludicrous; without logic, backed only by fears. Mum wants me away from that, but it's not like, I, too will shave my head, pierce my nose and other parts of my body and get a massive pyramid tattoo on my back. I don't have the same illness that Evelyn has, my mind doesn't work like hers.

No one's ever said it, but I'm convinced Mum knows it too, we've both seen the signs that we know all too well. If I were to guess. I'd say that Evelyn has bipolar disorder, as high functioning as she might sometimes be. I lay my head on the pillow in the dark of my room, staring into blankness. I don't know how long I lay here for, but if I didn't have the pot on the stove and three mouths to feed I bet I'd stay forever.

'The food's ready!' I shout, ladling the stew into a large bowl. Amara, Ashanti and Zandé file out of their bedrooms, Zandé with a phone in his hand, talking to a boy through the screen.

'Zandé, say goodbye to your friend, we're going to have dinner,' I say.

He goes to argue but stops when he sees the look on my face.

'I gotta go, Braiden, I'll call you back later,' Zandé complains.

The eleven-year-olds of today are the twenty-five-year-olds of last year.

'Alright,' says the boy on the screen, 'talk to you later, Sunday.' I exchange a look with Amara and Ashanti in the silence that follows.

'Zandé, what did he call you?' I ask.

'Oh yeah,' he says, loading lasagne onto his plate, 'some of my friends call me that. Sunday.'

'Why? That's not your name,' says Amara, opening the fridge and pulling out some lemonade.

'Well duh!'

'Zandé, watch yourself,' I warn, plopping some rice onto Ashanti's plate.

'Your name's Zandé,' Ashanti chimes. 'If your friends aren't willing to learn how to pronounce it properly, then they're not really your friends.'

'Whatever, it's not even that serious. I'm gonna eat in my room.'

'So Mum can have a go at me?' I protest. 'Sit!'

I fix myself a plate of food after I've tin-foiled the stew and put it in the fridge, put the dirty dishes in the sink and wiped down the bench. I sit next to Ashanti, across from Zandé and Amara, who are down to the last bites of their meals.

I stare down into my plate, trying very hard to suppress the thunderstorm within me. I stab my fork into a cube of potato and suddenly realise that I'm not hungry at all.

In an instant I'm overcome with such a feeling of dread that sits on me heavily, stretching the seconds into an eternity.

It feels like all that is wrong with the world is beneath my skin, inside my bones, in my veins. It happens, this feeling, often without a trigger, manifesting itself inside of me until there's none of me left.

It reveals itself to me in many forms, right before major exams, at the loneliest hour of the night, after an argument with Mum. The last time I felt a fraction of the way I feel now was a few months ago when I found Evelyn in the backyard outside my window, passed out in her own vomit.

But these feelings of premature hurt, invisible turmoil, are always somehow worse on the eve of a tragedy than in the eye.

We hear a knock on the door and I jump.

Amara and Ashanti look at me and giggle at my reaction.

'Evelyn?' Amara questions.

'No …' I say. 'She usually rings the doorbell, or calls.'

Though I don't know who else it could be.

I look at the three on the dining table. 'Stay here.'

I walk up the hall and close the door behind me, my footsteps slow and soft, as if the ground is made of glass. I step to the front door. The person on the other side knocks three times, this time with their fist, not their knuckles. I stand paralysed, terror spreading to every inch of my body. With my knees weak and my arms trembling, I find that I'm too afraid to look through the eyehole of the solid wooden door, fearing that the person on the other side would see me. Am I having an anxiety attack? Or is the person behind the door someone who wishes me harm? I don't know who it might be, I just know it's not an intruder; those are common in Norlane, but one wouldn't knock.

Through the sound of my heart thumping loudly in my ears I hear their heavy footsteps outside shuffle across the pavement. I see glimpses of their shadow at the bottom of the blinds, slowly moving back and forth. The figure stands outside the window and taps his fingers on the glass three times, I feel it as I hear it, as if he were tapping on my spine.

Silence falls, a silence so deep it feels like time has stopped, like the whole world has frozen. Then, just as quickly, a shiny metal pipe crashes through the front window. Shattered glass fragments fall to the ground and the blinds fall with it. The front door flies open before I realise that it's me that is undoing the locks. I step out into the front porch.

'What the hell do you think you're doing?!' I shout at the black figure, a very large man. He stands up straight and takes a step towards me, towering over me. For a split second I swear I've never seen this man before, his face gaunt beneath the yellowy light from the street.

'Santo?' I whisper to myself as I come to the horrifying realisation.

No. It can't be. When did he get so tall? So skinny, so … *terrifying.*

He looks at me with black eyes that turns my blood into ice and my body into stone.

Santo? … *Santo?* After all these years.

I can't find the words to say to him, paralysed by this incarnation of a brother I love, but I'm shocked when he looks at me like he doesn't know who I am.

'Move,' he grumbles, and I can't, for the life of me, form thought or move my lips to speak. Santo tightens his grip on the large metal pipe he smashed the window with. He lifts it above his head and strikes the place where my head would've been.

I watch my body move, dodging the weapon Santo swings at me, with no thought or feeling attached to it.

I feel my soul trickle out of my body as it becomes a vessel of pure instincts.

It isn't until Santo strikes me on the forearm with a loud crack that reality sets in.

I scream, hunching my body over to protect my injury, kicking at Santo to keep him away. He strikes me on the head and I feel the world shift beneath my feet. My eyes water from the pain, but I can't bring myself to cry out again.

I go to run, but Santo grabs me by the collar of my shirt and throws me in the air off the front porch. I land face first into the lawn, my teeth digging into the soggy soil. I cough grass and mud out of my mouth, and I heave a harsh breath, only to have it crushed out of me again when Santo presses both his knees on my chest.

'I told you to move!' he shouts, foam coming out of his mouth, his yellow eyes wide with derangement.

I cry out, in agony, in fear, in absolute terror, begging for this to come to an end. My chest tightens from the weight of Santo, pleading for air. My heart thumps so loudly in my ears I fear it's going to burst. I dig my nails into the grass and try to kick my legs in an attempt to fight back.

I start to feel my body weaken, giving up in a battle I never prepared for, a battle I had no hope of winning. Santo looks at me, his beady eyes so full of malice, so full of evil, eyes I do not recognise. Slowly, everything fades out of the view and into blackness as my eyes roll to the back of my head. I feel my body go limp as a final breath escapes my lungs.

* * *

I float upwards, so high. I'm not sure what I see, where I'm going, just that this all feels so familiar.

And I, weightless.

Free.

It's when the pain spills in from the gash on my head that I start to drift in and out of consciousness.

I feel the weight and breath in the familiar scent of my tartan blanket, feeling heavier than ever before. It takes me a few moments to realise that I lie in my bedroom.

I see a small streak of light that grows bigger and clearer beneath my bedroom door.

I blink at it, trying to remember my name and the colour of my eyes. I roll over with an effort and stare at the ceiling, every inch of my body aching a different ache. Sharp beneath the skin of my chest, dull in my bones, excruciating from the surface of my body to the depths of my soul.

I take a breath in and hold it as I pull myself off the bed.

Even my breaths ache.

I rise to my feet and walk out the door with shaking steps.

All the house lights are switched off except the kitchen lamp and the light in the hallway. I press my hand firmly against the wall to keep myself upright. The house is silent, still. I can only assume everyone has fallen asleep.

What time is it? How long was I out?

I reach for the throbbing pain on my head, feeling thick bandages that cover the wound above my left brow. I have to go see Mum, I have to check to see if the kids are alright. I take a step toward the hall when a sharp pain shoots up my spine, the weak groan that escapes my mouth sends shockwaves through my body.

My ribs rattle, and I feel as though I'm going to break in half completely.

I hear something rustle in the back living room. A moment later someone emerges from the shadows.

'Akita?' asks Evelyn's voice in frantic whisper, riddled with worry.

'Akita, are you okay?'

'I – Santo, he – where's Mum?' I struggle to speak.

'Go back to sleep, Keeks. I'll lie with you if you want?'

'Ev – no! we need to – ow – call the police,' I heave.

'Hey, hey, calm down. Look, why don't you lie down, and I'll go get Aunty, okay?'

Why isn't she listening to me? We don't have time to waste! Does she know what happened?!

Has Santo gotten away? Why is she acting like it was all a bad dream?

I shake Evelyn's arm off and make my way to the front living room in search of Mum. Evelyn trails behind me, walking uncomfortably close, begging me to get back in bed, a second later, I find out why.

Mum sits in the dark living room, illuminated by a singular lamp by the front door. The blinds have been erected; the pieces of glass cleaned off the carpet.

Santo lies asleep on the couch as Mum ices the bump just above his temple.

'M–Ma?'

'Akita,' Mum looks at me, then she glances at Evelyn behind me. They exchange a look, transmitting invisible information to each other.

'How are you feeling?' Mum asks gently.

'What's he doing here?' I ask, my voice shaky with all the nasty feelings in the world.

'He's sick.'

'But he–'

'I know what he did to you, Akita, and I'm sorry.'

'Ma, he's dangerous! He tried to kill me!'

She looks at me for a long time, with sad eyes.

'Get him out of here!' I shout as loud as I can, which isn't loud at all.

'Akita, you'll wake him,' she says with a sternness in her voice, a sternness she only uses when I'm in trouble. I feel like I'm a kid again.

I feel an unholy rage build up inside of me. I start to shake as if I'm going to burst into flames and engulf everyone in my fire.

I turn to walk away, the very sight of my mother and my brother making me feel sick to my core. I grab my car keys from my bedroom and I walk out the front door, the pain in my side no match for the sudden surge of adrenaline pumping through my veins.

'Akita, what are y–' I walk out the front and slam the door shut behind me.

I hope I have woken Santo with the noise, I hope the pain on his head lasts forever. I hear the door open and footsteps behind. Evelyn hobbles after me.

'Akita, please, you're not thinking straight what are you – no!' I get into the front seat of my car and lock the doors.

'Akita! Don't do this! You're – you're concussed! You can't drive!'

Evelyn frantically taps on the driver's window. When I start the engine she moves to the front of my car and puts her arms up.

'Evelyn, move!' I growl with such a ferocity that I feel Evelyn's courage dwindle.

'Please, Akita,' she mouths.

I wait a few seconds, sitting in the driver's seat, looking beyond this street that I've spent the past five years living in, the neighbourhood that's been my home for over a decade. I take a deep breath and count to ten, half expecting my mother to come out of the house and stand beside Evelyn, half expecting the very fabric of time to tear into pieces.

When neither of those things happen after I get to ten, I roll down my window.

'Get in,' I say slowly, 'or fuck off.'

We drive in silence for the first ten minutes, my fingers gripping the steering wheel tightly, my foot heavy on the accelerator.

'Where to?' Evelyn asks tenderly as I merge onto the freeway.

I, having no idea, say the first thing that comes to my mind.

'To see the stars.'

We arrive at the beach at two in the morning.

I step into the cold sand and I feel the grains shift beneath my bare feet. I take a few steps, every single one with intention. I see the ocean before me, obsidian in the night, reflecting the full moon's light in silvery streaks as black waves rise to the dark sky and rush over to me by the wind's command. I stare out for a few moments, sinking my feet into this atmosphere, becoming one with it. Ever so slowly I feel my troubles bleed out of me and into the air, disappearing into nothing.

The sky is so clear, so black, and studded with more stars than I can count. I collapse onto my knees and stare into the ocean as the wind whips my hair and waters my eyes. Waves crash into the sand with such force, the sea mist envelopes me into its prehistoric scent, loosening summer's grip on the warm night. In the vastness of the never-ending sky and the depth of the ocean, I feel so small.

I press my back against the sand, easing my head down. With a jolt I feel the pain above my left brow travelling to the bottom of my foot, and my broken arm throbs, screaming for attention, my spirit, drained, my heart, exhausted.

I'm surprised to feel the calm that washes over me. I've been freefalling for so long that I'm relieved to have reached the ground, even if I am broken from this crash-landing. I stare at the stars, sending silent prayers for one of them to beam me up there. If I belong anywhere, please, let it be there.

I hear the sand crunching under Evelyn's foot as she lays beside me.

'How are you feeling?' she asks over the crashing waves.

I swallow hard, trying to suppress the memories of the past however many hours it's been.

Evelyn looks around, then stares at me. 'You didn't drag me out here to kill me, did you?'

'For the love of god, Evelyn, please shut up.'

'Sorry! ... sorry ... bad joke.'

I feel as if I'm in a dream; my body in the sand feels like it's floating upward. I close my eyes, focusing on the crashing of the waves and the whispers of the wind.

Nothing makes sense.

Santo showing up and doing what he did caused a ripple through reality, creating a new one that I've been thrown into, one I'm not equipped to live through.

How did it get to this?

I think back to a time, back in our childhood. Things were easy, things made sense.

Cause and consequence, night and day, Santo and Akita.

One thing I could always count on was Santo, moreso than seeing the stars at night.

Everywhere he went, I followed. Best friends, although at the time neither of us would admit to that repulsive truth.

We played together, imagined worlds together, in between the fights over whose turn it was in the gaming console and hitting each other when words simply weren't enough. That Santo, and those memories of him are what I carry with me when I remember my brother. I feel those memories begin to die as the new ones of him today take their place. We both grew, changed. Spent less time together, more space apart. Santo grew to become someone else completely. Someone I hardly recognise. Someone who doesn't recognise me.

His face obscured, draining colour from the world, his soulless black eyes, his jaw misshapen from his vices. His body covered in scars and dents from things, places and people I cannot even imagine.

Santo, a monster, a physical manifestation of what's going on between his eyes. Looking at him was hard, yet I couldn't peel my eyes away; now his image is tattooed onto my mind, forever haunting me. Staring into the black abyss of his eyes was like looking at the dead. The memory of him on top of me, squeezing the breath out of me, sits so heavily on my thoughts that it feels like I'm there again, lying helplessly in the grass, crushed under his weight.

I sit up and my head spins. Evelyn watches me warily.

'You alright?' she asks for about the millionth time.

I shift my weight to the palms of my hands behind me and bury my feet into the cool sand, breathing in the cold air.

'Maybe there's a hospital nearby?' Evelyn says, searching our surroundings.

I laugh at her and my ribs rattle. I lie back down and gasp for air until I can breathe again.

I stare upwards to stop my head from spinning, to be as still as what I see above.

I've always been stunned by and drawn to the sight of a starry night sky for as long as I can remember. Most people are. But as I've grown older and the sky's grown dimmer, occasions like these are rare.

When I was little, when Dad, Santo and I used to stargaze in Giza, something wonderful always happened. The stars would summon my soul and make me one of them, every single time. I'd gaze up in awe, I'd see all the dreams I've dreamt, all the tears I've wept. In those moments I'd forget who I was, I only knew what I felt, among the stars, as a tiny speck of light.

I'd gaze up at the night sky, at the stars, and I knew with absolute certainty that they were staring back at me.

For a long time I believed they were just dreams, imaginings of a six-year-old. But now, as I lay here, my breath one with the wind, I feel the stars whispering to me. They ask why it's been so long.

I breathe a hot breath into the cold night.

'Hey?' says Evelyn, her voice is somewhere distant.

'Hmm?'

'What do you think of love?'

'W … what?' I ask, turning to her. For the first time tonight, Evelyn doesn't look back at me.

'I mean … do you believe in it?'

I don't answer her, my mind still elsewhere.

'Have you ever been in love, Akita?'

'Yeah,' I laugh.

'Yeah?'

'Yep.'

'Jacob?'

'The one and only … though I – I didn't know it at the time.'

'Huh …'

'What about you?' I ask.

'Yeah, I've been in love,' Evelyn says, and I can feel her smile in the words she speaks.

'I'm still in love with her, I think.'

'Who is she?'

'Erica. I met her in a club last year in South Melbourne.'

'Sounds romantic.'

'She was out of this world, Akita,' breathes Evelyn, her voice twisted with endless affection.

'What happened?'

'The same thing that always happens. She got tired of my shit.'

Neither of us says anything for a while.

There are so many things about Evelyn that I admire. I'm proud that she's finally decided to get her shit together, but tonight I've realised that even if she relapses, even if she falls and breaks apart again, she isn't mine to fix.

I start to feel myself and begin to drift off to sleep when Evelyn speaks again.

'Do you still love him?'

'Who? Jacob?'

'No. Santo,' she says. 'I'm kidding! That was a bad joke, I'm sorry!'

'Evelyn,' I laugh, then I start to cry, the pain pulsing down my spine from my ribs, and Evelyn apologises profusely.

'It's complicated,' I sniff when I get air in my lungs.

'How, Keeks? You either love someone or you don't. The way I see it, it isn't complicated at all.'

I wipe the tears from my eyes and face the stars.

'Do you remember when we were younger and Haboba would tell us the story of the sky and the sea?'

Evelyn falls quiet, the weight of my words sinking into the folds of her brain.

I don't say anything else. I don't need to. The story of the sky and the sea speaks all the words for me.

* * *

A long time ago, there was nothing.

The universe was all but an infinite void of darkness, and in it lived a lone star.

In its death, the tiny, lone speck of light exploded, giving birth to millions of other stars.

Some stars were ice-cold, others burned with a fire so fierce they illuminated the atmosphere.

Before too long, the dark void became what we now know as space.

Then there came a period of sudden energy bursts, and from those explosions, planets were born. Before space knew it, it had become a sky to the stars, suns, moons and billions of planets in millions of galaxies that keep her company.

The sky, as beautiful as she was becoming, embedded in stars, painted with stardust, and dotted with galaxies, took her time in admiring all that had become.

She found herself fascinated by all the planets, their shapes, sizes, colours, anatomies.

She was most especially fascinated by the strange, glistening matter that these planets carried.

Every planet she visited, no matter how different it was from the last, she found the same substance.

Water.

Some planets carried more water than others, but with every planet the sky explored she was elated to find her familiar friend.

Then one day the sky stopped to explore a planet with the most water she had ever seen. More than half the planet was covered in the strange substance that moved so freely and glittered so similarly to the stars the sky is covered in.

The sky leaned in, pressed into the planet's atmosphere, peering into the water's beauty. He went by many names and came in many forms. Ocean, river, waterfall, lake, streams. But she called him the "sea" because her eyes have never seen such beauty. The closer the sky got to the sea the louder he roared, and the more time she spent with him the higher his waves rose.

The sea was mesmerised by the beauty of the sky. The sea loved the way the rotation of her suns made her skin explode with hues of extraordinary colours.

He loved how she could become so dark yet so full of light.

The sea fell in love with all her stars and all the suns and the moons that he could and could not see.

When there were times of uncertainty, when the sky and the sea could not see each other clearly, they could do nothing but wait. The sky refused to command her suns to manipulate time, and the sea could not lift the fog and only waited for the clouds to pass. When they would reunite, the sky and the sea painted worlds in colours. The sky loved how the sea reflected her beauty back to her between the ripples of his tides, the way her stars would glimmer in his waves, the colours of her creations mirrored on the surface of his being.

Things were as they should be because they were meant to be, but like all else in nature, not without the test of time.

As centuries went on, each began to notice flaws in the lines and the dots that made the sky, the sky, and the sea,,the sea.

One day, without the sea's permission, as he lay flat and still, without waves, tides, or ripples, the sky submerged herself in the deep layers of the sea, and only then realised that all had not been as it seemed.

The sky was deeply shocked by what she saw.

The beautiful surface of the sea was so different from the dark and murky layers beneath him that seemed unending.

The sky began to drift away from the sea, fearing their connection because of how much he saw of her and how little she knew of him.

The sea, however, was confused and hurt, unsure if the only reason the sky ever loved the sea was because of the magic he made with the colours she shone on him.

As centuries passed, the sky found herself drifting back to the sea, because though her mind was made, there was no denying the affinity that tied the two together.

When the two reunite, she lays herself bare and the sea parts his waves, making way for her return.

Chapter 35

Geelong

Taresai

I trace my fingertips along the cracks of the timber dining table.

It's a shame.

Six seats line the edges of the table, five years spent living within these four walls, under this roof, and yet I can't name a single instance where I've sat with all my children and broken bread together on this table.

Not even on the rare days I'm home. If it's not me, who's absent, it's Akita, who spends more time out there than she does in here.

I stare out into the backyard through the glass doors, glaring at the overgrown grass, the concrete pavement stained with charcoal and red cordial, underneath dreary grey skies. The trees sway gently in the autumn breeze. Every so often a leaf parts with a branch and surrenders to the wind.

This house has seen better days and so have the people in it.

I don't understand.

Life isn't as much a struggle as it was back then. And yet during those years of difficulty, when I couldn't speak English and my children were preparing to be fatherless, there was always a reason to laugh.

Joy was never a difficult thing for us to find in the dark days that passed.

There are many reasons to smile in this house, but at times it feels like nobody does.

When Santino first left, things were difficult, but we managed. I'd thought back then that when my children grew, when Akita graduated high school, when Zandé knew the way home from school, when Amara learned to drive, I thought I would at last be able to breathe easily.

But as my children grow older they don't become easier to parent. With every age comes a new set of challenges. Things aren't simpler; in some hours of the night, I feel like they're more complex than ever before.

Sure, the food lasts longer, the house stays cleaner, I have more disposable income, but I'd take a conversation with eight-year-old Akita over an argument with my twenty-one-year-old daughter any day.

My daughter Akita has never been a speaker, not as a child, not today.

She doesn't talk to me, but it strikes deeper now that she's older because she chooses not to.

I sit and wait patiently for Akita to arrive at the table.

I called her name once a few minutes ago from outside her bedroom, and I know she heard me, so I will not call on her again.

We had an argument a few days ago and she hasn't spoken to or even looked at me since. She wants to move out, and I forbade her from it. It goes against everything that I am, and I refuse to wrap my head around it. Just because we were forced to leave our country doesn't mean we abandon our ways. Albeit, today, out of all days, might be the day she breaks many century-old rules.

That thought quickly shrinks when I sense her presence nearby. Akita walks out of her bedroom toward me, her footsteps slow and gentle. I don't turn.

She stops, and I, unmoving, feel her staring at the back me.

I can almost hear her contemplation to retreat into the safety of her bedroom, less than a step away.

Akita then does what I'd hoped, but not as I expected.

She walks towards me and sits on the opposite side of the dining table. A palm over her fist, staring at me with a look I can't quite translate. Her face has a hardness to it, one worn out of wisdom, and eyes swimming with pain no person her age should know.

Akita's left eyebrow twitches every now and then, but her eyes remain focused. She's become used to this, this game that only she and I know to play.

She's better at it than I am. Defiant.

In my greying age these arguments weaken me, creating a chasm between us when all I want is to reach out and touch her.

I'm kept awake at night, missing a daughter who sleeps a room away from me.

I bring myself to look at her.

As I stare, I see glimpses of the face Akita bore as a child, the largeness of her almond-shaped brown eyes, her small flat nose, the roundness of her cheeks which now sit higher on her matured face. I watched her face change with the seasons and years, but the magic of a mother is to look at the face of her child, at any age, and in it, see the one at their birth.

How badly I want things to go back to the way they were. When she couldn't form words to speak but had a mind full of them, when she would look at me like I carry the sun on my shoulders, not the way she looks at me now.

I can't tell the colour or the depth of the sea that lies behind those brown eyes.

I feel exhausted. We sit in silence for a few moments as she waits for me to speak. A stark contrast to the last time we were eye to eye.

'Where were you last night?' I ask her in my mother tongue.

'I went out with a couple of friends.' She speaks firmly in the language of this country, without missing a beat.

'Until four in the morning?' I ask again in Dinka.

'What's the big deal?' she replies, slipping her hands into the pocket of her hoodie. 'I came home, didn't I?'

'The big deal,' I repeat, 'is that you didn't call, and you didn't pick up when I called either. What if something happened?'

Akita looks at me for a long time, as if she's going to say something, then she looks away and scoffs.

'Akita, either spit it out or keep it to yourself.'

'Nothing happened,' she says quietly, but there's such a hardness to her voice it makes my skin prickle, 'and even if it did Ma, what could you have done?'

'Akita,' I warn, 'watch yourself.'

Akita kisses her teeth and I shoot her a look of caution.

'Was there anything else?' she says looking away, her voice mingled with tones of despair. Yes, there is so much more. I want to ask her what is it she can find out there that I can't provide in here?

I want to know if things could go back to the way they used to. I want to ask her why she tortures me with her silence because of that one night all of three months ago.

Santo went to prison for what he did to her, it was I that reported him to the police the following morning.

Still, I remain appalled and completely shattered for both my children, unable to erase the horrifying memory from my mind. To arrive home and find them both unconscious on the grass. One from injuries and bleeding from the head, the other foaming at the mouth and twitching.

'No,' I say softly. 'Is there anything you want to say to me?' I ask her in Arabic, the only other language Akita knows how to speak.

'Yes,' she responds simply in Arabic, 'I need to go.'

'Go where?' I ask in English without meaning to, and she falls into the same linguistic pattern.

'I don't know, Ma, away from here.'

'Not this again.'

'You never want to talk about it.'

'Because there's nothing to talk about! You leave this house when I say you can! I'm not letting you live on your own – you've been twenty-one for three days for goodness' sake!'

'I'm so sick of this, Ma, I'm so sick of you!' she cries. 'You have four other kids and none of them have had to deal with the shit that you've put me through!'

'Akita!'

'Stop pouring all your hopes and dreams into me, Ma,' she says, her voice breaking in soft exasperation. 'I have no room for my own, and if I continue to live my life trying and please you, I will die a failure!'

The palm of my hand collides with Akita's face in a vicious slap.

She steps back, holding her cheek, her eyes low. She gets up from the table and shuffles to her room.

'I'm going to bed.'

My eyes sting as they well up, my body frozen in shock.

I sit at the empty dining table, in the empty kitchen, feeling further away from my daughter with each second that passes. A single tear runs down my cheek and falls on the wooden table, seeping into the cracks of the timber.

Akita

I roll over on my side. My cheek still stings from the slap. I don't hear Mum outside my bedroom door, so I know she still sits on the dining table where I left her. I roll over once more and stare at my ceiling. My room is lit only by my bedside table lamp, in such a way that it feels like I'm inside a lantern.

I take a deep breath in and slowly exhale.

I have everything I've ever wanted.

A nice car, a generous paying job with my own desk and sick leave. I have three different groups of friends, independence, and freedom – a form of it anyway.

I don't have to worry about my future anymore, because this is it for me. I can just take each day as it comes. All the facets of my life are predictable, everything fits into each other like clockwork in the snakes and ladders of the corporate world.

On weekdays I wear pantsuits with closed-toe black heels, and jeans and a blazer from Zara on a Friday. I park my car on the third floor of the parking lot, between the white lines of the letter 'L,' and I get a soy milk vanilla latte every morning from the cafe beside the building that I work in inner-city Geelong – which houses the offices of the Australian Bureau of Statistics.

My day starts and ends in this city. So do my weeks, my months, my years.

Sometimes it feels like Geelong is the only place left in the world and everywhere else vanished.

I hear the dining table chair slide across the kitchen floor outside my room as Mum walks up the hall, into her bedroom and closes the door behind her.

I contemplate my movements on this Friday night.

My weekdays are when I am in this world, this world of protocols and procedures, of rules and order, of cause and consequence. My weekends are when I take myself out.

* * *

Most the friends I had in my youth have fallen and faded out of my life just like most people do as they grow up, they grow apart.

Chloe is an exception.

She went on a year-long meditation retreat in India after we graduated, and she came back with a different air to her. Something I can't see, but feel.

Chloe has discovered all the secrets of life, though she's yet to find what she wants to do with hers. For the moment she works at one of the stores Jacob's mum owns.

Chloe's invited me and a few of her other friends over for a 'full moon party', which is code for slow music and psychedelics.

I park my car at the end of the cul-de-sac in front of Chloe's mum's new house. They live in Leonard, on an affluent estate in a picture-perfect neighbourhood with rotten bones.

The crimes that happen here are no different from those which occur back home in Corio and Norlane, drug dealing, theft, violence of all sorts, but the people who commit them are European-car-driving, 9–5 working people. Chloe opens the front door and pulls me into the living room, a place of coloured smoke slowly swirling above the faceless heads that sit on the carpet in a circle. A place of slow music that hits with a force that slows time.

I take my place, put my lips on the joint when it has been passed to me, inhaling deep, exhaling softly. I breathe it in and cough it out, surrendering to it, staring at the ceiling as a smile forms on my face.

Though my chest burns and my nostrils sting, I start feeling lighter, and I greet the familiar feeling with glee and open arms.

I remember there was a time when Santo used to say: you don't need wings to be free, to fly.

For once, I think I agree with the lunatic.

I start to disentangle from reality, drifting further away from my thoughts, from the unrelenting heaviness that burdens my soul when I'm sober. I drift with the smoke towards the ceiling, watching my limp body from above, my head rolling, my chest rising and falling to the rhythm of my breath. This is what it's like to be free.

Taresai

I knew it the second she walked out the front door last night.

I knew it would be a sleepless night, a night that would turn to day before I'd hear back from my daughter.

'A work party,' she'd responded when I asked her where she was going yesterday. I couldn't stop her; she's twenty-one, she's capable of making her own decisions, but damn it, why must they be so reckless?

It's 11.34 on this wintery morning. For all I know my child could be dead.

With every ring of the phone going unanswered my heart sinks deeper.

She must still be asleep.

Heavens, please Akita, be asleep.

I should be glad that her phone rang at all.

I sit on the edge of my bed, running my fingers through my hair, untangling the braids I wove, wondering what happened to my daughter.

I know her heart is heavily burdened, and I know I have hurt her.

I know Santo has hurt her, and he was the person Akita loved most.

I know my daughter has been searching for ways to erase him from her memories to ease her ache. But it is my torture that she expects me to do the same.

When they were younger, Santo and Akita would fight as brothers and sisters do. After the storm, I'd sit them both down and resolve it, pointing out their wrongdoings and emphasising their right doings. That part was always tricky, but they never needed their mother to embolden their love for each other. That was something they did freely, naturally, so effortlessly.

When they were younger, my dilemma was choosing who had a turn on the gaming console first, who got the apple juice box and who got the orange.

Now, it's choosing one's life over another. How do I make them see each other when they face complete opposite waters, when all love has been lost?

I felt it in my spine the moment my son began to change, began to slip, the moment Santo's light began to dim. It was before he threw out his medications and abused his sister. No, it was when he stopped calling me 'Mum,' when he stopped calling me anything, and the light in his eyes wouldn't change when his gaze would settle on me.

Akita's change was subtle, so subtle that I only ever noticed when it was too late.

My mind often wanders to the days when Akita sat between my legs as I twisted her hair into various shapes. In those hours we were spirit to spirit, communicating with more than just words in a language of love. I'd comb and wrap my fingers into the coils of her every strand like a sacred ritual.

All I can do is bask in those memories, because that is all they are now.

I haven't touched Akita's hair since she was sixteen.

Sometimes I drift in grief, allow the tides of sorrow to wash over me. Other times I fight the crashing waves of resentment, of bitterness, but they pull me under.

All I do for my daughter, all my efforts in being the mother I didn't have.

How could she be so blind to me?

That question vanishes every moment from my mind when I remember Akita could ask me the same thing.

And I would have nothing to say.

How could I, when she is lost in all the ways that I am found? And she, certain in all that troubles me.

I'm separated from Akita, I'm separated from all my children, by much more than only the times. Once that realisation dawned on me, it no longer gripped me with despair, but held me with hope. I realised it's the very plight every migrant mother and refugee father has with their progeny.

I'd have thanked the skies for the blessings in my life, the privileges, the freedoms, the rights, if I came here as young as my children did, but only because I know what it's like to go without.

In this country, my daughters will never need to worry about being sold and married to men twice their age and having their every move dictated. My children won't witness the horrors that their parents have endured, and that is an eternal blessing – but at what cost?

Back in Sudan it was law of the land, that life and death went hand in hand.

That life is a cloth of pain and hardship, where moments of happiness are golden threads that only few could afford to weave.

I realised that wasn't true much before we came here.

This life is different.

Nearly sixteen years we've been in this country, and still I find myself unable to fathom the stark contrasts between and nuanced hues of the life my children live and the life I have lived. Sometimes I feel worlds away from them.

When I'd go days without food, they go days without seeing the sun.

My sons don't have to worry about being forced into the military, no, Santo sold his soul to the devil instead. My children, their kinfolk and skinfolk who look like them in this country, have severed roots, roaming this land, seeking to belong, disconnected from their tribes, and yet we wonder why they're so lost.

In the ebb of identity, the flow of the stereotype, they grow in a place where the streetlights shine brighter than the stars, where they are told who they are before they've had a chance to figure it out for themselves.

Yes, young Taresai would be grateful to be in wonderful Australia, but there's no doubt that I too would be lost.

Living in a rectangular box of cement and brick, one that is numbered, on a street that is measured, in a city built with calculated precision.

Back home in Sudan you'd never find a straight line, only obscure shapes. The curves of sand dunes, the jagged edges of the mountains and rock formations, the grooves of the terrain, ripples of the rivers, the humps and bumps of the red dirt that would colour our village when the wind felt like it.

In the rare seasons when it rained, my siblings and I would take down the fabric hung from the opening of our hut and lay on the floor of our home, allowing the scent of wet mud and sand to drift inward and take us away.

As I'd lay there, I'd feel the heartbeat of the land thumbing on the skin of my back, and I could taste the mud on my tongue. I knew who I was, I knew who I was going to be, and I knew where home was.

But I would hope with all my heart, to be somewhere else, because hope was the only thing I could do.

Akita

It takes my eyes a few blinks and my chest a few breaths before I can make sense of who I am, where I am, and why I'm lying next to a topless Chloe.

I roll over the bed and land on the orange shaggy rug with a thud. I groan, but also welcome the pain of feeling something after being numb for however many hours it's been this time.

I pick up a nearby phone. It's 3.46pm on a very cold Saturday. I stretch out my limps and shuffle into the bathroom.

The house is still, silent and quite frankly trashed in the way young people with savings accounts trash homes. Crocheted blankets on the carpet, cushions stained with malt liquor, the picture frames on the wall askew, a mint-green bong left on the dining table like some sort of centrepiece.

I wash my face with cold water, rubbing the mascara from my eyelashes and the powder off my skin. I stare at myself in the mirror.

I have the rest of today and tomorrow to get back to looking like the woman who works at a government office. The woman who shows up to her desk fifteen minutes early wearing YSL perfume and Tom Ford lipstick. A version of myself I hardly know in this state. I'm startled when I feel my phone vibrate in my back pocket. I pull it out. Twenty-three missed calls from mother dearest. I fill a cup with cold water and gargle. I spit it out in the sink and wipe my mouth, gazing at myself in the mirror, unable to meet my own eyes.

Chapter 36

Geelong

Akita

I'm nearly always the last to leave the office on Friday.

The building is deserted; me, the cleaner, and the two security officers are all who remain. Stuart, a sixty-something-year-old man, is cleaning the floor above me, and the two security officers, Hayden and Josh, remain on the first floor.

They're all nice enough. Stuart often asks me about my heritage and shares his encounters with people who look like me. Hayden and Josh, from what I see, are footy fanatics. I don't care to have small talk with them, but I don't mind them. For the most part, they don't bother me when I stay back and do my work.

I work in the diversity and integration department, on a desk by the window on the third storey of an eight-level building.

I collect data and statistics from local schools and places of learning and evaluate the effectiveness of the education provided to migrant children. I like my job enough; I get government paycheques, and I like to think that I'm working for the kids in a position that I was once in.

I like the people I work with, except for Maurice, the only other black person in this entire building.

Maurice is a couple years older than I am, and works in the finance department. When I first started here Maurice was in his third year on the job, everyone was warm and welcoming, except him.

I didn't understand what his problem was, and I still don't.

I was initially disheartened by his dismissal of me, but suspected it was only a matter of time until he and I got along. Eleven months later and Maurice still avoids me at the office parties and potlocks, and talks over me whenever someone asks about the motherland, even though we're from completely opposite sides of the continent.

Whenever we have staff days out for friendly games of footy, kickball or softball, Maurice insists on going head-to-head with me. Every time.

I don't understand him, but I know what he is.

He plays a game where I am his only competition, his only enemy.

I've decided to let him play those games on his own. I refuse to partake, to set fire to his match. I don't want anything Maurice has; I've shrunken his existence down to a pesky little fly that I ignore when I can, swat when I can't.

I drink the last of my coffee. Everyone else clocks off early on Fridays, leaving unfinished work on their desks to be resumed on Mondays, emails unanswered, phone calls unreturned, documents incomplete.

But I can't.

At first, everybody, including the department manager, thought that I was putting in the extra hours and the extra effort in my work to prove myself, to earn some sort of promotion or recognition. I've been here almost twelve months; I've got nothing else to prove.

I can mess up as many times as my project partner, Brenda, and still have the position I have now. But there's something that's been hardwired within me that forbids me to do that.

To relax. To open myself up to the possibility of, well, anything short of excellence.

I can't accept anything that isn't to or greater than the standard I have set for myself.

They all applaud me for it, everybody here in the diversity and integration department, all the way to finance, accounting and HR, admiring me, my work, my efforts.

I've been invited to all the weddings, baby showers, birthdays, christenings, after-work hangouts, even Georgia's divorce party.

I've been an asset, they say, with an impeccable work ethic. I should pride myself on it. But I just think there's something very wrong with me. I do it all because I fear I've lost every other sense of who I am, so if I hang on to this job then I hang on to myself, even if it's by the thinnest thread.

When I'm here the disconnect is nuanced, dull, quieter than it is when I lie awake in my bed at night. I have everything I've ever wanted, everything I've worked so hard for, so why do I feel so empty?

It's almost 11pm by the time I park my car along the nature stripe outside Mum's house. I hang my leather bag over my shoulder and walk up the driveway. I pause, looking up at the faint dots shimmering in the blue-black sky, stained with the yellow lights of the city.

I walk inside, mildly interested to notice that most of the lights in the house have been switched off. The hallway light is the only one on, glowing from the ceiling.

Mum must be asleep; nothing else commands this kind of silence, especially when all of us are home. I walk to my bedroom and switch on the light, throwing my bag and jacket on my desk chair. I collapse onto my bed and sigh heavily. Something feels off.

Usually Amara, Ashanti or Zandé come to my room to greet me when I come home from work. Even on late nights like this. Though I don't think that's what's getting to me.

The energy in the house feels strange, like it's been corrupted.

I sit up, sensing the calm that the air buzzes with, the kind of calm that only awakens in the dying of a thunderstorm.

I walk into the kitchen, the timber floor cold on my bare feet. I open the fridge and I see something move in the corner of my eye in the hallway. I jump back and race towards the kitchen light and flick it on.

A man stands in the middle of the hallway. Smiling up at me with great pain in his eyes. A man I haven't seen in years. I open my mouth to speak, to curse, to express my feelings of anger and resentment, but when I part my lips, hold stale breath, a word is all I can utter.

'Dad.'

Taresai

It's truly bizarre to sleep next to someone again. I'm unfamiliar with the weight of his body next to mine, the warmth of his breath on my skin, the sounds of his snores echoing through the silence of the night.

I've dreamt of this day when Santino would come back. I've had visions of what it would be like, the relief I would feel, how things would go back to normal again.

I was wrong. Normal died a long time ago.

Santino told me he was coming back three weeks ago; I didn't believe him. That was the last time we spoke. Last night he arrived at the doorstep of a house he's never seen to greet the wife and children he's been away from for nearly a decade.

I turn to Santino, asleep beside me. I stare at him. The light that creeps in from the window sits atop the edges of his face, settling in the deep lines etched on his forehead from all the forgotten nights spent worrying. The wrinkles around his mouth from all the tireless words he'd uttered, the greys in his hair from all the thoughts he's had, unspoken.

Time has been a friend to me compared to what it's been to Santino. He looks so much older, greyer, skinnier.

I look at him deeply, unable to believe my own eyes. Unable to comprehend his materialisation, his body, his shut eyes, his head, with all his thoughts, secrets and memories, lying on this pillow, inches away from me.

Akita

The first few days of having Dad back in the house were strange.

It was like life had broken and we all pretended not to see the cracks. It felt like a stranger was in the house, a guest, a long-lost relative coming to visit and stay with us temporarily. I felt like I needed to look presentable at all times, like it was wrong to sing in the shower and play my music when I did the dishes or cooked.

But after a few days of small talking and Dad trying to take up as little space as possible, I'm starting to care much less.

'I don't know, Akita, I think I kind of like it,' says Zandé, his head on my lap as I attempt to twist his hair into a braid. 'I like him, Dad's nice.'

'That's good, Zandé,' I say as he winces.

'Akita, are you hearing this boy?' Amara scoffs. 'He's talking about his Dad like he's a new friend.'

'It's not a bad thing,' says Ashanti, lying belly down on my bed with her feet in the air.

'Yeah, but it's weird,' argues Amara.

'I don't care,' says Zandé defensively.

This all must be so strange for him. He's pretty much meeting his father for the first time. A man who's has been a mystery all his life is now sleeping in the room on the other side of his wall. We've all congregated in my room as we do on most days when I come from work; all we've been talking about this week is Dad.

Dad's been having very long and deep conversations with Mum and a lot of small talk with us, surface-level stuff. He took us out to dinner on Friday, which felt like we were all actors in a theatre show, performing for an invisible audience. Pretending that this is normal.

There will be a day when Dad and I will sit down and catch up on everything he's missed in the past ten years. For my sake, I hope that day never comes. There's too much to say, too much to ask and all the time in the world wouldn't be enough to speak them.

Everybody and their fathers have come to visit Dad in the past week, welcoming him back to the country. Uncles and friends that Dad has stayed connected with, some he even met over there in Sudan who've come back years before.

That night after dinner, after all of Dad's friends have gone home and all of us have retreated into our bedrooms, I hear the doorbell. I pretend to be asleep to avoid having to serve some more guests.

I hear a knock on my door, too harsh to be Mum's.

I wait a few seconds before I respond. I see my doorknob twist and the door slowly swings open as a large figure walks in. I sit up, my muscles tensed as I stare into the vacant eyes of my brother, Santo.

'Hi, Akita,' he says, his eyes unfocused.

'They let you out,' I say quietly, almost to myself.

Santo was imprisoned after that incident last year, but I didn't expect to see him roaming free for at least another year.

That night nobody speaks of, not even Mum.

She was the only one who stayed in contact with Santo when he got sent to the slammer. He tried to call me several times from prison, but I always hung up after the courtesy announcement from Port Phillip Corrections. They kept my number on the call list from the last time he was in there.

That night last year was the last time we looked into each other's eyes, the last time we exchanged words. I wasted no time thinking of him, no breath in speaking his name, yet here he is, standing at my door.

'Yeah, mentally ill and whatnot,' he smiles, his teeth sharp, his head shaven, his eyes obsidian. Santo's huge figure stands at the threshold of my door, dressed in black, blocking out any light from coming into my room. I hardly even see Zandé standing behind him.

'You alright, Akita?' Zandé asks when I catch his eyes, arms folded, chest puffed in his Spiderman pyjamas.

'Yeah, I'm okay Zan, go to bed.'

Zandé reluctantly walks away.

Santo watches Zandé with a look in his eyes that I can't read. He turns and looks at me. My glower must be extreme because Santo lets out a dry chuckle.

'It's alright, Akita, I'm not gonna hurt you. Mum let me in.'

Those things don't equate. I can have one as well as the other.

'Listen,' he says, rubbing his jawbone with his fingers.

I see the deep scars on the back of his hand, wrapping around his skin like a string made from lightning. Without realising I trace my fingers along the scar on my head, above my left brow, a stain on my skin left by Santo and a metal pipe.

'A–Akita, I want to apologise. For ... everything. But mostly for–'

'Trying to kill me?' my voice is softer than I'd intended.

'That wasn't me, Akita I blacked out.'

'Yeah, I figured.'

'It was all the shit I was pumping into me, it made me sick.'

'Then why did you do it?' I ask. Santo puts his hands in his pockets and smiles wordlessly. I look away, the sight of him making my blood boil and freeze over at the same time. There is so much I want to say to him, so much I want to tell him, and yet nothing at all.

'Are you on your medications?' I ask calmly.

Santo considers the question.

'I'm feeling much, much better now.'

We both fall quiet, unable to meet each other's gaze now that the tension has eased.

'Hey, are you … are you free these days?' Santo asks,

'What do you mean?'

'I wanna show you something. Something I found. It's not far … by car.'

'Ah, listen, Santo, not tonight, yeah?' I say, as tenderly as I can.

Guilt grips me when I say the words. I'm not sure why I'm worried about hurting his feelings. But I feel I'm too much in a state of bewilderment to go wherever he is suggesting, not to mention my terror. I'm not even sure I've breathed a single breath since he opened my door.

'Alright, well … let me know when. I'll be around.'

I pull my knees to my chest and hug them, feeling like I'm in some sort of fever dream.

'Okay, I better go, but, um, think about it okay?'

'Yeah, okay.'

Santo turns to leave, but stops in his tracks.

'Dad's here,' Santo says, eyebrows furrowed. 'How crazy?'

'Yeah,' I say tiredly. 'Didn't you know?'

'Oh, no, I've known for a while,' he says coolly, 'Mum told me a few weeks ago that he was coming back.'

Santo smiles, nods his head, and closes my bedroom door.

Of course, she did, of course Mum told Santo about Dad before any of us. But I'm not upset nor surprised. I understand why she would.

If it meant her son had something to hold on to when all has been lost to him, I'd like to think that I would do the same

Chapter 37

Geelong

Akita

Santo comes over nearly every day to have a meal with Mum and Dad.

Some days he remembers my name, other days he only recognises my face. He is confused most of the time, his mind a pool of transient memories and loose thoughts. Santo listens to music with a constant feeling and look of déjà vu, to songs we've listened to since we were kids.

He has a worker named Daniel who has explained to Mum and Dad that the damages done to his brain by Santo's abuse of himself, are irreversible, but not unmanageable, so long as he stays away from that dark and twisted world of violence and narcotics.

But it's all he knows and I feel to ask that of him, is to ask Santo to prolong the inevitable.

He is a shell of the person he used to be, an echo of the voice that was once so familiar and the more time he spends here, the further away I feel from him.

It's bizarre: our family is whole again; we have dinner with all seven of us at the dining table. Mum, Dad and Santo sit together on the other side of the table, Amara, Ashanti and Zandé on the other. I sit in the centre of it, between two different worlds, two different lifetimes, taking it all in. For most of it I feel as though I'm in limbo, looking into a mirror of the past and one of the present.

Things are normal; we seem like a normal family. But I've gone so long without normality that this display of it is disturbing to the spirit. I try to let myself enjoy it, to drown out the feelings of resentment and dread of what's to come once the foundations begin to crack.

I try to be happy for Santo – he's trying to turn a new leaf even though his brain has turned to mush and his soul has parted ways with his body, only to visit in moments like these. I look to Zandé, who smiles ear to ear, his presence casting a bright light on us, rivalling the sun of the afternoon. Ashanti stares at Dad with such curiosity, as if he is going to vanish into thin air before he speaks his next word. Amara throws jokes at Santo about being a jailbird, most of which flies over his head but he laughs anyway, confusion in his eyes, a disconnection in his soul.

On a Sunday evening, while Amara and Mum pack up the dishes, I walk to the front living room where Dad and Santo sit on the leather armchairs opposite each other. They both fall silent when I walk into the room, but I feel like what they were talking about wasn't of great importance.

'Akita …' Santo recalls with no difficulty.

'Hey Santo, what was it you wanted to show me?'

* * *

Santo and I walk down the restless streets of Norlane.

This neighbourhood is usually terrifying on a night so dark, though tonight there's a delicate sense of calm lingering in the air. The moonlight blankets the streets with a silvery glow, making even the most rundown milk bars, graffitied walls, overgrown grass, charred dumpsters and broken fences look beautiful.

Santo and I walk in silence for the first couple of minutes before I speak.

'So … where are we going exactly?' I ask, taking long strides to keep up with his walking pace. 'Somewhere really cool,' he beams, and I see his teeth gleam in the moonlight. 'We'll be there soon, only a couple more minutes.'

I agreed to walk the thirty-minute journey after Santo confessed that he felt anxious about cars, a phase he hopes to see the other side of.

When he said those words to me it made me want to cry. I want to protect Santo – from the world, but most especially from himself. He has support workers, counsellors, but it seems that all the people in the world can't save Santo from Santo.

'This feels nice,' Santo says after a while. 'Walking.'

'Yeah,' I laugh. 'I don't do it enough.'

'I walk everywhere. One time I walked for three days straight. The cops found me passed out on the side of the freeway. I don't even remember where I was going.'

Santo laughs. I laugh too, to stop myself from crying mostly, but also because I don't know what to say to that. What do you say to a broken boy with a broken life, a broken soul, a boy who doesn't see that he's broken?

'But when I walk, Akita, I notice all the little things.'

'What little things?'

'The little things in people, what they think, how they are.'

'How?'

'I see people … getting scared of me on the street, without a reason to,' he says pulling up his hoodie.

'They cross the road, lock their cars, clutch their purses, as if there's anything in there worth stealing!' He chuckles. 'And what would I be doing jacking cars and stealing purses in broad daylight anyway?' Santo sniffs and blows white air out of his mouth into the sky. After a small pause between us, he speaks again.

'Those people, they think they're important. More important than me, than *us*. They think we want to take what they have, its why they hold onto it so close.' Santo presses his hands deeper into his pockets. 'But I don't get it: what's scary about a big black boy? A–A big black man? I mean, did *we* invade their lands and take it as our own? Did we enslave their people?'

I watch Santo as he speaks, moved by his words.

'If anything, *we* should be afraid that they're gonna steal *our* shit,' Santo laughs.

It's the very first time in a lifetime that I'm seeing this side of him, a side I hadn't known survived. I didn't know there were still traces of him left.

'I don't get it, Akita – this whole world is backwards.'

We walk to the edge of Norlane and cross the train tracks, walking along the bay which reeks of poverty and rotting seaweed.

The full moon glows brightly, casting an iridescent orb in the black sky, making passing clouds gleam like opal.

'So,' Santo says suddenly. 'Are you still seeing that lanky boy?'

'Wha–Jacob? No ... no, we broke up a long time ago. I don't remember telling you about him,' I say, embarrassed, but I don't know why.

'No, you didn't. Mum did.'

'Ah . . .'

'She didn't need to, though, I already knew.'

'How?' I cackle in disbelief.

'The streets talk, Akita.'

'Oh, do they now, Santo?' I question, still chuckling.

'Yeah, they do,' he tries to convince, but even in the dark of night I see him suppress the smile that creeps onto his face.

'What do these streets say?' I enquire, wiping a tear from my eyes.

Santo's face changes suddenly; in the moonlight I see the amusement wiped from his mind, the light draining from his eyes.

'The streets talk in a voice that only I can understand. A voice only *I* can hear. All I need to do is press my ear to the ground.'

Santo looks at me intensely and I feel disturbed by the sudden change of his aura, his disposition, disturbed by how quickly I can lose him, even if all I do is blink.

'What about you?' I ask before he sinks deeper. 'Are you seeing anyone?'

'Not anymore,' he says to my complete and utter surprise. 'She broke my heart, though.'

'Huh, I didn't know you had one,' I think out loud before I could stop myself.

Santo stops in his tracks and stares at me, his eyes enormous.

I might have gone too far.

For a split second I feel my heart quicken and my breathing stop, then Santo smiles, his sharp teeth ripping through his mouth in a hearty chuckle.

We walk to the edge of the bay, to a place where the grainy sand meets the shrub and soggy patches of grass. Santo leads me towards a hidden track between the bushes, a downhill path that twists around the corner and arrives at a place I cannot see. Santo walks down the path as though he's done it many times before.

I ignore the anxiety swelling in the pit of my stomach and follow.

I take a single step and stumble downhill, my canvas sneakers weighted by the wet mud. I grab onto what I can only assume are branches of trees or bushes and trudge on in near pitch-blackness. When I don't hear Santo's footsteps ahead of mine I start to panic.

I feel my foot sink into a deep muddy puddle, and before I know it I'm tripping and tumbling down the rest of the way, sliding down the steep, muddy track.

I land at the bottom of the hill in a puddle of water with a squelch, mud staining the front of my jeans and jumper. I get to my feet and walk toward Santo, who stands still, unfazed by my fall, his eyes fixed on something mine can't yet see.

Santo points towards something in the distance when he feels me beside him.

'Do you see that?' he asks, pointing at what looks to be a small shack sitting in the shallow water in the distance.

'Yah-huh.'

'We're here. Let's go in,' he beams. Santo searches my face, trying to read me. 'It's not haunted,' he professes solemnly.

That's not my worry. The house, if that's what it is, looks like it may sink into the water if so much as a leaf is blown in through the broken windows. But how do I explain that to Santo?

'Akita,' he says, 'I cross my heart.'

* * *

Our footsteps echo on the rotting timber floor. Santo pulls out a torch and shines it around the space. I catch glimpses of moth-eaten curtains and exposed nails poking through like broken bones of a body that still stands. I don't know how long this house has been here. I hadn't even know it existed until now.

We tread through, the foul stench of decay filling my nostrils.

'Santo, why'd you bring me here?'

Santo takes a long time to answer. He wanders through the space in a trance, as if he's been enchanted; I follow closely behind. I can't see his face, but I imagine his eyes wide and his mouth open, like he's seeing this place for the very first time.

'This house was built by and belonged to Frances O'Hare.'

I think for a moment, trying to remember if that name should mean something to me.

'Who?'

'Frances. He was an Irish prisoner, Akita. A philosopher, way ahead of his time. He came here as a convict, and he was hated by everyone because of his thinking.'

'What was his thinking?'

'That people are not good or bad. We make decisions, but it's not the consequences of those decisions that is the true marker of a person's character. It's the intention. The world gave him nothing, so he took things, without asking.'

He speaks those words, and I know I'm not the first to hear it come out of his mouth.

I don't know if I agree with Santo's and Frances' ways of thinking, but this very moment isn't about me, so I hold my tongue and watch as Santo speaks, his face illuminated by the white light of his torch.

'I read about him when I was locked up. Gus, my cellmate, told me about Frances. The cell that I slept in was the same one he was in when he was locked up too.' When Santo smiles I get a flash of the face he had when we were kids, the face I love so much. His dimples deepening, the deep pools they create on his cheeks, his gentle brown eyes, his wide smile, and ever-gleaming teeth.

'I feel like I know him, Akita. I read his journals, I read all the books about him, and … and I feel like we're the same person. Connected by everything but at the same time … by nothing either.'

I stare at Santo for a very long time, my brain struggling to see him as the figure standing before me. Every second it seems I'm getting a different version of him, someone I've known all my life and lifetimes before this one, and yet he is someone I've just met.

Speaking with a voice and looking with the eyes of a young child and the wisdom of an old man.

'What?' Santo says after observing the look on my face.

'Nothing.' I smile weakly, hoping that he doesn't see the tears in my eyes. 'It's just … I'm trying to understand you, Sunny.'

Santo looks at me, his eyes softening, his mouth curving into a sad smile.

'Don't,' he breathes, 'don't try to understand me, Akita. You'll spend the rest of your life trying to find answers but never getting them.'

'Okay,' I say, more to myself than to him.

I've dreamt of this day. The day he and I would meet again. I rehearsed what I would say, imagined every possible scenario. But here I am, shaken by the same epiphanies that ground me, these very moments stirring and dredging up that which sits deepest and burying it all again.

Santo and I stand alone, together, for the first time since our childhood. Much has changed, yet so much has remained.

In my eyes, Santo was never afraid of faceless beings and malevolent monsters of the dark. Of terrible things that haven't happened and those that have.

What I admired him for as a child, I hated in him as we grew. I now realise that he was frightened, terrified, more often than I was.

He just never showed it.

I watched as he collapsed into himself, made friends with his demons, slipped through the cracks and fell into the belly of the world.

I never understood why. Why it was so hard for him to just be *fucking* good.

In time, I've come to know that trying to make sense of Santo was like venturing out into the unknown with nothing but the promise of losing oneself. And still, I look.

He alone is a prisoner of his own creation; he got lost, deep in the labyrinth of his mind, and he does not want to be found.

There are parts of him that I have lost, and I have to make peace with the fact that I'll never get them back. But as we stand here, I realise that I am forever tied to Santo through the glorious gift of blood and bone.

Santo looks at me, looks beyond me like I'm made of glass, like I could shatter at any moment, and with my broken pieces I'll become one with the floor and this old house.

I sniff and wipe my tears, smearing the mud from my sleeve across my face.

'There's one more thing I want to show you before I say goodnight, Kita.'

Santo leads me to a room at the back of the house. I walk through the threshold, following him closely. I realise we are standing in a bathroom when my vision adjusts.

Santo walks toward the sink and waits for me to stand beside him. He shines the torch on our faces, so we see our reflections in the dirty, cracked mirror.

I stare at myself, I stare at Santo through the murk, through the brown spots, stains and all that is broken. He bends down and gazes at the rusty metal sink, and I bow my head with him. Santo opens his mouth and spits down the drain of the sink.

He turns to me, and he watches as I do the same.

Chapter 38

Geelong

Akita

The clouds thunder long before the rain starts to pour.

I stare at the sky, clouded in complex hues of grey, concealing above, soothing below. Every so often lighting strikes within the clouds, giving life to the storm, thumping within it like a heartbeat, a pulse.

Even though those moments are but a mere second long, in them the whole world stands still; everything stops. Lightning bursts through the clouds and extends her hand out to me. For a second it feels like we could touch, like I could feel her electricity on my fingertips if I were to just reach out my hand.

But I don't.

I stand here among everyone else, dressed in black, celebrating the colourful life of Santo, mourning the loss of him and the lightning that stays trapped within those clouds.

It's a beautiful day. The first day in a while where I feel light.

It's been five weeks of heartache, devastation, of sorrow, but in it I have found there can be comfort, and rest in the moments I am able to breathe into it.

At times I find it hard to wrap my head around the fact that he is no longer here and other times, during my many sleepless nights, Santo's parting with this world is the only thing that makes sense, even though my mind can't yet seem to move beyond that.

Santo was in so many ways, was not of it, this time, this place.

There is a relief, above all else, which is beginning to settle. I'm relieved that his tortured soul is finally free, but with it comes a selfish kind of sadness. An anguish for all that has been lost and an anger in him and in the universe and all the gods and goddesses that ever existed that didn't allow Santo to stay long enough on this earth to right his wrongs. To pick up his broken pieces and be the person we all wanted him to be. Needed him to be.

But this was the way it was meant to be, for Santo to pass peacefully in his sleep. His time had come, and I know that all of who he is will wait for me.

After some time the thunder stops, the clouds slowly part, and I am reunited with the line that separates the earth from the sky.

* * *

I lay on the square of concrete in the backyard, basking in the afternoon sun. Amara's tabby cat, which she named Leo, paces around the space where my head lies before she curls beside me with her head resting on my neck.

It was Dad who'd adopted Leo, ten days after Santo's funeral and her presence has been a distraction as well as a nascence.

She's a sweet kitten; ginger fur, jade eyes and a brown freckle on her pink nose. She didn't like me for the first couple weeks, but now I catch her searching around the house for me, only resting when I'm found.

We lie in the sun with our eyes closed, breathing out of sync to a rhythm only the two of us know. The birds fly over us and call to each other, and the trees sway and rustle in the breeze.

I don't know how long we lay here for, but I don't think I would mind if it were all day.

The doorbell sounds off and Leo jumps off me, scratching my neck with her delicate claws. I get to my feet and walk into the house.

Leo and I are the only ones home. Zandé and Ashanti are at school for the final day of the year, Amara is at rehearsals for her upcoming recital and Mum and Dad are at work. I walk down the hallway and open the front door, expecting to see the postman, one of our neighbours or Jehovah's witnesses.

But instead, a tall brown woman with a wide nose and wild black hair stands before me.

'Hello?' I say, stepping out onto the porch, closing the door behind me.

'Hi,' she says, her eyes softening with relief.

She beams at me, her eyes darting back and forth as she searches my face.

'Can I help you?' I ask awkwardly.

I see my words cut through to her, extinguishing the light in her eyes, shrinking the thoughts in her brain.

'Ah, yes!' she says, closing her eyes and shaking her head, struggling to form words. 'Sorry, you must be, um, Akita?' she asks, squinting her face as she says my name.

'Yeah, that's me,' I say slowly.

'I'm Emelé ...' She grins at me expectantly.

'Oh!' I say, trying to rack my brain if her face and her name should be things that I know or remember.

'Is your family home?'

'No ... no, just me for the time being. I'm sorry, are you a friend of ...'

She looks too old to be a friend of Amara's; she looks a little older than I am actually, and she's too young to be a friend of Mum's.

'No, that's okay,' she says, her eyes focused on mine.

She takes a long time to speak. 'It's just, well ...' She looks at me dreamily, then snaps back out of it and whips her head around, coming back into reality.

I stare at the strange women warily.

'Stay right there, Akita, I'll be back.'

Emelé paces down the driveway and opens the rear door of an SUV parked behind my small car. I have no clue what to make of the situation, befuddled as it unfolds. I watch as she unbuckles something, pushes another thing to the side, then she pulls out a small brown child. He looks two, maybe three, years old. Emelé carries the child on her hip and walks towards me.

'There's someone I want you to meet,' Emelé says to the boy.

He has large brown eyes and curls as wild as his mother's.

The boy looks up at me shyly and meets my gaze. A small gasp escapes my me as I look into the eyes I've seen a thousand times.

'Sunny,' Emelé smiles. 'Say hi to your aunty.'

Taresai

In Sudan, war came without warning, but I knew every time it was near.

Before there were explosions and gunshots, the rumble of feet on the hot earth desperate for an escape, the thuds of falling bodies hitting the ground as their soul would part. Before all that, there was a sickening buzz in the air that would make the hair on my skin stand, so venomous I could almost taste it.

Each morning leading up to the day I'd wake up with every muscle tensed, ready to flee, to run as far as my legs could carry me.

I was ten when my first home was blown out of existence.

Messai and I ran, he with Anette in his arms and I with Asélle clinging onto me. Our mother wasn't home. She'd been in the city, on the other side of the country, receiving treatment in a hospital for nearly two years.

We walked for three days before we arrived at a camp. Walked as our feet bled in the day, and slept in the bushes by night. Except I didn't do much sleeping. I'd stay wide awake, counting the stars, listening to the sounds of the night. The cackling of the hyenas miles away, the screeching of the monkeys, the giraffes across the savanna, but only when they'd fight. The rustling of the lion cubs and the trumpet of the elephants just as the sun would creep up, exploding the sky wide open in absolute silence.

I used to think I stayed awake because I was afraid, but in truth I felt safer in the animal kingdom than in the ruins of what was mine.

I stayed awake because I came alive in the night-time: my spirit awakened and travelled someplace far.

I pick up a chair from the dining table, walking with it to the front of the house and place it in the sunlight on the front porch.

The street is quiet today, the trees on the nature strip sway in the breeze gently, announcing their presence amongst everything else.

I lost Santo, my eldest living son, years before he died. When he was just a boy. The man he became after was something I didn't recognise. But the absence of every form of him in this world creates a deep pain that is chasmal and everlasting.

It didn't come as a surprise, but it knocked the breath from my lungs, drained the blood from my body. For years, losing my Santo came in waves of pain, sharper in the earlier days when he began to slip. Those waves have turned to currents, washing over my feet, at times rising to my knees and steadily past my waist. At times I find myself underwater, heart heavy, but without a trace of fear or panic.

I hear Akita's footsteps approach and I ready myself.

All that is lost in life may be found in death.

In his death there's a finality, a permanence that breaks me as much as it soothes me.

But Santo will never really be gone.

Not ever.

He lives through his memories, his siblings, his son.

The setting sun casts an incandescent light on the afternoon, soaking everything in its orange glory. I sit on the chair on the front porch and Akita sits between my legs. I twist her hair into knots and braids as she shares with me the secrets of her universe.

When I look up to the sky I see the first star of the night, its light ushering in the dawn of a new era.

Chapter 39

Geelong

Akita

I hold the flower stem between my teeth and bite down, leaving a delicately sour taste on my tongue.

I remember getting into trouble as a kid for doing such things, for 'eating grass' and spending too much time with my knees in the dirt.

I think if anybody had come from where I came from, they would be no different.

In Giza, green was not a colour I'd often see. Sure, the sand came in tones of orange, the sky would burst into hues of red, and people's faces would glow in all the shades of brown, underneath the North African sun.

It was beautiful, but my young self didn't see beauty in the everyday.

At the state school we went to I didn't have many friends: I had none at all if I don't count Santo. During lunchtimes, when the girls would sit and talk about goodness knows what and the boys would kick balls between each other, I would walk around the campus on my own in search of the little green weeds that would poke through the cracks of the pavement. They were ugly little things, most of them splintery to the touch, but I loved them, and I didn't understand why for a long time – nobody did.

With these eyes that see clearer today with the gift of time, I've come to understand little Akita's big heart. Finding those weeds, seeing the life that formed, breathed, and grew through the cracks, gave me hope.

That's all it was.

If little ugly weeds could survive in the hot and infertile soil of Giza, so could I.

I lay my head in the soft patch of grass, still warm from today's heat. Staring up at the clear evening sky, I see the stars twinkling faintly.

Norlane, a chaotic ecosystem with many intricacies sounds off in the evening with a rhapsody only few can appreciate. Most nights there are police sirens or ambulance cries and yelling from a fight down the block or a brawl down the street. People speak in abbreviations and shortened words that fall out of their relaxed mouths in a twang only this neighbourhood can forge.

Illegal fireworks from the commission housing units on the next street over, stray cats in the alleyway where there was a stabbing last week, and a drug deal across the road.

I probably shouldn't be lying in the front yard at this time of night, but this hood has been my home long enough for me to know I'll be fine, and leaving when those feelings change. Besides, I've adapted to this; I've lived here so long that the shouting and the sirens sound like lullabies. If growing up in Corio and living in Norlane have taught me anything, it's that the key to survival is minding one's own business.

Our next-door neighbour, Roger, is a friendly beer-bellied man who has more hair on his face than he does on top of his head.

He's a nice guy, a solid bloke, save for the fact that he fixes stolen cars and sells them as his own.

Every day there's a new car without licence plates in his driveway, but hey, all I know is that he's a mechanic – a ghetto mechanic, but a mechanic, nonetheless.

I can understand why people wouldn't want to live here, in this rundown part of Geelong, where poverty and hardship hangs over like a permanent dark cloud. But there are moments when that silver lining shines brighter than the sun.

In those afternoons when I'd just lay in the grass after a long day, sucking on the hard lollies from the milk bar that stain the tongue and scrape the roof of the mouth. Summer evenings when the sky is painted in pink and white just after sunset and the air hums a soft melody, times when the birds gather around as we eat fish and chips on the oval of the locally funded park.

I often say that Norlane has the prettiest sunsets, not because most of the streetlights don't work and the sky is clearer, but because when the sun shines around here, in the roughness of this place, the beauty of this neighbourhood – which not a lot of people can see – glimmers and gleams with a light no eye can deny.

I smack my thigh instinctively when I feel my first mosquito bite of the night. I wipe my hand on the grass blades as memories of a time before all this flash in my mind.

When I think about all the places I've lived, I don't remember any of them with as much fondness as I do the house on Edgar Street, Silverwater.

Number 23, I think our house number was.

It was small, according to Mum, old and in a swampy part in the middle of nowhere. It probably doesn't stand where it once stood.

It was my castle, no matter who or what I wanted to be.

I watched as entire worlds sprung from the damp grass: kingdoms, forests, the rising and falling of empires with each setting sun.

I would feel the grass beneath my feet, catch the fireflies in my hands, watch as the ladybugs crawled from my palm to my fingertips. I'd smell the mud in the soggy patches of the grass, I would taste the algae from the ponds that dispersed in the air and hear the birds chirping as dawn turned into day, day turned to dusk and as dusk turned to night.

It was different from Giza, different from the little village we lived in, different from the only other place I was told was home.

My memories following our move from Edgar Street are a little scattered. I'd turned ten, I had an infant baby brother, Santo was on numerous medications, I met Evelyn. I started reading chapter books, I became really good at jigsaw puzzles, and I started colouring inside the lines of my drawing books.

I stopped playing outside, stopped riding my bike because it would either get stolen from our front yard or the tyres would pop from the broken glass on the pavement.

It was the end of one era and the start of another that I surrendered to in its misery without looking for its magic. It was like I'd discovered the worlds other people had built and I'd settled into getting lost in them and grown tired of creating my own.

But I want that again, to run barefoot in the grass, to feel the sting of the sun on my bare skin, I want the world and the life I knew before freefalling into responsibility, before being governed by things with false importance.

I want to swallow entire worlds, entire universes.

I hear the front door swing open and footsteps rustling in the grass coming my way.

'May I join you?' asks Dad, his tall figure standing above me.

'Yeah, sure.'

He exhales and settles down beside me.

Neither one of us speaks for a long time. The crickets chirp, the bats screech, and the trees rustle in the gentle breeze. All my conversations with Dad in the five months he's been here have been small, mild and so very shallow.

I've had to conceal my anger, my resentment, my disappointment in him, having worn a facade for so long now that I don't think I have much anger left in me.

I don't know what I have left in me for Dad.

My wounds have begun to scar, and yet sometimes it feels as though they still bleed as freshly as they did ten years ago.

'Ah,' Dad breathes. 'A crescent moon.'

'Yeah … crazy …'

I can feel his contemplation, his mind trying to find ways to connect with me, but failing, once again, because he doesn't know his daughter.

'It's beautiful,' he whispers.

'Yeah, it is.'

A feeling of remorse grows in the pit of my stomach; my body knows from memory what is to come.

'You know, Akita, my mother always used to say that the moon has magical powers.'

'Oh yeah?'

'Indeed,' he says, his eyes misty. 'In its every phase, the moon's power up there has special forces and in a way governs what happens down here.'

'What does a crescent moon mean?' I ask, turning to him.

Dad looks to me, the silver light of the moon dancing in the silvery linings of his brown eyes.

'New beginnings,' he says with all his breath, smiling with his entire face.

It's the first time that I've ever heard Dad speak about his mother, my grandmother, my Haboba. All the stories of her I know were told by my mother's mother.

I look at him, his hair and beard greyer than they are black. I'm not sure if he's always looked this way since he's been back, or if learning he's somebody's grandfather has made him look like one.

'Hey, Dad? What was she like? Haboba?'

Dad inhales deeply and chuckles softly, staring at the stars as if they are her eyes.

'She was crazy,' he smiles, 'like all remarkable women are.'

'Really?'

'She was a force, Akita, an outer worldly being. She saw things before they happened, spoke to people who weren't there, said things without opening her mouth.'

Dad speaks to me like I am a friend, no authority in his tone, no air of being wiser.

'But … being her seventh and only son to make it past a week … I found it hard to connect with my mother. She had all under her spell, on this physical plane and in the next, but she was all *I* had.'

I stare at the faint stars, taking in things I never knew.

'I love my mother, she gave me everything I needed, but in her shortcomings I had to be the one to make myself a man. I wanted to study, I wanted to go to school, to university, and she was supportive too, until she learned I wanted to study medicine.'

I catch myself before I laugh out loud.

'Really?' I press, in disbelief. A doctor child is every African parent's dream, above marrying into royalty and inheriting all the riches of the world.

'Yes,' Dad laughs softly. 'She didn't believe in modern medicine. She believed in herbs and natural elements.'

'Seems fair.'

'I wanted to help people, and so did she, and everyone else in our village. It wasn't uncommon, to want to heal when death walked so closely among us.'

We both fall quiet. My father's mother sounds incredible, a woman I would've liked to have met, and yet I feel like I know her, like my father is describing a friend who visits me in my dreams, puts thoughts into my mind and guides me through this life.

'Why didn't you pursue medicine?' I ask.

'I did for a couple of years … and then I met your mother. I realised I wanted to be a husband and a father more.'

This time I can't stop myself from laughing. I snort at the irony, only laughing harder when I see the guilty smile spreading across his face.

'Obligation, Akita. I did what needed to be done,' Dad says after the laughter stops. I try, I try very hard, my judgement withheld, to see how leaving one's wife and young children in a country for nearly a decade was obligatory, to no avail.

'I think it was my mother who brought me back here.' Dad says to the sky. 'Of course, I yearned for it to, but in my mind the time was not yet right.'

I try to look away from him, to display my censure, but I can't peel my eyes away.

'I dreamt of her. For three nights straight. She'd say nothing, she simply looked at me, and when I looked into her eyes, I saw each one of you. You, Santo, your sisters, your baby brother. Your mother.'

I blink away the tears that sting my eyes.

'You have her spirit. Her strength,' Dad says after a while.

'Who? Haboba?' I sniff.

'Yes, that goes without saying, but I meant your mother.'

I smile to the night sky and hold that sentiment close to my chest.

'You've got so much light in you, Akita, so much light ... please, don't let it go out.'

I feel my body tense as suppressed anger awakens and slowly begins to leak. Conversations with Dad are all well and good until he tries to parent me, to give me his fatherly guidance that he deprived me of for too long.

I clench my eyes shut until I see galaxies and entire universes form in the confines of my eyelids. When I open my eyes I feel weak, exhausted.

I think I resent him most for leaving me with the burden of forgiving him, the burden that sits heavily on my conscience, invades my emotions and threatens my thoughts. In the beginning it felt good to ignore Dad, to meet him with unrelenting coldness, but now the thought of doing that makes me want to cry.

'Thank you,' Dad says softly. 'Thank you for all you have done, Akita.' He looks at me, his eyes misty again, and I force myself to meet his gaze. I feel like I'm going to burst.

We've each searched for parts of him, parts of our father in other people. All the kids in there, in that house, searched for those parts, in me.

I look at Dad, deep into his eyes, transmitting to him all the words I cannot say. Not in this lifetime. Not as Akita, his daughter, to Santino, her father.

I sit up on the grass, my legs crossed.

'I quit my job,' I say, gazing ahead. Dad sits up and looks at me.

I uncross my legs and stand, the grass tickling my bare feet.

'I no longer feel the pressure of obligation, Dad.'

I stare up at the sky; the stars shine brighter than ever before in Norlane.

'Something has been calling for me. All my life,' I say, walking towards the front door and standing on the porch. 'I thought it was wisdom, telling me to ignore it. But now I see that's so far from the truth. It always has been.'

Epilogue

Taresai

I've lived a life.

A life that knows the pain of my darkest nights. Knows the love that burns with the heat of a thousand suns and a hope that orbits mine like the moon orbits this earth. To have lost. To pour love into children I bore, to watch them be, become and live evermore. To have memories line the folds of my brain, stained with feeling in a golden hue. I watch their bodies move with the years, their faces change with the seasons as I come home to a house, with different coloured lights shining out of every window.

At the start of each day and at the end of each night I realise that there is hope in my kingdom, because I have seen all my wounds turn to scars.

Akita

The open road, the world before me.

Saying hello, and within an instant we're saying goodbye. The landscapes shift as we move through a year's worth of seasons in moments. Watching as the colours of the leaves change from spring green to autumn yellow.

I sit on the passenger seat, leaning out the window as the wind whips my braided hair loose. He sits beside me, his fingers gently grasping the steering wheel. The sky follows us, thin clouds dance in the blue beyond, the birds fly each way.

But maybe, just maybe, it isn't so.

Maybe the terrain stays the same, all the birds fly in the same direction, the trees are all the same shade of green. The mountains kissing the unchanging sky look as they always do, as they always have, since the very beginning of time until this very moment.

Maybe nothing moves, maybe nothing changes but us.

ACKNOWLEDGEMENTS

I give my thanks and express my deepest gratitude to the First People of this land. *Hopeless Kingdom* was written in its entirety on unceded Wadawurrung land; I acknowledge and pay my respect to the People, their country – which continues to inspire me each day, their history, and elders past and present.

Thank you to the remarkable team at UWA Publishing. I consider myself lucky to have had my first novel shared in the hands of women who worked with me to make *Hopeless Kingdom* what it is and for treating the manuscript with such care in every step. Thank you to Kate Pickard, Nicole van Kan, Lauren Pratt, Colin Barr, and my publisher, Eleanor Hurt, for taking me under your wing. Thank you to Elena Gomez for editing the manuscript and to Mika Tabata for the magnificent cover art.

I am ever so grateful to the judges of the Dorothy Hewett Award 2021, Tony Hughes-d'Aeth, Eleanor Hurt, Leni Shilton, and Will Yeoman. It's an honour to have had my work recognised by you.

To my family, without whom, I would not be who and where I am today. To my older brothers Akek, Atway and Akec, my little brothers Kual and Thocriel and my little sisters Ayak and Ashot, thank you for your love and light. Growing up, I believed there wasn't a thing I couldn't do, so long as I put my heart to it, the rest would follow. I'd like to thank my parents for instilling that in me. Thank you to my Baba, Valentino Malueth Akec and my Mama, Anyang Muorwel Gum. Everything I am is because of you.

To my friends and colleagues at Somebody's Daughter Theatre Company – Hayley, Kiara, Cath, Alix. Justin, Sam, Emma and Laura. To Maud Clarke and Kharen Harper for nurturing my very first steps into the peculiar world of the arts and seeing a light in this story from its very first incarnation to this one.

Thank you to my good friend and soul brother Djarlar.

And to my partner and best friend Reece, for being the sky and sometimes, the sea.